Also by Gene Thompson
Published by Ballantine Books:

LUPE

MURDER MYSTERY

GENE THOMPSON

BALLANTINE BOOKS • NEW YORK

The lines quoted on page 156 are from "I Wake and Feel the Fell of Dark" by Gerard Manley Hopkins, reprinted courtesy of Oxford University Press.

For the quotation from Sir Max Beerbohm on page 279, I am indebted to Arthur Sheekman.

"La Fornarina" is on permanent exhibit in the Galleria Palatina in Florence.

Library of Congress Catalog Card Number: 80-5295

ISBN 0-345-29892-6

This edition published by arrangement with Random House, Inc.

Manufactured in the United States of America

First Ballantine Books Edition: December 1981
Second Printing: February 1983

Cover photograph by Anthony Loew

*For my mother
and in memory of my father*

I

On Thursday, Dade Cooley came home to an empty house. It was only five o'clock, but since it was February it was already getting dark. He turned on the lights, almost stumbling over the luggage which was everywhere, lit a fire in the small marble fireplace in the sitting room and mixed himself an Old Fashioned. On the coffee table was the copy of *Vogue* they had both been waiting for. It contained Ellen's piece on their trip the year before to Italy. He picked it up, turned to the article and began leafing through it. There was an illustration showing Ravello, a thousand feet above the Amalfi Drive, carved out of the cliffs.

He glanced at his watch. He was late. He put down the magazine and went upstairs to bathe. Turning on the radio, he heard the announcer say that Dr. Dan would be with them in a moment to tell everybody what kind of weather he had in store for the Bay Area. Stripping off his clothes and putting them on the window seat in the bedroom, Dade looked out across San Francisco and the dark clouds over the Bay and decided that the storm might break before Dr. Dan had a chance to predict it.

A few minutes later, the twangy voice of Dr. Dan said, "From the mountains to the sea, a good, good evening. Well, tonight's a night to snuggle under the covers—or maybe under the bed if thunderstorms scare you. The storm system that hit the Los Angeles area on Tuesday, bringing the southland a Valentine's Day present of three point two inches of rain, has been working its way north for the last two days and is expected to dump at least that

1

much on our fair city starting tonight, with a pretty strong possibility of the same thunder-and-lightning show the folks down south just enjoyed."

Dade switched off the radio, annoyed. He had to be on the plane to Los Angeles at eight that night. That meant flying in a thunderstorm. It didn't bother him, but when Ellen found out she would try to stop him. Going into the bathroom, he turned on the steaming-hot water in the walking tub Ellen had insisted on buying with the money she had gotten from the *Vogue* piece. ("Darling, it's deep and it holds the heat far better than the new ones and it's six feet long." "Goddamned thing looks like a sarcophagus.") He studied his naked body in the mirror, trying to decide how much of his sixty-year-old paunch was fat and how much sagging muscles, tightened his stomach, looked at the result with satisfaction and decided he did not need to diet, only to exercise, something he would think about come spring. Slapping his left hand against his lower belly and holding it in, he thrust his right hand into the air as if brandishing a trident, like the Poseidon in the Athens Museum, shook his hoary locks and recited the opening of *The Iliad* in Greek, ending with the words "divine Achilles," then got into the tub.

Fifteen minutes later, he had shaved and was dressing when he heard Ellen's key in the lock. He went to the hall and looked down the narrow staircase. "Billy Blue Hill! I thought I told you to ring the bell when you come home to an empty house."

"It isn't empty. You're here."

"You didn't know that."

"What good would it do?" She was carrying packages through the sitting room into the kitchen.

Dade hurried downstairs, still finishing dressing. "It's to scare burglars, honey." He followed her into the kitchen and began taking things out of the paper bags she had set down on the drainboard. He picked up a can of albacore and whistled at the price. "I told you to buy the cheap kind."

"It has porpoise in it."

"Oh, bullshit. Porpoise won't hurt you. Next time, you ring that bell."

"Darling, what use is it to scare him? I mean, he has no way out. There's no back door. Where on earth do you expect the poor burglar to go?"

"Just do like I tell you and don't you go feeling sorry for criminals."

She looked at him. "Why are you all dressed up?"

"I saw your piece, darling. It looks just wonderful."

"I asked you a question."

"I've got to go out in about an hour."

"Where?"

"To see a client." He avoided her eyes and went back into the sitting room, asking whether she wanted a drink.

"No. Yes." She followed him into the room, looking at him steadily. Her eyes were lidded and dark-blue. In the half-light, she looked thirty. She was forty-five, with a face like a Watteau miniature. When he had anything important to say to her, he found himself looking away to collect his thoughts. She saw him avert his eyes now and asked what was the matter.

"We'll talk about it later." He began mixing her a kir. "I wish we had children."

"We have four."

"I meant small ones."

"Abigail is only sixteen."

"But she's never home."

"Darling, what's the matter?"

"I said, we'll talk about it later." He had finished making her drink. He handed it to her. She sipped it. He looked at her. "Well?"

"It's fine."

"Well, then, say so."

"Must you always have praise?"

"I go to trouble."

The doorbell rang repeatedly. She said, "Jonah," went to the front door, opened it and, standing at the top of the stairs, pulled on a lever to open the downstairs door. A tall boy with curly blond hair, a black leather jacket, leather pants and boots ran up the stairs and put his cold cheek to his mother's lips, then went toward his father.

Dade said, "Where is my little boy and what have you done with him?"

"Papa." The boy hugged him. "I have to talk to you. Right now."

"I have him first," said Ellen.

"Come in and sit down," said Dade.

"I can't. She's downstairs. The girl I'm with."

"Why didn't you bring her up?" asked Ellen.

"I'm parked in a red zone. She has to watch the bike or they'll tow it away. Papa, can we use the cabin?"

"For immoral purposes?"

"Oh, Papa."

"No."

"What do you want me to be, furtive?"

"Discreet."

"We'll be discreet."

"Be discreet somewhere else."

"Why?"

"I just don't like it. Sonny, I've told you before, you can do whatever you like, just so long as you don't attract attention."

"But that's all changed."

"I haven't."

"The world is different now."

"The world has made a mistake. And it's not the first time."

"Mommy—?"

"Your father has spoken." Behind her husband's back, Ellen nodded at her son, a finger to her lips.

"Do you need some money?" Dade pulled out a twenty-dollar bill and gave it to him. Jonah kissed him.

"Thanks." Jonah grinned and started out, then turned and said, "I read in the paper about your friend. The one down south who got killed. I'm awfully sorry."

"Thank you."

"The girl—the daughter—I forget her name—"

"Rachel?"

"She tried to reach you."

"I just talked to her this afternoon."

"Well, she called here yesterday morning. I was here, getting some stuff. Anyway, she was all shook up and when I said that the two of you were in France, she said"—Jonah imitated a girl's voice—"'Oh, *no!*' And then

I explained you were due in late last night and she said she'd call you back and that was that. Oh, and a cop came by asking to see you."

"When?"

"Yesterday morning. When I said you were both out of the country, he just thanked me and left, but afterward I got to wondering—"

"I'm her executor," Dade said. "That must be why they sent him."

Jonah glanced at his watch. "Hey, I've got to get out of here!" He kissed his parents, then ran for the door, clumping down the stairs two at a time.

Ellen called out, "Wait! The chicken!" She started after him.

"Never mind the chicken," said Dade.

"But I made it for him."

"He doesn't need the chicken and you don't need to get a look at that girl." He closed the door and headed back into the sitting room. "You told him yes, didn't you?"

"Well, of course I did. Why did you have to put him through that?"

"I'm an old-fashioned man."

"Oh, come off it, Dade. When you were his age—"

"When I was his age, I was just a country boy at Muskingum College—"

"Not to mention Oxford and Harvard Law School."

"I'd as soon you didn't."

Ellen looked away, pointing out the window. "Here it comes," she said. It began to rain. Dade stole a glance at his watch. Ellen took a sip of her drink, then set it down and said, "All right, what's going on?"

"It's time for the news." He turned on the television.

She turned it off. "I am interested in *your* news."

It was raining heavily now. Dade looked out the window at the storm and said, thinking of Jonah, "God damn it, I don't want him on the goddamned motorcycle in the goddamned rain."

"He's twenty-two and it's his own life."

"There's a old fairy tale about this here giant nobody could kill 'cause his life was hidden somewheres, I mean, he didn't have it on him, so to speak. You know where he hid it? In a egg in the hollow of a tree. You understand what I'm saying to you, Ellen?"

"These aren't storybook children and you have to let them alone! They're grown up now!"

"I don't care to discuss the matter further."

"Good. Then we can talk about where you're off to."

"Tell you the truth—" There was a clap of thunder. He grimaced.

She picked up a tablet by the phone with something scrawled on it in his handwriting. It read "Cleave. Conjure. Toilet." "What is 'Cleave. Conjure. Toilet'?"

"I'm making a list of words that mean their own opposites. I'm going to call them Cooley Opponyms. Fella bet me I couldn't think of more than three."

"I don't think you can get away with 'toilet.' "

"Clean, dirty?"

"No."

"I guess not." He took out a gold pencil and ruefully crossed it out.

She looked over his shoulder and saw the name of a cemetery in Los Angeles scribbled at the bottom of the page. Pointing at it, she asked, "Isn't that where—?"

"Yes."

"The funeral's tomorrow, isn't it?"

"As a matter of fact, I thought—"

"Well, you can stop thinking it. You're not going. Not in this weather."

He put his hands on her shoulders and looked at her steadily. "Honey, I have to go." There was a flash of lightning and then more thunder. He braced himself for a fight.

She looked at him for a moment and then surprised him by saying, "All right. My God, poor Miriam!" She picked up a clipping from a rosewood sewing stand and handed it to Dade. "Here. I cut this out for you."

Putting on his glasses, Dade read it carefully, pointing at the words with a thick forefinger and moving his lips. It said:

Miriam Buffet Welles Dies: Wife of Art Collector Jensen Welles died at the age of 36 after an accident at her home in Malibu, California. A former member of the Los Angeles Art Commission, Mrs. Welles was also prominent in numerous charities associated with the art world. Well-known in art circles, she was considered by many one of the country's leading authenticators of Renaissance painting.

For many years, Miriam Buffett acted as curator of the Welles Collection, arranging for exhibitions and for the acquisition of additional canvases. On the death of the first Mrs. Welles after a long illness, the betrothal of Miriam Buffett to Jensen Welles was announced the following spring. In recent years, Miriam Welles has been associated with Proulx Galleries in Los Angeles, through which many important acquisitions have been made, adding to the already distinguished private collection of Jensen Welles, the most recent of which is the Botticelli "Venus of the Grotto."

Mrs. Welles, who died Tuesday, leaves her husband and a stepdaughter, Rachel Welles, who resides with her father.

Dade frowned. "When Rachel called, she was crying so hard I had trouble understanding her. When I got her calmed down, she said she had something important to tell me. Just then, she was interrupted. She said, 'Wait a minute.' When she came back on the line, she kept her voice down and said, 'I can't talk now.' I told her I'd phone her back and she said, 'No, don't,' and asked me not to tell anyone she'd called. She sounded scared to death. I said, 'You want me to come down there?' and she started crying to beat the band and said, 'Please help me,' so I said I'd go."

"Well, she's only eighteen and you said they were close. Girls at that age can be very dramatic."

"We'll just have to see. Want to come along?"

She shook her head. "I can't."

"Sure?"

"I promised myself I'd start on the new piece."

"Which one?"

"Ancient magic."

"I wish there were a magical way of getting me out of this trip."

"It may just be magic that's gotten you into it."

"Come again?"

"The kabbala says that the souls of men and women who die prematurely are driven to haunt mankind until they are laid to rest."

He stared at her. "Are you serious?"

"Yes."

"Then I think you should go back to writing about travel."

"Spoilsport. But you know, the kabbala may just turn out to be right." She helped him pack an overnight case and called a cab.

"I'll just get Miriam's papers together and make a few calls. I'll stay over tomorrow night."

"Want me to pick you up at the airport Saturday?"

"I'll call you from the inn." At the door, bundled up in his overcoat, he gave her a kiss and said, "Wish me luck."

"Merde!" she said with a grin.

"Merde!" His eyes lit up. Taking out his pencil and his pad, he triumphantly added the word to his list, then hurried out into the rainy night.

II

The services were private. They were held at ten o'clock in the morning in a small cemetery in Hollywood. A tall hedge of yew separated it from the back lot of a movie studio. High stone walls and dense planting made the place seem like no more than a garden and kept out the curious. Inside the wrought-iron gates, birds sang and muted fountains plashed. The little stone houses of the rich dead lined the gravel walks, reminiscent of the villas of Pompeii. Once inside, one forgot that this was now the wrong part of town. Neighborhoods change. The rich move elsewhere. But it is difficult to move a cemetery, and this one was now an oasis in a slum.

Inside the chapel, the invited guests sat in respectful silence while the minister delivered a eulogy, referring briefly to the way in which the deceased had died and seeking to discover the hand of God in a freak accident.

The services ended. Ushers whispered requests to the mourners, asking them to file by the coffin row by row, beginning with those sitting at the rear. Dade got to his feet and walked up the side aisle. He looked down at the body of Miriam Welles. She was dressed in an antique Persian robe, saffron silk embroidered with birds and flowers in rich colors. Her thick dark hair, long and lustrous, framed her head in soft waves. Dade studied the beautiful face. It looked different, almost unfamiliar. He wondered why. Then it occurred to him that someone else had put on her make-up. He took the rose from his lapel and placed it gently on the body. As he turned to go, he saw Jensen sitting in the front row, a tall lean figure with hooded eyes and a long nose. His elbows were balanced on the arm-rests of the pew and the powerful hands were clasped as if in prayer. Dade looked around for Rachel. He did not see her. The seat next to Jensen was conspicuously empty.

Dade went outside and waited with the crowd. A hearse was parked there, a uniformed attendant furtively drag-ging on a cigarette behind the open back door.

A woman's voice said, "Dade." It was Nettie Proulx. She squeezed his arm. He patted her ringed hand. "Oh, Dade," she said. Even in the way she spoke his name, he could hear the slight French accent. She looked up at him, her soft plump face puffy with grief. She was fifty but Dade had never before seen her look her age. She asked in a low voice, "How did she look? Tell me the truth. I just couldn't go up there." She looked at him with her two-colored eyes, one blue, one brown.

"Very nice, same as always, just like somebody sleep-ing."

"Are you serious?" When he nodded, she said, "But I heard that when they found her—oh, it's too awful!" Her voice had become a hoarse whisper. She put a hand to her mouth, shaking her head.

Dade said, "I don't see Rachel. Where is she?"

"I'm sure she's here. She must be."

Gil and Chloe Ransohoff moved toward them. They had been sitting near Dade at the back of the chapel. Chloe had the body of a girl, full breasts, a small waist and a flat stomach. She wore a nutria coat over her shoulders and had a way of standing, arms akimbo, so that the expen-sive coat did not hide her figure. The doll's face under the perfectly groomed platinum-blond hair was almost hard, the lips compressed, the expression set. When she caught Dade's eyes, her features relaxed into a conscious social smile.

"She was my best friend," Chloe said.

Gil nodded to Dade, who nodded back. Gil was a hand-some man in his forties with greenish eyes and a curved goat's smile. He smiled at Dade now. Dade did not like Gil's smile. It was insolent, familiar, like a stranger calling him by his first name.

Turning away, Dade saw a woman he thought he knew.

He was about to speak to her when he realized that she was not a friend but an actress he had only seen a few times on television. She was about the same age as Miriam. Her eyes were extraordinary. They had a remarkable clarity but were almost expressionless in the way that the eyes of Greek statues often seem, as if their gaze were fixed on eternity. Her glance brushed over him. An older man leaned on her arm. They turned away and started strolling down the gravel path. The man walked unsteadily, clinging to her arm.

All the mourners had come out of the chapel now and they were gathered in groups, their voices low, waiting for Jensen. Attendants wheeled the now-closed casket out of the chapel and lifted it off the gurney into the hearse. Jensen had still not appeared. Dade remembered that he had left his hat on his chair and, excusing himself, went back into the chapel to get it. As he started out again, he caught sight of Jensen, glasses perched on his long nose, bending over a guest book on a lighted lectern in an alcove, the funeral director standing at his elbow.

Jensen said, "You're quite sure? These are, after all, private services."

"We did not invite them, Mr. Welles."

Jensen grunted, turning away. Catching sight of Dade, he held out his hand. Dade grasped it. The hand was dry and firm. Jensen tightened his grip. For a man his age, his strength was impressive.

"May I offer you my sympathies, Jensen?"

"Thank you for coming. We'll be gathering at the house afterward. If you'd care to come by—"

"Something's come up. I'm afraid I have to wait around at the inn for a phone call."

"I understand." Jensen took his elbow and steered him toward the doors of the chapel. The funeral director bowed to him. Jensen turned and stared at him. "Don't do that," he said. He walked out into the sunshine with Dade. Faces turned toward them. Jensen remained standing in the doorway, looking slowly around, as if he were about to issue a statement. Then, dropping Dade's arm abruptly, Jensen walked over toward Chloe and Gil, extending his hand. Gil shook hands with him and began to express his sympathy when Jensen interrupted him, saying, "I am sorry you won't be able to stay longer."

Taken aback, Gil started to say something, then broke off because Jensen held his eyes with an unflinching stare. Taking Chloe's arm, he gave Jensen a brief nod and then hurried his wife away toward a gate in the hedge leading to the parking lot.

Jensen offered Nettie his arm. Together, they began to walk toward the burial place, the mourners following. Dade thought, I should ask him about Rachel. He decided against it.

III

The gathering after the funeral was at the Welles house in Malibu. Sighing, Dade drove his rented car back toward the beach, brow furrowed, the crocodile eyes narrowed in thought. Rachel had asked him to wait at the inn for her call. "Let *me* call *you*," she had said. She had been very definite about it. He checked his watch. The guests would be at the Welles house for an hour or two. Probably she would wait for them to leave before calling him. It was a sunny day. He would lie on the beach and read a book.

He drove north now on Pacific Coast Highway, climbing up past the low stucco tile-roofed buildings and sweeping lawns of the university, then past a cluster of expensive new tract houses high on a hill. It was a gray day with not too much traffic on the road. The highway, four lanes with a center divider, sliced through the hills above the water. Malibu was not picturesque. It faced south because of the northern curve of Santa Monica Bay on which it was built, but it was a long curve, almost twenty-six miles, unrelieved by inlets or islands, which made the flat calm sea wide and monotonous. To his right the cliffs were deeply eroded, which gave the place an insubstantial look. The hills and the mouths of the canyons were all covered with low-growing natives like sumac and chaparral. The trails up into the hills were dry and uninviting. But now in February, the mustard had come out and all the hills were dusted with gold, giving the stark landscape a sudden beauty.

On impulse, Dade made a U-turn on the highway and headed south again toward the Colony, making a left at

13

the Civic Center, which looked like a model of the stoa in Athens, and pulled up in front of the sheriff's station. He might as well ask for details of the accident. Then, if Rachel had questions, he could answer them.

He got out of the car in front of the long low colonnaded building, climbed the shallow steps and went toward dark-tinted plate-glass double doors.

The waiting room was large, with a counter at one end. Dade walked up and gave his card to a uniformed young woman, a deputy. "I want to ask a few questions about the Welles case. I'm the executor for the estate."

Behind the counter, a door at the side was open and Dade could see into the squad room. A lieutenant came into the squad room from a glassed-in cubicle at the back.

The woman deputy pressed a lever on an intercom and said into it, "Lieutenant, who's handling the Welles case?"

Dade watched as the lieutenant stopped, leaned over a desk, his back to them, and depressed a key on another intercom. "Wait a minute," they heard him say. At a table, two young deputies were playing cards. Their hair was sun-bleached from spending all their off-duty time surfing. The lieutenant threw a paper clip at one of them to get his attention. "Brandt, who's got the file on the Welles case?"

"You have," the deputy said, looking up. His young face was cracked with fine lines and the blue of his eyes was washed out, as if by the sea. "I put it back on your desk. Accidental death." Brandt turned to his partner, putting down the cards in his hand. "Gin."

"We're playing poker."

"I just wanted you to get a look at a really lousy hand."

"I'm handling it," the lieutenant said into the intercom.

"Someone here wants to talk to you," said the deputy.

"Is he a reporter?"

"No, sir, he's an attorney." She read from the card Dade had given her. "A Mr. Dade Cooley."

"Who's he representing?"

"He's the executor for the deceased."

"Ask him to wait a couple of minutes." His back still to them, the lieutenant released the intercom key and went back into his cubicle. Dade saw him pick up a telephone and punch out a number.

The deputy at the counter said, "The lieutenant asks—"

"Yes, I heard him. Many thanks." Dade walked away, pulling a magazine out of his inside coat pocket, and followed a sign which read MEN down a hall to a lavatory.

He was washing his hands, the magazine under one arm, as the lieutenant came into the men's room. A nameplate on the breast pocket of his uniform read LT. REFUGIO VALDEZ. Dade whistled under his breath, shut off the faucet and reached for a paper towel. As the lieutenant turned toward the washstand, Dade dropped the magazine and the lieutenant retrieved it, handing it to him. Thanking him, Dade said, brandishing it, "You know, there's a Hottentot tribal ceremony during which a respected elder urinates on the bride and bridegroom at a wedding?"

"No, I didn't know that, sir."

"Fact. Says so right here in the *Smithsonian*. An apt remark, given our present business, wouldn't you say?"

"Yes, sir, that is true."

Dade stuffed the magazine into his coat pocket and began blotting his hands on a paper towel. He glanced up, briefly studying the lieutenant's face in the mirror. He had straight black hair, large moist eyes, a thick mustache and a wide smile with big white teeth.

"Piece also suggests some adults can distinguish sex by the odor of the urine." Dade glanced at the lieutenant's uniform, then added, "Now, there's something fits right into your own line of work, isn't that so?"

The lieutenant busied himself at the basin, saying, "Especially considering that my work often involves a process of elimination."

Dade's eyes twinkled with appreciation. "Son, this has been a felicitous conversation." He strode out of the men's room and then watched as Lieutenant Valdez went through a side door into the squad room and hurried across it toward the cubicle. After a moment, Dade followed him.

Valdez picked up a report lying on his desk and, his back to Dade, began leafing through it quickly. The report was in a manila folder and there was a supplemental sheet clipped to the outside. Removing the supplemental sheet, he reached over and stuffed it into the top drawer of his desk, after which he depressed the intercom key and said, "Okay, send him in."

"I'm already here, Lieutenant."

Valdez turned and saw Dade standing in the doorway. Surprised, he grinned. "Mr. Dade Cooley?"

"Lieutenant Valdez? Well, well, it is a small world. Larger, certainly, than the one in which we met but smaller than we know." Dade took a business card from a dog-eared leather case and placed it on the corner of the lieutenant's desk, then, at a gesture from Valdez, settled himself in the visitor's chair.

The lieutenant sat down, picked up the card, glanced at it and then said in a matter-of-fact voice, "How can I help you, sir?"

The sound of the sheriff's helicopter landing on the pad outside the window made it impossible for them to talk for a moment. Dade got to his feet and walked over to the window, watching the landing. A moment later, the pilot switched off the engine. Dade turned and said, "I was out of the country when this thing happened. Tuesday, wasn't it?"

"That's right."

"I just learned about it yesterday."

"We tried to find you, sir." The lieutenant consulted the report on his desk, then looked up. "You reside at 3614 Jackson Street in San Francisco?"

"That's correct."

"The Northern station sent a car up to Pacific Heights the morning after the body was found. He telephoned this office at nine-ten A.M. saying that you were out of the country and couldn't be reached, at which time, having made the appropriate efforts to notify you, we released the name of the deceased to the press." His tone was slightly defensive. It changed then, became apologetic. "We did try, sir."

"Mrs. Cooley and I were in France. We were going to take a canal trip but they don't start up until about mid-April. Very restful. Those barges go slower than I can walk, you know that? Once I did three miles on the tow-path and beat it to the next Cistercian abbey by half an hour. Well, no matter. You tried and you have my thanks."

"So long as you understand, sir."

"Anyway, we got back to San Francisco Wednesday and Rachel called me the following day, yesterday. You know Rachel?"

"No, I don't, sir."

"She's Jensen's daughter. Well, she went to tell me what all had happened and started crying so hard, I couldn't understand most of what she said. But of course I came straight down. For the funeral."

"That was today?"

"That's correct. I wonder if you'd set my mind at ease? Just tell me what happened."

Nodding, Valdez called out, "Brandt!" through the open door. The sunburned deputy put down his cards, got slowly to his feet with a creaking of leather and ambled toward his superior, putting his hands on the door frame and leaning into the lieutenant's office.

"Yes, sir."

"I read your report. Some of it."

"Uh-huh."

"What was the cause of death?"

"It's in my report."

"That must be the part I couldn't make out." The teeth gleamed white under the bristling mustache.

"Look, the coroner give me all that. You know how he talks. All them bullshit words, me standing in that goddamn downpour, it's a wonder I could read my notes at all. Her spine snapped, okay?"

Valdez gave a quick, apprehensive look at Dade, then said, "Brandt, this is Mr. Dade Cooley, an attorney. He's—"

But Dade interrupted him, saying, "I'm just an interested party. I wonder if you could tell me what happened? In your own words."

"Well, lady was hit and killed by her own car."

"Her own car. I see. What kind of car?" Dade took out a notebook and began jotting things down as he questioned Brandt.

"A Rolls. She left it in drive, got out to close the garage

door 'cause the automatic thing wouldn't work, and I guess she really didn't have the brakes on 'cause the damn thing suddenly took off and smashed into her."

"Any idea how fast?" Dade asked him.

"No tire tracks in that rain. Didn't matter. Coroner said it was just how she was hit, that was all there was to it."

"A Rolls? You say she drove a Rolls?"

"Well, it wasn't her car. See, hers was down to the Arco station being fixed. It had just been fixed, that is, and the old man—I'm sorry, sir—"

"He's sixty-seven. You can call him an old man."

"Well, the sixty-seven-year-old man—her husband, that is—went down to the Arco station with his daughter to pick up hers, her being sick in bed."

"Who was sick in bed?"

"Decedent. Mrs. Welles. Not what you'd call real sick, she just had a cold and went to bed, and since her husband and his daughter was both going out, they offered to bring back her car."

"They went together?"

"Yes, sir."

Valdez handed the report to Dade, who leafed through it, asking, "What time was this?"

"Around eight-thirty. It was raining like hell, had been for hours. Father and daughter, they go out front and get into this Mercedes coupe—"

"Whose car?"

"Hers. The father, he always drives the Rolls—he's the only one drives it—the dames both hated it—but the mud was so bad in the driveway, he didn't think he could get the car out. See, you have to back out of the garage and then back up this steep little hill and then swing around—see, the garage is down on a cliff, out at the end of the house. There's a long driveway. Nobody would want to back up it, so they've got themselves this steep little road like a bunny slope up at a ski resort, and that's where you have to back up to turn around."

"I remember that driveway," Dade said.

"She lets her father off at the Arco station and then drives on into Venice to meet her boyfriend at a café there."

"It says here," Dade murmured, leafing through the report, "that Mr. Welles drove into Beverly Hills to go to his office."

"Yes, sir."

"Must have been quite a drive for an old man, all the way from Malibu into town in a storm like that."

"Yes, sir. Especially with a couple of belts in him."

"Oh?"

"Stopped off afterward at a bar downstairs from his office. But the bartender says he only had two and they weren't quick belts, he was there a good half-hour."

"I see. And then?"

"Well, the daughter—Rachel, I think her name is—she returns about eleven-thirty, goes down the drive and at first, she thinks her stepmother is backing out because the garage door is open and the motherfucking Rolls is going full blast. Christ, I'm sorry I said that—"

"Just keep talking, sonny."

"Yeah. Well, like I say, it's going full blast, belching fumes. She honks so's her stepmother won't back into her—the maid heard that—and then drives into the garage, gets out of her own car and then sees there's nobody in the Rolls. Then she sees the decedent. There's this block wall at the far end of the garage and the Rolls had pinned the decedent right up against it. She was dead, of course, dead for hours is what the coroner says, and slumped over, pinned by her hips and legs, which is why the girl didn't see her at first.

"Anyway, the girl starts in screaming and the maid hears her. She comes charging out just as the Welles girl is getting into the Rolls, trying to pull it the hell out of the way. Maid runs to the body, which hits the garage floor at that point. Girl backs up Rolls and smashes into a tree, which is damn lucky because the shape she was in, I think she'd've gone right over that cliff. Anyway, girl barrels into the house and calls the paramedics. We get there with them, less than ten minutes after we get the call. It's a mopping-up operation, all the while this broad screaming at them to help—"

"To help?"

"She wanted the Pulmotor. She wanted mouth-to-mouth.

She wanted any frigging thing she could think of to save the lady, yelling at everybody, 'How do you know she's dead?' and, man, I never saw a body so dead in my life. Coroner says she'd been dead somewheres between, oh, two or three hours. She was dead, all right."

"Time of death sometime between eight-thirty and nine-thirty, that what you're saying?" Dade asked.

"Yes, sir," Brandt answered. "Decedent last seen alive by the stepdaughter at eight-thirty, and death occurred sometime in the next hour."

Dade studied the deputy's pale-blue eyes for some moments and then asked, "What happened when you checked the transmitter?"

"The one in the Rolls?"

"That's right."

"Wouldn't work. Our guys brought it in and took it apart."

"Battery?"

"Nope. Battery was fine. What went wrong is what usually happens. You know how women handle them things, just like they was tubes of toothpaste, and you mash down hard on that little button and you bend the metal so that it wcn't make contact anymore. Happens all the time. What I figure is, she backed up that little hill, pushed the transmitter, garage door wouldn't work, she put on the brake but not enough, ran down the hill to close the door manually, the Rolls slips the brake and comes charging toward her, she runs into the garage to get out of the way and the damn thing smashes the lady against the back wall."

"But you just told me the ladies didn't like that car and didn't drive it if they could help it. They can't have used the transmitter in it much."

Deputy Brandt hadn't thought of this. He frowned, thinking.

"Check the idle screw?" Dade asked.

"Yes, sir." Brandt gave Dade a look of admiration. "Set too high. That could have been the reason. If the brakes gave, the thing would've taken off. I guess that's what happened."

"A last question," Dade said. "Your report says the lady

was sick in bed, that that's how come she didn't go down with her husband to get her own car."

"Yes, sir. Maid told us that, and the husband and the daughter both."

"Any idea where the deceased was going? Your report doesn't say."

"No, but I thought it was away on a trip. There was a suitcase in the trunk. Way it turns out, she'd just come back from one. She and the husband went on a trip somewheres. Up to Santa Barbara a few days before. Came back and just left her suitcase in the car. Forgot about it."

Dade looked at him, surprised. "I don't find that in the report," he said.

The lieutenant looked at Brandt with amazement.

Brandt's face reddened. He said, "It's not there."

The lieutenant got to his feet, leaned across the desk and said in a low, cutting voice, "Just why the hell not?"

"I forgot, sir." He swallowed, embarrassed. "Jeez, it was pouring rain and me trying to calm down this broad and write a report with the husband showing up in the middle of it and him collapsing, chest pains, it was, so they had to take the body out of the ambulance to put him in—Christ, when the coroner told me, 'Death by misadventure'—he said, Don't quote me yet but that's the way it looks—well, I just kind of wrapped things up. I came back here and wrote my report, and the next day I remembered I hadn't put in about the suitcase but by then the coroner had already made it official and I couldn't see it meant Jack Shit, I mean, about the damn suitcase—hell, these rich folks are always running off to hell and gone—people like that leave town if you fart out loud—"

Dade asked softly, "What was in the suitcase?"

"Just a few clothes. Hers."

"Did you impound it?" the lieutenant asked him.

"No, sir. Didn't seem any reason to."

"You make a list of what was in it?" Valdez asked.

"I didn't open it, sir."

"Then how do you know what was in it?"

"The old guy—the husband—told me. I was going to check it out, just for form's sake and I started to ask the husband to open it but . . ." He trailed off.

"You started to ask him?" Dade prompted him.

"That's right when he collapsed. He just grabbed at his chest and fell down in the driveway."

"You call a doctor?"

"Well, by then the coroner had arrived, so we had him take a look at Mr. Welles. Sounds kind of funny, having a living person examined by a coroner, but he is a doctor, and when he said, 'Get him to a hospital,' well, we just took the damn body out of the ambulance—I mean, she was dead, she could wait, you can see my point—and they took him off to Santa Monica. I figure it was nothing because when we got ready to release the body, he was on the phone making the arrangements to have the mortuary pick it up."

There was a silence. Valdez looked at Dade inquiringly.

Dade asked, "The girl—Rachel Welles—did she ever make any suggestion that something was amiss?"

"Sir?" Brandt looked blank.

"I mean, was she satisfied?" Brandt's pale eyes looked puzzled. Dade gestured, explaining. "When you talked to her later. After the shock had worn off."

"I never talked to her later, sir."

"Why not?"

"Well, there was no reason. The coroner, he said it was an accident, and I mean *we* didn't investigate. There was nothing *to* investigate."

"What about you, Lieutenant?"

The lieutenant shook his head. "I've never even met her. Case was never assigned to us to investigate."

"But Welles," said Dade, "he talked to somebody. According to this report, he talked to the coroner."

"To the coroner's office, that means. I was there, as it happens," said the lieutenant. "Welles asked to talk to him, but the coroner didn't even know who he was, and he was busy, so when he heard that Welles just wanted to know when the body would be released, he said, 'Now.' Wouldn't have been any delay at all except that in cases like this, an autopsy is routine and his office was backed up. Anything else?"

"No," said Dade. "Nothing else." Dade thanked Brandt for his trouble.

The lieutenant gave Brandt a short nod of dismissal, saying, "We'll talk about this later. That's all for now."

Brandt nodded at Dade and left the room hastily, banging the glass-paneled door behind him.

"I'm sorry," Valdez said.

"It's all right."

"I'm blaming him. I should blame myself. Trouble is, once the coroner called it accidental, there was no reason to investigate any further." He drew a long breath. "I can see what happened. We had some bad fires this year. A storm like that usually means mud slides. A coroner has to have a pretty good reason to tie up a crew going over the ground for clues, and if it looked to him like nothing but a freak accident—"

"And that's what you think it was?"

"Well, I suppose people always smell something when there's money involved."

"Family has money. Miriam, she didn't have a dime." Dade got slowly to his feet.

"If you have any other questions—"

"Seems to me you've answered them all. Many thanks. Oh, and don't worry about that suitcase. I'll be taking charge of it. It's my responsibility now."

The lieutenant went over and opened the door for Dade. As Dade pushed open the heavy glass door of the squad room, it reflected the room behind him. Dade hesitated, pulling on his hat and watching the reflection of the lieutenant jerking his head at a nondescript man sitting in a chair against the wall, reading a newspaper. The man folded his paper, rose and came toward him. The lieutenant indicated Dade's retreating back, then went into his office and closed the door.

IV

It was almost one o'clock when Dade drove into the parking lot at the inn. He stopped at the desk. There were no messages. Grunting, he headed for his room. It was down at the water's edge, newly remodeled, since the last series of high tides had flooded the lower level and washed half of it away. Most of the inn was on the bluff above. There had been a small pool and a terrace but the torrential rains of the year before had caused a landslide and the terrace had caved in. The expensive suites on the beach reached by a tiny funicular had suffered from this. What damage they had previously escaped from the raging surf had later been done by falling masonry. The debris had been hauled away and the thin-walled suites rebuilt, each with a fireplace and a kitchen and sliding glass doors opening onto a small deck above the sandy beach.

Dade stomped into the room, banged shut the door, poured himself a stiff drink from his flask and then stretched out on the king-size bed complete with vibrator attachment into which you were supposed to put coins. Curious, he put in a couple of quarters. The bed began to vibrate. He had felt the same thing before, during a minor tremblor in San Francisco. The motion made him queasy. He walked across the room and lowered his bulk into a chair placed so that one had a view of the sea. The phone rang. Finally. He grabbed it and said, "Hello? Hello?"

The operator said, "A Mr. Caldwell is in the lobby asking to see you, sir. May I send him down?"

"I don't know anybody named Caldwell. You must have the wrong room."

24

"Excuse it, sir." There was a click. He put down the phone. He was about to change clothes when the phone rang again. The operator said, "This is Mary at the desk. Is this Mr. Dade Cooley?"

"Yes, it is."

"Well, the party here insists that you know him. He says he's the attorney for a Mr. Welles. He apologizes for intruding on you at a time like this but would like to see you."

"Oh, Caldwell *Ballinger*. All right, send him down." Dade took off his jacket and vest, pulled on a sweater, then went to the door, watching the funicular descend. The man in it was heavyset, his weight concealed by a double-breasted pin-striped suit. The funicular jarred to a stop.

Ballinger got out, looked around and then headed for Dade's open door. He was an ugly man with a thick nose, thick lips and dark eyes behind thick glasses. Ballinger extended a fleshy hand. "Good afternoon, Mr. Cooley."

Dade shook hands with him. "It's been a long time," he said. He led Ballinger into what the brochure on the bureau described as a "cabaña suite." Two chairs were drawn up in front of an empty blackened fireplace. Dade nodded toward them.

Ballinger set down his brief case on the rickety table and said, "This is a sad time for all of us."

"Yes, indeed." Dade seated himself and Ballinger did the same.

He snapped open his brief case and started fishing for something inside, flicking through papers, unsnapping pouches and looking in them.

Dade said, "I had a third-grade teacher used to do that. Every morning at the start of the school day, she used to go through all the drawers in her desk, looking for something. Never did find out what it was."

"Is that so?"

"Miss Barrett, her name was. Nice woman. As a favor she used to let me stay after school to clean the erasers."

Ballinger found what he was looking for, a thick manila envelope, and handed it to Dade. "This is yours, I believe, sir. It's a court order giving you power of attorney as executor for the late Miriam Welles. You'll find the keys to her safe-deposit box in it."

"Thank you kindly." Dade put the envelope in his pocket.

Ballinger said, "Her papers, bank statements and the like, both the personal ones and the ones for the gallery, are all at the house. I can arrange to have them sent to you here or in San Francisco, whichever you prefer."

"You got my address up in San Francisco?"

"Yes, sir."

"Just send them along."

"Mr. Welles asked me to deliver a message to you."

"All right."

"He wanted me to express his appreciation to you for attending the services."

"Thank you."

"He knew you weren't planning to come by this afternoon." When Dade looked up as if he were going to say something, Ballinger held up a fat hand. "No, it's quite all right. He understands." Ballinger hesitated for a moment, then said: "They tell me you had some questions about the sheriff's report. I was called just as a matter of form. I told them to give you the fullest cooperation."

"Thank you very much."

"I hope the questions were answered to your satisfaction?"

"Um-hm. Jensen, I suppose he's satisfied?"

"Certainly."

"The investigation, it doesn't amount to much more than an on-the-scene report from one patrolman."

Ballinger stretched out his hands, touching the palms and rotating them, like a conjurer about to perform a trick. He said, "There is nothing to investigate. Mrs. Welles died in a tragic accident. A prominent man like Mr. Welles is quite aware that if an investigation is protracted, it would be bound to attract the attention of the media. And to what end? Mr. Welles has suffered quite enough. He has accepted what happened to his wife and wants only to be left in peace." The brown skin wrinkled around the eyes, magnified behind the thick lenses. A pink tongue moistened the thick lips.

"And poor Rachel, how is she taking it?"

"As well as can be expected."

"Of course, the young regard death as an affront. That's because they have no experience of it."

"I'm sure that's very true." Ballinger began snapping shut the compartments of his brief case.

"My wife told me about a tribe of aboriginals that regarded all deaths as caused by witchcraft. Reason was, they had no experience of any person dying of natural causes. I guess accidents are always hard to accept."

"Very interesting." Ballinger got to his feet. "I'll be getting along," he said.

Dade saw him to the door, saying, "You tell Jensen for me that I appreciate this, you hear?"

Ballinger smiled, showing a little row of brownish teeth. "I'll tell him."

Dade saw him out, and then called room service and ordered fresh sand dabs, asparagus, new potatoes and a pear with a wedge of Roquefort. "You folks got any of the Spring Mountain Chardonnay left?"

"Just a minute, sir." A pause, then: "No, sir. But I can send you down some Chalone."

"That'll do nicely." He put down the phone, went into the bathroom and took a shower. Afterward, he dried himself with a big rough towel, then stomped out into the room, pulling fresh clothes from the suitcase and muttering, "I got my hair and I got the dick of a man of forty and that's the secret, that's the fountain of youth and don't let anybody kid you."

V

A few minutes later, the phone rang. He answered it and Ellen's voice said, "Dade?"

"Ellen! Hi, honey."

"How are you, dearest?"

"I miss you."

"I'm sure you do. Oh darling, are you comfortable?"

"Sure."

"I can just see you in that awful place. It's so damp there. Why on earth don't you build a fire?"

He stared at the empty fireplace. "How do you know I haven't built a fire?"

"Because you left the back curtains open."

"Where the hell are you?"

"In the lobby. I'll be right down."

When he went outside, she was already descending in the funicular, wearing a long beige coat with a fur collar, her arms around herself as if she were cold. The car stopped. He opened the cage door and tried to embrace her. She stopped him.

"Be careful."

"What is it?"

"I have two logs under my coat. I got them from the lobby." He took them from her. "Watch out. One of them is still smoking."

Then went into his room and he built a fire. There was a knock at the door. Ellen opened it and let in a bellboy, his arms full of groceries.

"You want me to put these things in the kitchen, lady?"

"Whatever gave you an idea like that?"

The boy carried the bags to the pass-through, then started taking the groceries out of the bags and setting them down on the sideboard. He was a lean, muscular boy in his mid-twenties with lank blond hair and a deep tan. Holding the package of bacon Ellen had bought, he weighed it in his hand and said, "Nitrites. Bad."

"Your mother raised you right," she said.

The boy checked the refrigerator to see whether it was working, tried the sink faucet and then glanced at the stove. "We had trouble here after the rains. I just wanted to make sure things were working."

"I guess that was a pretty terrible storm," Dade said.

"It was bad."

"Were you here?"

"Down the road."

"Well, you're a good boy and you can tell your mother I said so," said Dade.

"She's not here, she's back East." He grinned at them. His teeth were white, straight, with shovel-shaped incisors.

"Where do you live?" Ellen asked.

"In an ashram." Seeing her puzzled look, he explained. "Like a commune."

Dade came toward them and gave him a dollar. The boy thanked him and stuffed it in his jeans pocket.

"Why do you call it that?" Ellen asked.

"That's what Mahatma Yaksha calls it."

Ellen's face was suddenly full of interest. "You belong to that—what do you call it, Mission of Light?"

"Holy Light. Yes, ma'am."

"May I ask you something?"

"Sure."

"You won't mind?" He shrugged. She said, "Well, doesn't it bother you, his driving around in a custom Mercedes?"

He said, his face serious, "I wish there were a better car in the world—you know what I mean? more expensive—so we could buy him that."

"How much do you give him?"

"Everything." He turned to Dade. "This money you gave me. I don't keep it. It goes to the ashram. Everything I make."

"And that makes you happy?" Dade asked.

"The Mahatma makes me happy. Happy isn't the word. The Mahatma is my life. Everything." He took a card out of his pocket, offering it to Dade. "Here." It read, "Help! We clean up after everybody. No job too small. Ken and Pete." There were two telephone numbers printed in the corner, one for days and one for evenings.

"There are eight of us but we just put two names on the card. I'm Pete. We do everything. Floors, windows, pools—"

"You ever work at the Welles place, boy?"

"Where that lady was killed? Gee, that was a pretty sad thing."

"You ever work there?"

"We bid a job."

"But you didn't work there."

"She was going to call us. Tell you the truth, I thought we had the job. I drove by that night and I was sure I saw Ken's car there."

"What night was that, son?" Dade asked softly.

"Night of the storm."

"Tuesday?"

"For a fact."

"And Ken—that's your friend on this here card, is that right?"

"That's Ken."

"Was Ken working there?"

"That's what I thought, so I started to pull in—see we all work together, and I thought I'd help him out. But then I saw that it wasn't Ken's car. It was a blue Mustang fastback, just like Ken's, all right, but Ken's has a white interior. This one was dark. Besides, Ken's is in better shape. So I saw it wasn't Ken and I just drove off. After, I heard what happened, so I figured there wasn't going to be any job, no way."

"You happen to remember what time this was, Pete?"

"Right after I got off work. I was driving home. Let's see, I get off here at nine. The Welles place is right down the road."

"About ten minutes, wouldn't you say?"

"Yeah." The boy put his head to one side and looked at Dade. "How come you're asking?"

"Just curious."

"You know the lady?"

"I knew her."

"I'm sorry, mister."

"Thank you."

"The way we look at it, there is no death."

"Well, I'm glad the question has been settled after so many years. Tell me, sonny, what was the job you were going to do for Mrs. Welles?"

"Patching a leaky roof."

"What were you going to do about the dogs?"

"Let me clue you in about them dogs." Dade looked at him sharply. A grin, slower this time. "They got these big attack dogs. They're funny. You know, I heard a story once about this guy who had to go back to somebody's office late at night to get some papers. They had an attack dog. The guy gets inside and the dog, he just looks at him, sitting down, wagging his tail. Well, the guy gets the papers and starts to leave and the dog goes ape. The poor guy spent the whole night trapped in the corner with this big dog nailing him down, growling at him. See, the dog had been trained to let burglars in but not out. Well, he wasn't a burglar but you see what I mean. Anyway, these Welles dogs are like that, but in reverse. Once you're inside, you're all right. The maid, she took us inside and then we went out the side door and those dogs, they were pussycats."

Dade gave him another bill, thanking him. "You going to be at these numbers you gave me on this here card?"

"I guess."

Ellen went into the bathroom to freshen up. Pete started to leave. Dade stopped him.

"I may be asking more questions about this lady's death. If I come looking for you, I better find you. You understand me?"

"I told you everything. For a fact."

"I still may have more questions."

"I don't want to get involved, mister, okay?"

"You talk to me or you might end up talking to the sheriff, understand?"

"Yes, sir." Pete left.

Ellen came out of the bathroom. "I'll start lunch."

"I ordered lunch."

"I cancelled it. Besides, I'm sure the fish I brought is fresher." She went behind the bar of the kitchen and began cooking.

"Better do some more shopping. I got a feeling we'll be staying a day or two longer."

Ellen looked at him, surprised. "Is something wrong?"

"Yeah."

"What?"

"I don't know." There was a knock at the door. Dade opened it and found Pete standing there.

"Okay if I come in?" Dade opened the door wider and Pete entered. He rubbed his palms on his trousers and looked at the floor. "I just wanted to tell you this. A while back—this is a few years ago—I was with some guys back East when they held up a liquor store. Nobody got hurt but we all got busted. I was a minor. They gave me six months' detention. I don't know about that dead lady and Ken, I'm sure he don't, neither, and I hope you believe me."

Dade walked up and down for a few moments. Then he said, "The rabbis tell us that if a strange woman arrives from a foreign country and says she is divorced, we must believe her since she would have no reason to lie. Do you understand that?"

"No, sir."

"Do you know who the rabbis are?"

"Jew folks, right?"

Dade opened his mouth and then shut it again. "Thank you."

"It's all right," Pete said.

"I'll see you tomorrow."

"That's what I wanted to talk to you about. I won't be here tomorrow."

"I hope there's not another liquor store in your sights."

"Pardon me?"

"Why won't you be here, son?"

"I got laid off."

"I see."

"You got my card. Anything you want to ask me, just call up." He went to the door. "So long, sir." The boy left.

Rummaging in his pockets, Dade found his small leather-covered notebook and his gold pencil and made a note to himself, lip-reading the words as he wrote them, allowing Ellen to sit him down at his place. He put the card Pete had given him in the notebook, put away the pencil, stuffed the book back into his pocket and then sat staring into space.

Ellen said, serving him lunch, "How was this morning? I suppose it was awful. How could it have been anything else?"

"It wasn't too bad."

"Did you talk to Rachel?"

"No. She wasn't at the funeral. And I haven't heard from her, either. When I think about how she sounded on the phone—telling me she was afraid and had to see me and to wait for her call—"

Ellen said, "Are you telling me Miriam could have been murdered?"

"Any death could be murder. Ever think about that?"

"Well, this just sounds to me like adolescent imagination."

"I stopped by the sheriff's to find out just what happened to Miriam."

"My dear brave detective, did you learn anything?" When he told her what he had found out from the sheriff, something in his expression bothered her.

"What is going *on?* You act as if—"

"Jensen wants me out of here." She stared at him in disbelief. "Fact. He sent Ballinger here to make sure I got Miriam's papers right away—translation: to speed up my departure." He glanced at his watch impatiently. "I've waited long enough." He snatched up the phone and dialed a number.

The number rang twice. Then a voice answered, saying, "Miriam Welles speaking." Dade reacted in shock, then he caught himself. He was listening to a recorded message. He had forgotten and called her private number. There was a beeping signal. Ellen saw the look on his face and said, "Dade?" He put down the phone quickly, his hand trembling. He went to the bureau, picked up his wallet, took out an address book and checked the number of the Welles house. At that moment the phone rang. He picked it up.

"Yes?"

"Dade?" It was Rachel's voice now. She spoke softly.

"Rachel, honey, is that you?"

"Dade, can you come to where I am? I'll give you the address. Now, it sounds complicated but it isn't really—" She gave him directions.

"I'll be right there." He put down the phone. Ellen helped him into his coat.

She said, "I'm curious about something. Ask Rachel if Miriam tried to stop Jensen."

"Stop him?"

"From going out. It was the worst storm of the year, wasn't it? I wouldn't have let you go out. Not without a very good excuse."

"Maybe he had one."

"Find out."

"Jess Watmough still own this place?" Dade asked.

"I think so. We haven't seen him in years."

"Well, call the manager and send Jess our regards. Then mention how much we appreciate Pete." He kissed her and hurried away.

He drove south on the highway through what, in his childhood, had been a private rancho, all twenty-two miles of it fenced off from the rest of the world, with cowboys riding shotgun along its boundaries, while the old lady who owned the whole thing, the Queen of the Malibu, built her castle in the center, filling it with wall-to-wall Persian carpets made of tile and fought a lifetime battle for her privacy, galloping side-saddle with her guards around her realm. Now the highway through the legendary rancho was public, and Dade drove across the old Spanish land grant, legally called Rancho Topanga Malibu Sequit, on his way to visit the girl the newspapers called "the Billion Dollar Baby."

VI

He drove along the water's edge past the dilapidated amusement park on the Santa Monica pier and then down the narrow thoroughfare of Main Street into Venice. On his left, the long-abandoned canals were ditches overgrown with weeds. Above them stood shingled weatherbeaten Victorian houses looking out on the wide blank expanse of the sea. The air was different from that of Malibu. It was pungent with iodine because the beaches here were shallow and broad and strewn with kelp thrown up by the high tide.

Following the directions Rachel had given him, Dade turned left and went up Rose to a ramshackle three-story Victorian mansion with turrets and a widow's walk, the outside covered with shingles cut in the form of fish scales. It had been turned into apartments. As Dade parked, he could see a sign reading NO VACANCY. He got out and walked toward the front door. There were nameplates and buzzers for almost a dozen tenants. Dade found WELLES, 307 and rang the bell. He had to ring it twice before a scratchy voice came through the grating over a speaker, asking, "Who is it?"

Dade said, "It's me, honey. Dade."

A buzzer made a prolonged vibrating sound. Dade pushed open the heavy front door and went into a linoleum-covered lobby and up a broad flight of stairs to the second floor, where a gallery ran around the stairwell. Another stairway doubled back and up to the third floor. There, an arrow above the numbers of four more apartments pointed to a corridor at the back, leading to what were once servants' quarters. Dade walked down a narrow hall. At the far end, he heard a sound of bolts being drawn. A chain rattled. A door opened, slightly at first, then wider. Rachel stood there. She was barefoot and dressed only in faded jeans and a fisherman's sweater. Her hair was even redder than he had remembered it, a tousled mop.

She looked at him without expression, twisting her thin hands together, the blue eyes dark, almost hard. Then she threw her arms around him, burying her face in his coat and murmuring his name over and over. He patted her head. She lifted her freckled face and smiled at him and he found himself remembering the freckled faces of his childhood and wondering why one didn't seem to see them so much anymore. She took his hand and led him into her room.

"Well," she said. He looked around. The room was small, containing a brass bed with a chenille bedspread, a dropleaf desk with a Windsor chair and a bridge lamp and a shabby wing chair. On the back of the door hung a black dress, freshly pressed. It was a corner room with small casement windows looking down on the intersection below. Rachel rubbed her palms on her jeans and gestured at one window. "If you lean out of it, you can see the ocean. It's very nice."

"Yes. Yes, very nice."

"Please sit down." She indicated the wing chair and sat opposite him, elbows on her knees. On the desk, he could see a photograph in a little cardboard frame. It showed Rachel on the beach next to a young man with his arm around her. He had the build of a weightlifter and the face of Baryshnikov. He was dressed in a wet suit and his other arm held a surfboard. Seeing Dade looking at it, she handed it to him, saying, "His name is Nick Levin. He's beautiful, isn't he? He's Russian. That is, he's from Russia. He lives here now."

"What does he do?"

"He makes money. Lots of money."

"How?"

"In commodities. We're going to be married, Dade."

"My felicitations, Rachel." He returned the photograph.

"Thank you." She put the photograph on her desk carefully, hesitated and then took another one out of a drawer and gave it to him. It was a picture of Miriam and Rachel on the pool deck of the Welles house, both of them in bathing suits, both shading their eyes in the bright sun. Rachel was grinning. They had their arms around each other's waist. "That was the last picture taken of her," she said. "It was just a few weeks ago."

Dade nodded, handing the picture back. Rachel stood it up next to the photograph of herself and Nick. He looked around the room, seeing a hot plate with a kettle on it. It was sitting on an old sea chest, and there were cups and spoons beside it. Above on a shelf, was a little store of provisions. To the right was a small refrigerator. Following his glance, Rachel smiled and gestured, saying, "My kitchen." She pointed in the other direction. "Bathroom down the hall. Would you like tea or anything?"

"Not just now, thanks, honey."

"Well . . ."

There was a strained silence. Rachel looked away. The smile remained on her lips as if she had forgotten about it.

Dade said, "I looked for you today at the funeral."

"I—I didn't go," she said unnecessarily.

"How's that, honey?" She answered him with an exaggerated shrug, still not meeting his eyes. "How come you didn't go to the funeral, Rachel?"

"He asked me not to." She looked at him now with a bright blank smile and said, "I was upset, very upset, and finally he said if I didn't stop it, *he'd* be upset and so would I please either control myself or stay home? so I didn't go." Then she burst into tears, crying in the voice of a lost child and rocking back and forth in her chair. She turned away from him, put her head down in her arms on the desk and gave herself up to sobbing.

After a moment, Dade hoisted himself out of his chair and went to her, patting her thin shoulders and murmuring words of reassurance. She lifted her head, let out a shuddering sigh and, grabbing for a Kleenex, wiped her eyes quickly and blew her nose.

"Maybe he was right," she said finally. "I'm sorry, Dade."

He nodded, sitting down again and lacing his fingers,

squinting at her through half-closed lids. Then he said, "There a school around here somewheres?"

"A school?"

"I thought maybe you moved in here to be close to campus."

"I'm taking a year off." He could hardly blame her. She had graduated from high school at fifteen and had already completed three years at Vassar. "I was going to go abroad and then I met Nick. It's because of him."

"Nick?"

She nodded at the photograph. "He asked me to marry him. My father doesn't approve of him. This has gone on for months now. It got so he wouldn't even let Nick in the house. I said I was eighteen and I was certainly going to go on seeing him and Dad said, 'Fine, if that's the way things are, you can move out and see him on your own.' So—well, I did."

"What did Miriam say?"

"Oh, she tried to make me wait. She kept saying Dad would change his mind and to give him a chance. Well, I'd given him a chance for about three months and things just got worse and I finally decided this was all I could do."

"How are you living, Rachel?"

"I got a job as a waitress. It's just one of those counters, so I don't get tips, but after I get experience I can do better."

"You mean he's not helping you?"

"Dad? Oh, no. He made things very clear. He told me if I moved out, that was that."

"Hard for me to believe that Miriam went along with that."

"Oh, Miriam didn't! She was terribly upset and kept trying to sneak me money, but it's his money"—there was an edge to her voice now—"it's his money and I don't want it. Since it means so much to him, he can keep it. Every last cent."

"It's your money, Rachel."

"When he dies. Not before. You know that, Dade. Look, it's all right. I don't need anything. Nick tried to help me, too. After all, Nick makes about ten thousand dollars a month, for God's sake, but I wouldn't let him. I told him he could support me after we're married. It's just the way I am."

"I respect you for it."

"Thank you, Dade."

He got up from his chair again, went to the open window and leaned on the sill, looking out to his left. Above the rooftops, he could just catch the shimmer of the sea. He stared out at the view for some moments, then grunted and ducked his head back into the room. Rachel had gotten up and poured herself a diet drink from the refrigerator. She made a sign offering him one, but he shook his head. She sipped it, watching him over the rim of her glass.

"I've been waiting to hear from you," he said.

"I'm sorry. I waited to call because I thought you'd gone to the house with everyone else."

"Something's really bothering you, isn't it?" She nodded dumbly. "Why don't you just take a deep breath and tell me about it?"

"I don't want to make trouble—"

"Why don't you let me worry about that?"

She nodded again and then looked up and said, "Shall I just plunge right in?"

"Go ahead."

She began pacing up and down the far side of her little room in her bare feet, measuring her steps, talking slowly at first, then more rapidly. "Yesterday, Dad got the body released from the coroner's. I was at the house going through her things when the funeral director called, asking for clothes. It was stupid because nobody thought of it. Dad had gone by and chosen a casket and then they were stuck because the body was supposed to be ready by yesterday afternoon and they didn't have any clothes for her. Dad came home just then and I said I wanted her to have the Persian robe. Did you remember it, Dade, when you saw it today?"

"Yes, indeed."

"It was her favorite thing in the world. You know, it's two hundred years old and absolute perfection. It's a work of art. She's only worn it half a dozen times. She kept it in her cedar closet in a special camphor bag she had made for it. Well, I went to get it and it wasn't there. I mean, it wasn't there."

"Uh-huh." He watched her through lidded eyes, taking out an old briar pipe and filling it from a chamois pouch.

"Well, at first I thought Dad had had the same idea but when I went to him, I don't think he even knew what I was talking about. He was impatient with me. He said everybody would be kept waiting and to choose something else and get it over to them. Well, I just wouldn't. Miriam adored that. Of course, it belongs in a museum, not a grave, but I—" Her lips quivered.

"Now, just take it easy."

"I made them wait. I searched the whole house. It just couldn't be gone. At one point I thought maybe it had been stolen—it is worth thousands, of course, but nobody would break into the house to steal a thing like that, not with Dad's paintings all over the walls. My father got mad. He followed me from room to room while I searched and finally said he'd just choose something himself— maybe that dress she'd worn in Santa Barbara. He went slamming out to look for it. She liked it, so I gave up. I was going to get that. I remembered it was in that suitcase she'd left in the car. We found it there the night she was killed. It's the one they had taken to Santa Barbara with them for the weekend and she just hadn't bothered to have it brought in. The night she was killed, I brought it in myself and put it in her room. I was going to unpack it but I couldn't bring myself to open it. She used to put sprigs of lavender from the garden in with her clothes and I thought, if I see that all wrapped up in tissue paper—well, I just couldn't open it, that's all.

"But now, it had to be opened because that's where the dress Dad wanted was. I unlocked the suitcase—it's one of those combination locks and I knew the combination, it was her birth date—and when I opened it, there was the Persian robe in its camphor bag!"

"She'd taken it with her to Santa Barbara, is that it?"

"Dade, she would never have taken it there. You think she'd crush something like that in a suitcase for a weekend at San Ysidro? She would have looked like a fool, wearing that at a ranch! It's just impossible, you have to believe me."

"I see." But he didn't. He was trying to think through the implications of what she was saying. She put a slim hand on the sleeve of his tweed jacket and looked at him with imploring eyes, as if she were afraid he wouldn't believe her.

"There's more. Wait. I didn't stop and think. I was late. I called out to Dad that I'd found it and then took it into town for her myself and left it at the funeral parlor. They said they were just doing her hair and face and if I came back in an hour, she would be ready. It sounds like a doll, doesn't it? It's horrible, Dade. I don't know why we do it, I really don't.

"I went out and had coffee. I couldn't think. My hands were shaking and I was afraid I was going to faint. Then I went back and Dad was there, they had Miriam ready—I could see just her hair from the back of the room but I couldn't bring myself to go up and look—and then people began to arrive and I stayed near the door the whole evening, never once going up to see her until they'd all gone. Then I went back to the house. I went into Miriam's room. I could face the suitcase then. I was restless, I wanted something to do. I thought, I'll unpack for her. So I started to. Dade, you just won't believe what I found. In that suitcase was every bit of jewelry she had in the house—not the stuff in the safe-deposit box but the things she wore all the time and cared about—Japanese combs covered with bright blue velvety designs, all made of tiny birds' feathers, a leather-bound journal she kept when she was a student years ago in Florence, photographs, letters from you, from me, well, I don't have to go on. She must have been packing for days! You see what I'm saying. She was running away!" She broke off, breathless.

The eyes Dade fixed on her were points of light. "Where *is* that suitcase?"

"In her study. I saw what was in it and I just left it the way it was. Do you want to see it?"

"Later, I want to see it. What happened then? You tell your father?"

"Not right away. I just kept trying to make sense out of

everything and I couldn't. It couldn't have been some sick practical joke. The suitcase was locked and I don't know whether anybody but me knows the combination. I don't think Dad knows or even remembers but even if he did, why on earth would he do something so crazy? No, Miriam did it. There isn't a doubt in the world."

"You say you went in and told this to your father?"

"Yes. At first I was in a state of shock. I think I must have waited about half an hour. I went through all her things. You see, all the things she took were from different places. I knew where she kept them. No, it was Miriam. Nobody else put those things in that suitcase. It was that she was running away—as if she were afraid! But when I said maybe it wasn't an accident, he got just furious and told me I was crazy and to shut up!"

"Wasn't it obvious to him that she was leaving?"

"He says she's dead and that asking questions won't bring her back. You know why he's afraid? He's sixty-seven. He's proud. He's possessive. He knows if there's any investigation, people will find out she was leaving him and he can't stand that! He'd rather bury the truth than have that known!" Her voice had grown louder and louder.

He sighed, pinching the bridge of his nose, trying to think. Then he said, "Miriam say anything to you that last night that might give us a clue? Sheriff's report says you were there earlier."

She shook her head. "We just talked about how things were going—mostly about Nick and me."

"That's why you went there? Just to see her?"

"Oh no. It was Dad. He had called and said he wanted to see me, that it was important. Well, I—I went over to the house around five. Dad wasn't due back until later but Miriam was sick and I wanted to look in on her. She asked me to do a few things for her and I did. I turned up the monitor on the answering machine so she wouldn't have to answer the phone if she didn't want to. And I made her some tea with honey in it. I stayed with her until about six, when Dad got home. Then, a little while later—"

"How did she seem?"

"Oh, she was sick. She was coughing and I kept telling her not to use her voice. She told me the Arco man had

called about an hour before and that her car was ready
and asked me if I'd drive down with Dad when he went
out and pick it up for her. I said yes and that I'd just
leave it in the garage and not wake her."

"I mean, how were her spirits?"

"Oh, well, you know what she was like—always gay,
full of life."

"So, you didn't have the impression that anything was
bothering her?"

"Oh, heavens, no! As a matter of fact—well, you know
how you feel when you've got the flu. I expected to find
her like that. But she was just glowing. She kept talking
about Nick and me—she was crazy about him, she didn't
share Dad's feeling at all—and what she wanted was for
me to be patient, because she was sure Dad would come
around, and I promised I would be."

"In other words, if anything was worrying Miriam—oh,
say, if she'd had a fight with your father or if she was in
some kind of trouble she didn't mention, you saw no sign
of it?"

"No. That's why none of this makes any sense."

"I see." Dade put his fingers together and gazed into
them, as if they contained an invisible crystal ball. He
said, "You say your father came home around six?"

"Yes."

"What happened then?"

"Oh, he came in for a moment—just put his head in the
door because he didn't want her germs—to ask how she
was and then went into his own room to shower and
change. About half an hour later he called through the
open door, saying he'd be in the library watching the
news. Miriam said I ought to go down and sit with him, so
I did."

"Did you talk?"

"No. He had a drink. I think I had a Dr. Pepper. We
watched the news for almost an hour and then it was time
for dinner."

"Miriam join you?"

"Dad asked Rosarita to tell her dinner was ready. Rosarita said she was sleeping. Just then, the house phone
rang. It only rang once, so that meant Miriam had an-

swered it. Dad was annoyed and said, 'She is not sleeping!
Go tell her dinner is served.' So Rosarita had to go and
call her and apparently Miriam had been sleeping and said
she didn't want anyone to wake her again, so that ended
that."

"I see."

"Well, I was having dinner with Nick. I was meeting
him at nine."

"Did your father know that?"

"No. I had learned never to mention Nick around him.
To avoid scenes. He doesn't get into *arguments*. He thinks
they're vulgar. He just says something cutting and walks
out of the room. Anyway, I sat with Dad and had a little
to eat and it was arranged that we would go out together
and get Miriam's car around eight-thirty. Well, anyway,
we just sat there, with me wondering why he had wanted
to see me and knowing it must be something serious because he wasn't talking about it over dinner." Dade
nodded. Rachel looked away, smoothing the wrinkles in
her jeans. After a moment or two, she went on: "When
dinner was over, he asked me to excuse him for a few
minutes and went into the library. I went into the game
room and looked out the windows and watched the storm.
In a few minutes, he called me on the intercom and asked
me to come in and see him.

"I went in. He was standing there with his hands behind
his back. He'd had detectives on Nick for months. I
thought maybe this was going to be about that but he
didn't mention them. He looked as if he could barely control himself. His face was absolutely white. I thought
something terrible must have happened. But all he said
was that he wanted me to move back into the house and
to promise him that I would never see Nick again. Then
he went over and sat down behind his desk and that was
when I saw there was a gun there."

"There was a gun?" Dade looked at her sharply.

"Yes. Lying on the desk in front of him. You know,
he's a crack shot. Well, of course you know. You must.
He said that if I loved Nick, I would want to protect him.
I knew what he was talking about, of course. I was terribly frightened."

"When you say you knew what he was talking about, you mean that he was actually making a threat against Nick."

"Yes."

"Did he ever mention the gun?"

"No."

"Did he ever pick it up?"

"No."

"Did he toy with it—with a pencil, for example, or in any way draw your attention to it?"

"No. Anyway, that was all. He left the room. I was scared to death. I called Nick at his apartment and told him what had happened. Then I said, 'You get out of there right now.' Well, Nick acted like a damn fool. He said he wanted to come over and have it out with Dad right then and there and that was just more than I could stand. I said, 'Please, please don't do that. Just meet me at nine o'clock as we planned.' I could hear Dad coming down the hall, so I didn't dare talk any longer."

"Your father knows where Nick's apartment is?"

"Oh, yes. It's just five minutes down the Old Road, a little beach shack. He moved in there so we'd be near each other. Anyway, I wanted to talk to Miriam but that meant waking her up when she was sick and I couldn't do it. Just then, Dad came in, looking around for his raincoat. He said it was time to go and I said, 'I'll just run up for a second and see if Miriam is all right while you get the car, and then I'll meet you out front.'"

"But you said you drove."

"Well, Ballinger called him just then and when I came back downstairs, Dad was still on the phone so I went in to the game room and turned on the floods so I could look out the window and see the driveway. There was mud everywhere. I wasn't even sure Dad could get his car out. I went in to Dad and told him. I said mine was in front and if he wanted, we could take that and he could drive Miriam's into town. It was either that or risk getting his stuck in the mud. Well, he just loves that car—you know, it's got a bar and a television set in the back—so he decided he'd better play it safe and take Miriam's. Am I telling you what you want to know?"

"Just keep talking, honey."

"Well—we left then and I drove him down to the Arco station."

"What is that, about ten minutes from here?"

"About. So then, well, I let him out and waited to make sure he didn't have any trouble starting Miriam's car, and then I made a U-turn on the highway—you know, the Arco station is on the other side—and drove on in to meet Nick. When I got to the restaurant and I didn't see him I was in an absolute panic. He drove up just then. I can't tell you how relieved I was. He got me calmed down and we spent the whole evening trying to decide what to do.

"That's why I called Miriam. I had to talk to her and tell her what happened. And when I didn't get any answer, I thought, She's gotten worse, and I drove back because I had to see her. And then when I got there—" She broke off, shocked at the memory.

He asked, "Honey, was Miriam upset at the idea of your father going out?"

"No. Not in the least." His question puzzled her.

"She didn't try to stop him?"

"I don't understand."

"From going out in that storm."

She considered this, a line furrowing between her brows. Then, "No."

"Did you?"

"You don't try to stop Dad from anything."

"Why did he have to go into town?"

"*I* don't know." She was impatient. "To go to his office."

"Why at night?"

"I haven't the slightest idea. Why don't you ask him? What I want to know is, where was Miriam going?"

"Where do you think, Rachel? You got any idea?"

"She wouldn't have left without telling me. I mean, she just wouldn't have! You must believe me. It's impossible! Not even a note—nothing! Something happened after we left—I think something scared her to death. Dade, what should I do?"

"Rachel," he said, "you know where her papers are?"

"In a box in her study."

"I wonder if I can pick them up today?"

She dialed a number and got no answer. "Gone," she said. "Party's over. Dad generally goes to the club Friday afternoons to get a rubdown." She pulled a long face and croaked in a deep voice, imitating her father, "If anyone calls, I'll be at the club." Then her face brightened and she said, "Why don't I just meet you at the house and give them to you?"

"When?"

"Let's go right now." She picked up her keys and wallet and walked to the door, opening it to let him out.

"You don't need shoes?"

"In Malibu?" She grinned, shaking her head as she locked up behind them and then led him downstairs. In separate cars, they drove back to Malibu, Rachel ahead of him, speeding out of sight.

VII

The Welles house was not visible from the highway, and there was no address. Dade drove by it, missing it altogether and only realizing that he had when he found himself headed up toward the Malibu Inn. He pulled into the left-turn lane and sat there for a minute or two before he could make a U-turn and head back south again. It took him another few minutes to find the driveway.

Turning into it, he curved around through a screen of eucalyptus and then, ahead of him at the end of a dirt road, he saw the gates. They were wrought iron, not the cheap imitation shown in catalogues and referred to as "wrought-iron style." The automatic lock was also the real thing, heavy duty, and a sign on the top of a stone pillar said that the land on which he now stood was private property, that it was patrolled, that trespassers would be prosecuted (the particular ordinance which applied here was cited by number) and that the house and grounds were protected by the Westinghouse burglar-alarm system.

Dade climbed out of his car and walked around to have a look at things. There was very little to see. The dense row of eucalyptus, topped so that the foliage hung down almost to the ground, screened him from the highway. Myoporum, oak and pine grew in the stretch of land between the highway and the fence, so that even the sea wasn't visible from here. Inside the fence, a neat row of ficus towering up twenty feet effectively blocked the view. The air was scented with rosemary. Dade walked toward the gates and rang a bell with a microphone-speaker set in the pillar above it.

Suddenly two Dobermans with nail-studded collars charged straight at him, eyes glaring. They began to bark furiously. A sign on the fence read WARNING! ATTACK DOGS! Over the intercom, Dade could hear Rachel's voice answering his ring. She was saying something but he couldn't hear because the dogs kept leaping toward him and barking. Finally, Rachel's voice said, "Dade! Your car! Please get back in your car!"

He climbed into the driver's seat. The voice called out over the intercom, "Are you back in your car?" He tooted his horn. The gates then swung open automatically and he drove in. The gates closed behind him and the dogs, suddenly quiet, trotted off as if they had no interest in him at all and never had had.

The road was gravel, wide enough for two cars and marked by railroad ties set on end deep in the ground, with small green-hooded garden lights mounted beside them every ten feet or so. He drove past a tennis court with the fencing screened against the wind and sun with green canvas and then, finally, the house was visible, a big California beach house looking like a picture out of *Sunset*, all huge dark beams and walls of glass, with a big circular drive made of upended railroad ties close-set, something like ajuga growing between them and a giant California live oak welled in the center.

Dade climbed out of his car and went toward the entrance. It was shaded, set at the back of a Japanese garden with mounds of azaleas clipped close like boxwood, and from somewhere just out of sight, the sound of falling water. Rachel came out.

"I'm sorry," she said. "I would have left the gates open but the dogs would run out." The Dobermans trotted up and nuzzled her. She patted them.

Dade looked at them. "Safe, are they?"

"Here, yes."

"Who trained them to do that?"

"Nobody. It's their own idea."

"They look mean."

"I think they are. Oh, it's so stupid to have attack dogs." She looked around quickly toward the half-open door, as if afraid of being overheard. "I mean, friends of ours had one and a boy climbed the fence—he was just a kid, maybe nine or ten—and it was just terrible, what happened. People say dogs know. They don't know. I hate dogs like that. I wouldn't have one. It's all Dad and his paintings. Well, come on in!"

She led him into a wide gallery walled with white stucco and floored with Mexican tiles. Dade looked up at the gilt-framed Renaissance paintings covering the walls.

"I hear he's bought himself a Botticelli."

"He has to keep it locked up. He can't take it out unless the Pinkerton man is here or else they cancel the insurance."

He frowned. "Something like that gets too big for one man to own. It's like owning a Bach partita or a Shakespeare sonnet. I guess I just don't understand it, honey. Not much room left. What does he do when he buys new ones, sell off a few?"

"Dad sell a painting? Oh, never. You know how he started. At first he just bought paintings as investments. Then, when Mother fell ill, Miriam went to work for him. Miriam trained his eye. She taught him practically everything he knows. Well, something funny happened. She found a Michelangelo drawing he really wanted. It was terribly overpriced, but the man who owned it wanted two small paintings of my father's and Miriam thought it would be a perfect trade. They weren't important, they weren't even that good, but they both happened to be mentioned by Vasari. Well, Dad just hit the roof. He wouldn't sell, he wouldn't trade—something had happened to him and he just couldn't let go of anything. It got to him, do you know?

"It's hard to understand if you're not like that, just the way gambling doesn't make sense to people who don't gamble. Anyway, that's what happened. He keeps buying paintings, saying they're a hedge against inflation, but it's not that. This collection is *him*. It's what he hopes to be remembered for. He's going to leave it to a museum on the condition that they keep it intact and call it the Jensen Welles Collection. What he really wants is for the whole hundred million to be spent adding to it. He can't ever touch the money, of course, but if I went into it with him, then he feels I would carry on after he's gone. That's his dream. And that's why Nick is a threat. He doesn't want someone else to get his hands on my money. At least, that's what I think."

They walked past the open door of the library. Inside, Dade could see a portrait of Miriam hung at the end of the room, the lips about to break into the familiar smile, the oval face framed in the dark lustrous hair.

Dade said, "That one I suppose he'll never part with."

Suddenly serious, Rachel said, "I wish it were mine so I could give it to you."

"I'll take the thought for the deed."

A handsome Mexican woman with a sullen face came out of the library, carrying a vacuum cleaner.

"This is Rosarita," Rachel said. She introduced them in rapid soft Spanish.

Rosarita looked tired. There were dark circles under her eyes. "Will you be needing me?" she asked. "The *señor* said I could go to my family."

"No, it's all right."

"Thank you, *señorita*."

"I want you to have something of hers. Would you like the silver earrings from Taxco?"

"Thank you, *señorita*." Rosarita plugged in her machine, vacuuming her way down the hall, cleaning up after the guests.

Rachel said. "You have just met the staff."

"One maid? A house this size?"

"Servants steal. That's what Dad says. We have a cleaning service. Miriam used to have to stand there and watch them when they went through the house."

She led him up a curving stairway to the second floor. They turned left down an open hall from which one could look into the foyer. At the far end, Rachel unlocked a heavy carved door with a rounded top set in an embrasure and led him into a cluttered study. There was a large partners' desk in the middle with a bookcase behind it filled with recent books, all of them still in their dust jackets. Clothes were piled on chairs. The walls were covered with paintings. The tall casement windows were all shuttered and curtained. Rachel went to the windows behind the desk, yanked open a pair of velvet drapes on gold rings, unlatched the windows and then reached out and threw open the green shutters. The bright sun sparkled on the dark-blue sea below them.

Rachel went over to a suitcase on the floor. Stooping down, she worked the combination lock and lifted the lid. Dade squatted on the floor beside her. Swiftly, he went through everything in the suitcase. Apart from a few travel clothes, it contained only the objects Rachel had described. Rising, he scratched his head. Scrambling to her feet, Rachel said, "I'll get her papers." She went to a closet and tugged at a medium-size cardboard box. In it were check stubs, bank books, a ledger-size checkbook and stacks of bills and canceled checks, all bound with rubber bands. Dade took the box from her.

"Thanks. That'll do nicely."

She stepped back, tripping over a cord. He grabbed at her, steadying her.

"Oh! *Sorry!*" she said.

Dade looked down at the cord. It was plugged into a wall socket and ran across the floor and carpet, then up the leg of the desk and into a drawer.

Rachel said, "Oh, that's just the answering machine."

Dade put down the box slowly, balancing it on the cluttered desk. "May I have a look-see?" Then, when Rachel nodded, puzzled, Dade pulled open the drawer, lifted out the machine and experimentally turned the switch from Playback to Announcement and pressed the Test button. After a moment, they heard, "Miriam Welles speaking. I'm sorry, but I'm not able to take your call at this time. If you'll leave your name and number after the signal, I'll get back to you as soon as I can."

Her voice filled the room as if it were her scent. For a moment, she seemed to be there with them. Dade saw suddenly that Rachel had turned terribly pale. He took her arm.

"Here, you sit down."

"I'm all right."

"Just sit down for a minute, honey, like I tell you." He helped her into Miriam's desk chair.

She said, half whispering, "It's just hearing her voice again."

"I know."

"I'm all right now."

Dade turned the switch back to Playback, pushed the Rewind button for a second or two and then pressed the On button again. In a moment, they heard Ellen's voice faintly in the background calling out, "Dade?" and then the sound of the phone being hung up.

"That was me," Dade explained. "I called this afternoon. Mind if I play a bit more?"

"No, please. Go ahead."

Dade backed the tape up some distance, then set the switch on Playback and turned the machine on again. They heard a woman's voice with a French accent say, "Miriam? Are you there?" There was a click as Miriam's phone was picked up.

Then they heard Miriam's voice saying, "I'm here! Nettie?" Then, after a banging sound, Miriam's voice said, "Nettie? Nettie, don't hang up! The drawer's stuck and I can't shut the damn machine off! Nettie, can you hear me?"

"I'm here, Miriam. Listen, that stupid man called again—"

"On Sunday? Nettie, I told him it would be ready tomorrow. What is the matter with him?"

"Not that stupid man. The other one. Mr. Schiller."

"Oh, him! Well, if it's about the Wyeth, I don't want it. Schiller is a damn fool. In the first place, he didn't even know there are five Wyeths and when I tried to tell him that, he thought I meant paintings. Just get rid of him but make up some excuse because, for all I know, he could show up with something good one of these days."

"If we just took it on consignment, somebody would probably come along. After all, Wyeth is a big name."

"So is Rouault, but not if his first name is Sam. No, if we take it on consignment, he'd expect us to hang it and, on the whole, I'd rather hang myself. But right now, all I can think about is tomorrow. Listen—" The recording ended. The tape advanced to the next call.

Dade shut off the machine, looked at Rachel and asked

her, "Sunday. Hm. What was supposed to happen on Monday?"

"I don't know. But Nettie would."

Dade grunted, turning on the machine again. There were several messages in a row, all of them social, inconsequential. In some cases there was nothing on the tape but a beeping sound, indicating that the caller had hung up in the middle of hearing Miriam's recorded message, not wishing to leave word.

Then there was a man's voice on the tape. He identified himself as Ed at the Arco station, said Mrs. Welles' car was ready and would be left parked over by the fence. Dade pushed the 'Off' button. His eyes met Rachel's.

"That's the night she was killed, I mean, that same day!" Rachel said.

"Let's see. He would have called around four. Let's have a listen here." Dade pressed the On button again and let the tape run. There was one call with the click of the receiver at the end of the message cycle. Dade pushed the Off button, with a perplexed expression.

"What is it?" she said.

"That's a damn peculiar call."

"Why? Somebody called and got the answering machine and hung up. What's so odd about that?"

"Wrong. Somebody called, waited for her message to end, waited for the tone and then waited almost forty-five seconds before hanging up. You can hear the sound of the person hanging up on that tape, just the way you heard me. But why wait almost forty-five seconds? That was somebody waiting for Miriam to pick up that phone. Hm. Let's hear some more." He pushed the On button again.

Rachel's voice came on the tape, calling out, "Miriam? Miriam, it's me. Can you answer the phone? I want to know how you are. Miriam? Miriam?" There was a pause, Rachel called Miriam's name a few more times and then there was a click. After that came the call with Ellen's voice calling Dade and then the indicator showed the tape back in the position where they had found it.

Dade said, "End of the line." He shut off the machine. "This much is clear. She never answered that phone from the time you last saw her Tuesday night till the time she died." Dade frowned, then pointed to the other phone on Miriam's desk. "What about that number?"

Rachel shook her head. "Her friends never called her on the house phone."

"Is it listed?"

"Yes."

"How many phones you got here?"

"Three. These two and Dad's private line, but nobody ever uses that but Dad."

"Unlisted?"

"Yes. And with no extensions. Just the line in the study." Dade grunted, straightened up, arching his back, then walked over to the window and gazed out at the flashing blue field of the sea. He was silent for a long time. Rachel said, "What do you think we ought to do?"

"Let me think about it." He tapped the cardboard box. "I'll take this along. I want to have a look through it. I'll take it back with me to the inn. Ellen's just arrived, so I think I'll be staying on a day or two. Forget all this. Just don't talk about it to anybody. Understand, honey?"

"Yes."

Dade picked up the box and started toward the door. Rachel ran ahead of him, opening it for him. He followed her down the stairs to the front hall. A grandfather clock chimed four. "You might just tell your father I'm sorry I missed him. How's his health, by the way? I heard they took him to the hospital."

"Oh, he's fine. When they told him it was just gas he was almost affronted."

"I guess that left you with a lot to do."

"It was just awful. The police had the garage sealed off and they wouldn't let us in there until the coroner had made his report, which was yesterday. And on top of that, the insurance company had guards here all day Wednesday and Thursday while they went through the house inventorying everything, so we didn't even have any privacy. And here I was on the phone calling everybody, telling them where the funeral would be and what time. I had to help make the funeral arrangements and since—" Her face got very pale, so that even the freckles seemed to change color. She went on in a half-whisper. "I didn't know how much there was to do. But at least I kept busy and—" A sob broke from her. Suddenly she cried out, "She's dead, she's dead! And that son of a bitch is off at his club getting one of his goddamned rubdowns! All right, he's an old man, he's all broken up, he's running away, but Jesus Christ, what about me? Look at this place! Does this look like a house of mourning to you? It's nothing but a goddamned art gallery! All he cares about is his goddamned Botticelli!"

"You made her happy," Dade said.

"Did I?"

"She said so. Many times. Think about that."

She nodded. Then she asked quietly, "How would I get the investigation reopened?"

"You'd have to give the sheriff new evidence."

"But how am I supposed to get it? Isn't that his job?"

"Not after the investigation is closed."

"What should I do? I can't just leave it like this!"

"Well, you could hire an investigator."

"You mean a detective?"

"Yes."

"I don't have any money."

"That's not something we have to worry about." Dade walked up and down, pulling at his lower lip. Then he said, "You want me to find you somebody?"

"Yes. Please."

"I think I can do that."

She twisted her fingers together. "I wouldn't even know how to talk to him. Oh, please help me!"

Dade walked up and down again, examining alternatives, then finally nodding. "Let me explain my legal position in this. I do not represent Miriam. A dead person is not an entity who can be represented. I am her executor. It is my job to marshal the assets of her estate. That's why it's hard for me to represent you."

"I don't understand."

"I drew up the will. You're one of her heirs. There could be a conflict of interest."

"One of her heirs? That's ridiculous! In the first place, she didn't have much, and in the second place, she told me she was leaving everything to charity!"

"Well, that's so, that's so. She's just left you a few personal things to remember her by. The will says they have only a sentimental value."

"And that's a conflict? Dade!"

"All right, here's what I'll do. I will agree to represent you, Rachel, and to conduct an investigation into the death of your stepmother. But with this caveat: Under the law, it is conceivable that a conflict could arise between my interests as attorney for the estate and attorney for you."

"That's absurd."

"Still, the law requires that I make you aware of that possibility, and if, in my judgment, such a conflict arises, I will promptly inform you and withdraw from the case, urging you to seek other representation. Have I made myself clear?"

She threw her arms around him. "I'll do all I can to help."

They left the house together. He put her in her car.

"Will you be home this evening?" he asked.

"Yes," she said. Then, remembering, she gave him her phone number. "Will you call me tonight? Even if you don't know anything new?"

"All right, honey."

Rachel hesitated. Then she said, "I don't understand Dad. The way he reacted, you'd have thought I was suggesting that he had something to do with all this, which is really ridiculous, when you come to think of it, because the two of us left the house together, and he didn't get back from town for another three hours."

"You told me you thought he just couldn't bear the idea of having people find out she was leaving him."

"I suppose that's it."

"Is it possible that he had some idea she was going to leave him?" He watched her, waiting for an answer. When she didn't speak, he said softly, prompting her, "Rachel?"

"I don't know," she said finally. "God knows *I* didn't."

VIII

Back at the inn, Dade looked up and saw Pete crossing the courtyard. Dade tooted his horn, waving at him out the window. The boy saw him and came toward him, wiping his hands on his long white apron. Dade got out of his car, opened the trunk and started to lift out the cardboard box full of Miriam's papers. Pete said, "Here, let me," and picked up the box. The two of them rode down in the funicular. Ellen opened the door and Pete carried the box in and put it down on the table, then turned, waiting.

Dade fished in a pocket, then stopped, saying, "Whatever I give you goes to that Mahatma, that right?"

"Yes, sir."

"Well, you give him my blessings."

"Thanks. I'm sure he'll be grateful." Pete looked disappointed.

Dade thrust a bill into his hand. "And you take this and buy you some food for your household, you hear me, boy?"

"Yes, sir. I'll do that."

"Get yourself a chuck roast, something like that."

"We don't eat meat, sir."

"Well, learn. You look kinda peaky. Time you was putting some flesh on your bones. Now, one other thing. When you called on that lady, the one who got herself killed, tell me exactly what happened."

"How do you mean?"

"What was she doing?"

58

"You asked me before about her—" he said, somewhat defensively.

"Well, I'm asking you again."

"Mister, I don't want any part of this!"

A glint of suspicion sharpened Dade's glance. "She didn't happen to belong to the Mahatma's temple, did she? I mean, she wasn't one of his followers, now, was she?"

Pete backed away. "I don't answer questions about the others," he said, the eyes watchful.

"Well, you'll answer this one, sonny, and if you don't, I might have a chat with the Mahatma—only if I do, he'll be sitting in a cell down at the sheriff's, and I want to tell you, son, that I have argued many a case before the U.S. Supreme Court and I'm pretty good, so if you want to protect that fakir, you answer my questions."

"Mister," Pete said, rubbing the knuckles of one hand in the palm of another, "we're not supposed to talk about Holy Light on account of all that stuff that gets in the papers that isn't true, but, mister, believe me, I never seen the lady in my whole life before this, never heard of her, never said anything to her but about the job."

"All right, son. Now let's hear from you about that job. You say you were going to patch the roof?"

"On the garage. What with the storms, the roofers are all backed up and she wanted us to tack some waterproof canvas or something like that up over where the water was coming in."

"You talk to her a long time?"

"Just for a minute. The maid let us in and she took us through the house and into the garage. The lady, she was on the phone and she kind of nodded at us and then she came out and showed us the job, told us the problem, and then went back inside. I guess she was still on the phone because after we figured the job, we had to wait—I rang the back doorbell and she came outside—"

"How do you know she was still on the phone?"

"There's an extension in the garage. She picked it up and said something like, 'Those kids are still here.' "

"She use a name?"

"I don't remember a name."

"But whoever it was must have known what you'd come about."

"It sounded like it."

"She talking to a man or woman?"

"I don't know."

"You left after that?"

"Yes, sir."

"But you say you didn't get the job."

"Well, like I told you, this was the day before the big storm. See, the storm was forecast and the work had to be done right away. That was it. If we wanted the job, it had to be done right that day. Well, we couldn't do it, what with me working here and so forth, and the next night, when I saw Ken's car there—it wasn't Ken's car, honest it wasn't—I thought maybe he'd managed to get by."

Dade thought for a moment. Pete shifted uncomfortably. Dade said, "That's all she said? 'Those kids are still here'?"

"That's all I remember. After that, she just hung up and we talked more about the job."

Dade put a heavy hand on the boy's shoulder. "You're a nice young man. You tell your mother I've said that twice now. Your father living?"

"Yes, sir."

"He got much use for your present mode of life?"

"No, sir."

"Given up, has he?"

"I suppose."

"When did you last write him?"

"Oh . . . a while back."

"You write him tonight, you hear what I'm telling you?" The boy had a scared look on his face. "Now, you get along out of here and let me do some work."

"Yes, sir." The boy remained standing, looking at Dade expectantly, as if he hadn't heard.

"Come on, move it!"

The boy scurried out the door. Dade closed it behind him, went over to the closet, pulled off his jacket and hung it up carefully, loosened his tie and sighed. Ellen came in from the deck and got him a sweater.

"What did Rachel say?" He began to tell her, putting

things in chronological order. Interrupting him, she said, incredulous, "Jensen actually threatened to kill Rachel's boyfriend?"

"Well, he managed to convey that impression without saying so in so many words. Anyway, that's what Rachel says."

"Do you believe her? I mean, could she just be being hysterical and imagining things?"

"She wasn't hysterical. And we know Jensen hated Nick so much that he forced Rachel to choose between them and then forced Rachel out of his house. Jensen's like that, you know, and if he'd wanted to threaten Nick's life, that's just exactly how he'd do it. Besides, there's no reason I can see for Rachel to make it up. What would she gain? No, honey, I can believe he did it. It's just his style. Reminds me of how he insulted Gil Ransohoff at the funeral. That's Jensen, all right."

"Well, go on. Is that what Rachel wanted to tell you?"

"No. No, it was something else. About a suitcase." When he had finished summarizing Rachel's story, Ellen sat down suddenly, as if all the wind had been knocked out of her.

She said, "So, she was running away. She was leaving him."

"You know," he said after a moment's reflection, "it almost sounds as if she did it on impulse—as if she were running for her life."

"Yes, but people who run for their lives don't stop and pack first." Ellen said. "And from what Rachel says, that suitcase was already packed. It must have been. It would take all day to collect things like that."

"That's perfectly true, honey. I've got no argument with it. But if she'd been packing all day, that doesn't mean she planned to leave that night. Hadn't told Rachel and she used to tell Rachel everything. She'd had her car serviced. Sounds to me as if she planned to go away in that. Why would she take the Rolls? According to Rachel, she hated to drive it. And I'll tell you something else, Miriam had a weak chest. She once had pneumonia, and she had it bad. She was always afraid of getting it again. Why would a woman like that go out in the worst storm of the year?

"Let's say she packed planning to leave sometime later. She left when she did 'cause she had to. My own guess is, she was scared to death. No other way of explaining the facts."

Ellen frowned, clasping her hands in her lap and looking away, as if resisting his explanation. When he gave her a questioning look, she said, "Then why on earth get out of the car and run down that hill in a downpour to close the garage door? A woman who's scared to death just wouldn't do that!"

Dade's eyes widened with surprise.

He got to his feet and began pacing up and down, eyebrows twitching, glancing off to one side as if he imagined a jury box there.

"What is it?" she asked.

He shook a large forefinger at her. "You got something! You got something, Ellen, honey!"

"What?"

"She's scared to death. Everything she's done, she's done 'cause she's scared to death. That's so, isn't it? Well, that means if she got out of that car, it had to be for the same damn reason, honey. She didn't get out of the car to close a damn door. She got out because some other car was blocking the drive. High fence on both sides, mud everywhere! Whoever she's afraid of has just showed up. That person gets out of the car. She jumps out of her car—doesn't even bother to shut off the ignition. Now she literally is running for her life—back to the house! Whoever is after her starts chasing her, sees her car, engine running, door still open. A big heavy car is one hell of a weapon. Person jumps in the car and chases her into the empty garage, slamming her up against that concrete back wall and killing her."

"And the whole business about the broken transmitter is just coincidence, is that what you're saying?"

"In that case, it would have to be."

"Then it's an accident that it looks like an accident, is that your point? Are you saying somebody used a car as a murder weapon and the coroner misread it and called it an accident?"

"I'm saying it's possible." He made a face. "Trouble is,

now that I've heard myself say it, I don't believe it. I don't know what happened. That's what I've got to find out. And the first step is, why? We got to get us a motive."

"Do you want to call Arnolphe Motke? Get him down here?"

"Maybe."

"You're not a detective."

"No, but I don't want to go off half-cocked, either. I told Rachel I'd get her somebody, but first I want to see how the land lies."

"Now that I think of it, who stands to profit by Miriam's death?"

"Nobody. She left her half of the gallery to Nettie—nothing more than a lease and some furniture—personal things of no value to Rachel—and the rest goes to charity."

"Well, God knows Rachel doesn't need it. She's got pots."

"She has nothing at all."

"What? She has a hundred million dollars!"

"But she can't touch it."

"You're not serious!"

"I was Arnold Welles' lawyer. That's Jensen's daddy. I made out his will before you and I were married. I know what she's got. See, here's what happened. Old Arnold had two sons. One of them was Rachel's father, Jensen, and the other was Philip. Now, Philip was a spendthrift, a drunk and a philanderer but Old Arnold was crazy about him. Christ, how he loved him! But Old Arnold had worked hard for his money and he didn't want some dame taking Phil for it, he didn't want Phil boozing it away or losing it at the track—he just didn't know what to do. He wanted the money to stay in the family but he didn't want Philip to squander it.

"So he left Philip and Jensen the *income* from the hundred million dollars but had me put in a spendthrift clause so nobody could ever borrow against his expectancy. Jensen was furious and blamed me but the idea wasn't mine, it was his father's. Arnold didn't want Philip to think his father would play favorites and he thought that the income from a hundred million dollars was more than two men could reasonably spend anyway, no matter how much Philip drank. On their deaths, all the money was to go to charity.

"But he had me stipulate if there should ever be a grandchild who satisfied the rule against, perpetuities, all the money would go to him, her or them but all the income from the money was to continue going to the sons or the survivor of them—in this case, Jensen—as a life estate. At the time. Jensen and Philip were both married, but neither had any children."

"I don't know what 'the rule against perpetuities' is," Ellen said.

"Technically stated, it says that money must vest to a person who was born not later than twenty-one years after the death of a life in being at the time of the death of the testator."

"Must you talk that way?"

"You asked me a question!"

"Well, answer it!"

"The rule against perpetuities is just a way of stopping people from leaving money in the family indefinitely. Satisfied? You can't leave it to unborn great-great-grandchildren, for instance, do you understand? Otherwise, all the money in the country would tend to get tied up in estates. But I told Arnold he could leave it to unborn grandchildren, for instance. Arnold was very big on family and that went down well. So he left his money to a hypothetical grandchild, in this case, Rachel, who was born two years after his death. Philip and his wife were killed ten years ago in a plane crash. They had no children. That left Jensen.

"Rachel is sole heir. She owns the whole hundred million dollars. She'll get the use of it when Jensen dies. In the meantime she's working as a waitress. Hasn't got a dime. So just put your checkbook back in your purse. This is no time for a spending spree."

Ellen poured some hot water in the tea and served them each a cup. Picking up the thread of what they had discussed, she asked him, "But who on earth was there?" Then she gasped, remembering. "The blue Mustang!"

"It wasn't blocking the drive. It was out in front, near the gates."

"I see." She stirred her tea thoughtfully, then asked, "Did you find out if Miriam tried to stop him?"

"Rachel says one doesn't try to stop him from anything."

"But did she try?"

"No." He thought for a moment. "Rachel says she didn't."

"Then Miriam knew where he was going."

"Not necessarily. Maybe she didn't ask him because they were having one of their quarrels. They quarreled a lot."

"I thought you told me Rachel said that Jensen never got into an argument."

"He thinks it doesn't count if you keep your voice down."

"She would have tried to stop him anyway, for form's sake. Wives always do. No, I'm right. And it must have been important, don't you think?" Suddenly, her expression changed, as if she had caught a glimpse of the truth coiled, about to strike. "Dade," she said, "maybe it's very simple. Maybe he was going out to kill Nick and she found out about it and tried to stop him!"

They looked at each other. He sighed and shook his head. "We keep forgetting about the suitcase," he said.

"Oh, God damn the suitcase!"

"Honey?" He looked at her with surprise.

She made a face. "I was almost right."

IX

Dade dumped the contents of the box onto the bed and began to leaf through papers, glancing at old letters.

Ellen said, "Don't you hate doing that? Snooping, I mean?"

"Somebody has to." He went on reading for about twenty minutes, sipping his wine. Then, she saw him hesitate, frowning. He got up and walked to the windows, a paper in his hand.

"What is it? Can you tell me?"

"Well, she's dead now, poor Miriam is, and I guess it won't hurt. It just surprised me because she never mentioned it, not once. She was married before, Miriam was."

"Lots of women have been."

"To a Richard Monkhaus." He looked at the decree, then reacted with surprise. "Well, looky here."

"What?"

"She was only married to him a week."

"Then you mean an annulment."

"No, I mean a divorce. She made a five-thousand-mile trip to get it. After one week." He showed her the divorce decree. She scrutinized it and noticed something.

"Why did she marry a man twice her age?"

"Watch yourself."

"She did it twice," Ellen said.

"Come again?"

She pointed at the decree. "She married Monkhaus when she was eighteen. He was thirty-six. And you're not twice my age."

"Well, I look it and I think you're responsible."

66

She kissed the top of his head. "Then, I must see that I take better care of you." He put his arms around her and tried to pull her to him but she freed herself, saying, "Men have died from overexertion, did you know that?"

"But women, never, come to think of it!" He settled into a chair, a pad of paper and a pencil on the rickety table beside him and, on the floor, the cardboard box. After a few minutes, he asked her to help him. She sat on a stool across from him and together they went rapidly through the stub books and checks, making occasional notes of the largest sums and the bills Miriam had paid.

At five o'clock, he got up, stretched and poured himself more wine. Ellen went out on the deck for a breath of fresh air. Dade returned to his examination of Miriam's records.

Most of the bills for over a few hundred dollars were to department stores or for credit-card charges. Regular deposits appeared every month in her personal checkbook. Dade guessed that represented the allowance Jensen had given her. Checks were written against this and, each month, she wrote a check to her savings account for the balance. It was all in order. Despite the physical confusion in which she kept her desk, Miriam was meticulous in the abstract. Her checkbooks were balanced and there were no missing entries. No, there was nothing out of order, nothing to attract any attention.

He was about to give up on her financial records when he found her savings passbook. It was five years old and contained regular entries made every month, indicating that Miriam had saved a total of something over forty thousand dollars.

There was one withdrawal. The passbook showed that she had taken thirty-five thousand dollars out of her savings account and a crumpled receipt showed that the money had been transferred to a cashier's check. The receipt did not indicate to whom the check had been made out but the date attracted his attention. It had been made out the day before her death. Dade whistled with surprise, then rapped his knuckles on the table several times, as if trying to call his thoughts to order. But, after all, it made sense. She had packed carefully. She was leaving Jensen.

What more natural thing than to take cash with her?
Maybe the cashier's check was .just a way of transferring
funds to another bank. He would not jump to conclusions.
He would wait and see. All he had to do was ask the bank
to have a look at the cashier's-check register.

From the deck, Ellen beckoned to him. She pointed.
High in the air, he saw what looked like a huge colored
kite launched from a bluff circling slowly over the busy
highway, spiraling down toward the beach. It was a hang
glider. Spread-eagled above them was the body of a boy
suspended by a harness from the cradle of the undercar-
riage, hands grasping the guide bars, ankles hooked over
the guy wires running back to the tail. Above the flying
boy, like brilliant plumage, stretched the taut sails of his
little airship, floating above the cars like an illustration
from a book of fairy tales. Gusts of wind buffeted him,
shaking his sails, and he turned, just as the gulls flying
above him turned, and rode an air current down across the
power lines and the wide beach, where bathers in their
bright-colored trunks and bikinis were scattered over the
sand like confetti at a party, then out over the water,
wheeling back toward shore and floating over the heads of
the black-suited surfers as they raced him back to shore on
their narrow boards, skidding to a stop on the strand at
the edge of the sea.

"Nice here, isn't it?" Dade said. "Last night I slept with
those windows open and you know what I dreamed? I
dreamed I heard the great blue whale singing to itself as it
swam through those big waters. They sing to themselves,
did you know that?"

"Yes, I know that."

"Breaks the heart, don't it? The Lord God, you know,
he was mighty proud of the whale. Boasted to Job about
it. Went on and on. 'He maketh the deep to boil like a pot
. . .' and 'Upon earth there is not his like, who is made
without fear.' No wonder he sings to himself. I'd like to
hear it, upon my soul, I would." He looked at his watch.
"I want to stop at the bank."

"I have money."

"Not for that." He pulled on his jacket and straightened
his tie. Making sure he had with him the envelope Ballin-

ger had delivered to him, Dade locked the box of Miriam's papers in the closet and they left the room, heading back up toward the parking lot.

They drove down the hill to Miriam's bank. The bank manager looked at the piece of paper Dade put down on the desk before him, glancing at the clock and at the tellers counting up their money and snapping rubber bands around stacks of bills.

Dade said, "I realize it's late—"

The bank manager said, "You need to know today?"

"I'm afraid I do."

The manager gestured toward two wooden armchairs in front of his desk. "You just make yourselves comfortable." He went quickly behind the counter to a microfilm retrieval system and began punching buttons. He returned with a scrap of paper on which he had written down a name. He handed it to Dade, who studied it. On the date in question, Miriam had purchased a thirty-five-thousand-dollar cashier's check, all right, and had it made out by the bank to Proulx Galleries "for the purchase of a Giulio Romano."

"I wonder if I can speak with the person who helped her."

The manager said, "Nadine always did. She's not here today. Anything I can do for you?"

"I just wondered when she purchased it—what time of day."

"First thing in the morning. I let her in myself."

"Ten o'clock?"

"Yes. She went right over to Nadine's desk and left shortly afterward."

"Thank you very much."

"A great loss." Dade nodded. "Will there be anything else?" the manager asked.

"Mind if I use the phone?" The manager picked up his phone and put it where Dade could use it, then excused himself. Dade consulted his notebook and punched out a number, saying to Ellen, "So that's where it went. She bought herself a Renaissance painting."

"On the day before she died? What an odd thing to do."

"I want you to think about that remark for a moment and then tell me what you find wrong with it."

She looked at him steadily and crossed her eyes. He turned away. She said, "Whom are you calling?"

"Jensen. I have to arrange to have it appraised and so forth." Jensen came to the phone. Dade said, "Jensen, this is Dade. Would it trouble you if I came by for just a minute now?"

There was a pause. Then Jensen said, "No, of course not."

"Look, if it's inconvenient, we can make it another time."

"Not at all. I know how eager you are to get back up north, and it's no trouble at all for us to meet now. A few neighbors have stopped by but that's no problem."

"Ellen's with me. Just got down this afternoon."

"Make sure she comes with you, will you do that, Dade?"

"In, say, about ten minutes, then."

"Fine. Look forward to seeing you."

Dade put down the phone and went to the car with Ellen. He said, "Afterward, I'm going to take you to dinner. I'm going to take you to a place out in the Valley where they got seven mariachi bands taking turns. Food's so-so but that music—that'll blast you right out of your chair."

Ellen saw him glance in his rearview mirror. His expression changed. She said, "What's the matter?"

"I kind of thought so before but now I'm sure. Honey, you just hang on to your seat!" He gunned the car and raced out of the parking lot and up across the highway, white hair blowing in the wind, the crocodile eyes squinting at the road. His jaw tightened in anger. He swerved into the right-hand turn lane.

"What is it? Where are you going?" she asked.

"I'm gonna burn his ass!" He slammed to a stop in front of the sheriff's office, asked Ellen to wait and charged into the building. Dade went to the counter and, through a glass partition, saw Valdez crossing the squad room on his way to his office. A tall skinny deputy with blotchy skin got to his feet.

"Yes, sir?" asked the deputy.

Dade pointed. "Tell that Lieutenant Valdez I want to see him."

"He's not on duty now, sir."

"Fine. Then we won't be interrupted. Name is Cooley."

The deputy hesitated, then picked up a phone, punched a buzzer and spoke into the phone in a low voice, turning away from Dade. He put down the phone and turned back to Dade. "This way, sir." The deputy led Dade around to the lieutenant's office, then closed the door and went away.

Valdez looked up from the report he was writing out in longhand. "Yes, Mr. Cooley?"

Dade sat down in a chair opposite him. "Still working, I see."

"What can I do for you? It's kind of late."

"I'll talk fast."

"I don't mean to be rude but I've got to get this report out."

"See, there was this hayseed Waldo—now, this is years ago I'm talking about, back in World War Two. You've read about that war."

"Yeah."

"Waldo was a damn fool. Fat. Head like a peeled onion, with this wavy red hair sitting up on top of his head. Always chewing Juicy Fruit gum."

"I wonder if I could ask you to get to the point."

"Old Waldo, he was a snake in the grass. You couldn't trust him, not even to tell you the time of day. We decided we'd teach him a lesson."

The lieutenant looked at his watch. "Mr. Cooley, please—"

"Well, we set up this thing in the barracks. This was over in France. When Waldo came in, he found us all sitting around swapping stories. Only they wasn't stories, see, they was confessions. Each one worse than the last. About all the disgusting things we'd each done in our lives. We explained that we were cleansing ourselves. Spellbound, he was. Just plain spellbound.

"Come on, join us, we said. First time Waldo'd ever been invited to join anything. Waldo rubs them fat white hands of his together and says, 'Well, since you guys is all being so honest, I'm gonna level, too. Back on the farm in Kansas, I once fucked a heifer.'

"Well, I want to tell you, I never heard such a yell in all my born days. Laugh, I thought I'd die. At first, this poor son of a bitch didn't know what the Christ was going on. It hit him kind of slow-like. Then, he figured it out and his face turned redder than his hair. He just got up and walked out. Got hisself transferred. Never saw him again.

"I'm the one thought it up. Now that's a sample of the kind of thing I got in store for you unless you give me a goddamn good explanation how come you've had a tail on me for six hours." Dade took out his hunting watch and opened it. "Refugio, you got exactly ten seconds to start talking."

Valdez jumped to his feet, his dark skin flushing. "You have no right—!"

"Folks my age tend to get farsighted, you know. I can read that report you're writing right here from where I'm sitting, even upside down." Hastily Valdez grabbed the top sheet and turned it over. "It appears to me that the Welles case is anything but closed."

Valdez sat down and clasped his hands, leaning on his elbows, as if at times of stress he reverted unconsciously to prayer. He sighed, bit a knuckle and then said, "Orders. I can't discuss the case, okay? You want to make trouble for me, Mr. Cooley, go ahead. I'm sure you can."

"I see." Dade got to his feet and headed toward the door.

Valdez said, "Look, I'm sorry—"

Dade waved the apology away. "Don't worry, boy. I already got what I come for."

X

They drove to the Welles house. Ellen asked, "What happened to his first wife? What was her name, Alice?"

Dade nodded. "Rachel's mother. Jensen and Alice had a lot of trouble. He wanted to own her. She just couldn't stand it. Felt like she was being eaten alive. You know, the English say, The thing that beats you first will beat you last. Well, he squeezed her so, she couldn't bear having him around her. Wouldn't let him come near her. Then, when Miriam first came to work for Jensen—now, this is about ten years ago I'm talking about, when Rachel was still a little girl—Alice fell ill.

"It all started out with her imagining there was a bad smell in the house. They had a great many servants in those days and Alice, she had all of them scrubbing the house from morning till night, trying to get rid of the odor. Those who said they couldn't smell it got fired. House stank of Lysol. That reassured her. She knew the place had been cleaned. But according to Alice, the stink persisted. Kept her awake nights.

"After that, Alice started to have fits of delirium and convulsions. Jensen, he sent her to the Mayo Clinic. In no time, everything began to go wrong. The doctors there spotted the disease, even though the course, in her case, was atypical. They told Jensen his wife had general paresis. Jensen didn't recognize the term, forcing the doctor to be painfully specific: Alice had tertiary syphilis of the brain.

"Obvious to Jensen where she'd got it. He himself had gotten it years before, been cured of it in two weeks and never let his wife know that he'd had it. He postponed saying anything, reasoning that he'd know if she was infected. He waited for symptoms. Well, there weren't any. In poor Alice's case, disease skipped the first two stages, so when it surfaced, there wasn't a thing that the Mayo Clinic nor anybody else could do about it. Jensen couldn't bring her home and, after a few months, she didn't even know who he was half the time when he came to visit her. She lived that way for five years and then died raving."

"Good God."

They reached the house. Rosarita opened the door for them. Dade greeted her by name. She barely nodded, looking at them both with smoldering eyes, as if in her, grief expressed itself only as anger. She showed them into the library, where an armed Pinkerton man guarded the door. A dozen people were standing around with drinks, helping themselves from trays of canapés, their speech soft and rapid as they looked at paintings, their voices a collage of little reasonable arguments, like Bach inventions.

At one end of the windowless room stood an empty easel. An adjustable spotlight on a stand pointed at it. Jensen came toward Dade and Ellen, chin lifted, the long thin nose seeming to seek them out. He wore black. In the lamplight the bald domed head gleamed like the skull of a specter on Halloween. Dade wondered whether he oiled it for effect.

"You remember Jensen Welles," Dade said.

Ellen held out her hand. Jensen took it. "Please accept my sympathies," she said.

"Thank you. Dade, thank you again for coming." He shook hands with Dade, then gestured at the empty easel. "We're about to view the Botticelli. I'm so glad you could join us." The voice was strained. Jensen smiled at him with an effort.

Dade said, "We can't stay."

Jensen said, "I understand. You just want Miriam's papers." He looked suddenly relieved.

"I stopped by and got them earlier. Rachel gave them to me."

"I see. I didn't know she was here."

"She came out to meet me."

"Then this is just a social call. Well, I'm very grateful."

His expression changed abruptly. A bony hand gripped Dade's arm. Jensen drew him aside, his eyes bright and hard. "Was he with her? That—that friend of hers?" It took Dade a moment to realize Jensen meant Nick. Ellen moved toward the group of guests.

"No. I haven't met him. Rachel told me that they—"

"I can well imagine what she told you! Well, it's not going to happen! I'm not letting my daughter marry a crook!"

"You're sure he is one? Rachel said he makes a lot of money."

"You know how? Commodities! In my life, I have never known anybody who ever made a cent in commodities! The market is dominated by speculators, and betting with them is like playing poker with card sharks. Commodities, I said! He'll lose his shirt! I told Rachel so! That was last fall. A few weeks later, he came to me to show me a profit of ten thousand dollars he made in a single month buying copper. I thought it was beginner's luck. The next month, he made even more in pork bellies. I couldn't believe it. He showed me the broker's receipts. I made inquiries the next day. My man told me Nick Levin made every cent of that money just as he said!"

"That should set your mind at ease, Jensen."

"Nonsense! He's a liar! First, he told me he had a system, then he said it was luck. That was after he'd made money in December, just as much, the same way."

"Jensen, maybe the boy's got a gift."

"He has no gift! He's a liar! It's a trick! Don't you understand, he's a crook! I've warned Rachel but she won't listen! She listens to you. I want you to warn her."

"Jensen, right now we've got to have us a little chin about another matter."

"Right after we view the Botticelli." He moved toward the open lock room at the end of the library, signaling to the Pinkerton guard at the door. The guard picked up a large shrouded canvas and started carrying it over to the lighted easel.

Dade said, "Jensen, the Botticelli's going to have to wait."

"I don't understand." Jensen's profile lifted in indignation. He looked to Dade like a battered Roman coin.

"If you don't mind——" Dade said.

"Come this way, please. Excuse us." Jensen led Dade out of the library, murmuring excuses to his guests, and across the hall to a book-lined study with leather chairs and green-shaded lamps. He remained standing, looking at Dade with annoyance. Dade closed the door. That irritated Jensen even more. "Look, if this is about Miriam's estate, I don't know why we have to take it up right now. Can't it wait?"

"One of the things I have to say can't, no."

"She didn't leave much. Nobody knows that better than you do. What's the problem? Some kind of unpaid bill I don't know about? What's so urgent?"

"There's nothing urgent about her estate, Jensen. As a matter of fact, the only thing I haven't been able to account for is the Romano."

"Pardon me, I didn't understand."

"The Romano she bought on Monday."

"A Giulio Romano? Bought for whom?"

"Herself, it appears."

"Miriam never bought herself a painting in her whole life."

"Well, she did this time."

"I'm telling you——"

"Jensen, I don't want to get into an argument about this. She drew the money for it out of her savings account and I've got a record of the cashier's check she used to pay for the picture."

"There is no Giulio Romano in my collection."

"Well, maybe you better have another look."

"You listen to me! It was only yesterday I had the insurance people in—it was their idea. I mean, the garage door had been open, the house had been empty for hours, somebody could have broken in. I've got an inventory, right up to date. It does not include a Giulio Romano. It does, however, include a Botticelli, and if you don't mind——" Jensen started out of the room.

Dade took hold of his arm. "I got something else to tell you."

Jensen stared at the hand on his arm. "My guests are waiting," he said.

"There seems to be a question about Miriam's death."

"Question?"

"From what I have been able to determine—"

"Who asked you to determine anything?" Jensen's face mottled with anger.

"I'm representing Miriam's interests in a broader sense than I think you understand. There seems to be some question about her death and your daughter has retained me to conduct a private investigation."

"How dare she do such a thing! How dare she! I'll have my attorneys file against you for harassment, obstruction of justice, anything they can name!"

"I'm not the only one who holds this opinion," Dade said quietly.

"We all know what Rachel thinks!" Jensen's eyes were as cold and hard as onyx.

"I mean the sheriff. Their investigation isn't closed, despite what they told you."

Jensen moved toward a chair and leaned on its back. "Are you sure of this?"

"I have myself seen a fragment of a handwritten report saying that 'Jensen Welles continues under surveillance.' Jensen, I don't know what's going on, but for Miriam's sake, I had to come here and tell you what I know."

"My God!" Jensen looked suddenly ashen, ill.

Dade looked at him, concerned. "You all right?"

Jensen nodded and said, "I'll have to ask you to excuse me, please." He went out of the study, making his way back toward his guests.

Dade picked up the phone and dialed. A woman's voice said, "Yes? Who is it?"

"This is Dade Cooley, Nettie honey. Say, Ellen and I are coming into town and I got a few papers for you to sign, nothing important, just to get that gallery in your name. I wonder if it'd trouble you if we stopped by?"

"No, please. When?"

He took out his watch, opened it and saw that it was six-thirty. "Now, I don't want to interrupt your dinner—"

"Don't worry about it. I live here. Behind the gallery. Just ring the bell." The phone clicked. She had hung up.

He suddenly remembered Miriam's laughter, telling him about Nettie on the telephone. She never said goodbye. The first time it happened, Miriam had thought Nettie was annoyed at something but it wasn't that at all. She simply put down the phone when a conversation was concluded. Miriam had said, "Honestly, I don't know how we stay in business! Nettie has hung up on half of Southern California society!" He could still hear her laughter, like a contralto vocalizing.

XI

Dade turned off the freeway at La Cienega and took the boulevard north to Melrose Place. The gallery was on the first block. They arrived shortly after seven, parking on the quiet side street, which was lined with shops filled with antiques and the wholesale showrooms of fabric houses and furniture makers. The sidewalk was decorated with small trees trimmed as standards and set in large stone planters. On the street was a tile-topped stucco wall a hundred feet long. A brass plaque read

PROULX GALLERIES
PARIS, NEW YORK, PALM SPRINGS, LOS ANGELES

That was a brave boast. Nettie lent others her name in exchange for representation abroad and in the East. The Palm Springs gallery, little more than a narrow storefront, had long since closed.

To the left of the plaque, wrought-iron gates opened into a flagstone courtyard with a fifteenth-century marble fountain in the center. Around it were the heavy closed doors of various offices. One belonged to a firm of architects, another to an attorney and a third to a film-production company with an Iranian name. Dade knew that Miriam had gotten Jensen to buy the location. Proulx Galleries was only one of the tenants. At the back of the courtyard was a long, low stucco building with a tile roof jutting out over a terrace. Small barred windows were set high in the wall. A nameplate on one side of carved antique double doors repeated the name of the gallery, and

79

there was a small brass doorbell above it. The door was unlocked. Dade rang the bell and then they went in.

On the walls of the thickly carpeted gallery were half a dozen portraits by lesser-known painters of the fifteenth and sixteenth century, each one exhibited in an ornate gold frame and illuminated by a picture light. Dade called Nettie's name, then went with Ellen through an open door at the back into a small sitting room furnished with heavy carved Italian furniture. A fire burned in a fireplace with a green marble chimneypiece. In the center of the room was a canvas on an easel. It was a portrait of a woman in an elaborate jeweled dress of the sixteenth century. There was almost a sly look to the sidelong glance of the eyes. The lips were parted in a simpering smile, showing spaces between the teeth.

Dade looked around. Through the windows, he could see the lights on in Nettie's apartment. "You think we ought to go on up, honey?"

"We rang the bell. Let's give her a moment." Ellen sat down and studied the portrait.

Dade looked at it with distaste. "Damn shame to do that to a woman."

"Well, you had to paint people as they were or you didn't get paid."

"Lady with a face like that ought to have more sense."

"Do you know what Nettie once told me? Now, wait a minute. I want to get it right." Ellen took a deep breath and then said quickly in an imitation of Nettie's rapid nasal cultivated speech, 'A cousin of the Duchess of Alba was dreadful-looking, enormously rich and unspeakably vain. She had herself painted as a raving beauty by Goya, then hid the portrait away in one of her castles and when she got old, she took it out and told everyone that was how she had looked as a young girl, when Goya had loved her!' " She broke off, seeing Dade's troubled expression. "What's wrong?"

Dade looked around restlessly. "Where is she?"

"On the phone, maybe."

"I don't think she heard the bell."

"Give her a minute," Ellen said. She walked around the gallery, examining paintings. When she turned back to say something to Dade, she saw that he had seated himself on a small gold chair at an inlaid Carleton desk with blown-glass doors opening on to a tiny curio cabinet at the back of the writing space. He had taken a ledger check-book out of a drawer and was leafing through it. Ellen went over to him and slapped his hand.

He said, "I'm the executor, remember?"

"You still ought to ask."

"Jesus!"

"What?"

"Here." He pointed a broad finger at something. Ellen had to borrow his pince-nez to read the small handwriting. It indicated there was a deposit on February thirteenth for thirty-five thousand dollars and next to it, "$35,000.00—13 Feb.—one Giulio Romano—Dick Monkhaus," followed by a scribbled address. He noted it.

She said, after a long pause, "All right, her first husband turned up and offered to sell her a Romano and she bought it. The fact that she died the next day in a freak accident is coincidence."

He said, "God damn it, you confound me with common sense. But where's that painting?" Like a hunting dog, he went to the back door of the gallery and looked up at the outside staircase to Nettie's apartment. Dade sniffed the air, then walked around to the right toward a little shed. It was a workroom. He peered through a dusty window and saw a can of turpentine on a shelf. Next to it were bottles labeled Alcohol, Ammonia and Oil of Rosemary, and cans labeled Benzine, Copaiba Balsam and Trichloroethylene.

Ellen's voice said, "I didn't know she did restoring." He turned. She had followed him out and was standing at his elbow, looking through the window. "You never mentioned that."

"I don't think she did."

"What's all that for?"

"Maybe just for cleaning," Dade said.

"Well, maybe Nettie—"

"Wait a minute. What was that?"

She listened. They both heard it: a sound of moaning. They hurried up the outside staircase to Nettie's apartment and knocked at the door. There was no answer. Dade tried the knob. The door was unlocked. They went inside. The little room had been ransacked, paintings torn from the wall, cabinets overturned. Dade strode toward the door to the bedroom and listened for a moment. Hearing nothing, he turned the knob and threw it open.

The bedroom was a shambles. It had been searched and there were also signs of a struggle. Furniture was knocked over, lamps and cloths pulled off tables. Dade tried to keep Ellen out but she saw something, let out a cry of alarm and ran to the other side of the bed.

Nettie lay there on the floor, moaning, blood oozing from a wound in her scalp.

"Dade!" Ellen cried out.

He rushed for the phone and called the police. By the time they had arrived with an ambulance, Nettie had recovered consciousness. She said she had hit her head on the corner of a table and they could see traces of blood there. Ellen and Dade had her stretched out on the bed, Ellen had gotten ice from the refrigerator and was applying cold compresses to Nettie's head. The ambulance attendants came into the room wheeling a stretcher. Nettie shook her head.

"You have to go," Ellen said.

"I'm all right." The two police officers tried to argue with her. She said in a low voice, "I am all right. No."

One of the policemen, a burly man with rimless glasses, shook his head at the attendants, opened his notebook and asked her if she could tell them what happened.

"I don't know. I spoke to Mr. Cooley on the phone"—she gestured at Dade—"that was from the gallery. Then I came upstairs to start dinner. There was someone here. I knew it the moment I came in the room."

"Can you describe the person?"

"I didn't see whoever it was. I was in here, you understand. I tried to run out the door. I remember grabbing at that table. I guess I was falling. Then I hit my head and that's all I remember."

"Door downstairs open?" the policeman asked.

"You mean the gallery door? Yes. I left it unlocked for my friends here. It all happened so fast."

The burly officer turned to Dade. "You say you and

your wife found the gallery open?" Then, when Dade
nodded, he said, "Well, that's how he must have gotten
in." He turned to Nettie. "Any idea what he was after?"

"What they're always after, I suppose."

The officer said, "What they're always after is that stereo
you've got in the front room and that television. It's still
there. Lady, this place wasn't robbed, it was searched. Furniture smashed." He held up a broken gilt table. "I'm going
to ask you again, what were they after?"

Nettie put a hand to her mouth, astonished. "Smashed?
My beautiful table?" The other officer held up a small antique lacquer vanity table. One leg was broken and the
lift-up top was splintered. Nettie looked at it and let out a
little moan of dismay. "Oh, of course! They were after my
jewelry. They must have been."

"You got jewelry here, lady?"

"Only paste. Everything good is in the safe-deposit
box."

One of the paramedics said something quietly to the
burly officer, glancing two or three times in Nettie's direction. The officer nodded, folding up his notebook.

"We're going to let you rest now, lady. Again, we have
advised you to seek competent medical treatment. If you
wish to refuse, that is of course your privilege. I'd like
your friends here to lock up for you when they go. Tomorrow, if you're feeling better then, we'd like you to give
us a more complete statement."

"Thank you," Nettie said weakly.

"In the meantime, do we have your permission to examine the premises, including your personal effects, for evidence?"

"By all means." She turned to Dade. "Please show them
anything they want. The keys to the locked drawers are in
that Federal desk in the living room. If it's not open—"

"It's been broken open, lady," the officer said.

"Oh, no!"

The paramedics and the ambulance attendants had left.
The two officers followed them out, Dade going with
them. He offered to help them but the officer in charge
shook his head.

"I just wanted to know if we'd run into any resistance.

If it was drugs, she wouldn't know whether whoever it was had found them. Permission like that means no drugs."

"Well, if there's nothing more I can do for you . . ." Dade moved them to the door.

They started out, then the officer turned. A trick of light refracted from his rimless glasses gave him for a moment a blank, blind look. "She's a real bullshitter, isn't she? What's the score?" He stood waiting. When Dade didn't answer, he turned and followed his partner down the stairs.

Dade came back into the bedroom. Nettie was sitting up in bed, an icebag in one hand held to the puffiness on the side of her face.

She said, "Oh, Dade, isn't this incredible? I just—"

Dade interrupted her. "I want to ask you some questions, Nettie."

"Oh, do forgive me, Dade, but won't they keep?" She looked at him pleadingly with her two-colored eyes, one of them now swollen.

"No, they won't." He spoke in a flat, hard voice. "Somebody searched this place. What for?"

"I told the officer—"

"You told him a lie. I'm sorry to be so blunt but you see, I knew from Miriam when she bought into the gallery it saved your neck. You were almost bankrupt. There is no jewelry."

"Of course there isn't. I just said that to get rid of them. My head aches and I didn't want hours of questions. I don't know what they were looking for. Good God, the last three days have been a nightmare, ever since Miriam was killed." She wept, remembering. "I called as soon as I heard. They told me Jensen had been taken to the hospital. Rachel couldn't even talk on the telephone. Her voice was gone. She had cried so much, it was just in rags. All she could do was whisper. At first, I was afraid I'd waked her up. I was so upset, I didn't realize how early it was. It was only eight o'clock and when I saw the time, well, I was just mortified."

"This was the next morning?"

"Yes."

"How did you hear about it?"

"It was on the news. I listen to the news all day on the radio. Isn't that silly? It's like an addiction. They mostly keep saying the same thing, elaborating along the way, hour by hour, but I just keep listening. Really I think I do it for company . . ." She trailed off, her eyes closed in pain.

"Dade, please," said Ellen.

"When I called you from Jensen's, I had something else I wanted to ask you about. There's a painting missing."

Nettie said, "Well, everybody warned him not to leave all that stuff in a house that's empty half the time, but he wouldn't listen."

"This isn't one of Jensen's, Nettie. It's that Giulio Romano that was bought the day before Miriam was killed."

She looked at him blankly. "How do you mean, missing?"

"Well, do you have it here?"

"No. No, I don't have it. Miriam took it away with her Monday."

"I can't find it and nobody seems to know anything about it."

"Well, there's nothing to know. Someone came in and offered it for sale. All I can tell you is she worked on it every day for a month, day and night, even had meals sent in."

"Worked on it?" Dade asked.

"Cleaning it. Place stank to high heaven. Then she found a buyer for it and sold it. I'm sure the payment was deposited." She looked ill. She put a hand over her eyes for a moment. Ellen shot Dade a warning look.

"Do you know who the buyer was?"

"Really, I haven't the slightest idea. Miriam handled the whole thing herself."

"What would you say if I told you the buyer was Miriam?" She stared at him. "It was paid for by a cashier's check drawn on her savings account."

"Well, that happens. Sometimes clients need a few days to have money transferred."

"So far as I can tell, no money was transferred. The check was issued the day before her death."

"Oh!" She looked as if she weren't quite following his argument.

"If she hasn't got the money, she should have the painting."

"Yes, I suppose that's true."

"Well, where is it?"

"I have no idea. I simply have no idea." Now she looked quite unwell.

He patted her hand. "We'll let you rest now."

She struggled to her feet. "I'll let you out. I have to lock up after you." They went downstairs together. Outside, they heard the dead bolt sliding into place and saw the alarm light go from green to red.

XII

Finding a pay phone on the street, Dade parked beside it and telephoned the Welles house. There was no answer. He called the number Rachel had given him. She answered right away. He said, "I'm not calling you too late, am I?"

"Dade? No, of course not."

"Rachel, honey, Miriam bought a painting last Monday. You got any idea what happened to it?"

"Well, she bought paintings all the time. You should ask Nettie. Do you know who she bought it for?"

"Bought it for herself."

"Dade, she never bought paintings for herself."

"She bought this one. It's a Giulio Romano."

"Nettie's the one you should ask about it."

"Nettie doesn't know where it is. And I don't think I'm the only one looking for it." He told her what had happened at the gallery.

"Oh, my God!"

"Now, she's all right."

"Wait a minute! Dade, I just remembered something! Miriam did bring home a painting! She was storing it."

"I talked to your father. He says the insurance people just went through the house and there's no such thing there."

"He's wrong. You tell him—"

"He's not there, honey. I just tried the number."

"Why don't I meet you there tomorrow?"

"All right. What time?"

She hesitated. Then she said, "I can't. Nick and I are

driving down to Tijuana and he wants to leave at some godawful early hour. Dade! I just realized I have to go to the house to get some things for the trip. Is there any reason I can't meet you there now?"

"Would you do that, Rachel? Say, in about an hour?"

"I'll see you then."

He hung up without saying goodbye, curious to know how it felt. It was satisfying, bracing, he decided. Abrupt, yes, but it put an end to all those "Well, it's been nice talking to you" and "Well, I guess I'd better get going" noises.

He drove out Pico Boulevard instead of the freeway. Ellen rested her head on his shoulder. He hummed "The Blue-Tail Fly" under his breath, and then sang to the melody:

> *"When I was young, a lusty buck,*
> *Forty women I did—"*

Ellen sat bolt upright. "What's the matter with you?"

"I just wanted to find out if you were awake."

"Oh. Well, yes. I'm wide awake."

"Good. I got to stop by the Welles house."

"Not tonight!"

"You that tired?"

"No. But I brought down my research and I have to read my quota of pages today."

"I'll take you back first." He thought. "But what about that dinner I promised you?"

"I'll fix us something."

After he had left her at the inn, he drove down the dark, almost deserted highway to the Welles house. Rachel was waiting for him outside the gates. She got out of her car and ran toward him, hugging him. He looked around. "I thought you'd be with your friend Nick."

She shook her head. "He wanted to take me down to the Fox Venice to see a revival to cheer me up. I want you to guess what the name of the picture was."

"No idea, honey."

"*Ivan the Terrible.* In the first place, I am in no mood to sit through *Ivan the Terrible.* And certainly not with him sitting there the whole time, his left hand up in front of him to blot out the subtitles. Last week I had *The Stone Flower* and *Potemkin* and that was enough. Tonight, I just want to go to bed. He doesn't understand what I'm feeling. And, frankly, there are times when I thank God for that." Then she took his hand, pulling him along with her. "This way," she said.

Instead of going in through the gates, she led him down the steep driveway which ran just outside the fence and curved down toward the garage at the end of the house, the dogs running alongside and barking at them. Rachel and Dade made their way down the dark driveway, hanging on to each other.

"Monday, that's when it was. The next day was Valentine's Day," she said. "I wanted to do a great big valentine for Nick. I was over visiting Miriam that day, so I went to where we keep the paint and there was this crate there. It was maybe, oh, about two by three and not more than a few inches thick. Well, I was curious. I'd never seen it before. It was open at one end. I reached inside and pulled out this painting. I started to, I mean. Miriam showed up just at that minute and she yelled out, '*Don't touch that!*' I said I was sorry. I didn't know what I'd done. She must have seen my face because she came running over and put her hands on my arms—you know, we were very close and Miriam just didn't talk to me like that."

"I know that, honey."

"Well, I was just completely taken aback. I said, 'What's the matter?' And she said—she was very apologetic—she said it was just that it was terribly valuable and wasn't hers—oh, then it can't be the same painting, can it?"

"Never mind about that. Go on."

"Well, she begged me not to touch it again. I asked her what it was but she just shook her head."

"You say this was the day she was killed?"

"No, the day before. See, I had to get this done because the paint had to dry, so I did it the thirteenth. She was killed the next day. Some Valentine's Day." She put a key into a lock and the garage door opened automatically, lights in the garage going on. Jensen's car was gone. Miriam's was parked on the right.

Rachel stopped suddenly, turning away. By the glow of the lights, he could see her face. She looked sick. She held on to his arm. He embraced her, patting her.

"I'll be all right," she said.

"You sure?"

She gestured at the steep slope. "They couldn't get the ambulance all the way down the drive, what with the mud and the rain, so the men had to wheel the stretcher down. They were slipping around in the mud, trying to get the body on it." Behind them, the lights in the garage suddenly went out. "The damn timer," Rachel said. She broke free of him and went back into the garage, flicking a switch to turn on overhead work lights. Ahead, at the end of Jensen's empty parking space, was the concrete block wall against which the car had crushed Miriam.

Going to a row of cabinets built on the left side of the garage, Rachel opened one and Dade saw a crate inside. "Here it is, Dade." She lifted it down and handed it to him.

He took it, glancing at it. "When's the last time you saw this? The thirteenth?"

"Yes, I think so." Then, catching herself, surprised, she said, "No, wait! It was there that night! Remember, I told you she asked me to do some things before I went out? The garage was leaking! Some men came and put a tarp over it but she was worried and she made me come out here to make sure there was no water coming in on the painting. I did. I pulled it out and looked at it and it was perfectly dry. There were no leaks anywhere. I told her so and she said 'Thank God' or something like that."

Dade looked around. "Was the Rolls here that night when you came out?"

"Yes. Dad had just gotten home. I backed it out. See, you have to do that to get the cabinet open—"

"—just the way she did."

"Oh, my God, my God!"

"That's what she was doing out in the rain, Rachel. She wasn't closing the door, she was getting the painting."

Rachel stared at the empty parking space, at the driveway, then at the cabinet, as if trying to reconstruct what had happened. "She was running away. She had everything she cared about with her. And the last thing she went after was that painting. It was an accident, that's what you're saying, isn't it? It really was just a ghastly accident."

"That's how it looks, honey. And I'd be prepared to go along with that, except for one thing." She looked at him blankly. He held up the crate. "There's no painting in here."

She looked at him in utter amazement, then took the crate and looked into it herself, as if she thought he was playing some cruel joke on her. Gently he took the crate back from her and put it away where they had found it and closed the cabinet.

On the back wall of the garage, he could see a faint smudged chalk outline where the police had sketched the position of the body. He walked toward it. Rachel followed him. The chalk marks were in the middle of the concrete block wall. He glanced from there back to the cabinets on the left, then crossed to the cabinet where she had shown him the empty crate, opening it again and measuring an invisible distance with his eye. Rachel watched him. He grunted to himself, satisfied, closing the cabinet.

"How did you find this when you came back that night, open or closed?"

"Closed."

"Just the way it is now?" His tone was insistent.

"I—I think it was closed." She furrowed her brow, then her face cleared. "Yes. I'm sure of it. After I backed the car out, I was trying to bring her around and I kept screaming for Rosarita, and when she came out I told her to get a flashlight. We keep one in there somewhere and she was opening and closing cabinets looking for it."

"Hm. See, Miriam had to back out the car to open the cabinet, all right, but she was hit here"—he pointed toward the center of the rear wall of the garage—"so the cabinet could have been opened afterward without any need to move the car. Seems to me she was killed before she ever had a chance to open that cabinet and take out the painting. Otherwise, if she already had it in her arms, the murderer took a risk of smashing it with the car, or, if she dropped it, running right over it, which is a strange thing to do if the painting's the motive."

"You mean she was killed for a painting?"

"All I'm saying is, it's possible."

"But that's absurd! I mean, nobody even knew it was here!"

Dade saw that staying in the garage was upsetting her. He patted her arm. "There's one other reason I'm fairly sure she hadn't yet gotten the painting out. I can't imagine why she wouldn't have left it in its crate to protect it, since she had to carry it through all that rain up to the car. No, my guess is she never took it out of the cabinet. Someone else did."

"The murderer?"

"Well, that remains to be seen, doesn't it? Now, I just want to make sure I've got this straight. It was just after six when she sent you out to check on that painting, right?"

"Well, Dad had just gotten home—yes, I guess it was."

"And the transmitter in the Rolls. Was it working then?"

"I—I don't know."

"How did you get the car out?"

She looked abashed. "I have a thing about being closed in—whenever I'm going out through the garage, I open the door with that switch on the wall there first." She walked over to a switch beside the garage door and next to the row of cabinets and pressed it. The garage door closed. "Come on in," she said, leading him to the door into the house, "I'll let you out the front door. It's easier than going up that driveway."

"All right."

"Just wait till I turn off the alarm." Rachel took out a key and inserted it into the alarm system in the wall. She turned the key and then punched out a code in a row of buttons. When the alarm light went from red to green, she unlocked the door leading into the house. "Isn't that wonderful? They tell us it's for our protection. To keep people out. The truth is, we're all our own jailers living high on the hog in the Sing Sing Hilton."

They walked down the back hall together. Rachel

stopped to open a storage closet and pulled out a pair of hiking boots, a zippered canvas bag and a black plastic poncho. "Army surplus store," she said, gesturing at her things. "Less than ten dollars for everything. You learn a lot, living in Venice."

Dade fingered the poncho and looked at the clumsy boots. "You don't care too much for dressing up, do you?"

By way of answer, she pulled the poncho over her head. It was nothing but a big rectangle with a hood. She peered out at him, grinning. "When I wear it, Nick says I look exactly like a garbage bag."

"I think he's right." She made a face at him, pulling it off and bundling it under her arm. "Don't you like to dress up?"

"I was dressed up like a doll from the day I was born. I may never get dressed up again." She stuffed the boots and poncho in the zippered bag and then, carrying it, walked with him into the game room and then down through the gallery toward the front door.

Finally, Dade said to her, "I don't want you to talk about that painting for the time being, understand?"

"Should I go to the sheriff?"

"No. Not right now."

"Why not?"

Dade didn't answer. He walked up and down on the tiles in the hall, eyes on them as if counting them, tracing out an arabesque with the toe of his shoe. Then he said, "You want a lawyer's opinion?"

"Yes. Yes, please." Her eyes were watchful, alarmed.

"Let's say somebody stole that painting. Stole it and killed Miriam in a rigged accident to hide the theft. Well, honey, right now nobody knows. Once you tell the sheriff, you tell the press. There's no use pretending. The sheriff, they try to keep things confidential. But a lot of things are a matter of public record. The media is very curious, especially about the death of a rich lady. Word gets out. Result: You don't just tell the sheriff, you tell the murderer. And you don't want to do that. You stay out of it."

"Are you going to say something yourself?"

"I'm just going to report it as missing. I'm her executor.

It's my job. But I don't want anyone getting the idea that you might know something, understand?"

She nodded, then opened the front door for him, leaving it open behind her. "What shoulld I do?"

"Nothing."

The dogs ran up to her, nuzzling her. "Come on," she said. "I'll walk you to your car."

"Don't you want to lock up?"

"I still have to collect a few odds and ends." She went with him to the gates and let him out.

Dade watched her walk back to the house and go inside.

XIII

He went directly to the sheriff's office and was surprised to find Valdez still there. As soon as he was shown into his office, Valdez threw down a pencil impatiently and said, "I understand that Mrs. Proulx you went to see tonight, that French lady got herself assaulted"—he consulted his notes—"she was partners with the deceased Mrs. Welles, isn't that correct?"

"Yes."

"Mind telling me the reason for your visit?"

"I'm Mrs. Welles' executor and Mrs. Proulx is one of her heirs."

Valdez gave him a look. "I thought Mrs. Welles didn't have any money of her own."

"Not in the sense you mean. The bequests are small."

"I see." Valdez sat back, tilting his swivel chair and locking his hands behind his head. "Look, I understand your beef about the tail. It's just routine. What can I do for you at this late hour, Mr. Cooley?"

"I came here to report some property missing."

"Taken from your room?"

"No, from the Welles house."

"When?"

"Sometime this week."

"How come they haven't reported it?" Valdez asked.

"From what I judge, they didn't know it was there."

"But you did."

"Part of her estate."

"Value?"

"Thirty-five thousand dollars."

"Look, Welles is on record saying there's nothing missing."

"I understand that," Dade said.

The phone rang. "Excuse me," Valdez said, picking it up. He said "Valdez" into the mouthpiece, listened for three seconds and then jumped to his feet, saying, "Get me a car!" and slammed down the phone. "There's been a shooting at the Welles place," he said, striding to the door.

Dade followed him. They ran out of the building and got into the back of a waiting squad car, then raced down the highway, lights flashing, siren on, two squad cars and the paramedics' truck following them up the long slow curve of the dark highway. Minutes later, the cars and the truck turned left across the center divider, then headed back south to the Welles drive. Valdez and Dade got out of the car. Rachel's car was parked where Dade had last seen it, under the trees at the side of the drive, outside the gates. The grounds were dark, lit only by the headlights of the sheriff's cars. The gates were locked. One of the men yelled, "Watch out for them goddamn dogs!"

Valdez aimed a flashlight through the wrought iron, then said, "You don't have to worry about the dogs." He played the beam of his flashlight across the drive and they could see the dogs lying on the ground, blood-splattered. A deputy yelled for a ladder. Brandt, the deputy who had been there the night Miriam was killed, knew his way around. He tried a hidden switch on the gatepost which controlled the garden lights. It didn't work.

"Power's out," Brandt said. Two deputies ran up carrying a rope ladder with grappling hooks and threw one end of it over the eight-foot-high spiked wrought-iron gates. Brandt scrambled up in the dark, balanced and then jumped, opening the gate with a manual release hidden in a stone pillar.

Valdez and Dade went along the path, preceded by four deputies with drawn guns, the paramedics driving slowly behind them. An owl hooted. There was no other sound. One of the deputies went up to the front door and listened, then tried the knob. It was locked. Valdez said, "Somebody could be in there with her."

"Want me to get the bullhorn?" Brandt asked. Valdez

hesitated. Brandt said, "It's either that or we'll have to break in. Want me to get the ax?" He signaled to his partner, who ran back toward the squad cars.

Dade turned to Valdez and said, "The garage. It's a lot easier."

Valdez nodded, pointing at another deputy. "You and your partner wait here." Valdez and Dade hurried back through the gates, then down the steep driveway which ran outside the fence to the garage at the end of the house, clambering down the narrow road with the dirt piled high on either side. Brandt and his partner ran ahead of them, his partner carrying an ax.

There was no need to break in. The garage door was wide open. On a wall, Valdez spotted an electrical box, pulled out a handkerchief and opened it carefully, holding his light on it, then flicked the power switch from Off to On. The lights came on in the garage and all over the garden.

"Get the print crew on this," Valdez said. Dade's eyes raked the garage. The cabinet where the painting had been stored was open now and the empty crate lay on the floor of the garage. Valdez walked to the back door leading from the garage into the house. Dade went with him. A deputy stepped in front of them, stood to one side, gun upraised, turned the doorknob, found the door unlocked and kicked it open. Silence. The hall was empty. They went down it quickly, then into the game room and from there, into the gallery. The lights were on and there was no sign of anything wrong. Valdez nodded toward the front door. A deputy strode toward it, sliding back the dead bolt and unlocking it, letting in the other two deputies and the paramedics. Valdez reacted as if he had heard something. He motioned them all to be quiet. Nobody moved. Valdez made a gesture. All four deputies began rapidly searching the entire downstairs, guns drawn. They worked in silence, treading lightly and opening doors suddenly, without warning, always standing to one side. There was no sign of anyone anywhere. Nothing seemed to have been disturbed.

Very quietly, while the paramedics waited in the front hall, the six men mounted the stairs to the second floor. While Valdez and Dade waited, the search was repeated.

Everything seemed in order until they tiptoed into Rachel's old room and a deputy tried the door to the bathroom and found it locked.

Rachel's voice called out, "I have a gun and I know how to use it!"

"It's the sheriff," said the deputy. "Throw down the gun and come out with your hands in the air." There was no sound.

Dade said, "Rachel, honey?" Immediately there was a click of the door being unlocked and Rachel appeared, a .32 dangling from one hand. She looked as if she were about to collapse. Dade went toward her. She dropped the gun, almost falling into his arms.

"Oh, God. I thought you were him."

"Search the grounds," Valdez said to the others. They ran out. Dade and a paramedic helped Rachel to sit down. Pulling out his flask, Dade made her take a big swallow. She looked at the lieutenant in front of her. "What happened, Miss Welles?" Valdez asked.

"Is he gone?"

"There's no sign of anybody."

"Is Bad dead?"

"The Doberman? I think they're both dead."

"Both? Oh, no!"

"What happened? Can you tell us?" Valdez asked.

"Take it easy, honey," Dade said.

"Just after you left, I heard a popping sound, like fire-crackers. I thought it was that damn car of Nick's—he's always having trouble—and I went out the front door and there was Bad. I just stood there for a second. I couldn't think. I wanted to get away but I was afraid to go get my car. I was sure he was out there. I ran back in the house and bolted the door. Then I thought, I'll go through the house to the garage and get Miriam's car! I just wanted to get out of here! But when I went in there, the garage door was open and there was a man there. I guess I screamed. All the lights went out and then he shot at me. I could see the flashes, just like in the movies.

"I ran back into the house and slammed the door and then ran upstairs in the dark and got the gun Miriam always kept in the drawer by her bed. I locked myself in the bathroom—there's a phone in there—and I called the sheriff. I just whispered and then I hung up because I was afraid he was after me. I was in there on the floor in the dark, with the gun in my hand, it seemed like forever, and I kept thinking, He's coming. Then the lights went on and I could hear somebody opening doors. I was so afraid."

A deputy had come into the room. He said, "Skid marks in the drive. Fresh. A few footprints in that soft dirt. They're on the way up here with plaster. Bullet holes in the garage. Plaster came down from over the door leading from the garage to the house. Gun fired from inside the garage. We found some slugs. The guy's got a forty-five. Whoever it was shot off the lock on the garage to get the door open."

"How come no alarm?" Valdez asked, looking around.

"Oh, God, I had it turned off," Rachel said. She looked at Dade. "Remember, when we came in? I was going right out again, you see, and . . ." She trailed off.

"As for prints—" the deputy continued.

"I think he was wearing gloves," Rachel said.

"What else?"

"A raincoat. And boots. Black, shiny rubber boots."

"You didn't recognize him?" Valdez asked.

"He had on one of those stocking masks. Do you know, they're horrible? My God, I never realized it before. They're like the hood of an executioner. Anonymous. It was nobody. There was no way I could have recognized him."

"Did he say anything?"

"Are you serious? When I screamed, he turned out the lights and then fired at me. I ran away! How could he say anything?"

Dade said, "The lieutenant, he wants to know whether you heard his voice."

"No."

"Then how do you know it was a man?"

"I—I just know. I mean, I—I think it was. It was dressed in men's clothes."

"Could you have made a mistake?" Valdez asked.

"What?"

"If it had been a woman in men's clothes, could you have told?"

"I . . ." She began to tremble. Dade got out his flask and forced her to take another swallow. Holding on to him, shuddering from the brandy, she said, "I don't know! It all happened so fast!" Suddenly, realization flooded her face. "My God, he tried to *kill* me! Why?"

"We don't know that," Valdez said. "You had him trapped in the garage. Maybe he was just trying to scare you off so he could escape."

Dade said, "If he wanted to shoot you, he wouldn't have turned off the lights. Seems to me he turned them off so you couldn't see *him*."

"He shot over your head," Valdez spoke gently. "That plaster over the garage door is a good seven-feet high."

Dade pulled out his address book, checked a number and called Jensen's club. "I don't want you to be alone, honey." He waited a moment, then: No, Mr. Welles wasn't there and the man at the desk had no idea where to reach him. Dade put down the phone, thinking.

Rachel gave him Nick's number. "Call Nick."

"Let's not do that, honey, okay?" Dade patted her shoulder. Rachel's pallor was marked. Both Valdez and Dade were aware of it. They exchanged glances. The paramedic offered her smelling salts. Dade said, "What's the name of your doctor, honey?"

"I don't want to see a doctor!"

Dade took one of her hands in his, squeezing it. "I want you to tell me the name of your doctor." She compressed her lips. The blue eyes looked away defiantly. Dade put his head near hers and said, "What's his name, honey?"

She thought for a moment or two. Her expression softened. She sighed. Her eyes met Dade's. "It's Gil Ransohoff."

"You know his number offhand?" She rattled it off. Dade punched it out. They could hear the slow ring, ring, ring, and the sound of a woman's voice answering. "Chloe?"

"Yes."

"This here's Dade Cooley. Listen here, we got us a little

problem with Rachel. Is that doctor husband of yours in shouting distance?"

"What's the matter? What is it?"

"Could he come to the phone?"

"You should be able to reach him at the hospital. Has there been an accident?"

"Somebody broke in here—"

"What!"

"Now, it's all right—"

"At the Welles' house?"

"Yes, ma'am. Rachel, she's kind of shook up—"

"I'll come right out."

"That's not necessary."

"I'll talk to her," Rachel said, reaching for the phone. Dade patted her hand.

Chloe asked, "Who's with her?"

"She's alone. Jensen doesn't seem to be at home—"

"She has to stay here," Chloe said. "I'll come and get her."

"I think we can deliver her right to you." Dade looked inquiringly at Valdez, who nodded. Rachel started to protest. Dade put a hand over the phone and said to her, "You pack some things. Now, move." Rachel left the room.

"What's going *on*?" Chloe asked.

"There was a bit of a shooting affray, to be honest with you. Now, nobody's hurt."

"Oh, my God! I don't understand!"

"Most understandable thing in the world. Crooks read newspapers, just like the rest of us. Best day in the world to rob a house is when there's been a funeral. Nobody's home. Now, I'm sure that's all there was to it. We'll send her right along. Chloe, I'm much indebted to you."

As soon as Rachel was packed, Valdez told one of the deputies where to take her. Rachel insisted on driving her own car. Valdez agreed but told one of the deputies to ride with her, the other to escort her.

"But if I'm not in any danger—"

"You're not now." Valdez walked into the corridor, giving orders to his men in an undertone.

"Do what he says, honey, will you do that for me?"

"You'll call me tomorrow?"

" 'Course I will. I already wrote down the number. See?" He held up his address book. She nodded and started out, the deputy carrying her suitcase. On impulse, she ran back and hugged Dade, kissing him. He gripped her shoulders, saying in a half-whisper, "You take it easy, hear?"

"Ready?" It was Valdez, putting his head in the door.

Rachel said, "Yes. Yes, thank you, I am."

They both went out the door, following Valdez down the hall. They walked down the stairs in silence. Valdez asked Rachel for the house keys. She went to get them.

"Thanks," Dade said to Valdez.

"I have no objection to taking precautions." Then in a low voice, he said, "Look, I know what you're thinking. But it was just an intruder trying to rob the place on the day of the funeral. We run into that kind of thing all the time. Mr. Cooley, you've got the wrong idea. Back in my office this evening," he said almost impatiently, "I don't know what you saw or what you think you heard, but there's been a misunderstanding. There is no ongoing murder investigation in the Welles case. And unless you've got some new evidence why there should be—"

"All right, you've made your point."

Voices of the paramedics floated toward them as they loaded the dogs' carcasses onto a stretcher. "Watch out, the bag's coming open."

"Where do we take this thing? The morgue? It don't seem right."

"Take it to the vet," Valdez said. "The one we use."

"They're dead, sir."

"Do what I fucking told you."

"Yes, sir."

They heard the sound of vehicles starting up. Valdez nodded at Dade, who was escorting Rachel. A deputy brought Rachel's car around. Rachel got behind the wheel, Dade got in beside her, and with the deputy in back, Rachel drove Dade down to the sheriff's station to get his car. They drove for a while in silence. In the parking lot, she said, "You think he's right? That it was just a burglar?"

"No." He told her about the crate in the garage. She

gripped his arm. "As I said before, try to stay out of it. Right now, the less you know, the safer you are."

"Did you tell the sheriff about the painting?"

"I told him it was missing. That's all I told him. Then we were interrupted with that call from you. Rachel," he said abruptly, "what I want to know is, can you keep your own counsel?"

"What are you trying to tell me?"

"Everybody talks. Now, I want to know if you can keep your mouth shut. For your own sake."

She looked at him levelly. "Yes."

"After what happened to Nettie and then this tonight, I'm sure you see why."

She turned away from him, hands over her ears, as if trying to drown out the sound of something that frightened her and was closer now. "Then she was murdered. That's what you're saying, isn't it?"

He didn't answer. She got back into her car with the waiting deputy and Dade headed back to the inn.

Ellen stretched out her arms sleepily as he eased into bed beside her. She murmured, "What time is it?"

"Late. Go to sleep."

She looked at the clock in disbelief. "What happened?"

"It's a long story." Reaching across her, he picked up the phone and called San Francisco.

She mumbled sleepily, "Ring Lardner once described someone as a man of few words, most of them ill-chosen, and I think he was talking about you."

"He also said his wife was an inveterate umbrage-taker and frequently took more than was good for her." He got Arnolphe Motke's answering machine.

The voice said, "Motke," and then there was a beep.

"Name. Nick Levin. Subject: Commodities. Base: Los Angeles. This here's a first-class ticket, Arnie, okay? This may help you: Somebody's already been over a lot of the ground." He rang off and began to tell Ellen what had happened at Rachel's, breaking off at the point when they were searching the house, when he realized Ellen was fast asleep.

XIV

Dade slept well. He was up at seven and found a note from Ellen reading, "Out getting gas." She had made coffee and he sipped a cup while ordering breakfast, then went for a dip in the ocean. Emerging shivering, he toweled himself dry in the brisk morning air, standing on his deck and looking out at the flat, bright sea, then got out of his wet trunks and pulled on a terry-cloth burnoose. At seven-thirty, breakfast arrived, brought by a smiling Pete. Dade sat down and, tucking a large napkin at his neck, he addressed himself to a hearty breakfast of ham, eggs, fried potatoes, toast and jelly and coffee laced with cream and sugar, meanwhile reading his newspaper and commenting on it aloud, occasionally turning to one side to address the President, the head of the Teamsters, a convicted terrorist and the editor of the Los Angeles *Times*.

It was eight o'clock and he was on his fourth cup of coffee when the phone rang. It was Motke.

"About Levin. Been in the country for a year. I ran a ten-twenty-nine on him. No criminal record. But I'm still checking. There is something."

"What?"

"I'm still trying to pin it down. There's a discount broker down there says he knows Levin. Started to laugh when I mentioned his name. Wouldn't say what he thinks 'cause it's still a guess. Guy owes me. I sort of reminded him about that. So he says, okay, he'll lean on some friends and get back to me around three. I'll call you then."

Dade had no sooner put down the phone it rang again. It was Rachel, worried because she hadn't been able to reach Nick. She had called him from Gil's but he wasn't home yet. Gil had given her a sedative that was stronger than she realized and she had gone to sleep immediately. When she woke up, it was already eight and Nick's phone didn't answer.

"We're supposed to go to Tijuana today. He won't know where I am."

"He'll find out. I got an idea he's smart enough to ask questions."

"Dade? What are they going to do?"

"About what, honey?"

"What happened."

"I'm sure they're on it." He drank more coffee, wondering if she had ever told Nick about the painting.

"Aren't they going to investigate anything?"

"Why don't you ask them? Ask that lieutenant fella—Valdez."

"I thought maybe he'd said something to you."

"I don't know beans. You talk to your daddy?"

"I called his club. He wasn't there. He left early. And he's not at the house yet."

"I'll get hold of him. Something bothering you?"

"I just want to see Nick."

He remembered that she was a young girl in love. "He'll turn up. I already told you that."

"And I want to go home."

"Why don't we talk about that in a little while? I got a few things that need doing this morning. What say I give you a ring after lunch and we'll talk about it, that okay with you?"

"What do you mean? What are you going to do?"

"I'll tell you later."

"Something about all this?"

"I said I'd tell you. Only if you promise to stay put all day. Now, I want to hear it, Rachel. Say, 'I promise.'" There was a silence. "And I want you to cut out the telephoning. Just don't talk to anybody until I call you, you promise me that?"

"I have to call and tell them I won't be at work."

"You let me do that. What's the name of the place?"

"It's the Taco Bell on Lincoln. Just tell them—"

"I know what to tell them. Now, you just sit tight. Bye-ble, honey." Dade put down the phone and returned to his newspaper. A few minutes later, the phone rang again. The operator announced a Mr. Levin. Dade told her to send him on down, then went to the door.

Nick, ignoring the funicular, came running down the long steep flight of stairs. Dade shook hands with him gravely, introducing himself. Nick was even handsomer than his photographs. He seemed shaken. His face was drawn. He asked, "Was an accident? You tell me." Dade ushered him in and offered him coffee. "I don't want coffee. I want truth."

"What makes you think there was an accident, son?"

"I go by Rachel's apartment. Rachel not there. I wait. Then I go to her house. Is a policeman. He ask me questions. I say, 'Where is Rachel?' He don't tell me. He just ask me questions. For half an hour. 'Where you were last night? Why not home?' I say finally, 'Rachel is dead?' He ask me why I think that. I start to yell at him. He say Rachel not dead but won't say no more and to go away. You tell me now what happened. I think you know. Where is Rachel taken?"

"Now, she's just fine. She'll tell you all about it herself."

His voice was flat and hard. "You don't tell me where she is."

"You going to be home at like three this afternoon?" Nick nodded slowly. "Well, what say you give me your number and I'll call you then?"

"You do not trust me?"

"Why don't you sit down a minute and help yourself to coffee? I got some questions."

"Just like the police, is it not?"

"Now who's not doing the trusting?"

Nick's lean, angular face broke into a wide smile, frank like a child's. He sat down. Dade went to the kitchen and got another cup and saucer and brought them to him. Nick helped himself. Dade sat back, watching him.

"Say, tell me something. Where do you do business?"

"I don't have it an office. Here, I do business." He tapped his head. At the mention of "business," the smile evaporated. Business appeared to be a very serious affair to Nick.

"What business you doing lately?"

"Say it again, please?"

"I was asking what you're investing in now." Dade spoke clearly and slowly.

Nick nodded like a mandarin. He wrinkled his nose and pursed his lips. His eyes narrowed. The play of expression had variety, degree. He said finally, "At present times, I am in currencies."

"Which?"

"Swiss francs. I have this good feeling about Switzerland."

"Nice clean people."

"Pardon?"

"Never mind. You think silver's going limit up Monday?"

Nick gave him a surprised look and then grinned. "You are needing money?"

"Son, money's like poontang. The more you get, the more you have to have."

"What is it, poontang?"

"Women. I mean girls, son."

"Oh, is girls!" The grin widened.

"Let's get back to money. What about silver?"

He opened his hands and shrugged. "Anybody's guess."

"What's yours? Look, I'm not going to quote you."

"I have no opinion."

"Well, what do you like?" Dade picked up the newspaper, folded open to the financial page, and thrust it at him. "Here."

Nick took the paper, glancing at the stock quotations and made a face. "Up, down, up, down! Like never before. Why?"

"It's the Arabs."

"Yes? You think so? Why?"

"See, they got a lot of money in the market and they sell when it goes down and buy when it goes up. That's your answer."

Nick thought about this for a few moments, a frown on his face. Then he got a look at Dade's amused expression and burst into shouts of laughter, repeating Dade's words under his breath as if committing them to memory. "You know what is with the Arabs," he said after a moment. "Is like with an old servant. She works. Is happy. Why to pay her more? So it is with the sheik. He is sitting there all the time on the sand and all the time is the people bringing him toys, they give cars and watches and jewels and the great banquets and all the time, he is eating and focking girls, oh, how happy he is!

"And then one day, the son, he grows up and goes away to Oxford and he sees what is what and then he go home and he say to his father, 'You dummy!'" Another wide smile. Then the face changed suddenly, becoming serious. "I am honest with you. All questions I answer. But when I am asking you where is Rachel, you don't tell. What is reason?"

"Now, Rachel's fine. While we're on the subject, she tells me you know she has no money."

"I think she is having one hundred million dollars."

"Yes and no. She has the money but she can't touch it."

"Is exactly what I understand. And the father is giving to her money all the time. Is called an allowance. I understand."

"Not anymore and he won't give her another penny if you two get married."

"I know this, I know this." Nick waved it away impatiently. "We wait. We wait."

"To get the allowance?"

"Not for me. For her. For why do you ask me all this?"

"Just getting to know you, son. Me, I got a feeling that money isn't all you got on your mind. I know a fellow sinner when I see one. No, it's all right. Bible, it says the love of money is the root of all evil but it don't say a thing like that about poontang!"

Nick laughed a loud, ringing laugh and then said with the candor of a Shakespearean character confiding in the audience, "All times, I am thinking about focking and the pissy."

"Pussy."

"Is what I say. I like it, the pissy, and that is what I think about the most. Some men, they thinking all the time about the titties and I like that but what I am thinking about most times is the pissy, you understand?"

"How are you going to manage with just one?"

"Say it again, please?"

"When you're married."

"Oh! I still think about all the girls, how can I help it? In my life, I fock two hundred eleven women. Is good?"

"Rachel, she understands that?"

"She is understanding. Besides, what I do? I don't do nothing now, just think. At least, this is my hope. If not possible, that is very bad. I don't wanting Rachel like trapped. I wanting her therefore to be having her money. Me, I have money. No problems, correct? Rachel, she must be having money, too. Her money. Otherwise, come problems—she can't go. I am realist. I tell her I love her but I not know the future but she say, 'We must marry now,' so I want her protected, do you see?"

"Have you told her all this?"

"Many time. And to Miriam I tell it. So Miriam is saying to Rachel, 'You wait. Your father, he is changing his mind. Wait, wait.' "

"Oh, he changed his mind, all right. He decided to solve the problem by threatening to shoot you, isn't that so?"

"Is true. All like Rachel says."

"This was Tuesday, correct?"

Nick nodded emphatically. "On the Valentine's Day. We don't have it, the Valentine's Day, in Soviet Union, you know. Rachel call me and say what is happen."

"When was that?"

"After eight. Maybe fifteen minutes after."

"And what did you do?"

"Like Rachel says. I go out of apartment."

"Were you afraid of him?"

Nick gave him a contemptuous look. "Why to be afraid? A man try to kill me, I kill him first. But with the papa is a different thing."

"Yes, I understand that. So you went out?"

"Exactly."

"Where?"

"To restaurant to wait."

"You went straight to the restaurant?"

"Yes. Is called Land's End."

"But look here, you're five minutes closer to the restaurant than Rachel's house and she didn't leave for another fifteen minutes, and yet you arrived there the same time she did. She said so herself. So where did you go?"

Nick shrugged, his expression untroubled. "I am driving around, thinking what to do. First, I think, this man he is crazy. Maybe he shoot Rachel, too, isn't it? I am, how you say"—he made a roiling gesture—"like this inside. Then, when is time, I go to restaurant."

Dade nodded and grunted. "You've been very open with me and I'm grateful to you."

"I am not holding nothing back. For what is the reason? For whose benefit is it to tell the lies? I do not pretend to live. I live. All the lies is why I am leaving Soviet Union. Here is my life. You can see me. In Russian, we are saying, *Derzhi karman shire*—how does it say?—Hold open your pockets wider. Because every man, he hide something. Me, I don't hide. I like it, the money, the pissy, Rachel."

"Well, you got one big thing in your favor, son. Miriam liked you."

The boyish face sobered. "She was friend. Was terrible thing."

"When was the last time you saw her, by the way?"

"Is when Rachel move out. The papa, he don't want me to go there."

"Well, Jensen or no Jensen, I still think you should have fixed that roof for Miriam. What with that painting in there—"

"She did not ask me." He tried to catch himself but it was too late. The eyes hardened. He got to his feet, hands flat on the table.

Dade said, rising. "Son, you've been very helpful. Now, just run along and wait for me to call you."

"I don't like it, what you do to me. I don't think I understand you, what you are."

"In case you're still working on your English, the word is 'captious.' " Nick's hands tightened on the table's edge. Dade opened the door. "You'll be hearing from me," he said. Nick left abruptly.

Dade went back into his room, pulled off his burnoose and stepped into the shower, singing and scrubbing himself. A little while later, shaved and dressed, his pink face redolent of Jean Marie Farina, he came out of the bathroom to find Ellen seated at the table drinking coffee and reading the newspaper. He kissed her good morning. She did not look up.

"You mad at me?"

"What on earth ever gave you an idea like that?" Then in a sugary tone she asked, "Did you and Rachel have lots and lots to talk about last night? Ooooh, I bet it was exciting for you!"

"Ellen—"

"The company of a girl of eighteen must be a treat for a man of seventy."

"*Sixty!*"

"Picky, picky."

"Truth is, I stopped by last night to see that lieutenant. The one I met in the men's room."

"I didn't know you were working there anymore, dear."

Ignoring her, he went on, "Then we got word someone took a shot at Rachel."

"Oh, my *God!* Was she hurt?"

"No." He told her what had happened. She was aghast. "I'm going to call on Mr. Monkhaus. I want to find out what he knows about that missing Romano. Meanwhile, you run down to the Getty—you know that museum he built in Malibu, looks just like a villa in Herculaneum?"

"I know where the Getty is, dear."

"Well, they've got a little art library down in the basement, right behind the garage where they've got tomb friezes and such, and I want you to get me a list of the missing Romanos. Berenson's got a book on lost art—"

"*Homeless Paintings.*"

"That's it. But that's stuff they've lost recently. See what else is missing. Oh, and would you make a call for Rachel? I don't know the number but she works at the Taco Bell on Lincoln, and she wants them to know she won't be in today. Tell them—"

"Oh my land!" She had just caught sight of something in the paper. "I won't have to tell them anything. They can read all about it." She showed him an article in the newspaper. The caption read, "Burglar Shoots Dogs, Terrorizes Bereaved Heiress."

"Oh, boy." He kissed her briefly.

Upstairs, he paused at the desk to leave his key. A balding man with the pasty complexion of a tourist stood there in a Hawaiian shirt, a large woman in a polyester slacks suit standing beside him. Dade leaned in front of them and said to the sharp-featured woman who was trying to answer the telephone and wait on them at the same time, "Thank you, Madeleine."

"The name is Mary."

"Whatever it is, I loved you last night."

She slapped the flat of her hand hard down on the desk. He hurried away into the parking lot and, after checking the address he had copied down from Miriam's records, he drove south on the highway toward the freeway, singing Mozart's "Là ci darem la mano" along with the baritone from the Met on the radio.

XV

A new slide had blocked the highway at Big Rock. Dade turned around and went up Rambla Pacifico, climbing several miles up to the spine of the mountains separating the narrow coast from the rest of the city. Then he turned right onto Saddle Peak and drove for miles, finally making a right on Topanga, a boulevard that ran from the Valley through the wall of the Santa Monica Mountains to the sea. It swept down through a forest where there were campgrounds at the edge of a stream, past the shanties and shopping center of what once had been the refuge of the flower children. He emerged once again on Pacific Coast Highway, not much more than a mile south of where he had started. He had driven twenty miles out of his way to get around the slide. Malibu was an inhospitable coast. Only the Chumash had really lived there well, had adjusted the rhythm and style of their lives to that restless land where every year there were fires, floods, high tides that washed away houses, mud slides that engulfed whole districts, earthquakes, destructive winds and where every few years the records for heat and cold, precipitation, frost, everything, were broken.

Even though it was a Saturday, it was a good hour before he got to the house. It was a pink stucco bungalow on a tree-shaded street just below Fountain Avenue in Hollywood. The patch of lawn was overgrown with crab grass, and unkempt oleander bushes screened the windows from view. At first, Dade thought he had the wrong address. When he got out of his car, he could hear voices raised in argument, a man's and a woman's. The speeches were punctuated by banging and the occasional crash of dishes breaking.

As Dade started up the concrete path, the sounds stopped. Inside, a door slammed. Stepping up onto a porch that leaned to one side, Dade rang the doorbell. There was no answer. After a few moments, he rang it again.

The door opened abruptly and a woman stared out at him through a screen door. She was the actress he had seen at the funeral. She wore no make-up. Her thin, straw-colored hair was unkempt. She wore a dirty white terry-cloth wrapper and he noticed that her bare feet were dirty. She looked at him, not saying anything.

"Mrs. Monkhaus?" When she didn't answer, Dade introduced himself, taking out a card and offering it to her. "I'd like to talk with your husband for a few minutes."

"He can't talk to you now."

"It's important."

"Can you tell me what it's about?"

"I'm the executor for the estate of the late Miriam Welles."

"Just a minute."

The door closed. He could not hear anything. He waited a long time. He began to wonder whether she was coming back and was about to ring the bell a second time when the door opened again. This time, she held the screen door open for him. He stepped into a stucco alcove, then followed her into a small living room in which there were a pair of overstuffed chairs from the forties and a matching sofa. Under an arch, dark double doors were closed. The door leading from the entry into the rest of the house was also shut.

Mrs. Monkhaus followed him into the room. She said, "My husband really can't talk to you now. Do you have it with you?"

"I beg your pardon?"

"My husband's painting. Did you bring it with you?"

"We seem to be talking at cross-purposes, ma'am. I just came here to ask you some questions about it. Why don't you just begin by describing it for me?"

"Describing it?" She seemed at a loss. "Well, it's a picture of a woman, a very beautiful woman, done in the style of the Italian Renaissance." She made a self-conscious gesture. "She's wearing a sort of buff-colored shawl and she has dark hair and dark eyes. Does that help you at all?"

"Do you have a photograph of it?"

"No. Why would we? Anyway, my husband can identify it easily and I can't believe Jensen Welles would get it mixed up with anything else. I mean, he has everything catalogued, hasn't he?"

"And who was the artist, can you tell me that?"

"My husband's father."

"Your husband's father? But I had the impression—"

"Tillie!" a high thin man's voice called out.

One of the double doors was yanked open and the man Dade had seen at the funeral with her appeared in the doorway, a half-filled glass in one hand. He was unshaven and thick-set, with strong features. Dade noticed that his eyebrows were raised, as if in surprise, but that his face was expressionless, almost immobile.

"He hasn't got it, is that what he's trying to tell you?" he said to Tillie. Then, to Dade: I suppose Welles sent you. Well, you tell him for me he's got one hell of a nerve! I happen to know a thing or two and you can tell him I said so!" His voice was shrill and Dade was struck by the fact that the man spoke very slowly, moving his lips with care. His wife reacted with alarm, putting her hands on his chest, pushing him back into the other room.

"I said I'll handle it!"

"I want to talk to him! I want to talk to the man that son of a bitch sent to do his dirty work!"

"Not now!" She succeeded in making him go back into the other room, pulling the door closed behind her. Turning to Dade, she whispered, "It isn't a good time."

The door banged open again and Richard Monkhaus said, "That's my painting and I want it back!" Quickly, Tillie stepped forward, pushing him back again into the other room and once more attempting to close the door on him.

Dade pointed at a rectangle on the wall, lighter than the rest of the wallpaper in the room. "That's where it hung, isn't it?" When Monkhaus didn't answer, but only stared at him, the face still expressionless except for the raised eye-brows, Dade said, "Judging by that discoloration, I'd say it hung there for years."

Breaking free of his wife, Monkhaus walked unsteadily over to the wall Dade had indicated. A scrap of the wall-paper had come unglued and curled up. Suddenly Monk-haus reached up, grasped the paper and ripped a whole section off the wall. Crumpling it up in one hand, the drink sloshing in the other as he walked, he lurched back toward the other room.

"Dump!" he said shrilly. "That's what this place is, a dump! At least, that painting dressed it up some! I want it back and you go tell Welles I want it back now!"

Tillie forced him back through the double doors, mur-muring, "Monk, Monk, *please*," in a surprisingly soft, gentle tone. She closed the doors. There was a crash in the other room, as if Monk had fallen against something. Tillie gave no sign that she had heard.

"I have to ask him a few questions," said Dade. "Don't make me have papers served and drag him into court."

She looked suddenly frightened. "Can't you let him alone? For Christ's sake, he's made his contribution! Let people remember him as he was. You don't want to parade a drunk around a courtroom!"

"He's not a drunk, ma'am." When she continued staring at him levelly, not answering, Dade said, "How long has he had it?"

"I don't know what you're talking about."

"He has Parkinson's disease." Dade's voice was gentle. "The symptoms are unmistakable. For some reason, you're keeping it a secret. Or trying to. That drunk act is a cover-up." She reacted as if he had suddenly pointed a gun at her. The frightened eyes searched his face. "Why did he take the painting to Mrs. Welles?"

"They—they were friends." Her voice was low, hoarse. Her clear eyes continued to meet his.

"Once, they were a whole lot more than friends."

"All right, so you know. But that was years ago." Her eyes moved toward the closed double doors, then back to his. She spoke in a voice as soft as a sigh. "The painting was an excuse. It was worthless. He went to her with it because he was begging."

"Your husband must be a very successful beggar if he goes to somebody for a handout and she gives him thirty-five thousand dollars."

"My husband never cashed that check she gave him, even though we didn't have a cent in the world." She gestured at the shabby room. "We were broke. I haven't had a part in years, if you must know the truth. Anyway, the point is, my husband decided not to sell his father's painting after all."

"Then I take it you're not broke anymore."

"I work."

"Where?"

"What difference does it make? I don't know what Mr. Jensen Welles is trying to pull but we don't want charity—not from Jensen Welles or anyone else. We just want back the painting, in exchange for the check. That's fair enough, isn't it?"

Suddenly, they were interrupted by the sound of an engine revving up and then, through the dingy curtains of the windows at the other end of the room, Dade saw a car reversing fast down the narrow driveway, heard the screech of brakes, then the roar of the motor as the car sped off up the street.

Tillie stared out the front windows after it. Dade turned to look at her.

She said, "He heard us. He listens. All the time. Oh, God, he shouldn't drive. When he's upset, it gets worse. Much worse."

"Where will he go?"

"Sometimes he just drives for hours. I don't think he'll do that today. Please go now. He'll check the street. If your car isn't here, maybe he'll come back sooner."

"I'm sorry."

"You're sorry! I've told you what I know. I don't know what you hoped to gain by coming here. All Monk wants is the painting back."

"Enough to kill for it? Because that's how it will look if that picture is found in your husband's possession. See, there's good reason to believe Miriam Welles was murdered for it."

"It isn't true! My God, it isn't true!" She turned suddenly, twisting her right hand with her left, as if trying to keep herself from striking him.

Dade left the house, clapping his hat firmly on his head. He stepped down from the porch onto the concrete path, unable to forget that the car Dick Monkhaus had backed down the driveway in was a blue Mustang fastback.

XVI

Dade walked back down the cracked concrete path toward the tree-lined street, boys skateboarding on the sidewalk, the sky dull with smog. A workman in overalls staggered down the street, drinking from a bottle in a paper bag. Somewhere close by, Dade could hear the approaching uh-hunh uh-hunh uh-hunh of an ambulance and then, as he slid behind the wheel of his car, the rising siren of a police car.

He drove past the shabby houses toward Fountain Avenue, turned right, drove around the block and then turned up the Monkhaus street again, parking at the end where his car was half hidden from view by the spreading branches of a big avocado tree in front of a Green and Green style cottage on the corner. Dade settled back in his seat, taking out his notebook.

An old woman in a man's coat-sweater and a green visor opened her front door and shuffled out in felt slippers to pick up a newspaper. She stood on her porch and stared at his car for a few moments, as if memorizing his license number, and afterward went back inside and slammed the door shut. Dade thought for a moment, then got out of his car and went up to her house, knocking at the door. She didn't open it but she was watching him because a voice called out from behind a heavily curtained window. "What do you want?"

"Do you know what time the Radnitzes will be home?"

"I don't know any Radnitzes."

"They live across the street. I'm the adjuster from the

insurance company. They said they'd meet me at ten and they're not home."

"Why don't you park over there?"

"Shade. If I've got to wait, I don't want to park in the sun. That is, if it's all right with you. Nice tree you've got here, this avocado. It's a Bacon avocado. Did you know that?" She opened the front door and peered up at the tree through the screen door. Dade said, "It's unusual—it's a boy in the morning and a girl in the afternoon."

"Well, it's sure in the right part of town."

Dade laughed. He glanced at his watch and said, "I'm sure they said ten. It's really important that we get this matter settled. After all, it's money in their pocket. I don't understand their not being here."

"Well, I don't know anybody named Radnitz."

"Thanks anyway, ma'am. And have a nice day."

"You do the same. You just make yourself at home."

Dade heard a window bang shut behind him as he went back to his car. Settling himself once again behind the wheel, he returned to his notebook, writing slowly with his gold pencil. First, he made a list of names. After each one, he made brief notes of where each of them said he was between eight-thirty and shortly after nine, meanwhile keeping an eye on the street.

At one point he broke off impatiently and began talking under his breath. He reproached himself, saying that he had no business doing what he was doing, that he ought to call San Francisco and get Arnolphe Motke down there. Snorting, he pointed out to himself that he didn't even know the rules of the game.

Then he spoke in rebuttal. He was a damn good lawyer, wasn't he? Wasn't this a matter of examining the evidence, sifting it, looking for the truth? He raised his voice, began gesturing, breaking off only when he saw a woman with a shopping cart full of groceries hesitating, squinting in at him through round, metal-rimmed glasses. He lifted his hat and nodded in her direction. She turned and walked briskly on.

The defense had won. He was persuaded that he knew exactly what he was doing. Tapping the gold pencil against his teeth, he studied his notes.

A few cars had gone by and Dade had looked up each time but had been disappointed. He had waited half an hour, long enough. He started the car and was about to pull away from the curb when a car came around the corner fast. It was a blue Mustang and Monk was driving. He pulled into the driveway, disappearing from view.

Then Dade saw Monk coming down the driveway on foot, back bowed, arms held out stiffly. He made his way slowly across the patch of weedy lawn and then, the front door opened for him and he went inside.

Dade switched off his engine and waited, trying to decide what to do. He filled his pipe, smoking it steadily, ruminating. He had just about decided to go back inside and confront Monk when the Mustang backed into view again, but this time Tillie Monkhaus was driving and she was alone.

She headed up toward Hollywood Boulevard. Dade followed her at a distance. When she turned right onto the boulevard, he followed her more closely. She drove only a few blocks, then turned right and parked in front of the Greyhound bus station. Dade saw her take a small suitcase from the trunk, then hurry inside. Parking behind her, he followed her.

From across the waiting room, he saw her go to a wall phone. She did not, as with most people, turn toward the wall for privacy but looked straight ahead of her, out at the room itself. It seemed to be a local call because she only put one coin into the box. She spoke twice, briefly, angrily. She waited, composed. Then, apparently, someone came on the line and she spoke with animation, unconsciously expressing herself with gestures, as if whoever was at the other end of the line could see her. She glanced at her watch, shook her head, said one more thing and put down the receiver. Then she went into the ladies' room, suitcase in hand. Dade sat down to wait, watching the door from a vinyl-upholstered chrome armchair as he read his paper.

He waited perhaps fifteen minutes and when she finally emerged, he almost missed her. She had changed clothes, a cloche hid the unkempt hair, her face was made up and her whole bearing was different. She wore boots and her clothes were flashy, common. She took small, rapid steps and her gestures, when she took a vial of perfume from her purse and put a few drops on her wrist, were quick, decisive. Now he noticed her legs for the first time. They were slender and set off by the high-heeled silver boots which matched the color of her suit. Suddenly, Dade understood what she did for a living. She walked briskly toward the doors of the bus terminal. Dade followed her, going out a side door.

It was about eleven-thirty. The street was crowded. He got into his car and followed her as she drove down to Fountain, took it to La Cienega, went left down to Santa Monica and then right toward Century City, where she left her car with a parking attendant at the Century Plaza Hotel, then went inside. Dade got out of his car, leaving it in the line of cars to be parked, and followed her. She went toward the main bar, which was crowded with businessmen. She spoke to the headwaiter and was led toward a booth.

A man rose to greet her. He was thin, with a raised beak-like nose. Even in the dim light of the bar, Dade had no trouble recognizing him immediately. It was Jensen. And he was obviously upset at seeing Tillie.

Dade made his way toward the bar, ordered a martini made with Bombay gin, and sat sipping it, watching the faraway reflection of Tillie Monkhaus and Jensen Welles in the mirror over the bar. They talked heatedly for a minute or two. Then Dade saw Tillie lean toward Jensen. Suddenly, she got to her feet, an angry expression on her face, and left the room. Jensen had risen. He swayed on his feet. Dade hurried over to him. He managed to get Jensen to sit down in the booth again. Dade sat down with him. Jensen's face was damp with perspiration. He blotted it with a linen napkin.

"What happened?" Dade asked.

"Nothing." The sight of Dade seemed to bewilder Jensen. "What are you doing here?" he asked.

"Having a drink." Jensen's eyes strayed around the room nervously. "You expecting somebody?" Dade asked.

"Yes, as a matter of fact I am."

"You talk to Rachel?" Jensen looked at Dade blankly. "I thought perhaps she'd called you."

"I haven't been home."

"Then you don't know what happened last night."

"That? I know about that. The sheriff called me." Dade gave him a surprised look. Jensen said impatiently, "In my position, you get to expect these things. They told me, they told me. I understand. Day of a funeral, that element always tries to break in. I'm only sorry Rachel should have been there. You notice they got nothing."

"Somebody took a shot at her."

"And hit the ceiling of the garage."

Dade grunted and changed tack. "Oh, I happened to see you talking with Mrs. Monkhaus. Have you known her long?"

"You know that woman?" Jensen's voice shook.

"All I know about her is that she seems to be looking for a missing painting. The same one I'm looking for."

"I know nothing about it." Jensen compressed his thin lips, put on a pair of gold-rimmed glasses, picked up a menu and began reading it with great attention, as if checking it for spelling and punctuation.

Dade put the tips of his thick fingers together, looked around the dim, crowded bar and then said, "She telephoned you and asked to see you. You arranged to meet her here." Jensen's face showed nothing. "That is true, isn't it?" When Jensen remained silent, Dade said, "You mind telling me why you agreed to see her if you don't know anything about the painting?"

A dull flush mottled Jensen's cheeks. He said in an undertone, "It doesn't concern you and that's all I'm going to say."

Dade hesitated, picking up a fork and examining it carefully, as if it were a rare piece he was interested in buying. Then he put down the fork and said, "It does concern me. I'm the executor and the painting is missing. That is my problem. I'd be grateful for any light you could shed on it."

Jensen sighed, removed his glasses and, pulling out a handkerchief, began polishing them. "Very well, then: Her husband called me the day after Miriam died. The day

after, mind you! He told my secretary Miriam had gotten a
painting from him on consignment or some such thing and
he wanted it back and she promised to give it to him. I
didn't know what he was talking about. I said to get in
touch with Nettie and forgot about it. He called me again
that night. Said Nettie didn't know where it was. I said I
didn't either. I'm afraid I hung up on him. Hell of a time to
call a man, don't you think? He called a few more times
after that. My secretary got rid of him.

"When his wife called a little while ago, she was
abusive. My secretary said I'd better talk to her myself, so
I did and I agreed to meet her here to straighten things
out. Woman threatened me. I don't have the painting, I've
never had it, and I don't know what the Christ she's talking
about. 'Get a search warrant,' I said. 'Search my house.
Search everything. When you get through, I'll sue you for
slander and libel. Doesn't matter whether I win. By the
time I get through, you won't have one thing left in the
world.' She looked kind of shaken up. She knows I mean it.
Satisfied?"

"You say she threatened you? How?"

"It isn't important. Dade, I have told you what I know.
Now, if you'll excuse me—"

Dade rose and stood over Jensen, looking down at the
bald skull, the long nose once again buried in the menu.
Dade said, "Jensen, is there any way I can help you?"
Dade waited. Jensen ignored him. Finally, Dade said,
"Well, I tried."

XVII

Dade made his way out of the crowded bar and crossed the hotel lobby to a pay phone. He called Nettie.

"You feeling better?"

"I'm fine. You were very kind. You and your wife."

"Nettie, mind if I stop by, in, say, about fifteen minutes?"

"No, not at all."

"I've got some more questions."

"Dade, I'm going to beg off." Her voice was crisp. "After what I went through last night—"

"Incidentally, almost the same thing happened to Rachel a few hours later."

"What?"

"I'll see you shortly." He replaced the receiver, then turned to a cigar-smoking man waiting to use the phone and said, "By God, I hung up on her!"

"Attaboy!" the man said.

Dade called the inn and got hold of Ellen. She said with a note of relief in her voice, "Dade, where are you?"

"Century City. You find out anything?"

"It took me forever."

"Hey, that's too bad. I just ran into Jensen Welles. I should've asked him."

"Well, go ahead!"

"Now, Ellen—"

"No, I mean it. Go ask him. I'll wait."

"Honey, I don't want to ask him anything. Now, what did you find out?"

"All Romanos present and accounted for. There are

none missing, neither recently nor from long, long ago. None have been sold in the last couple of years, and the top price was twenty-three thousand dollars."

"Got another assignment for you."

"Ask Jensen Welles."

"I'm asking you. I want you to go back to the Getty and do a little digging. When I get home, I want you to give me a brushup course on authentication. What did Miriam do and just how did she do it?"

"I wish you'd thought of this earlier."

"What's the matter?"

"The bus only runs once an hour."

"Land sakes, can't you rent a car?"

"In Malibu? They don't even have cabs. Furthermore, there was another rock slide and half the highway is closed."

"I know. I took the detour."

"You'll be lucky to get back. When will you be, by the way?"

"In a little while. First, I have to see Nettie."

"Why don't you ask *her* about authentication?"

"Meow, meow!"

"Well, why don't you?"

"I'm more interested in finding out where that painting is. 'Course, I don't know whether I can trust what she says. You know, last night, she told me a barefaced lie."

"She lied? About what?"

"Now you know what I know. Just search your memory. Any messages?"

"Just a minute!"

"Ellen, I'm on a public phone in the lobby of a hotel—"

"I want to know what it is she lied about."

"Think about it for a minute, then I'll give you the answer. Any messages? Motke call yet?"

"Just Nick Levin."

"I'll get back to him later. This is turning out to be quite a little puzzle."

"Then you think she was murdered?"

"Oh, yes. It was murder, all right."

"Dade?" He could hear worry in her voice. "You stay out of it!"

"I'm jut beginning to put a few things together."

"Yes, and somebody's watching you do it." The operator came on to say his three minutes were up. "Dade?" Ellen said, "Dade? What was the lie?"

"Ellen, I don't have any more change in my pocket."

"What's the number there? I'll call you back."

"I don't have my glasses on."

"You have eyes like a hawk!"

"I'm late, honey."

"You bastard!"

He hung up the phone and walked toward the doors of the hotel, whistling.

When Dade arrived at the gallery, Nettie was on the phone, walking up and down in her high heels, dragging a long cord after her. She waved him to a chair, then said impatiently into the phone in French, "If you can't speak Russian, speak German!" then shifted to English, nodding and saying, "Yes, I know it's late. I said, I know it's late! Um-hm, um-hm," and at one point letting go of the receiver and dragging it by its cord she paced the floor, rolling her eyes and sighing with impatience.

Dade wondered if it was a bill collector. Miriam had told him that Nettie was always in debt. Five years before, when Miriam had first bought into the gallery, she had learned about Nettie's extravagance. Nettie had had the flu and Miriam, alone in the gallery, had been forced to go through Nettie's personal papers to look for an important bill of lading and had found a huge sheaf of unpaid personal bills and letters from collection agencies.

"Why didn't you tell me?" Miriam had asked her afterward.

Nettie had shrugged, taking the whole stack of bills and throwing them out. "Don't think about it."

"You have to think about it!" Miriam had said.

"One little pile goes down, another little pile goes up."

Nettie was French but had been educated in England. Her speech was British but with a faint nasal French intonation. Her family had been well-to-do. Her mother had studied at the Sorbonne and played tennis at Wimbledon. "She used to play with the King of Sweden," Nettie once said. "God, he was awful. Ninety or something, blind as a bat and he cheated. Mother was always yelling, 'Go to the net, Majesty!' to get him out of the way."

Now, still on the phone, she was obviously at her wit's end. "My name is Proulx!" she cried out. "Proulx, like *you*! . . . Yes, but just forget the last two letters. My late husband's family stopped pronouncing them five hundred years ago, probably because they couldn't read . . . Yes, yes, all right." She hung up, sighing.

"Well! Now, what is all this about Rachel?" He told her. She was shocked. "My God! And that Nick Levin, he wasn't there to protect her?"

"No."

"Pity. Wait till you meet him."

"I already have."

"Doesn't he just make your mouth water? No, I suppose he wouldn't. But seeing him makes me long to be a Roman empress with slaves. Oh God, the things I will go to my grave having left undone!"

"I'd sure like to know where he gets his money."

"Commodities."

"You have to ante up to get into the game. He's only been in the country about a year and he's been out here less than six months. Who staked him?"

"Oh, I see what you mean. You should have asked him. He's very open about it. It's a funny story. He and his mother arrived here from Russia with nothing. She had a brother somewhere in the East who had sponsored them but he wouldn't help, so they lived in two awful rooms and he worked washing dishes. She spent all her time lying on a sofa in her stocking feet reading Pushkin and Chekhov and playing the numbers! Really! She had once had a dream that saved their lives, and somehow she became convinced that the right number would appear in a dream and make their fortune.

"Every morning, before she served Nick breakfast, she used to make him tell her everything he had dreamed, to see if she could read meaning into it. She was like a kabbalist, reducing everything to numbers. Then all day long, while Nick washed dishes, she used to take little cat naps, to see if she could dream their way out of troubles. Then she got very sick and went to the hospital. She was dying.

She made him place one last bet. The next day, he got home from work and a neighbor woman told him she had bad news, that he must be brave. He said—she imitated him—'Is my mother?' Well, it was his uncle. He had died suddenly. That meant they got the insurance. Nick went straight to the hospital. His mother was barely conscious. He told her they had just gotten a hundred thousand dollars. She said, 'My number, *moychick*?' He told her yes. She died that night with a smile on her face. That's how he started, Dade. There isn't any mystery to it at all."

"Um."

"What does 'um' mean?"

"Right now, it just means 'um.' "

"What a beauty! I've only seen one other such specimen in a lifetime. During the war, I was in the Resistance with him. We all knew what they would do to us if we were caught, and we used to take turns holding each other's heads under water and so forth, practicing to see how long we could hold out. You see, if you got caught and you could hold out just a little while, it would give the others a chance to get away. I used to have fantasies of dying under torture for Michel. He wanted to make love to me but I wouldn't let him. He was married. Well, when you're young, you can't help making mistakes." She sighed. "At least Rachel's all right. I suppose, as usual, they haven't got a clue as to who broke in."

"No, but it's pretty clear what they were looking for. Same thing they were looking for when they broke into this place. That Giulio Romano."

"That painting? Why that? Considering what Jensen has in his collection, that particular canvas just isn't worth that much."

"It is to somebody. It was to Miriam. I think she was taking it with her the night she was killed. In fact, Nettie, she may have been murdered for it." She gasped. Her hands flew to her mouth. "By the way, you neglected to tell me that she bought that painting from her first husband." He studied her.

She made a little *moue* of disapproval. "Oh, so you know about that. A dreadful man!"

"I don't know about it at all. Never heard Miriam mention him."

"She married him when she was an art student in Florence and he was a poet there on a Fulbright. On their wedding night he took her to this apartment in a place like a slum, very noisy, with everybody around them screaming and fighting all the time and everybody's radio playing music full blast and then, once they were alone together, he went a little crazy. She didn't know him anymore. He did awful things to her, awful things, they were revolting, they were degrading and there was simply no end to it.

"When he went out the next day, he locked her in the room. She screamed and pounded but nobody in that neighborhood thought anything of it. He was very strong and she was helpless against him. She wanted to kill him. He must have known what her reaction would be because everything she could have used as a weapon had been taken out of the apartment. He raped her for a week. It was a nightmare. She thought she would lose her mind. The apartment was on the fourth floor and there were times when she thought of throwing herself out the window. The worst of it was that he made her feel a hatred she had never felt. She loathed him.

"At the end of that time, he sort of came to his senses. He offered her the money for a divorce. Oh, she wanted a divorce, all right, but she wanted to tell everybody what he had done. She wanted him put in jail. He knew what she was thinking and told her that in Italy her words wouldn't mean anything. She was legally his wife and there were no witnesses and, not only that, she couldn't even get a divorce there. The money he offered her was to fly home and divorce him in Las Vegas. Five hundred and twenty-eight dollars. That was the cost of the fare. She didn't see him again until he walked into the gallery with that painting. She told me she didn't even recognize him. That's all I know about him. Horrid man!"

Dade turned away from her, leaning on the back of a tall carved chair, and thought for several moments. He combed his fingers through his bushy white hair and then said with disgust, "Every time I ask a question about that painting, all hell breaks loose." He shook his hand at her like an Italian in the midst of a street argument and said, "Nettie, listen here, you told me a lie."

"I—I what?" She was taken aback. Recovering herself, she said, "Perhaps you ought to tell me what it was."

"You said you called Rachel at eight in the morning, after you heard on the radio about what happened."

"Well?"

"It wasn't on the radio then."

"Of course it was!"

"Just the announcement. No names. They didn't release the names until ten after nine. I know that because I'm the reason."

Her expression did not change. She looked at him levelly and said, "All right. I heard it on the radio after I talked to Rachel."

"How did you find out Miriam was dead, Nettie?"

"I don't want you to ask me."

"Somebody will and you don't want to be accused of withholding evidence," Dade said. "I think you'd better tell me."

"Gil told me. Oh, Dade, they were going away together the next day. She was leaving Jensen. I knew all about it. Miriam had confided in me. Gil called me at eight in the morning. He was desperate. He said, 'She's dead, Nettie! She's dead! It's on the radio! She's dead, my God, she's dead!' That was all he said. But I couldn't tell you I'd heard it from him because now that she's gone, nobody needs to know they were going away."

"This was eight the next morning?"

"A little before then."

"And he said he'd heard it on the radio? Well, I say he didn't. How do you suppose he found out?"

"I have no idea."

"Then I'll have to ask *him*."

"He'll know I told you."

"I've got another question for him. Maybe you can help me out with this one. What did he know about that missing painting?"

"Well, she was working on it, cleaning it for a month. What else is there to know? Oh, Dade, think of what he's feeling. That poor man! All I'm trying to do is protect him. That's why I wouldn't give his address to that dreadful Monkhaus."

"What are you talking about?"

"He's called me three or four times, trying to find the painting . . . Well, I'm not being entirely fair in putting it that way. I told him I'd make inquiries and to call me back. He called just before you did this morning, as a matter of fact. He asked me who that man was at the funeral—'that man named Gil.' He'd seen him there. Gil and Miriam used to meet up in my apartment. He must have known they were lovers. You only had to see them together once to figure that out. Well, I pretended I didn't know what he was talking about. I don't want him hounding Gil at a time like this. There's nothing to worry about. There must have been two hundred people at the funeral. All he ever heard was Gil's first name. There's no way he can find out any more."

"Oh yes there is. They keep a funeral book at the cemetery. If Gil signed it, it won't take Monkhaus any time at all." Dade strode to the phone on her desk, muttered a request for permission and punched out a number. Then: "Chloe? That you? . . . This here's Dade Cooley." He listened for a moment. His expression changed. "Chloe? Chloe, what happened?" A shocked look came over his face. Then he said, "I'll be right there."

Nettie took a step toward him. "What's the matter? What happened?"

"There's been a shooting."

"My God!"

"Monkhaus went over there, all right."

"And shot him? Oh, my God!"

"No, it's the other way around. Monkhaus, he's in the hospital. Critical. Gil . . . well, it appears that right now he's in custody. I better go look after Rachel. Now, if you'll excuse me—" He went out, banging the door behind him.

XVIII

Dade drove through the gates of Bel Air and then turned left up Bellagio, a narrow road lined with tall, dense hedges which screened the houses from view. Ahead, he could see a squad car parked outside the Ransohoff house. He turned left into the driveway. A patrolman waved him to a stop. Dade handed him a card and said, "Lady in there, she's expecting me. Miss Rachel Welles."

"Sorry, sir. Nobody in or out."

"I'm her attorney. Now, you wouldn't deny me access to my client?"

The patrolman hesitated, then waved him in. Dade rang the bell.

An eye appeared at the peephole and then the door was flung open by Rachel. She grabbed his arm and pulled him inside, saying, "Thank God it's you. I was afraid it might be somebody from a newspaper." He remembered that she had a fear of reporters. "I guess they haven't gotten the story yet." She closed the door and led him across a foyer toward a sitting room.

He said, "No reason they'll connect you with this, is there?"

She looked at him, puzzled. "But when they find out he was her first husband—"

"You knew him?"

"No, but I recognized the name. She had told me about him. And when the police asked me if I knew who he was, I told them. Was that wrong?"

"No, of course not. You tell them anything else?"

"I don't know any more."

133

"They didn't ask you what you thought he wanted?"

"Yes. But I don't know."

"Mr. Monkhaus is the one Miriam bought that Romano from. He wants it back."

"Well, what made him think Gil had it?" She broke off. "My God! You mean, he's the man who broke into the house last night? Of course!"

"You recognize him?"

"How could I? I told you, he had on that awful mask—"

"I meant, maybe recognized something about him."

"What?"

"What did you notice about Mr. Monkhaus today?"

"That way he walks."

"What about it?"

She thought for a moment, frowning, running a hand through her thick red hair. Then she shook her head. "Honestly, Dade, I'd have to say I don't know. It all happened so fast."

"All right, honey."

"Did you talk to Nick, Dade?"

"He came by this morning. He's just fine."

"Can I call him now?"

"Just be patient with me a little while longer. I don't want you calling anybody till I say so. The next thing is to get you out of here. You got anybody you can stay with? Someplace out of town, say, where you're not known?"

"Let's see . . ." She put her hands in the back pockets of her jeans and stared up at the ceiling. Then she brightened and said, "Aunt Julia!"

"Thought your daddy was your only relative."

"Oh, she's not my aunt. I just call her that. She taught me English at Lone Mountain. We got to be friends. She's retired now and always asking me to come visit her. She lives in San Marino."

"You give her a call right now and tell her you're coming. And don't tell anybody else."

"All right." She started toward the phone. Hesitating, she asked with an attempt at offhandedness, "Have you talked to my father?"

"Just a little while ago."

"Does he know about last night?"

"Yes, he heard about it."

She stood there, looking at her hands. Then she asked in a low voice, "Did he ask about me?"

"I told him you were fine."

She met his eyes. "Did he ask?"

"Rachel, when a man has just gone through the shock of losing his wife—"

"He doesn't care about me."

"Rachel—"

"He never has."

"If it's Nick you're thinking about, understand that your father's just trying to protect you."

"Trying to protect me! He's trying to own me! That's how he is! I'm not his daughter, I'm part of his collection! I can't stand it! Nobody can! That's why Miriam was leaving him. He drove her to it. Now he's done the same thing to me!"

"What say you make that phone call, Rachel?"

"Wait. I wasn't thinking, Dade, I can't leave Chloe alone."

"I want you out of here. Now, I mean it."

"Well, Nettie just called to find out what was going on. She offered to come and stay here, so I'll just ask her to take my place."

"Don't do that." He had spoken more sharply than he had intended. "Let's find out how soon Gil will be back first."

"All right."

"Right now, I'd like to talk to Chloe."

"Wait a minute." She started up the stairs, then paused, turning, and said timidly, "You didn't say whether you liked him. Nick, I mean."

"The important thing is whether you do."

"I love him." She went up the stairs, then came down right away, leading Dade into the sitting room. "She's very upset. She's pretending not to be but I can tell. She'll be down in a moment."

After a few minutes, the door opened and Chloe came into the room and held out a hand. "Hello, Dade," she said.

Rachel gave Chloe a quick kiss of reassurance and then went out and closed the door.

Chloe said, with a glance at the ceiling, "They're still up there. How long can they go on dusting everything for fingerprints and photographing? It's ridiculous. He already told them exactly what happened." She gestured at an armchair, making herself comfortable on a little sofa. Dade sat. She seemed absorbed in studying the polish on her fingernails. He remembered Miriam saying that Chloe was an extremely shrewd woman. ("She watches people as avidly as some men watch the stock market but she is very careful never to be caught at it.") And then that cascade of laughter, like a brook in spring.

Chloe said, "They just said they wanted to ask him some questions, and he's been gone for ages." She glanced at her watch and said impatiently, "Look, I really have to know what's going on. We're going out tonight and if this is going to drag on much longer—"

"Who's his attorney?"

"A man named Postel."

"Willy Postel?"

"Yes."

"You call him?"

"Gil asked me to. They said they'd get back to me, but I'm still waiting."

"Well, it's Saturday and he may be out of town."

"Oh, my heavens, I can't just let Gil sit there!"

"Look, I know Willy. You want me to go down and bring Gil back?"

"Can you do that?"

"I can try. But first you have to tell me what happened?"

"Rachel let him in. She'd been waiting all morning to hear from Nick. God, isn't he *gorgeous*! Knowing Miriam, I'm surprised she kept her sticky fingers off him. Or did she?" Chloe gave him an unpleasant smile. "Well, anyway, here it was lunchtime and she hadn't heard. Every time the phone rang, she jumped up, thinking it was for her. And then she heard the doorbell and ran into the hall from the kitchen to answer it, I heard voices, then I heard the door close and Rachel came back into the kitchen—we were both getting lunch together—and she said, 'There's somebody here to see Gil.' I asked who it was and she said his name was Monkhaus."

"Did you know who he was?"

"Not then. Rachel told me afterward. When I went up-stairs and told Gil, Gil was very upset and asked if I'd said he was there. Then he said, 'I don't care what you told him, just get rid of him.' Then I heard this sound, kind of like a thumping and I turned around and there he was, coming up the stairs with this strange walk, like an automaton, with a kind of inhuman expression on his face. He scared me to death. Gil said something like 'It's all right, I'll see him,' and took him into the study and closed the door. I heard the lock click. We have these old-fashioned French door handles with keys and keyholes, so when someone locks a door, you can hear it quite plainly. I could hear voices raised. They were arguing. I told all this to the police."

"What did they say? Your husband and Mr. Monk-haus."

"I couldn't understand them. Then Rachel called me and I was just about to go downstairs when it happened."

"You say you told this to the police?"

"Yes."

"They believe you?"

"Why shouldn't they?"

"I don't."

"What do you mean?"

"You were eavesdropping, you could hear the key turn in the lock, you told me their voices were raised—I don't believe you couldn't understand what they said and the po-lice won't either. You can lie to them but don't lie to me. And if you want to help your husband, I wouldn't lie to them either, if I were you. See, if they catch you in a lie, they won't tell you about it. They'll just let you dig a deeper and deeper hole."

She blinked back tears, then looked at him, eyes wide with fear. "They were talking about Miriam. I didn't tell the police that part. And they're not in my head. How would they know whether I heard her name?"

"What else did you hear?"

"It was very brief. The Monkhaus man was hard to understand. He has this high angry voice and all I really remember hearing is, 'You have it and I want it.' I heard Gil say, 'I don't even know what you're talking about. I had nothing to do with her affairs.' Then Gil's voice changed and I heard him say, 'Oh, Jesus!' Just then Rachel called me. I ran to the top of the stairs and signaled her to be quiet. I could hear shouting and scuffling and some crashing noises. I tried to get in. I couldn't. I banged on the door and called Gil's name. I was just going to run into the bedroom and call the police when I heard this loud popping sound. I thought, That was a gun!

"Then the door banged open and Gil yelled out, 'Quick, get the paramedics!' I could see the Monkhaus man lying on the floor and this blood was just pouring out of him, I never saw anyone bleed like that, just gushing out, and Gil was pulling off his own shirt and ripping it up to make a tourniquet and he looked up at me and yelled out, 'Will you call the goddamn paramedics?' and I did."

"What kind of a gun was it?"

"I don't know."

"What size?"

"A kind of big gun. Like this." She described the shape with her hands.

"A forty-five?"

"Yes. Yes, I heard one of the officers say that. You could ask them, of course. I think it was a forty-five." Her voice was low with a note of desperation now. "Why won't they let me go down and see him?"

"They won't until after they've questioned him."

"What for? It was self-defense!"

"Monkhaus say anything that you heard? After the shooting?"

"No."

"Was he conscious when the paramedics came?"

"No."

"Then they've only got your husband's word for it that it was self-defense."

"My God, the man practically forced his way into our house!"

"I understand that."

"And he had a gun!"

"Did you see it?"

"Of course not. If I'd seen it, I wouldn't have let him in."

"Could have been your husband's."

"Don't be ridiculous!"

"Your husband own a gun?"

"No! That is, he has a rifle. But it isn't here, it's up at the cabin. He doesn't own a gun."

"Most doctors own guns. Self-protection. Usually they've got drugs in the house. Or so people think. Maybe he owns one and he hasn't told you."

"Why are you talking to me like this?"

"I'm trying to help you. You don't want to go on record as saying something you'll have to take back. See, they might just not think it was self-defense. Be a nice way to kill somebody, wouldn't it? Trick him into forcing his way into your house, making him think you had something he really wanted, then locking the door, yelling, struggling, scuffling, finally shooting him with an unregistered gun. Air-tight."

She looked at him with absolute horror, then let out a whimpering sound. Dade gripped her shoulders hard. He said harshly, "Right now, I may be the best help you've got, now you listen to me." Chloe fell back on the pillows of the sofa sobbing hysterically. Gradually, the sobbing subsided. She began adjusting her lacquered gold hair.

Dade said, "You don't think it was just a straightforward case of self-defense. If you did, you wouldn't be upset, you'd be mad as hell, calling every influential friend you've got. But from what you say, the only person you've called is Willy Postel. That's because something's got you mighty scared. I can help you, but only if you tell me the truth."

She calmed down then. Her mouth grew hard. "I don't think I'll say any more just now."

"Where was your husband the night Miriam was killed?"

"He was home here with me." Her voice was a whisper.

"If you lie to me, I can't help you."

She searched Dade's face and asked in a ragged voice, "How much do you know?"

"I know they were lovers. I know they were going to go off together."

She got to her feet, walked over to the mantlepiece and helped herself to a cigarette from a cloisonné box. Keeping her back turned to him, she began speaking. "That was over a month ago. Jensen found out. He came to see me and told me what was going on. I can't tell you what that did to me. It was odd, really. Here we both were, eaten up with jealousy, but our reactions were so different. I went to pieces inside but Jensen was all cold logic. He told me Miriam wouldn't have a cent to her name if she left him, explained why and asked if Gil knew. I was sure he didn't." She lit her cigarette, then turned to face him. "That night, I confronted Gil. He was furious. Made all sorts of excuses, that he couldn't help himself, that they loved each other and that nothing else mattered. Well, I know him better than she did. When it comes to money, it matters plenty to Gil. He loves it, he needs it and can't live without it. He's in debt, you know. Deeply in debt. He never worried about it because I have money and he knows I'll always bail him out."

She lowered her voice, moving toward him. "Well, he thought Miriam had money too. What he didn't know was that Miriam had signed a prenuptial agreement saying that if she ever left Jensen, she wouldn't get one red cent. I realized, from the way he talked, that she had never told him. She'd never bothered to bring it up and I guess he would have thought it poor taste to ask. That meant I had to be the one to tell him, which is exactly why Jensen had come to me. I told him, all right. Well, he'd been living in a fool's paradise and this came as one hell of a shock."

Angrily she stubbed out the cigarette. "Oh, he tried to pretend that it didn't matter but I knew better. I didn't think there was anything left of our marriage. Then, from one day to the next, Gil changed completely." She went back to the sofa and sat down again. "He said he didn't know what had happened to him, that it had been just an infatuation, nothing more. He begged my forgiveness, telling me it was over. The crazy thing was, I believed him. I never found out whether she knew I knew. I had to act as if nothing had happened. She was busy. There wasn't much chance for just the two of us to be together. That was a relief. Gil was his old self again. He was happy. We were happy together. I thought I had won."

She rubbed lightly at her eyes, conscious that the mascara was smudged. She took a compact and a handkerchief from her pocket and turning away, began repairing the ravages of tears with a swift, skillful hand. Putting her compact away, she said in a matter-of-fact voice, "Then she telephoned here that night, the night she was killed. She hadn't done that for a month."

"When?"

"I—I'm not sure."

"Before dinner or afterward?"

"Afterward. We have dinner at seven. Gil always likes to watch the news. Let's see—what night was it? Tuesday. Of course. Well, there's a program I like to watch on Tuesday at seven-thirty. Gil hates it, so he left the room after dinner. When it was over, I went into the living room to get something. Gil was upstairs. The phone rang then. I remember now. It was eight o'clock. Or just after eight. Minutes after."

"How did you know it was Miriam? Did she talk to you?"

Chloe shook her head. "I happened to pick up the extension at the same time Gil answered the phone. I'm sure they didn't know I was listening. She said, 'He's found out. It has to be tonight.' Gil started to say something and she interrupted him, saying, 'No, it has to be tonight. Right away.' Then she hung up. I heard him hang up.

"I put down the phone absolutely shaken. I felt—oh, I don't know what I felt. I felt as if my knees were going to give way. I felt like a fool. I thought I was going to faint. I don't know how I pulled myself together. I listened at the door. I could hear him going very quietly down the back stairs. He was going to the garage. I went to the window and watched him drive away in the storm."

"Then what did you do?"

"I don't know. Nothing. That isn't true. I got out a

bottle of Seconal. I was going to take the whole thing. I just wanted to die. You know what stopped me? He would have inherited my money. I was damn sure Miriam wouldn't get a cent from Jensen! I don't know what I did. I got into my nightgown and had a couple of drinks. I've never felt at such a loss in my life. It was cold. I put a fur coat on over my nightgown and watched game shows and old movies for four hours. Then I saw the lights of a car coming up the drive. I jumped up, thinking there'd been an accident and they were coming to tell me and then, when I looked out the window, I saw it was Gil, so I ran upstairs, got in bed in the dark and pretended to be asleep.

"He came in, turned on the light, then, I suppose thinking I was asleep, he turned it off again, got undressed and got into bed. The next morning, I got up quite early but he had already left for the office. I found out she was dead when somebody called me. It was on the news. I called him at the office to tell him. He said yes, that he'd heard. We didn't say any more than that."

"You were afraid your husband killed her, is that it?" She wouldn't answer. "Let me tell you the law, all right? A wife is free to testify against her husband but she can't be forced to. But when the sky starts falling and you refuse to answer somebody's questions, it's going to seem like you have something to hide. You can see that, can't you?"

"But if I just tell them I went to bed, that I don't know anything—"

"Talk to your husband. Then the two of you sit down with Willy Postel."

"How could he be guilty? What reason would he have?"

"You talk to your husband, hear? Now, you dry your eyes and I'll go downtown and try to bring him home."

XIX

Because Bel Air is under the jurisdiction of the city of Los Angeles, Gil had been taken downtown to be questioned. Dade drove to the city offices and made his way to a crowded, noisy waiting room at police headquarters. There were two people ahead of him at the counter, a fat woman in a white cotton jacket with white cotton slacks and her name printed on a bar pinned to her lapel and a thin man in overalls. The fat woman said to him, slapping at a newspaper she held in one hand, "There's this four-year-old kid chews tobacco and spits it on the floor and you know what his parents say? They think it's cute. You believe that? Four years old, looks like a little old man and by God, there he is, chewing and spitting all over the place. Says so right here in Dear Abby."

"I don't believe it," said the man.

"Would Dear Abby lie?" the woman demanded in a loud voice.

"She makes those things up," the man said in an even louder voice, addressing the whole room. "Four-year-old kids don't chew tobacco. She made it up. She makes up all that crap, right? Right!"

"She did not make it up!" the woman yelled.

"Let's hold it down," said the black sergeant at the desk. "Let's all just hold it down, okay?" The sergeant, a heavy-set man, looked up from a ledger in which he was writing and said to Dade, "Yes, sir?"

Dade took a card from his wallet and handed it to the sergeant. "I'm here to collect Dr. Ransohoff. His wife sent me." Dade was taken down a hall to a guarded elevator.

The deputy who escorted him said, "They been waiting for you. They just brought him down." They got out of the elevator and went down another corridor into an oblong room containing only three straight chairs. Gil sat in one, arms folded, an angry look on his face. Valdez was standing in front of him. Straddling the chair opposite him was a saturnine, sharp-featured plainclothesman.

Gil was saying, "I've told you everything I know back at the house! For Christ's sake, I don't even know if the poor bastard is still alive! Can't you tell me that much?"

"We'd like you to tell us why the victim came to see you," the plainclothesman said.

"Don't ask me. Ask him. I get it. You can't ask him. He has to be dead, right? Otherwise, you wouldn't be asking me that. Is he?" When they didn't answer, he said, "Don't you have to tell me?"

"No, we don't," Valdez said softly.

Then, seeing Dade, Gil got up, surprised. Valdez turned and stared at Dade. fists on his hips.

Dade said formally, "Your spouse, Mrs. Chloe Ransohoff, sent me here. Do you desire representation. sir?"

"I told Chloe to call Postel two hours ago. What's going on?" He looked around at the others. His face was haggard.

"Your wife has not been able to reach Postel. Please answer my question."

"Yes!"

"Do you desire me to represent you on a temporary basis? I must point out to you that I also represent another interest which may have some connection with this matter."

"Miriam's estate?" Gil seemed bewildered.

"Please answer the question."

"Yes." Gil met Dade's eyes, drawing himself up and matching the formality of his tone.

"Good. Then I must inform you, gentlemen, that I intend to be present during any and all sessions when my client is questioned." He turned to Gil and added, "Now, I don't want you to say one more word."

The plainclothesman got to his feet and looked at Dade with surprise, then turned to Valdez, fuming with frustration.

Dade said, "Release him or charge him."

Valdez paced the floor, not answering. He jerked his head at the plainclothesman, who went over to him. They whispered together, staring at Gil from time to time. Finally Valdez said to the plainclothesman, "Okay, he can go." They were escorted downstairs by Valdez, and Gil was cautioned not to leave town.

In silence, Dade led the way to his car. Gil got into it. Instead of taking him home, Dade drove him to the Grand Central Market, a couple of blocks away. Gil looked at him, not understanding.

"I want us to have a little chat. There'll be somebody following us, so we'll just have us our chat out here, in the open market. That way, they can't follow us too close. You had lunch? I take it you haven't. Well, over here's a place you're going to like. They make great *gorditas*."

Dade walked over to a counter and bought them each a warm tortilla wrapped around roast pork, refried beans and chopped tomato and lettuce. They strolled together through the market. It was an immense warehouse of a building which ran all the way through to the next street, with huge sliding doors wide open at either end. The floor was lined with counters and aluminum-shaded lamps, such as photographers use in studios, hung from long metal rods the length of the building, illuminating all the displays of food. A row of white-aproned butchers were standing behind cases filled with pork, lamb, mutton, beef, veal, poultry, and fish. Racks of fruits and vegetables were piled high—fresh eggs, breads, cases full of grains and spices. The signs were in both English and Spanish. It was four-thirty and the stalls were closing up.

Gil said, "If for any reason I have to get in touch with you, why don't you give me your address?" His speech was New York but there was something under it, a shade of care. He took out a pencil and a notebook and carefully wrote down Dade's name and his address in San Francisco. Dade noticed the handwriting: small, erect, European. Dade remembered that Gil had come from Germany.

"You were born in Cologne, weren't you?"

"That's right."

"I know that town. You get out before the war?"

"Just barely. My father was a professor at the university. One day, he was walking to campus and a friend came up to him and said, 'Don't go to class. Go home and get your family. Now.' I was just a little boy. We left in the middle of lunch. We just got in the car and drove away. We even left the laundry on the line. My mother had to leave her fur coat because it was a hot day and it would have looked funny to carry it. That coat would have kept us for months. As it was, we had nothing."

"You came here?"

"First we went to Switzerland. then France. We hid out there, in different places. Then after the war we came here. You know what it's like to run? It gets so you can't stop."

"That's not going to work this time, son."

"I beg your pardon?"

Their eyes met. There was silence. Then, as Gil put away his notebook and pencil, Dade said, "I got you out of there because I don't want you questioned until Postel can be present."

"Thanks."

Dade grunted. "Now I'd like a favor from you." Gil eyed him. "I represent Miriam's estate. I also happen to represent Rachel, who has retained me to investigate Miriam's death. That's just to get the lines clear for your benefit. Now, I'd like to get your version of what happened. You were going away with Miriam. She called you and said it had to be now, so you left your house that night and went to meet her."

Gil said, "Chloe." The greenish eyes narrowed. "I'm not going to tell you anything!" Gil had finished his *gordita* and hurled the paper into a packing crate full of garbage. Dade walked very deliberately over to a stool at a refreshment stand, gesturing for Gil to join him, and ordered himself a glass of sweetened rice water called *horchata*. Dade seated himself, looking up inquiringly at Gil, who was standing in front of him, hands flat on the back of his hips. "I want to go home to my wife," he said. "If you're going that way, fine. Otherwise I'll call a cab."

"Take a seat."

"I said—"

"*Now.*"

"Do you understand what I'm saying? I want to go home. I don't want to talk anymore, okay?"

"You know why I told you not to answer their questions back inside there? Those fellas are investigating a murder."

"He's dead? Oh, my God." Gil sat down slowly, dazed. "I killed him? It was self-defense. I swear to God it was self-defense. It was his gun. That's crazy. I didn't have any motive for killing him!"

"That's one of the things I didn't want you to say. 'Cause it isn't true." Dade's eyes bored into Gil's. Gil returned the look, expressionless, but a tremor passed over his cheek. "Incidentally, I didn't mean Mr. Monkhaus. I don't know anything about his condition. I meant Miriam."

Gil's lips twitched. Abruptly, he turned away.

Dade said quietly, "They don't know that you went to see her that night, but it's only a question of time before they find out, just the way I did. At that point, you will have two choices: Lie and look guilty or tell them the truth and take your chances. Of course, you could always just not say anything, but after a while that tends to make a man look very bad. I don't know how much time you've got before they come knocking at your door, but I just thought you might like this opportunity to tell me your story."

Dade took out his briar pipe, filled it and lit it, sitting back and smoking contentedly, his arms resting on the counter behind him, his ankles crossed.

Gil said nothing for a long time. Finally, without looking at Dade, shoulders hunched, the surgeon's hands clasped between his knees, he began speaking in a low voice. "We were going away together. The next day. She called me around eight, saying it had to be that night. She said, 'As soon as you can get here.' She sounded scared. She was afraid of Jensen, and I figured that's what it was. I said okay and cut out of there. We had this place where we were supposed to meet. In Malibu. I went there and waited."

"What time did you get there? Got any idea?"

"Well, it's a good half-hour or more from Bel Air, and that night in the rain it took longer. I got there and she hadn't arrived. I looked at my watch and it was twenty of nine and I thought, What's happened? because it's only at the most fifteen minutes from the Welles house, so I called and I got no answer. I figured she was on her way and I went on waiting."

"How long?"

"More than two hours. I guessed that Jensen had showed up or something. So I went home. The next morning, one of the girls in my office had the radio on and I heard it on the news."

"Where was this place?"

"Jetty's."

"You go there often?"

"I've been there. You know."

"You think anybody there remembers you from that night?"

"I don't know."

"Talk to anybody?"

"No. I don't think they'd remember me. That bar is mobbed. Standing room only."

"And that's what you're going to tell the police?" Gil nodded. Dade said, "My advice is, Don't. You just told me three lies in thirty seconds. They're not stupid. They'll catch you same as I did. And they'll come to the same conclusion I did. A man who lies about something like that has a lot to hide. You want to try me again?"

"You know what I think? You're trying to fake me out."

"No need to. You called Nettie around eight in the morning, saying you'd heard it on the radio. No, you didn't."

"It was on the radio! I heard it!"

"There were no names. Not till ten after nine. When you heard just the news bulletin on the radio, you filled in the names. See, you already knew. Second point: When a man spends two hours in a bar where he is known, somebody remembers. My guess is, you said nobody would because you weren't there."

"I was there!"

"Not for two hours. Just long enough to make that phone call. Oh, you made it, all right. You waited forty-five seconds after the beep sounded, waited for her to pick up the phone, afraid to say anything because your voice would be recorded on the tape. At first, I couldn't figure out what that long wait was for. That was before I knew about you and Miriam. She was in trouble. You knew that when she called you. When she wasn't at Jetty's and didn't answer the phone, you knew something was wrong. And you had to get up there and find out. Now, when did you really leave Jetty's?"

Gil flushed a dark, unhealthy red. Dade said quietly, "Funny thing about murder. People love to find out who done it. They won't rest till they do. Everybody's like that. This is murder. And you've just made yourself a prime suspect—by telling Nettie Miriam was dead before anyone knew. It looks bad for you if you won't tell how you found out. You see that, don't you?"

Gil took a long uneven breath. Then he said, "Okay, I left Jetty's just before nine. See, I thought maybe she was on her way, so I waited as long as it would take her to drive there and then I left and drove up to the house to find out what was going on."

"Arriving when?"

"Well, I guess about nine-fifteen. All I could think about was that son of a bitch Jensen. He's a violent man. For all I knew—well, anyway, the lights were on in the house. It was raining like hell. I parked near the gates but I didn't ring the bell. Instead, I slogged my way down the drive. I wanted to see if her car was there. Then I heard what I thought was a car coming. It was really pouring, so I couldn't be sure. I stood to one side, waiting to see if it was Miriam. No car came. I went on down the drive, trying not to slip. It's steep and with that little mud slide they'd had, it was very narrow.

"The car was in the garage. Just the one car. It was Jensen's and the motor was running. I thought, Christ, it's him, and I got out of the way but when the car didn't move, I went closer and then I saw there was nobody in it and when I went in the garage, I saw Miriam and she was dead. I got the hell out of there. Fast."

"How long do you think you were there?"

"At the time it seemed like forever. Everything seemed to be happening very slowly. But I remember when I got back in the car I looked at the clock on the dash and it was only nine-twenty and I thought, Maybe it'll be on the news, and then I thought how crazy that was. Afterward, I just drove around in that storm for hours, trying to think. I didn't know what to do. Then I drove home."

"Of course, you examined her, to make sure she was dead."

"I'm a doctor. Of course I looked at her. I went to her and took her hand. She was dead. I knew that when I first saw her. Nothing looks like death."

"Was her hand warm?"

"Yes."

"How long do you think she had been dead?"

"I don't know. Not long."

"And you looked in the car. For the painting."

"I don't know what you're talking about."

"I'm going to give you a moment to think that over. Then I'm going to ask you again." Dade puffed on his pipe, then sipped his milky rice drink, gazing into the middle distance.

Gil dragged on his cigarette. Dade turned and faced him, eyebrows raised inquiringly. Gil crushed out his cigarette with his heel. Then he stood and thrust his hands deep into his pockets and said, "I told Monkhaus. Now I'm telling you. I don't know what the hell you're talking about."

"Of course, if you had known about the painting, you might have gone barreling over there the minute she said there was trouble. You might not have waited at Jetty's after making that call. And that would have gotten you there just before nine."

"You *are* trying to fake me out!" A curved smile broke across the lean face.

Dade got up slowly from the bench. "Come on," he said. "I'll drive you home."

They rode back to Bel Air in silence. Dade noticed that

the squad car was gone. Gil got out of the car, then leaned down and asked, "Want to come in and have a drink?"

Dade shook his head. "Thank you very much."

In the distance, Dade saw Rachel come out of the house carrying a suitcase. Waving, she walked over to them.

"Hi, Rachel," Gil said.

"You all right, Gil?"

"Yeah."

"My God," she said. "I mean, my God!" She forced a laugh. Gil ran a hand through the curly mop of her hair. She started to pull away involuntarily, then caught herself. Gil's eyes flickered. "Well, thanks," she said, "thanks for everything." She touched Dade's hand and went to her car.

Gil turned back to Dade. The goat's mouth curved into a sudden smile. "Well, I want to thank you for your time."

"You'll get my bill. I have done you a valuable service. I want you to go inside and start telephoning and don't stop until you reach Postel. Don't talk to anybody else until you talk to him, or else it's your neck. I give you fair warning. Now, I want to tell you something about Postel. Me, I would describe myself as likable. Easygoing. Mellow. All that sort of thing. Postel's first-rate but he's got a short fuse. You lie to him like you just lied to me and he'll walk off your case."

XX

It was after five. He stopped at a pay phone and called the inn. When he heard Ellen's voice, he said, "Honey?"

"Who is this?"

"Honey, it's Dade."

"Dade who?"

"I know you hoped I'd get back earlier—"

"Three hours earlier!"

"And you've been worried. Oh, dear."

"I haven't been worried. I'm not a stupid woman. When I heard about the shooting on the radio, I called Chloe Ransohoff. I've kept tabs on you all afternoon. The word is angry. I am angry, Dade. Why didn't you call me?"

"But if you knew where I was—"

"You didn't know that!"

"All right, all right. Motke call yet?"

"No, but Rachel did. To say she'd gotten San Marino."

"Good. She give you the number there?"

"I'd already gotten it from Chloe. Listen, I got what you wanted from the Getty." He grunted an acknowledgment. "When will I see you?"

"Soon, honey." After he put down the phone, he called the U.S.C. Medical Center, found out Monk's condition was stable and said in a quavering voice to a nurse, "I'm a friend of the family and I worry so about that poor man lying there all alone, with nobody as knows him to pray for his suffering soul."

"Oh, you don't need to worry about that, sir. His wife

has been here since just after they brought him in. Never leaves his side."

"Thank you very much." He drove down to the hospital, and took the elevator to the jail ward on the thirteenth floor. There was a long corridor sealed with heavy wire mesh and in the middle of the passageway was a barred door. A police officer sat at a desk in front of it, two phones at his elbow and a sign-in book with a pencil attached to it by a string. He was overweight, with thin wispy hair and heavy dark-rimmed glasses. He was reading a paperback book with a nude couple on the cover. He put the book in the open drawer in front of him, closing it. He said to Dade, "May I help you, sir?"

Dade took out a card and handed it to him. "Would you tell Mrs. Richard Monkhaus I'm here? I'd like to take her to dinner."

A few minutes later, he heard footsteps and saw Tillie coming down the hall. She wore a long coat and had a scarf on her head. Dade went toward her. The officer unlocked the door and she came out.

They rode down in silence. When they got out on the main floor, she turned to him and said bitterly, "I don't know what you want but I wish you would leave me alone."

"I invited you to dinner. Didn't you get my message?"

"So that you could ask me questions. I rode down with you because I wanted to ask you to go away. Please. I didn't want them overhearing us. Up there they listen to everything, do you know that? They've even got a patient in one of the beds who's a detective. I know. I was on the stage for years and if there's one thing I always spot, it's bad acting."

"How's your husband?"

"They just brought him out of recovery. He's sleeping now. How would I know how he is? All they said is he's stable."

"They don't have him in intensive care. That means they expect him to recover with no trouble."

"Does it?"

"Did you tell them he has Parkinson's?"

"How could I? When I got here, he was in surgery. He

was in there four hours. Afterward, the doctor didn't even come to talk to me. Just the detectives."

"What did you tell them?"

"What could I tell them? I don't know anything. God, they're so stupid! A man shoots him and they put *him* in the jail ward! What I want to know is, where is that son of a bitch who shot him? Do you know, they won't tell me a goddamned thing?"

"Did they tell you your husband went to that house with a gun?"

The wide clear eyes were incredulous. "That's ridiculous! My husband has never even handled a gun in his life! Is that what they said? Tell me, is that what they said? I have no idea what's going on! They kept asking me questions but wouldn't tell me anything!"

Dade took her gently by the elbow, steering her toward the elevator. "There's a cafeteria on the second floor," he said. "I think it's time we got some food into you."

The cafeteria was crowded and noisy. They took their trays to a table in a corner. Tillie sighed, poking at her food.

"Come on, now, you eat."

She began spooning up the chicken soup Dade had insisted on putting on her tray and then started on the stuffed bell pepper. "Thank you," she said, when she had finished. "I enjoyed that." Then a troubled look came over her face. She put a hand to her forehead. "I don't know what to do," she said. "I don't know what's going to happen to him." She looked at him, puzzled. "They *can't* believe he went there with a gun."

Suddenly she looked appalled. "My God, you don't mean they'd put him in *jail*? Oh, my *God*! I just thought he was in the jail ward because it was a shooting and—well, you know, protective custody and so forth and I—how could I have been so stupid? All those hours sitting there and it never occurred to me. I kept trying to put the whole thing out of my mind because I was so afraid he would die. A priest came and talked to me. I'm not Catholic but he was very kind and he made me talk about other things, to get my mind off the waiting and not knowing, and I just didn't think—!"

"Don't go meeting trouble halfway. There might just be something we can do."

"Are you saying you'll help me?"

"So long as you tell me the truth."

She nodded and sat very still for almost a minute. Tears welled in her eyes. She wiped them away with her fingertips. When she spoke, her voice was low. "He did have a gun. My God, I forgot about it!"

"What kind of gun?"

"A forty-five. He kept it on a shelf behind some books. I saw it once when I was straightening up. It frightened me. He said he'd gotten it because of all the break-ins we've been having, because of the neighborhood. I'm sorry, I just can't talk to you now. Please understand."

"Mrs. Monkhaus, listen to me. Now, I'm not trying to frighten you but I think you ought to know something. Your husband went to someone's house with a loaded gun and threatened him. There was a struggle and your husband ended up being shot himself. But under the law, do you know what the district attorney can charge him with? Attempted murder."

"That's crazy."

"But it's true. Now, Mrs. Monkhaus, I'd hate to see a thing like that happen. And it doesn't have to happen. See, if he went there because he'd been driven half out of his mind by what had been done to him and if you'd both cooperate by telling the whole truth—see, you didn't tell me the truth when we talked—we both know that, don't we?—well, then, I can even believe that the district attorney might not press charges against your husband. Certainly, I'd be glad to put in a good word."

She looked away, staring across the cafeteria at their reflection in a mirrored wall. She took out a cigarette, tamping it on a thumbnail. Dade struck a match and held it for her. "All right. What do you want to know?"

"First, I'd like to know where that painting came from."

She dragged on her cigarette, as if, like the Pythian, she needed to inhale fumes before speaking the truth. Then, with a little shrug of surrender, she began to talk rapidly. "Monk's father was a painter. Not a good painter. He was a very good draftsman, a good technician. I don't know when he finally realized that he didn't really have any talent of his own. It must have been very painful. He ended up working in museums, copying things. You've seen those people with their little easels set up, painstakingly copying the works of the masters? That's what he did for a living. There's a market for it. God knows why. He made a little money. Not much." She looked up and made a helpless gesture with her hands. "I'm telling this badly."

"Just go on."

She sighed. "Then he got drafted. Monk was about fifteen, I guess. He worshiped his father. All he remembers about the war is waiting for his daddy to come home. Well, Monk's father finally got himself shipped home at the end of 1945. The day he came home, he walked down the block right past Monk. He didn't even recognize him. A boy changes so much at that age. Monk ran after him and when his father realized it was his son waving and yelling, he turned around and ran toward him into the street—just in time to be killed by a truck. Don't you love the way they run the universe, Mr. Cooley?

"Anyway, I have a feeling that's what made him a poet. Lots of times, a poem is a cry of pain." She broke off, fumbling in her purse for a handkerchief. As she took it out, she caught sight of something, hesitated and then abruptly pulled out a folded piece of yellowed paper and handed it to Dade. "Here," she said. "I want you to see something."

Dade opened up the paper. The words on it were written in faded ink. He read:

O what black hoürs we have spent
This night! what sights you, heart, saw; ways you went!
And more must, in yet longer light's delay.
     With witness I speak this. But where I say
Hours I mean years, mean life. And my lament
Is cries countless, cries like dead letters sent
To dearest him that lives alas! away.
     I am gall, I am heartburn. God's most deep decree
Bitter would have me taste: my taste was me.

Dade looked up at Tillie. She reached out and took back

the paper, carefully folding it up again and returning it to her purse.

"That's how he used to sound," she said. "That's the last thing he wrote. I just wanted you to know."

"Thank you."

"Well, anyway, Monk's mother died a few years later and Monk worked his way through school. The one thing he had that he'd gotten from his father was that painting. You see, his father had brought it back from Europe. He'd copied it there. Monk treasured it."

"I guess it was very beautiful."

"No. No, it wasn't. I never said anything but I did study art a little, once, before I went into acting, and I have to tell you that it was a rather sloppy piece of work. But Monk valued it. To tell you the truth, it was all we had and we had to get money for the insurance premium."

"What insurance premium?"

"That's what all this is about. That's what he's afraid of. Preexisting conditions is the name of their game. He found out he had Parkinson's a few months ago. He suspected it, and we went down to Baja to a doctor to have him examined so there wouldn't be any record for the insurance company to find. When we got back, he took out a life-insurance policy. I'm the beneficiary. Even if he dies of Parkinson's, I get the money. Just so long as they don't know he already had the disease. It's a preexisting condition all right, but afterward they can't tell how long you've had it, and in five more months, the life insurance will cover him for everything, preexisting or not.

"All right, now you understand. He had to come up with the first year's premium. It was something like five hundred dollars. He went to Miriam with the painting to beg for the money. She was the only person we knew who could afford it. He hadn't seen her in eighteen years. He's proud. He didn't want to ask for anything. He was pretending to drink, as usual, to cover up the signs. He said he needed money for an operation. He needed it for me. For life-insurance money, to live on after he's gone. And you know what she said?" Here, Tillie stretched out her expressive hands, the tips of the fingers just touching Dade's vest, the eyes at the same time imitating Miriam's and managing to express her own incredulity, and said, 'I'll clean it for you as a favor. For old times' sake. It's the least I can do.' It's the least she can do!"

Then, in a way that forcefully reminded him that she had been on the stage, she yelled out in a terrible voice, "It goddamn well was the least she could do!" She swallowed, then said quietly, "Anyway, she changed her mind and gave him a check. He had just asked her for five hundred dollars but she was generous. She made it for five hundred and twenty-eight and don't tell me you don't know what that was for! It made him feel like shit. All right, he was wrong. What he did was wrong. But that was years ago and he's paid for it in more ways than I can tell you.

"When he came back with that check in his pocket, he wouldn't tell me anything at first, he just sat at the kitchen table with his head in his hands. When I found out what she'd done to him, I was just—well, it doesn't matter. I went right out and borrowed money on the car, even though I didn't have any idea how we'd pay it back. I went home to him and told him what I'd done and I said, 'Go over there and get the painting back.' So he did, that same afternoon."

"When was this?"

"A month ago. He returned the check and asked for the painting. Well, then she told him some of the paint had flaked off and she had seen what appeared to be something underneath it. She said she had had it X-rayed that same day and underneath there seemed to be another painting *exactly the same*. She wanted his permission to strip it. She thought the painting underneath was a Giulio Romano, a painting Vasari mentioned that hasn't been seen for four hundred years.

"Somehow, Monk's father had found it, knew what it was and painted over it so it would look amateurish and he could smuggle it out of Europe. She said it had to be kept quiet, that the smuggling could cause trouble. If the authorities found out about it, they would confiscate it. That scared Monk. And it was a risk. If she was mistaken, that is, after she stripped it, if she found that the painting underneath wasn't a Romano after all, that it was just an earlier attempt by Monk's father, then he would get nothing. But she couldn't be sure about it without seeing it.

"Well, it meant destroying his father's painting, which cost him plenty, but Miriam Welles said if it was a Romano, it was worth thirty-five thousand dollars. He said okay, that he was willing to gamble. That was how it started. The excitement brought on one of his spells—a very bad one—and I had him in bed nursing him for a month. Then, the day he was better, Miriam called. This was last Monday, the day before she was killed. He went over there. She said it was the missing Romano all right and gave him a check for thirty-five thousand dollars. I can't tell you how happy we were.

"But Monk couldn't leave well enough alone. Maybe it's that he can't work anymore and didn't have anything else to think about, but he just had to know all about that painting. So he went downtown to the main library and went through all of Vasari and then some other books on Romano himself. No such painting is ever mentioned and there is no Giulio Romano missing." She gave him a level look. "He knew Miriam and he knew she wouldn't give him thirty-five thousand dollars for a nonexistent Romano. It had to be something much more valuable. He wanted it back."

"So he telephoned her," Dade said.

"He may have tried to—"

"He called her on the house phone. On that number they have listed in the book."

"You would have to ask him."

"And threatened her."

"That isn't true!"

"I think it is. That's why she was running away. She was running from him."

"I think this has gone far enough—" She started to get to her feet. His hand shot out, gripping her wrist. She sank back in her chair.

"See, just a little while before she was killed, a witness heard Miriam Welles say on the phone, 'He's found out.' This witness thought Miriam meant Jensen but you and I, we know better, don't we, Mrs. Monkhaus?"

"I don't know what you're talking about." She had recovered herself.

"The sheriff doesn't know this yet but there's a witness saw your husband's car out in front of the Welles place just about the time she was killed."

She burst out laughing. He looked at her, surprised. She said, "That is something! That is really something! Welles told you he saw my husband there that night!" Her voice became harsh. "Welles has never laid eyes on my husband in his whole life! *I* told Welles that my husband saw *him*! Oh, yes, Monk would recognize Jensen Welles—anybody would who ever reads a newspaper—but don't tell me Welles recognized Monk! My God, did he really tell you that?"

Suddenly, Dade understood what she was saying. He spoke casually. "And that's what you threatened Welles with today—that you'd go to the sheriff with that information if he didn't give you back the painting?"

"Yes."

"Weren't you taking a risk?"

"Why? You mean that Welles could threaten Monk with the same thing? Oh, no, he couldn't. Monk could testify that he recognized Welles but Welles could never claim that he recognized Monk. No, no, I don't think so."

"Mrs. Monkhaus, I think I should tell you that the witness who placed your husband at the Welles house is someone else."

Her composure deserted her. She looked around as if for a way of escaping. She began stroking her neck and her cheeks, like a mother trying to comfort a frightened child. When she spoke, her voice was frayed. "All right, so they're going to find out."

"What time was this?"

"I don't know."

"The witness saw your husband's car parked in front of the Welles house at ten after nine, well within the period during which the coroner says Mrs. Welles was killed."

"Monk was only there for a few minutes! When he found her dead, he left as fast as he could."

"So you're saying he arrived when?"

"I can't believe that more than five minutes went by between the time he arrived and the time he left. When he got home, he was in a terrible state of shock and he said he had just driven there, found her dead and left."

"That means he couldn't have arrived there any earlier than five after nine, and possibly later."

"Yes, yes, I guess so."

"It was pouring rain, it was dark, he was distressed and with good reason and yet you tell me he instantly recognized a man in a passing car he'd never seen in person?"

"Oh, not at first. He thought it was Miriam."

"Why?"

"Well, it was her car coming out of the drive."

"And he recognized her car?"

"Well, she has her initials on the licence plate and he'd seen it parked in the courtyard at the gallery."

"And when you went to Welles with this information today, what did he say?"

"He was frightened enough so that I was sure if he'd had the painting, he would have given it to me. That's what made Monk think that the person who had it wasn't Welles but Ransohoff." She got up suddenly. "I have to go back to him."

Dade escorted her up to the thirteenth floor. He asked, "You got a lawyer?"

"Why—no."

"Get one. And tell him the truth. One of the things he's going to want to know is where *you* were that night."

The barred door closed on her. She stood there for a moment, looking out at him as if from out of a cell, then turned and walked away.

XXI

In the lobby of the hospital, Dade called the Welles house and got Jensen. "It's kind of important that we have a talk," Dade said. "You going to be there in about forty-five minutes, say?"

"Is it about Rachel?"

"No, it isn't, Jensen."

"You know where she is?" When Dade did not answer immediately, Jensen said, "I tried her at the apartment but there was no answer. She's off somewhere with that fortune hunter, isn't she?"

"No, she isn't. That much I can tell you. It won't take long but we have to talk."

"All right. I'll be here."

"I'll see you, then."

Dade turned into the Welles driveway at eight o'clock. He could hear the pounding of a high surf. The dogs gone, the grounds were utterly silent. In their place, a bright floodlight on the top of a gatepost glared down like the eye of a Cyclops at approaching strangers. He rang the bell. Jensen's voice came on the speaker, saying, "Dade?"

"It's me."

The gates swung open and Dade eased the car up the drive. It was a warm, windy night. The scent of acacia and jasmine was heavy in the garden. The wings of a great horned owl fanned the air. It gave a deep hollow hoot.

Jensen let Dade in, waving him toward the library and saying, "Maid's got the night off and I'm on the phone. Help yourself to a drink."

Dade nodded and went into the library. The big easel

and the standing adjustable spotlight had been put away, in the lock room, he guessed, which was closed now. He looked up at the coffered ceiling, then walked around, examining the painting. In a moment, Jensen came into the room. Dade said, "I got something to say to you."

"Yes. Well, all right, come and sit down." Jensen gestured at a pair of tufted red-leather English club chairs by the fireplace. They sat down together. Jensen said abruptly, "That young man is no good. He wants her money but that's all he wants. I've tried to tell that to Rachel but she won't listen. Well, she's going to find out. The Greeks say the truth is there from the beginning." He let the ash from his cigar fall into a round glass ashtray on the butler's table between them. Dade said nothing. "That was the sheriff on the phone, by the way. He wants to have a talk with me. At my convenience." He tilted his head back and emitted a high, humorless cackle.

"I would try to fit him in."

Jensen's face reddened with anger. He had the kind of skin which flushed easily. Dade studied him, remembering that he had once seen Jensen at the club naked in the sauna and that he looked exactly like a forked radish. Jensen looked up as if searching for words in the smoke, the long thin nose lifted and moved this way and that, finally jabbing toward Dade, as if trying to impale him like a shrike. "Well, what do you want?"

"I was expecting that call from the sheriff. You told them you drove straight downtown to your office the night Miriam was killed. But you didn't. You came back to this house first. Why?"

"You've been listening to that Monkhaus woman!"

"Who by now has probably told her story to the sheriff."

" 'Story' is exactly the word!" Jensen quivered with outrage. "Ballinger tells me Mr. Monkhaus hasn't regained consciousness yet and may not. If she got up in court and tried to repeat it, Ballinger says it would be nothing but hearsay—and as such, inadmissible!"

"If push comes to shove, such a statement *would* be admissible over objection. There are some subtle and rather serious exceptions to the hearsay rule. Didn't Ballinger tell you that?" Jensen was shaken. Dade gave him a moment to recover and then asked softly, "Why did you return here that night, before driving into town?"

"To get my own car."

"But you didn't."

"No."

" 'Cause if you had, Miriam couldn't have been killed by it. Unless, of course, she was already dead, in which case—"

"She wasn't dead!"

"How do you know that?"

"I—I talked to her." Jensen's eyes held little sparks of fear in them.

"Then she was still alive?"

"Of course she was!"

"There was a terrible storm that night. Yet you drove all the way back on a dangerous highway, adding maybe half an hour to your trip, just to change cars? Something, incidentally, you ended up not doing? Now, I'm going to ask you again why you came back here."

Jensen expelled the air from his lungs slowly. "For my code key. I forgot it."

"You better explain that."

"I had to telex Zurich from my office. There's a computer there with my affairs in it. You can't get into it without a code key. It's a sequence of numbers. I'm very careful with it. I would never leave it in the office. I keep it locked in the desk in my bedroom. I forgot to bring it. It was all that confusion about the cars and the storm."

"Since you were here, why didn't you switch cars?"

"Because I had to reach Zurich at a certain hour!" he exclaimed impatiently. "Time was running out! I didn't want to go down that steep driveway to the garage. I just drove through the electric gates to the front door and went inside and upstairs to my room. I told Miriam what I'd come for and then I went right out."

"What did Miriam say?"

"Pardon me?"

"I asked you what she said."

"She knew what I was talking about. She knew where I was going."

"What did she say?"

"Nothing."

"Where was she?"

"In bed, in her room."

"Didn't you even give her a kiss good night?"

"I didn't want to catch whatever she had."

"Did she just wave good night?"

"I don't understand."

"Did you go in her room?"

"We have connecting rooms. The door was open and I just—"

"Did you see her, Jensen?"

There was a long pause. As the implication of Dade's question forced itself on him, Jensen looked at Dade with horror, eyeballs protruding. "Do you mean she could have been dead at that time? That she could have been in the garage when I thought I was talking to her?"

"That's exactly what I mean. Monkhaus arrived as you left and he says he saw you leaving and then found her dead."

"My God, I didn't know that!"

"But you can see now how it would look to the sheriff if you pretended that you hadn't been here."

Jensen turned away. In the firelight, Dade could see little spangles of perspiration on the smooth bronzed skull. Jensen got to his feet.

"I suggest you get yourself on down to the sheriff's first thing in the morning and correct that statement you gave them," Dade said.

Jensen thought about this for some time, palms flat together, squinting into them like a poker player of two minds about his hand. Finally, he said, "I want you there."

"You don't need me."

"Nevertheless, I want you to be present."

"Why?"

"Because the whole thing is ridiculous! My wife died in a dreadful accident and, at the behest of my daughter, you have gone around trying to make everything seem part of a conspiracy involving some second-rate painting you say is missing, and you've kept this up until finally, you've got the sheriff calling *me* to clarify matters. Well, I will gladly clarify them, sir, but in front of you, so that you won't be able to put some different construction on all of this behind my back. I want this thing settled in the morning."

"Since you're on my way, why don't I pick you up?"

"All right, you can do that."

"Nine-thirty suit you?"

"Fine." Jensen walked him to the front door, then shook hands with him and said, "Look, there's nothing personal in any of this. We just disagree. You understand that, don't you?"

"Yes."

"Good!" Jensen smiled. Dade went out the door. Abruptly, Jensen turned back into the house, closing the door behind him.

Outside, Dade started toward his car. Through the lighted window, he could see Jensen, phone in hand, punching out a number. Dade hesitated for a moment. Jensen looked up just then and caught Dade's eyes on him. Jensen turned his back, almost as if he were afraid Dade could read his lips.

XXII

Ellen met him at the door with an Old Fashioned. Taking it from her, he said, "How'd you know when I'd be here?"

"I heard the funicular start up and I just took it out of the icebox. You sure you still want to be a detective, honey?"

"You're not mad anymore?"

"Oh, you're such an old fool." She kissed him, helping him out of his jacket. "Motke called. Said he was sorry for the delay. Said he's still working on it and that he hopes to have word for you by tomorrow." She kissed him lightly. "Of course I was worried about you. But I wasn't after I heard that they had him locked up."

"Had who locked up?"

"The murderer."

"And who's that, honey?"

"Monkhaus, of course. I heard all about it. How he showed up with a gun—"

"—to get back the painting he killed Miriam for but somehow forgot to take with him."

"Oh, don't talk to me like that."

"I guess I don't understand your reasoning."

"He showed up in a rage and killed her and then . . ." She wavered. "Well, I guess he thought the painting was there but he couldn't find it."

"And since he'd already killed her, it was now too late to ask her where it was, is that what you mean?"

She gave him a look of annoyed bafflement, took the drink from his hand and took a sip from it. "All right, what did happen?"

"When I find out, I'll tell you."

"So you don't know either."

"I'm afraid I don't."

"Then why try to make a fool out of me?"

"I was just teasing, honey. The crazy thing is, it's just possible. Anything is."

"Think about how he treated Miriam years ago when they were married. That was an act of rage." He nodded soberly. "Well, for goodness' sake, tell me what you found out. What did Nettie lie about?"

"Just let me catch my breath."

"Oh, Dade!" She put her arms around him. "Darling, I don't want you involved in all this. You're a lawyer, not a detective. If there's a murderer loose, I don't want you running around after him. What are the police for?"

"I've often asked myself that same question."

"Did I tell you that in Egypt, the soul of a murdered man had to be nailed down? You see, if a man was murdered, they believed his *ifrīt* would rise from the ground where his blood had been shed and the only way of restraining it was by driving a nail which had never been used into the ground at the spot where the murder was committed."

"And that's what you think I ought to do?"

"That's what you're doing. The ghost is the murderer's sense of guilt. And you nail it down at the spot where murder was done by showing just how it was done and who did it."

"Ellen, you're a wonder."

"Have you had dinner?"

"I had a cup of soup. With Tillie Monkhaus."

"Let me fix you something."

He waved a hand at her. "I'll make you a proposition. Let's us walk on the beach while you tell me what you found out, and we'll head on down to the point there where you see that light or any other shack that takes your fancy, and have a late supper."

They went out onto the deck and down the steps to the sand and started walking along the water's edge. In the distance, they could see the long curve of lights outlining the bay.

"What time of year is it they catch lemmings?" she asked.

"That's grunion and it's midsummer."

They took off their shoes and waded through the lacy fans of the waves, sinking into the sand, heading south. She put a hand on his sleeve and said, "May I tell you something?"

"What?"

"A black slimy thing is climbing up your leg."

"Oh shit!" He brushed it off quickly and it oozed away. He squinted after it, then filled his pipe and lit it, cupping his hands and shielding the match from the sea breeze.

She said, "What happened today?" He told her, finishing up with an account of his visit to Jensen. The mirror of the sea cast a faint glow at the water's edge and he could make out the surprised expression on her face. "So Jensen was there, Monkhaus and then Gil. Well, if two of them found her dead, the third must have killed her—the one who was there first."

"But which one is that?"

"You just said—"

"No, I only told you what *they* said. Pete told us he saw Monk's car there at ten after nine. Let's say we accept that. All that means is that Monkhaus was there at that time. Now, Monkhaus says that as he arrived, he saw Jensen leaving, but it could easily have been the other way around. Remember, we only have Monk's word for this. Jensen can't say anything because he'd never seen Monkhaus and couldn't possibly have recognized him."

"So it's Monkhaus or Jensen."

"Or Gil."

"You told me Gil was at Jetty's—no, wait—I see. That's just what Gil said."

"Right. See, if Gil had called her from Jetty's and gotten no answer, he might have driven straight up to the house without waiting. That would get him there just before nine. Any one of the three could have been there first."

"Well, Monkhaus and Gil both had the same motive—the painting. But what was Jensen's?"

"You tell me."

"Oh, I know! He's a violent, jealous man. Everybody's known that about him for years. Let's say he came back to get the code key, decided to swap cars—after all, people always prefer to drive their own cars, especially on a highway like that in the downpour—let's say he happened to catch her running off to meet Gil!"

"We don't know if Jensen knew anything about her plans with Gil."

"But if he'd caught her trying to run off—"

"Ellen, you'd have to point out to me what triggered his reaction. Remember, all he sees is his wife in a car."

"Suppose he saw something more?"

"What?"

"I give up. So that's it, then. You've narrowed it down to three suspects."

"You deserve all the credit for that, my dear."

"Thank you, Dade!" Then her expression changed and she punched him hard in the arm. "A fie on you!"

"Honey—!"

"All right! So they're all in it together!"

"Ellen, please—"

"Don't 'please' me!"

"I just thought you were being impulsive, is all."

"Is that so?"

"Yes."

"Impulsive! Listen, for a man who ends up representing practically everybody he meets—!"

"That's not true!"

"Well, you started out representing Miriam's estate, then you agreed to represent Rachel—"

"And that's it."

"What about Gil?"

"I just stood in for old Willy Postel for an hour or so— and incidentally found out a thing or two in the process—"

"Then there's Jensen—"

"I do not represent him. He just wants me to go with him to the sheriff's in the morning because he thinks it's my fault that he has to be there." He shook a finger at her. "And I don't like you making fun of my work, do you understand me?"

"I didn't mean to offend you. Especially as I was just about to retain you myself."

"You?"

"I may soon be charged with assault and battery." She eyed him.

"Oh, Ellen—"

/ "Don't talk to me!"

Dade tramped along on the hard-packed sand, hands behind his back, whistling soundlessly under his breath, Ellen striding ahead of him. Catching up with her, he put an arm around her and gave her a kiss. "Truce?"

"Truce."

He pointed with his pipe to the lighted windows of a café. "That place okay?" She nodded.

It was crowded. They were told there would be a wait of an hour and a half, so they had drinks in the bar. After fifteen minutes, Dade beckoned to the shapely young waitress. She walked over to him and bent down to hear him over the din of voices, her little brown plastic tray pressed to her full young breasts. He brought his face close to her bosom, reading her name tag.

"They call you Shari?"

"That's right."

"What a lovely name."

"Thank you."

"My name's Cooley."

"How do you do, Mr. Cooley."

"I want to tell you, I think you're quite a waitress."

"Oh, thank you, sir."

"And I'm not just saying that because I'm the new owner—"

"You're the what?"

"Dade! You promised!" Ellen gasped.

"I shouldn't have said anything," he muttered.

"No, please!" the waitress said.

"Well, I just bought it today. And I thought, why don't we drop in and see how things are going?"

"I'll get the manager."

"No. Now, I insist. You're not to say one word. Promise?"

"Yes, sir."

In five minutes, they were shown to a booth in the dining room with high-backed leather armchairs, the table set against a window looking out over the waves. He smiled at Ellen. She looked away.

"You said you wouldn't do that anymore."

"At my age, a man is forgetful."

"Oh, shut up!"

"Now, let's hear what you learned." A young waiter came up and recited the menu. Dade said, "I'd like a bully of beef and a ratchet of burgundy." The waiter frowned, puzzled.

Ellen interrupted, ordering for them. Alone, they sipped their drinks. "All right," she said, taking out her notes, "where shall I begin?"

"Here's my problem. A fella shows up with a painting. Crude. Something makes Miriam suspicious and she finds there's another painting underneath it. She X-rays it and finds out it's essentially the same painting and guesses it was overpainted to disguise it so it could be smuggled out of Europe. She says she thinks it's a missing Romano. Now, she starts stripping it to get at the painting underneath. She hasn't paid Monkhaus for it yet because she's not sure. Now, that part's all right. I got no quarrel with all that.

"A month later, she tells Monkhaus she was right, that it is a Romano, which we know is a lie 'cause there's no missing Romano. Now, here's the problem: What did she think it was and what the hell made her so sure at one glance? I feel the truth is staring us in the face and it's so obvious, we just can't see it. That's why I wanted you to dig up what you could on authentication. Refresh my memory."

Ellen said, "Well, the most interesting thing I learned is that there don't happen to be any books on the subject. I had a long talk with the librarian, who turned out to be a charming man, very understated. I'll just run through all this rapidly and you can stop me if anything isn't clear.

"First, you have scientific analysis—X-ray to see the drawing underneath, infrared, et cetera. Every important museum has its own conservation lab where they do these things. But of course one must remember that a scientific analysis can never yield more than negative results. That is, it can only tell us that there is nothing modern in the paints used in the picture or in the panel or canvas. The painting could still be a modern copy done by an artist using old canvas and old paint but if he slips up and uses even a single pigment known, say, only since the nineteenth century, then he gives the whole show away. But you know all that. You must."

"Just keep talking, honey."

"Well, he knew Miriam and he talked about how she worked. She was a follower of Berenson, who was something of a detective and actually pioneered the whole art of authentication, starting in around the eighteen nineties and continuing right up until the Second World War." She squinted at her notes, saying under her breath, "Leans on photography, sort of. Topaz-colored eyes."

"I didn't follow that, honey."

"Oh, that's the librarian. He has these very unusual eyes. I don't believe I've ever seen anybody with eyes that color, so I just made a note to myself, that's all."

"Uh-huh."

"Well, to resume—"

"You're blushing, honey."

"Never mind!"

"Just thought I'd mention it. Pray continue."

"Photography. Yes. That's what authentication leans on. The use of photography came into existence in the eighteen seventies and eighteen eighties—that is to say, at around that time the catalogues of museums and galleries began to have photographs in them. Before, an expert really had to depend on his memory when he wanted to make comparisons of style and technique."

"Well, we know all that."

"If we know so much, why do we have to keep reading?"

"Sorry, honey. Full speed ahead."

"Anyway, what Berenson did was to amass a huge collection of photographs so that he could spread out the works of a given master at a moment's notice, have enlargements made, if necessary, and then compare a given painting in terms of brush strokes, length, direction, palette, subject, composition, proportion and so forth."

She began reading her notes aloud. "Berenson actually owed much to man named Morelli, who felt one could best determine an artist's style by looking at those things not chief focus of artist's full attention—ears, for example. An artist in Renaissance would create style of painting ears and stick to that style for rest of life, and this not something imitator would pay much attention to—ears or fingers or noses, depending on artist. Greek nose."

"What was that last part?"

"Nothing."

"Is that another little note to yourself, honey?"

"Listen, for a man who's been tom-catting around with three women all day long, you can just forget all about my librarian!"

"All right, all right. Well, that last wouldn't do it because she knew right off. What comes next?"

"Provenance." She glanced at her notes again and read: "But of course if documentation exists, say, on back of painting, that would take precedence over opinion. Instance: It was often custom for nobleman of period who commissioned portrait to put his coat of arms on back of picture with red wax seal. Something like that fairly conclusive. And if we can find stencils on back of canvas by, say, Christie's or some other reputable auction house— well, then we know what we have."

"She wouldn't have to strip the painting to see the back of the canvas. No good. Next."

"Signature. But most paintings of the Renaissance were not signed. In fact, if a painting were signed, that would make it suspect."

"We can rule that out, too. Next?"

"Opinion." She read from her notes. "Authentication really only subjective opinion on whether a picture is right or not—a unanimous opinion of three or four of the best authorities."

"She didn't call in any three or four authorities. Next?"

She took a paperback book out of her pocket. "I got you this. It's the *John McPhee Reader* and there's a gorgeous piece in here on Thomas Hoving, written when he was director of the Metropolitan. This one paragraph explains Miriam."

She began reading. " ' "Get in touch with other scholars—everybody you think is expert. The idea that there is fierce competition among museums in this respect is laughable. Everyone helps everyone. . . . Then get the work of art with you and live with it as long as you possibly can. You have to watch it. Watch it. Come across it by accident. I used to have the staff at The Cloisters put things where I would come across them by accident. A work of art will grow in stature, and fascinate you more and more. If it is a fake, it will eventually fall apart before your eyes, like a piece of plaster. . . ." ' What is it?"

Dade had gotten to his feet, hands on his hips, and was looking down at her as if down at a witness who had just given crucial testimony by accident. "She didn't call anybody in. Couldn't have. Wasn't time. She didn't live with it and watch it, like Hoving says. Now, she was one of the great authenticators in the country. But she didn't do any of the things you'd expect her to do, so just how the hell did she know what she had on her hands with just one look?" Dade relit his pipe, filling their corner with clouds of blue smoke. The surf pounded in their ears, like the dull concussion of cannonfire.

Ellen said, squinting at her notes, "I suppose it couldn't be—"

"What?" He sat down, at a loss.

"I can't read my writing. He was talking so fast. Identificatory? Is that what that says? Oh, marks. I'm sorry, Dade. I don't know what he was talking about."

"Son of a bitch!"

"What?"

He shook a finger at Ellen. "I just remembered! It don't mean doodily-squat if you've got certain things."

"What things?" She had picked up her drink. Now she put it down, puzzled.

"Let me tell you a story. Back in my daddy's time, they stole the 'Mona Lisa.' " She looked at him with surprise. He said, "Didn't you know that? Fact. Stole it from the Louvre in 1911. It was gone for two years and then found in the possession of an Italian who said he had stolen it out of national pride. That part's not important. What they had to know was whether they had the real painting back. You know how long it took to authenticate? Forty-five minutes! And here's how they did it. Didn't even look at the thing. Hung it face to the wall, like the poor old lady was in disgrace, and then opened a sealed envelope containing certain secret identifying marks the museum had put on the back of the canvas, and then checked these one by one till they were sure. That's how they did it and I'll bet you that's how she did it. Only in this case, the marks must have been on the *front* which explains why she had to strip it to make sure."

"I never heard of marks like that before."

"Most people haven't. That's because they're only on a few paintings. But those paintings are the ones worth millions. That's the name of this game!" He burst out in a shout of triumphant laughter. Then he said soberly, "Poor woman's dead and I'm carrying on. Well, as my old daddy used to say, 'It's no laughing matter but it's no matter if you laugh.' "

After dinner they walked back up the beach to the inn, returning about eleven. As they went back into their room, Dade mused, "All we know is, Monk's father, he smuggled a stolen painting into this country thirty-five years ago. Stolen from where? And when? Hell's bells, Ellen, all we know is it's a picture of some pretty lady and there are thousands and thousands of those, for which I thank God, apart from this here particular problem. We don't even know what the damn thing looks like!"

"Yes, we do!"

"What do you mean?"

"It looks like a Giulio Romano. Otherwise Miriam wouldn't have pretended that that's what it was."

He put his hands on the small of his back and glared at her as if at a hostile witness. "Honey, I didn't just ride into town on a load of pumpkins! I know that much! So what the hell does that tell us?"

Ellen threaded a needle, eying a loose button on his jacket. "He painted just like the man he worked for." She met his eyes.

His jaw dropped. "Raphael! Christ-on-the-mountain, *Ra-*

phael!" He grabbed for the phone and called Arnolphe Motke in San Francisco, finally getting him after a dozen rings. Motke's voice was thick. "Arnie? You asleep or drunk?"

"A little of both."

"The subject is painting. Italian Renaissance. Get on the phone. Start with Interpol. Then use your own sources. I don't care where you call. I don't give a hoot in hell if you get 'em out of bed. Just find out how many Raphaels are missing and when they disappeared. Names, dates and places." Dade slammed down the phone and then began pacing up and down, hardly standing still long enough for Ellen to pull off his jacket. She made tea, which he spiked with bourbon. Then he watched the news with the sound off, tipping back in his chair, somnolent, inattentive, soothed by the silent pictures flashed on the screen. Afterward he went out on the deck and smoked his pipe.

It was one in the morning, an hour and a half after Dade talked with Motke, when the phone rang. Dade banged into the room, almost tripping over a chair in his haste to answer it.

Motke's voice said, "Julius the Second. Portrait. Intended for Santa Maria del Popolo and disappeared around 1513. Portrait shows old man with long white beard. Aforementioned is only Raphael that ever disappeared—"

"Goddamned son of a bitch—"

"—until the theft of 'La Fornarina'—"

"The what?"

"—also known as 'The Veiled Woman,' which was stolen from the Louvre. I will spell that name."

"Stolen when?"

"Nineteen forty-five."

"Sweet Jesus."

"That do it?"

"You old bastard, you really came through."

"What's going on?"

"I'll tell you all about it when I see you. Go back to bed." Dade banged down the phone and let out a cowboy yell of triumph. He told Ellen, then said, "First thing in the morning, you call up Pickwick. I want one of those big fat art books, you know, the kind with reproductions of everything the artist ever painted. Tell them to send it out here by messenger."

"I know what you want. Do you think that's it?"

"Has to be."

"Easy enough to find out. Monk would know. Tillie. Rachel. Gil. Nettie. They all saw it."

"Yeah, but I got me a little trick up my sleeve. Just get me that book." He broke off, seeing a shadowed expression on Ellen's face. "What's the matter?"

"Maybe I'm a little afraid for you."

"You being superstitious?"

"A little. Did you know that the soul of a murder victim is thought to be able to fasten itself on any mortal who had been in some way connected with it in this world and cause terrible mischief?"

"Ellen—"

"But isn't it true? Hasn't Miriam's soul fastened on you, Dade? And isn't it getting to be very dangerous?" Not letting him answer, she put him to bed, then joined him. In minutes, she was fast asleep. But he lay awake, staring out through the dark windows at the night and listening to the pounding of the surf.

XXIII

In the morning, Dade was up at seven, ordered breakfast for two, and then pulled on his trunks, climbed down to the rocky beach from the weatherworn redwood deck and waded into the surf for a quick dip. The weather was treacherous, the sky bright but the surf high, with gusts of wind blowing brief, ugly sandstorms in front of the bungalows fronting on the water. He breasted the breakers and swam out to the choppy waters beyond, paddling back and forth and ducking under the swells like a happy seal.

Looking down along the curve of the coast, dotted with glass-walled houses, each with its deck stretched out over the steep beach, he could see occasional plumes of sand kicked up by the winds. The Santa Anas were going to blow, the devil winds. There was something ominous about it. Floating on his back and paddling with his feet and hands, he thought about the strangeness of hot winds, about their names: *sirocco, mistral, föhn;* how they troubled men's minds; how even the law reflected this human truth, at least in Europe in places like Germany and Switzerland, where crimes committed during the harsh, hot blowing of the *föhn* historically drew lesser punishments.

He swam back to shore, then stood on the thick crunch of the rocky strand. The gusts were harder now, great sheets of it drying him in moments, a laundry of wind stretched out on invisible clotheslines, a world of small tempests, hot, dying away only to return again and again. He stamped up and down in the glitter of harsh sunlight, glancing out at the rocks, half-submerged in the rising tide, thick with mussels. He remembered a line Ellen had once written, that the plump gray ones had been the diet of the Chumash but the flat blue-black ones had crossed the seas on the hulls of Cabrillo's ships all the way from the placid lake of the Mediterranean and colonized here, a chance gift from the Conquistadores.

He looked up and saw Pete standing there, balancing a tray. Dade waved to him and clambered up to the deck.

"I'll have that inside," Dade said, stepping into his burnoose, toweling himself and shedding his wet trunks.

Pete set the tray on the table and uncovered the steaming breakfasts. Dade could hear Ellen singing in the bathroom, showering.

"I brought you ham and eggs as a treat."

"I just ordered Post Toasties and a jelly doughnut."

"I sneaked this stuff out. You don't have to pay for it."

"I knew you for a crook the day I first saw you." Dade took a swallow of coffee and blotted his lips. "You write to your daddy, like I told you?"

"I sent a card." The boy frowned. "You know," he said, "I been thinking. You shouldn't go around telling everybody what to do."

"Why not?"

"It's a free country. I don't have to think like you. Everyone's got a right to their own opinion."

"'And every other man has a right to knock him down for it.' You know who said that? Samuel Johnson did. You ever read Boswell's *Johnson*?"

"No, sir."

"Well, you should. It'll help form your character. I saw a paperback copy of it upstairs at the newsstand. I want you to buy it and put it on my bill and start reading tonight because I'm going to be asking you questions about it in the morning."

"I don't have much free time, sir."

"Make time."

"Mr. Cooley, try to understand—"

"You resent my helping you, son?"

"Oh, not at all, sir. You've been real nice to me. I won't forget it. Some folks, they act like you don't have any feelings at all."

"Is that so?"

"Treat you like dirt, you know? One guy, he'd call up and order things and then just hang up on me like I was a machine, not even so much as a . . . well, goodbye." Pete started out.

Dade made a pyramid of his hands, breathing into them, thumbs hooked under his chin. He was like a man listening for the fall of tumblers. "Just one moment, please." Pete turned, an inquiring look on his face. "I want you to cast your mind back to something you told me. You were in the garage and the lady of the house—"

"The dead lady?"

"That's the one. She picked up the extension phone and said. . .? Now, tell me those words again, those words you heard."

"She said, I *can't* move it!"

" 'I *can't* move it.' That's what she said?"

"Yes, sir."

"You didn't tell me that part before."

"Well, I just remembered."

"Go on."

"Then she said, 'Listen, those kids are still here. I'll have to call you back.' "

"Now, I want you to think very carefully. What happened next?"

"She put down the phone."

"You mean hung it up?"

"Yes, sir."

"Just like that? Kind of funny to hang up on somebody, isn't it? Didn't she say goodbye first?"

"No . . ." Pete hesitated, trying to remember something. Then his face cleared.

"What is it, boy? Tell me."

"She didn't say goodbye because the other person hung up. Yeah. That's what happened."

"You sure?"

"I'm positive. I just remembered. I heard the click."

"You've been very helpful. Now, get out of here. And thanks, Pete."

"Have a nice day."

"Yeah. You too." Pete left the room. Ellen came out of the bathroom dressed in a plum-colored wool jersey dress and sat down to breakfast. "Where are you going?" Dade asked.

"After I get your book, I'm going shopping."

"That stuff they got at the Getty's not for sale."

"For groceries. I thought I told you not to order jelly doughnuts."

"My doctor says I'm to force jelly doughnuts." Dade finished his breakfast and sat down at the table, a tablet open, and began making brief notes of what Pete had told him. The phone rang. He answered it.

A woman's voice said, "Mr. Cooley, this is Mary upstairs. Did you want the boy to bring you down a copy of Masters and Johnson?"

"Put him on the phone." Dade waited, annoyed.

Then, Pete's voice said, "This is Pete, sir."

"Put down the phone, go over to the rack and find that copy I saw of Boswell's *Life of Samuel Johnson* and come back and tell me when you have it in your hand."

"Yes, sir." Dade waited. After two minutes, Pete's voice said triumphantly, "I found it, sir!"

"Ten pages by tomorrow morning or your friend the Mahatma will find himself on a cattle boat headed east before the sun sets." Dade banged down the phone.

At eight-fifteen, he got up, pulled off his burnoose, went into the bathroom and showered happily, singing, "I love you as I never loved befor-r-r-e . . ." in a deep booming voice. Then, scrubbing himself with a towel and praising his reflection in glowing terms, he dried his thick white hair, scraped his pink face with a straight-edged razor, sharpening it from time to time on a leather strop he had fastened around the flush lever of the toilet, scented himself with cologne, dressed in tweeds and came out into the room.

Ellen said, "That sheriff called."

"Lieutenant Valdez?"

"Yes. He wants to talk to you."

Dade started out the door, saying, "Tell the lieutenant he'll have to take his turn, just like everyone else." Then he turned and saw Valdez blocking the door.

Valdez said, "It's my turn now. Gil Ransohoff disappeared."

Dade stopped in his tracks.

"Around nine P.M. last night. I must have called you I don't know how many times."

"We got back late."

"Don't you pick up your messages?"

"Not when I come in the back door."

"I had further questions I wanted to ask Dr. Ransohoff and I went over to his house myself. His wife invited me in. She called him a couple of times and then said he was in the bathroom. We waited. We must have waited about ten minutes and she thought perhaps he hadn't heard her because the water was running, so she went upstairs and banged on the door and then called me, saying she couldn't get any answer. The door was locked. We forced it. The room was empty. The water was on and the window was open. I wonder if you know anything about it."

"I do not."

"You must have some idea where he is, since you represent him."

"I do not represent him. I appeared as his counsel only temporarily in the absence of Mr. Postel."

"Mind telling me why?" Dade stared at him. "When you came downtown, you mentioned a possible conflict."

"If you will excuse me—"

"You're the one mentioned it."

"Lieutenant," Ellen said, "why on earth am I keeping you standing in the doorway? Do come in and let me give you some coffee. By the way, did you know that the ancient Semites believed that if you spent New Year's night in a cemetery, knowledge could be obtained? Of course, I suppose the first thing you'd learn is that it's a good way to catch pneumonia."

"I'd try anything at this point to break this case."

"Have some coffee."

"Thank you, ma'am."

She took his arm and led him into the room. Behind them, the door closed. When Valdez turned around, Dade was gone.

Dade arrived at the Welles house at nine-twenty. He was shown into the library by Rosarita, who had just returned half an hour before and had no idea where the *señor* was. Dade looked at his watch. "He was expecting me."

"Yes, *señor*."

"Maybe he's just out on an errand."

"Perhaps he is, *señor*."

"I'll just wait."

"May I bring you coffee, *señor*?"

"I'd like that." Nine-thirty came and went. When Jensen had not arrived by ten o'clock, Dade called his office and was told by the answering service that they had not heard from him. When he called the inn, there were no messages for him. He called Jensen's club. No, Mr. Welles had not been there at all. At ten-thirty he tried Ballinger's office. The exchange put him through to Ballinger's house. No, Ballinger had no idea where Jensen had gone but would be sure to get in touch with him if he heard. Irritated, Dade stomped out of the Welles house.

XXIV

When he got back to the inn, Ellen was out on the deck hanging up laundry.

"Did Jensen call? Son of a bitch stood me up." She shook her head. "You find out if they got that book at Pickwick?"

"They had it down the road, left over from the holidays." She picked up a huge art book and carried it over to him, ramming it into his belly. "Here. Merry Christmas."

"How'd you get down there and back without a car?"

"One of the neighbors gave me a ride."

"You mean one of the guests?"

"No. Just a neighbor."

"I didn't know we knew any neighbors."

"Well—"

"Who gave you a ride?"

"A nice man."

"What nice man?"

"A truck farmer. You see, he was kind enough to stop—"

"You trying to tell me you were hitchhiking?"

"In a manner of speaking. It's just that I'd never done it and I knew you were in a hurry and he was obviously a very nice man, big mustache, Italian accent, something of a singer—"

"How'd you get back?"

"I didn't hitchhike."

"I asked you a question."

185

"The Sparkletts man. He was delivering somebody's bottled water and I just—"

"You know you're something of a damn fool?"

"Well, thanks!"

"You're entirely welcome." He put the heavy book on the table. Ellen unwrapped another book and started leafing through it.

"What you got there—Vasari?" Dade asked. "He must have seen it when the paint was wet."

"No, but this author mentions him." She turned pages carefully, then began reading. " 'As a portraitist Raphael was second to no Renaissance painter. Whoever she may have been—and it is likely that she was the famous *Fornarina* ("baker's daughter") recorded by Vasari—the sitter for the so-called *Donna Velata* ("veiled woman") is the same dark-eyed creature Raphael used as a model for the *Sistine Madonna* . . . In color this is the richest of all Raphael's portraits.' It goes on to speak of '. . . the dazzling white-and-gold drapery of this enchanting portrait, the resonant depth of the dark eyes and chestnut hair, the brilliance of the pale flesh, the soft glow of the stones in the necklace, and the luminous marvel of the pearl hanging from the woman's veil.' "

"Let's have a look."

"Here it is." She opened the heavy book on the table to a full-page reproduction of "La Fornarina."

"That's the baker's daughter, all right. Now, it comes back to me. You know who she is, don't you?"

"No."

"His girlfriend! Fact. Vasari said Raphael had to have women around him all the time. Horniest bastard of the whole bunch. Michelangelo and Da Vinci, they sort of let a lot of poontang go to waste, so Raphael, he just licked everybody else's plate clean, so to speak. Toward the end, he slowed down. Working away in some fella's palazzo— Chigi, that's the man—and Raphael, he moved so slow, they brought in this baker's daughter to stay there with him, to stoke his fires. Loved her. Wrote his sonnets to her. So, there was the two of them, banging away night and day in that drafty palazzo, and then Raphael, he figured the end was near—only thirty-seven but you know when it's coming—and he sent her away, 'leaving her means to live honestly,' Vasari says. And after all, Vasari was his friend. He ought to know. Then, they put the 'Transfiguration' up at the end of the bed, where he could see it and, come Good Friday, he ups and dies. Know what Vasari says the poor bastard died of? Fucked hisself to death!"

"Dade!"

"Fact! And that picture, honey"—Dade jabbed a finger at the glowing portrait—"that picture's a painting of the woman who made him do it. Shame on you!" he shouted at the baker's daughter. "Thirty-seven years old—a mere slip of a boy—and you egged him on till he fucked hisself to death! Christ, what a story."

"How come you're still alive, dearest?" She put on her coat.

"Where you off to?"

"The Getty. I've come across the most marvelous books there for my piece. I've found something I want to share with you and that dear lieutenant. Did you know that the Talmud even has an incantation to exorcise the demon of a privy? I knew that would make your day!" She pirouetted, a finger on her head. His face reddened. She started out.

"Take the car," he yelled, "and don't talk to truck farmers. And while I'm thinking about it, stay away from the Sparkletts man as well. I'll overlook it this once but I won't sanction—"

"And you stay out of bakeries, especially those with daughters on the premises!"

He snapped his fingers. "By God."

"What?" She stopped.

"Overlook and sanction!"

"Overlook and sanction?"

"Cleave, conjure, *merde* and now, overlook and sanction! Take that!"

After she left, Dade went out and sat on the deck, propping his feet up on the railing, letting the salt air blow in his face, squinting at the water and trying to pretend he was on a ship. That was the thing. They'd have to take a cruise. To the Greek islands. He imagined a grateful client with a yacht. One big enough for four children. Oh, you are too kind, sir. A knock at the door interrupted his day-dreaming.

It was Pete with a letter. He said apologetically, "I was supposed to bring this thing down here on a tray but I couldn't find one. Oh, and the guy said to tell you he's sorry. The messenger. See, he was supposed to deliver this to you last night but there was a slide."

Dade waved him away, closed the door, ripped open the letter and began to read. It was in Jensen's careful handwriting. It said:

Dear Dade,

I have known almost from the beginning that Miriam was murdered. Upon reflection, I realize that suspicion may fall on me. That being the case, I must now tell you the exact truth of what happened. You will see from what I am about to write that everything I am telling you is in confidence. Naturally, I cannot put any of this on the record at this time. After you have had the opportunity to consider what I'm about to tell you, then, perhaps, we can meet and decide on a proper course of action. Meanwhile, maybe one will occur to me.

In 1945, Raphael's "La Fornarina" was stolen from the Louvre. As I'm sure you know, there is no statute of limitations in France on the theft of national art treasures. The French government asked Interpol for help. There was never any hint that the painting ever entered this country. For years now, it has been considered lost, hidden perhaps in one of those private South American collections, which I happen to think are more legend than fact.

A few days before her death, Miriam came to me and told me she had a surprise, that Raphael's "La Fornarina" ("The Veiled Woman," as it is popularly known) had turned up. She said the owner wanted to sell it secretly and that his price on the black market was three million dollars, which, of course, is a fraction of the price it would easily command in a legitimate sale. After my initial shock, I was hesitant. I have never trafficked in stolen goods.

Miriam proposed the whole thing as if it were a lark. She said to me, "How would you like to own a French national art treasure? A Raphael!" I was shocked at her. She said to me, "Look, it's the black market. If you don't buy it, it might go into the private collection of some very rich family or to some Mafia figure and it might be a hundred years before the Louvre gets it back, if then. Buy it," she said to me. "Buy it for the Louvre. But keep it. Keep it with you for the rest of your life. They owe you that much for buying it back for them. Think of it as rental. And then, just will it back to them and they'll get it on your death. After all, they haven't had it for years. They can wait a while longer."

The mysterious seller was to deliver the painting to my house on the night of the fifteenth of February, at which time I would hand over three million in cash. That's why I had to go into town on the night of the storm—to telex Zurich. Three million in cash isn't easy to raise, even for a man in my position. It had taken me days to get that much money together.

Well, of course, the night of the fourteenth, Miriam was killed in what all of us believed was a freak accident. Now, the question in my mind at that time was whether the seller might figure out that I was the buyer and try to reach me. The minute that Monkhaus man started calling me about a missing Romano, I knew everything. But what could I do? I didn't have the painting and I had absolutely no idea what had happened to it. On top of that, you started asking me the same thing. There was simply nothing I could say except, "I don't know." And wait—to find out who had killed my wife for it.

Jensen Crumholtz Welles

Dade put the letter down carefully on the rickety card table. He walked to the window and looked out at the windswept sea.

"Shithouse mouse," he said.

XXV

Dade called Pete. "What messenger service delivered this?" he asked.

"The Malibu one. There's only just the one."

"Thanks." Dade hung up and checked the directory. He got the dispatcher on the phone. Giving his name, Dade said, "I got a letter today that your man said was supposed to have been here last night."

"See, the road was blocked—" the dispatcher began.

"I just want to know when you picked up this letter. What time?"

"Just a minute." The dispatcher left the line for a moment, then came back on and said, "Log says we got there at nine thirty-seven."

"Mr. Welles give you the letter?"

"Our instructions are not to bother the house when Mr. Welles calls us. We just always pick up his stuff from that letter box he's got on that there gate pillar."

"Last night was no different?"

"Not so far as I know."

"Thank you very much." Dade put down the phone and stared off into space.

The phone rang. It was Valdez. Dade said, "I looked for you when I got back but I didn't see you."

"Very funny. Okay if I come by in half an hour?"

"Any time you like."

"This is official business. I'll be there at eleven-thirty and don't make me go looking for you." Click.

Dade got to his feet, studied the baker's daughter for a few moments, adjusting the book on the table so that it lay in plain view. He got himself a yellow lined tablet and a thick stub of pencil from the kitchen and started making himself a diagram of the Welles driveway and garage and a timetable, his brows flying up and down as he concentrated, little sounds popping from his lips as he talked to himself. He covered several pages. He had gotten to his feet and started to walk up and down, measuring the room, when he heard a knock at the door and went to it, throwing it open.

Valdez entered, his jaw clenched like a fist. He looked around. "Jensen Welles here?"

"No, he isn't."

"Been here?"

"No." Dade closed the door and gestured at a chair drawn up at the table. He said, "You asked me a question Friday night. About whether I had any new evidence in this case. I'm prepared to answer your question now. Take a seat." Dade himself sat down by the fireplace.

At that moment, Valdez caught sight of the open art book on the table. His face changed. Dade watched him. Valdez said, "Okay, so you know the score."

"What's the story?"

Valdez said, "I'll ask the questions."

Dade knocked the bowl of the briar delicately against the chimney wall, then began to fill it with little pinches of tobacco taken from the pouch cupped in his crotch. "I'm a slow study. You must have noticed that."

"Look, this is a federal case. Now, either you answer my questions or else—"

"Or else what? Sonny, you don't want to get me riled. Now, sit down like I told you and pay attention. I don't like folks standing over me unless they're waiters." Valdez sat down. "Malibu Lagoon, I'm told, is regarded by the Audubon Society as one of the greatest sanctuaries for birds of passage in the entire southern half of this splendid state—and being something of a bird of passage myself, I am entertaining the idea of strolling down there this very afternoon on the arm of my wife, in which case, I will ask you to excuse me, and that will put an end to our brief discussion. Your other option is to put your cards on the table."

"Mr. Cooley, don't push me."

"You can assume I know the whole story," Dade said, ignoring him. "What I don't know is how you got into it. Tell me that and I'll do what I can to help you."

Valdez thought a moment. Then, as if agreeing with himself, he nodded and said, "Okay. It's this simple. Nobody shells out millions for a painting without first finding out if it's the real thing. Welles has a friend who is an assistant curator at the Met. Welles called him and asked if he had access to the secret identifying marks on the canvas. Welles, of course, had no way of knowing that his friend the assistant curator also works for the FBI as an expert on art thefts. The FBI got in touch with the French government. They were only too glad to cooperate. Everything was set to grab the painting on the fifteenth, when it changed hands.

"Well, the lady was killed the night before, the painting was nowhere to be found and a decision was made to call the death accidental and close the case, just to throw everybody off-guard. We've had everyone connected with her under surveillance ever since. That means the husband, the daughter and her boyfriend, the attorney, the maid, the first husband and his wife and the man the deceased was going to run off with and *his* wife—oh, and the partner, that French lady. One of them murdered her and one of them's got that painting stashed somewhere."

"Twelve."

"Twelve?"

"You're talking about suspects, right?" Dade said.

"How'd you come up with twelve?"

"You counting my wife and me?"

"You think I'm crazy?"

"Well, you'd be just as crazy to count a couple of the others."

"Such as?"

"You have the floor."

"There's a word for people like you, Mr. Cooley."

"And you don't want to be quoted using it. Now, just carry on, son."

"We've found out this much: We leaned on Monkhaus.

He admits he was there. He says he found her dead. And he tells us that when he drove up a couple of minutes after nine, Welles was just driving away. He swears it's true. Now, I want to see Jensen Welles in my office today. All right, all right, you're not his attorney, I know. But if I don't hear from him by three o'clock, I'll send somebody out to bring him in. That's for the record."

The phone rang for Valdez. He listened, grunting, saying nothing until whoever was on the line had finished speaking. Then he said, "On my way," and slammed down the phone. He looked at Dade, his face dark with anger. He said, "That woman who was clobbered the other night? Mrs. Welles' partner?"

"Nettie?" Dade said, his eyes watchful.

"They just found her car at the bottom of a cliff in Malibu Canyon. They can't get to it yet but somebody with binoculars spotted the license and it took them about thirty seconds to get a make on it—"

Dade was already on his way to the door, Valdez following.

Malibu Canyon was a wild and spectacular pass through the mountains which encircled Malibu like a sea wall. A stream flowed through it, emptying into a lagoon at the edge of the Colony, but unlike other streams in those mountains, it flowed year round and, as a consequence, the canyon was lush, its floor thick with fern, willow and sycamore. The road was a shelf cut into the winding cliffs, rising higher and higher and then plunging into a tunnel which led to the upland meadows of Calabasas and oak-studded pastures where cattle and sheep grazed.

The squad car in which Dade and Valdez rode raced up past the lawns of Pepperdine University and into the canyon, lights flashing and sirens wailing. Cars on the right slowed to a stop, unable to risk pulling over onto the crumbling shoulder. Their driver maneuvered the speeding squad car from right to left, weaving back and forth on the narrow two-lane road. They climbed higher and higher, until they could see the black mouth of the tunnel ahead of them, to their right a lookout point where the road widened to allow motorists to park and admire the view. The cliffs plunged hundreds of feet straight down to the canyon below.

An ambulance was parked there, lights flashing. There were several squad cars and a crane, with a paramedic about to be lowered by cable to the floor of the canyon. The driver skidded to a stop and they got out and started toward the edge. The paramedic rotated slowly on his cable like a skydiver, then signaled to the operator of the crane; a winch turned and the paramedic plunged down into the abyss.

Valdez hurried toward his men. Dade looked over the edge of the cliff. Far below, smashed on the huge boulders through which ran the narrow creek, he could see a black Citroën. Valdez walked to another part of the cliff for a better view. The paramedic far below struggled to wrench open a door. When it wouldn't give, they saw him pick up a rock and then scramble onto the hood of the car, lift the rock and smash the windshield with it. Dade could see the glass pebbling, flashing in the sunlight. The paramedic crawled halfway into the front seat. He remained there for a couple of minutes and then wriggled back out, something in his right hand which he tucked in his shirt.

Straightening, he waved his arms. Abruptly, the winch began to reverse itself and the paramedic swam slowly up toward them through a sea of crystal air, dwarfed by the huge rocky outcroppings in the almost-perpendicular cliffs. He surfaced and the crane wheeled around, the paramedic suspended for a moment above their heads, like a circus performer about to attempt some extraordinary feat. Then the winch reversed again and the paramedic in his white jump suit descended in their midst like a giant marionette. He unhooked himself from the rig, looking around at the uniformed men everywhere, as if uncertain to whom he should give his report.

The lieutenant beckoned to him. The paramedic strode over to Valdez and spoke to him in a voice none of them could hear, turning his back on the semicircle of audience as if he did not want his expression read. He took an object from his shirt and handed it to Valdez. Valdez put a swift hand on the paramedic's shoulder as if challenging him and this made the paramedic turn slightly so that they could all now see his profile as he nodded vehemently. Valdez spoke to him again and the paramedic walked away.

Valdez hesitated for a moment, looking down at the wreck far below, knitting his dark brows, then turned and walked toward Dade, handing him a thick wallet. Dade opened it. Tucked into one side they could see a passport. The other side was full of credit cards. One of them fell to the ground. Dade picked it up. It read, "Gilbert Ransohoff."

Valdez nodded. "It's a man all right. Answers to Ransohoff's description. Alone in the car, brief case on the seat next to him. Empty. That's it. Nothing else in the car." Dade swore to himself. "It'll be some time before they can get the body out of there." Valdez and Dade walked toward the paramedic and two deputies, who were now taking acetylene torches out of a utility truck. "They'll have to cut him loose." Dade's eyes rested on Valdez, as if asking a question to which he already knew the answer. "It's too soon to be absolutely sure but it seems fairly certain he was shot to death."

"Jesus," Dade said under his breath.

The paramedic turned to them and said, "Dead for some time. Can't be sure how long until we get him out of there." He jerked his head toward the canyon.

"Can you make a guess?" Dade asked.

"The way he looks, I would have said three days. The sun does that. You'll have to get an opinion from forensic but they'll only be able to tell you give or take a few hours." The paramedic frowned. "But if somebody shot him, what was the point of driving the car off the cliff? I mean, what would it buy you?"

"Time," said Dade. "On a lonely road late at night, good chance the car wouldn't be spotted before daylight."

Brandt came running up, saying there was an urgent call from headquarters. "Okay, okay," Valdez said and followed Brandt to the command car. Valdez leaned into the driver's seat and picked up the microphone, speaking into it and resting his forearms on the sill of the open window. He listened for a moment. Dade could hear the blurred chattering of a response. Turning toward Dade, Valdez shot him a look of surprise, at the same time still listening to the radio. Valdez said into the microphone, knocking the dirt from his shoes by banging them against the car, "Yes, sir, I want him picked up. I want him brought in now for questioning." He paused a moment. There was a rapid, irritable reply. Valdez interrupted, saying, "Sir, please try to see it from my point of view—" Dade sensed rivalry in the air like acrid smoke. "Okay, sir, put him on." Valdez nodded at Dade, flashing his white teeth in a satisfied smile.

"Sergeant? Go out and pick up Daddy Warbucks. I don't want to hear about your problems, bring him in." Another voice spoke, softer, apologetic. Valdez's face changed. "Oh, shit! All right, all right, I'll hear your explanation." The other voice spoke quickly, too low for Dade to understand. Valdez listened for a few moments and then interrupted, saying quietly, "I have listened to your explanation, sergeant, and you know what I think? In my opinion, your explanation sucks!" His dark skin flushed. "Well, find him! I want you to put out an A.P.B. on him right now!" He tossed the microphone onto the back seat of the car. "They lost him!" he said. "They lost him! And you want to know how? Our tail sees Mr. Welles leave his house in his Rolls and follows him right down into Beverly Hills to the parking lot at his building. Mr. Welles takes out a card key and inserts said card key in a mechanical device, thus gaining admittance. But at night, said mechanical device is not an arm that goes up and down in the familiar fashion, it is a grill, a fucking grill like in front of a castle, and the goddamn thing down and our man is stuck and by the time he wakes up a janitor to gain access to said building, he ends up alone in a basement parking lot with nothing to tail but a goddamn Rolls Royce. Mr. Welles just never comes back again. Well, haven't you got anything to say?"

"I was thinking of 'Oh, shit!' but you beat me to it."

They walked toward the cliff, watching the men preparing to hoist equipment down over the precipice. Brandt came running toward Valdez. The two men walked a few steps away, Brandt talking to him in a low voice, both of them oblivious of the fact that a mechanic with an acetylene torch had now been lifted into the air and hung suspended over their heads for a moment; then, he was swung out over the cliffside and lowered swiftly into the chasm. Valdez nodded and strode toward Dade. He put his hands on his hips and spoke in a scarcely audible voice. "We've got a problem."

He nodded toward a station wagon with a big sign reading PRESS which had just pulled up. A photographer was scrambling out, getting his gear together, stringing cameras and leather pouches over his shoulders while behind him the competition in the form of a mobile TV unit was now parking and a man with a handheld minicam was hurrying forward.

"Wife doesn't know yet. We have to send somebody over to tell her. I wondered if you—?" He looked steadily at Dade. Dade's eyes swiveled toward the press, then he gave Valdez a nod of agreement. Dade went over and climbed into a squad car. He gave the driver the Ransohoff address and they roared north, lights flashing and siren blaring as before, shot through the tunnel and sped through the rest of the canyon to the Ventura Freeway, where they headed east on the wide ribbon of concrete at the foot of the Santa Monica mountains separating them from the Los Angeles basin, to their left, the huge San Fernando Valley, unusually clear that day because of the winds, with the high range of the San Gabriels, some of them snowcapped, bordering the valley on the north. At the San Diego Freeway, they swung south, climbing up through the pass. At Sunset, the driver turned east and, weaving his way as fast as he could through the never-ending traffic, drove the couple of miles to the gates of Bel Air and then roared up Bellagio, siren wailing.

Dade leaned forward and tapped him on the shoulder. "Shut that thing off, will you?" Startled, the driver reacted, and flicked two switches. The sound of the siren died, like a toy running down. The driver parked the squad car at the curb, discreetly sliding it alongside a hedge of pittosporum.

As Dade started up the stairs, he saw a car in the driveway: Rachel's. He rang the bell. But when the door swung back, it was neither Chloe nor Rachel who answered it. He found himself looking into Nettie's face.

XXVI

"Dade," she said. "Come on in. It's so terrible." It took Dade a moment or two to realize that she meant Gil's disappearance. Then she caught sight of the squad car. Turning slowly to Dade, she said in a toneless voice that was less question than statement of fact, "They found him."

"Yes," Dade said.

"Is he dead?"

"Yes."

"Oh, my God! What happened?"

"We're not sure yet, Nettie."

"Where did they find him?" She glanced apprehensively behind her at a closed door.

"At the bottom of a cliff. In Malibu."

"Oh, no!"

Somewhere, a door opened and Chloe came down the hall, saying, "Nettie? Who was—?" She broke off, seeing Dade. She looked at them blankly. Nobody said anything for a moment. Chloe turned at the sound of footsteps behind her. Rachel came down the hall. The silence lengthened. Chloe, slim in black slacks and a black pullover and seeming almost as young as Rachel, put a distracted hand to her smooth blond hair and looked at all of them in turn.

The expression drained from the porcelain face. She took a step toward Dade, stretching out her hand and touching him lightly, giving him a tremulous little smile, as if she knew that he was the bearer of ill tidings but that the tidings, like a punishment reserved for a child, could be softened by Dade himself, if he chose, so that she must be careful how she addressed him. The glossy lips parted. She tried to speak. No sound came out.

She looked around at the others with the same smile, then looked back at Dade, still trying to speak, but now there was the glisten of tears rising and welling in the china-blue eyes. Suddenly she could bear it no longer and with a ragged cry of "Oh, no!"—half-crouching in a woman's self-protective gesture, arms crossed over her breasts, head averted as if to ward off blows—she began to whimper.

Nettie quickly moved to her side, supporting her, Rachel ran to Chloe and took her hand. Chloe began slowly wrestling with them, as if with fate. Her eyes looked beseechingly up at Dade.

"He's not *dead*, is he?" And when Dade nodded, still not saying anything, she broke into wild cries of protest, the two women still holding her, Chloe still struggling to be free. "What happened to him? Please tell me what happened to him!"

"It was an accident," Nettie said soothingly. She put a comforting arm around her shoulders and tried to lead her away, as if she no longer trusted Chloe to be able to stand by herself. Rachel looked to the side. Her expression was unreadable. Nettie said, "Come with me, darling. Come on, please, please come with me."

"But I want to know—"

"He'll come and tell us. Now, let's go sit down." Nettie led her away.

Rachel released Chloe's hand and stood there, head to one side, as if hearing something approaching, something far off but ominous. Her head swung around and she peered up at Dade, as if through a jalousie. "It wasn't an accident, was it?"

"No, honey, it wasn't."

Rachel's swift mind went over everything, he could almost feel it, the way one feels the sudden, delicate brush of a blind man's fingers across one's face.

From the other room, they heard Nettie's voice calling. Dade hurried down the hall, Rachel following him.

Chloe sat in the middle of a small French sofa, Nettie beside her, holding her hand tightly, pressing it flat against the down cushion with both of hers. Rachel immediately sat on her other side, an arm around her. Chloe's eyes were blank, staring straight ahead. She began to shiver violently.

Dade found a decanter and quickly poured her a drink, holding it to her lips, making her swallow it, murmuring to her. He said in a slow, offhand voice, "Doctors say brandy don't do no good. They've made tests, see. Myself, I've never known how these tests were conducted. I happen to think it's the sovereign remedy. Here you are, take another swallow now."

Chloe relaxed a bit, sitting back and closing her eyes, the two women still holding on to her. She no longer struggled but gave herself up now to their creature comfort. Dade watched her, waiting for another shock of realization to jolt her back again to reality. There was no way of banishing pain. It would have to wear away.

He pulled over a petit-point footstool and sat down in front of her. She opened her eyes, looking at him with a trace of apprehension, as if perhaps he were going to bring her more bad news.

He said gently, "Why don't we just let them excuse us for a minute and you and me have us a word together, okay?" Chloe nodded dumbly. Nettie and Rachel rose slowly, patting Chloe's hands reassuringly. They left the room.

Dade moved to a seat beside Chloe and took her hand. It was limp and cold. "See, I got to tell you what happened, so's you don't end up reading it first in the paper or some such thing."

She said in an unnaturally low tone, as if having trouble finding her voice, "Then, there's more. I thought there was more."

"Now, I want you to be brave. Can you do that for me?" She nodded. "His car went over a cliff, but he was shot first."

"He was what?"

"He was shot." She seemed unable to absorb what he had said. "Somebody shot him? They say somebody *shot* him?" She repeated the words as one repeats a rumor. She looked around, as if trying to orient herself. "Who shot him?"

"The sheriff, he's just started his investigation—"

"He's dead?" It hit her all over again. Her voice was a wail.

"Chloe, I'm so sorry to tell you this."

"Oh, help me, please!"

"I'll do all I can."

"Who did it? Who did it?"

"We'll try to find out. You up to answering a few questions?"

"Yes. Yes, I want to help."

He took her hands. "I want you to cast your mind back for a moment—now, I know this is a painful subject for you—but I want you to think back to that night of the big storm, the night Miriam was killed." The ghost of an expression passed across her face, as slight as a wind scattering leaves in the garden, and then it was gone. Dade couldn't be sure but it seemed to him almost malevolent.

Now the porcelain face was expressionless again. Dade said almost casually, "You remember, you told me about your husband's coming home and how you pretended to be asleep in bed?" Her only reply was a slight nod. "But you saw him come home. You were looking out the window and you saw his car. Did he get out of the car?"

"No. He drove right into the garage."

"Did he bring anything home with him?"

"I didn't see anything."

"When he came into the bedroom, was he carrying anything, anything at all?"

"No."

"After he came home, did he come right upstairs?"

She tried to think, started to say something and then shrugged and answered, "I don't know. I suppose so."

"You were in bed?"

"Yes."

"You were waiting for him to come upstairs and find you in bed, so that he'd think you'd been asleep the whole time."

"Yes."

"Can you hear the garage door open and close from the bedroom?"

"Yes." She remembered now. "Yes, I heard it close."

"Can you hear the car motor?"

"I heard him shut off the motor." There was life in her eyes now and the hand Dade had been holding suddenly tensed. She lifted it, gesturing, trying to remember something, as if the act of remembering might somehow mean reprieve, might change the past. She said, "I heard him shut off the motor and I waited to hear the back door. I didn't hear it for a few minutes. I worried, about whether something had happened to him, about why he was just sitting in the car. I almost went down to him. I forgot that, I'm sorry. Then, I heard his key in the lock and after that, he came upstairs very quietly and into the bedroom."

"Tell me what he did then."

"He got undressed and came to bed."

"How did he look?"

"I didn't look at him. I was pretending to be asleep."

"Describe what he did. Take it slow, now. Go step by step."

She drew her brows together in an effort to remember. "He closed the door quietly and I could hear him throwing down his things, pulling off his jacket and then starting to get undressed."

"What things was he throwing down?"

"Well, you know, his jacket——"

"You said that first he threw down his things and then pulled off his jacket. What things did you mean?"

"Well, I guess his hat and his raincoat."

"He wore those upstairs to the bedroom?" Dade looked at her closely. "On the night of a storm, when they would have been dripping wet?"

She shook her head impatiently. "I shouldn't have said that. I don't know what I was thinking of. No, he always hung his coat and his hat on the hall tree. He was very methodical."

"In other words, if he went out wearing a hat or a raincoat or carrying an umbrella, he always left those things on the hall tree?"

"That's right."

"Did he ever leave anything else there?"

"No, he always brought his brief case upstairs."

"Is that what you heard him throw down?"

"I suppose so."

"What was he doing with his brief case?"

"Have you ever seen a doctor or a lawyer without a brief case?"

"But he wasn't coming home from the office."

"No." She looked at him sharply. "Why does it matter?"

"Where is the brief case now?"

"I—I don't know."

"You haven't seen it?"

"No. I suppose he took it with him—when he went." At the memory, she was close to tears again. Dade patted her hand. She said, trying to explain, "He had a lot of personal things in it. He never went out without it. It was always in the car when he went out."

"But see here, what you're telling me is, he locked himself in the bathroom, turned on the water so you'd think he was still there and then climbed out the window with his brief case."

She put her slender fingers to her forehead, frowning slightly. "Maybe he put it in the car first."

"But he didn't leave here in his own car. He went on foot, remember?"

"I don't know why you're asking me all this!" she lashed out suddenly, bright spots of anger in her cheeks. "What do you want?"

He patted her hand in a gentle, apologetic way, then got to his feet. "The sheriff, he'll be around asking questions. Sometimes, it helps to get things straight first. I'll call the others." Dade excused himself and walked into the hall. He could hear voices through an open door.

Nettie and Rachel were sitting in the breakfast room. Rachel said, "I'll go back in to her." She went out quickly.

Nettie said in a composed voice, "Someone should stay with her. She shouldn't be left alone at a time like this."

"Yes, I think you're quite right," Dade answered.

"I called the sheriff's. We have to make funeral arrangements and it's difficult when you don't know how long before they release the body."

"Are you going to make them?" Dade asked her.

"Yes, I am." Her two-colored eyes met his gravely. Rachel's voice called to her. "Excuse me," she said. She left the room.

In the hall, Dade could see Rachel whispering with Nettie. Rachel took Nettie's arm and led her toward Dade, half whispering to him, "I was just telling Nettie she says she wants to be alone but I don't think that's good."

Dade said, "I think she ought to get herself away from this house, don't you?"

"Sometimes it's better to stay and face things," Nettie said.

Dade shook his head. "In this case, that's going to mean reporters. Myself, I think she ought to go stay with her people. She's got family here, hasn't she?"

Nettie was doubtful. "Well, they're very social and they never really approved of Gil, so I don't know whether she'd be comfortable there."

"They have to be told," Dade pointed out.

"Yes. Do you want me to call them?" Rachel asked.

"I think that's a good idea," Dade replied.

Rachel said, "I'll go talk to her about it." She left the room.

Dade turned to Nettie. "That car they found him in. We got word it was registered to you."

She looked at him with her frank Parisian stare. "I lent it to him."

"Mind telling me why?"

"He came to me for help. He said the police were after him. He said they thought he'd killed Miriam. He swore to me that he hadn't but that he knew who had and he had ways of forcing that person to help him."

"That all he said?"

"We had no time. He was afraid the police would come looking for him at my apartment. He was running out to the car. I ran after him. I tried to stop him. I told him that you don't go cornering murderers, but he wouldn't listen. He just drove away and *pouf*! he was killed. My poor dear Gil. Well, he wouldn't listen—"

Rachel came back into the room. "She says she'll go."

Nettie said, "I'll go back in to her." She went out.

Dade said to Rachel, "I want you to pack her things and get her out of here. In the next hour, understand?" She nodded. "Come to think of it, what are you doing here?"

"I called Chloe this morning, just to see how things were, and when I heard Gil was missing, well, I came right over. I just had to."

"I understand."

"I haven't called anyone else, not even Nick."

"It's all right, Rachel. Now, as soon as they pick Chloe up, I want you to get back into your car and skedaddle out to Old Aunt Mary's or whoever the hell she is and stay there until I call you." He shook a warning finger at her and started out.

Rachel opened the front door for him, then set the latch and followed him outside, closing the door behind her.

He turned, thinking she had something to tell him privately but all she did was put her arms around him. He embraced her, stroking her hair.

"Dade?" she said. She searched his face.

"Yes, honey?"

"Where is my father? Do you know?"

He shook his head. "No, Rachel, I don't."

A gust of wind blew her red hair across her face. She brushed it away. "Nettie said they were looking for him. The police, I mean. I heard her tell Chloe."

"Yes, Rachel, I know they are."

"Why, Dade?"

"They just want to ask him some questions."

She turned away, frowning. Then, facing him, she said, "I'm going back to the house and wait for him. After I get Chloe settled, I'll go to the apartment and pick up some things and go back to the house. That's the thing to do."

"Are you sure?"

"Yes. I should just be there." She made an awkward gesture. "If he tries to reach me—"

"All right."

XXVII

At six-thirty, Dade was back at the inn. Ellen met him at the door of their room and put her arms around him, saying, "Oh, God, how *awful*!"

"Yeah." He walked out onto the deck, looking up at the first stars of dusk. He pointed, saying, "Honey, what color's that sky?"

"I'd say violet."

"Yeah. That's what I thought. Not often you see a sky that color. Kind of a watercolor palette they got down here." He took a deep breath. "I warned him, honey."

"I know," she said.

"He wouldn't listen." He started to say something and she shushed him, taking his arm and leading him down onto the beach and making him sit in the sand. She took off his shoes and socks. "I was going to take me a bath."

"You don't need a bath." He sighed. She asked, "What was he doing in Nettie's car?" He repeated what Nettie had said. She said wonderingly, "How did he ever figure out who had killed her?"

"I don't know."

"You know, if he'd only told Nettie the name of that someone."

"Yes. Unless of course that someone was Nettie."

"Oh, for God's sake, Dade!"

"Well, you asked." He looked out at the wide dark expanse of beach, at the dark cardboard mountains, two-dimensional against the pale evening sky. "Pretty country." He hugged her to him, gradually relaxing, letting his eyes wander across the unbroken horizon. A yacht stood at an-

chor off the coast. It was strung with lights and the crew
was scrambling in the rigging, furling the sails. He said, "I
ever tell you this place sold for ten cents an acre back in
1857?"

"No."

"You want Chinese? Szechuan? That vinegar-based soup
and the duck smoked with tea leaves and roasted over
cedar?"

"Nope."

"What do you want, Ellen?"

"Lobster."

"Where?"

"Here. It's going to rain. Isn't that wonderful? I bought
the lobsters."

"Show me."

"They're in the tub. We'll have a fire and watch *The
Maltese Falcon.* It's on tonight. Very late."

"How soon's dinner?"

"You tell me." They went back inside. He stomped into
the bathroom. When he came out again, buttoning himself
into a fresh shirt, it had started to rain. His face changed.

Picking up the phone, he called the Welles house. When
Rosarita answered, he told her his name and said he
wanted to come up and look at something in the house.
"I'm Mrs. Welles' executor," he said in slow Spanish,
"*abogado. Comprende?*"

"*Sí, señor.*"

He put down the phone, pulling on his raincoat.

"You're not going out again!"

"Just for half an hour."

"But it's raining!"

"I've got to find something out."

"What?"

"Jensen's a rich man. If he wanted to disappear, he
could afford to walk out of that house with nothing. Except for one thing. His code key. Without it, he'd be in a
lot of trouble. Now, I happen to know where he kept it.
And I want to know if he took it with him." He hurried
out.

As he left the inn, the rain got harder. He timed the
drive to the Welles house. It was, as Pete had said, just ex-

actly ten minutes. The clean, straight downpour was lit by the glow from the windows. Rosarita let him in.

"I want to go up to Mr. Welles' room, if you don't mind."

She looked at him uncertainly for a moment, then said. "The *señor* is away."

"Yes, I know. I just want to see his room." Not waiting for an answer, Dade strode toward the stairway, Rosarita following him, twisting her hands.

"Maybe you come back another time, *señor*?" she said.

"This won't wait," he answered briefly. He went up the stairs two at a time, Rosarita running along after him. At the top of the stairs to the right was Jensen's room. He opened the door.

The room was in perfect order. The bed was made. It was carved oak, a fourposter with a carved wooden canopy. The heavy red velvet draperies were drawn and he sensed that, behind them, the shutters were closed. The room contained very little furniture, only a carved oak armchair, a carved armoire and what looked like an Irish hunt breakfast table which served as a desk. It was made in the shape of a horseshoe and behind it was a tall, uncomfortable-looking oak chair, also heavily carved.

Dade went over to the desk. It contained one drawer, facing the chair which stood in the desk well. The drawer was secured by an old-fashioned lock. He looked in Jensen's bathroom, found a pair of tweezers and a nail file and, while Rosarita watched uneasily, picked the lock and opened the drawer. It contained only a few letters and mementos, nothing even remotely resembling a code key. Closing the drawer, he stared into space for a moment.

Then, abstracted, his eyes half closed, he opened the door connecting Jensen's room with Miriam's. Her bed was to the right of the door, near the windows. Standing where he was, he could not see it. He walked into her room and looked around and saw the down comforter neatly folded at the foot of the carved quattrocento bed, the heavy draperies drawn. The dark ornate furniture was dusted and polished. It gleamed in the lamplight. The soft colors of the antique Kirman rug glowed up at him. Everything was in readiness, as if the room itself expected Miriam, waited for her.

Dade stood there for some moments. Rosarita waited patiently, hands folded. Finally he went out the door of Miriam's room, Rosarita following, and into the upper hall.

He looked around, remembering the basic design of the upstairs. Miriam's and Jensen's bedrooms were in the center. Beyond Jensen's was Jensen's study and after that a service staircase gave access to the kitchen and Rosarita's bedroom. Turning, he walked past Miriam's bedroom, Rachel's old room and a guest room—and two other guest rooms across the hall—toward Miriam's study over the game room at the end of the hall, then turned a corner and went down the stairs to the rear hall which led to the garage.

Just then, the phone rang and Rosarita hurried away to answer it. He walked on down to the game room. As he went into the room, suddenly there was a sharp bang! at the plate glass window. He reacted, saw that it was a bird which had flown into it and now lay stunned on the lawn just outside, its head to one side. Picking up a bell on the bar, he rang it and Rosarita came in the room. She gave him a sudden, lovely smile.

"You people have a cat?" he asked.

"A cat?" she frowned.

"Yes. Is there a cat on the premises?"

"The red cat, *señor*?"

"Any cat. You see, there's that bird out there—" She followed his eyes to the window. "Ran into the window." He pantomimed a blow to the head.

A quick intake of breath showed him that she understood. She went out a side door, gathered up the stunned bird and came back into the house with it.

Dade said, following her, "You put it in your room and it'll come to and fly all over the place."

"Garage," she said briefly. He followed her down the back hall and through a door into the garage where she set the bird down on the concrete floor and opened a window giving onto a cliff over the sea, gesturing at it and wiping her hands dry with her skirt.

"You are a very resourceful woman," he said to her. He wasn't sure whether she understood him but she knew that he had paid her a compliment and she rewarded him with a dark, luminous smile.

He hesitated, seeing something. A buff-colored raincoat hung on a peg, a hooded Burberry. He examined it. There were faint brownish stains on the front: bloodstains.

"Is the one she wear that night, *señor*," she said softly. Dade nodded. He searched the pockets, finding a button. Jensen Welles' name was inked on the label of an inside pocket. He put the button back where he had found it.

"Nobody say have it cleaned."

He turned away slowly. She held the door into the house open for him. He glanced around the garage, empty now except for Miriam's car, then accompanied Rosarita back into the house. He stood in the rear hall, an abstracted look on his face.

The phone rang again. Rosarita excused herself and went off to answer it. Dade went back into the game room. He started toward the gallery, intending to let himself out, when Rosarita came into the room, gesturing. She picked up a phone on the bar and offered it to him. "You talk. This man, he does not understand me. Twice now he calls."

Dade took the receiver and said into it, "My name is Cooley. Can I help you with something?"

A man's voice said, "Mr. Welles there?"

"Not at the present."

"This here's Fred Dix. You know if he's expecting me tonight?"

"As I say, he's not here. I wonder if you can tell me—?"

"Thank you so much." Click.

He said good night to Rosarita and walked out to the car. He looked up at the dark sky. The rain had stopped. The skies were washed clean and a sickle moon showed him shreds of cloud and polished stars. He got into the car, sighing. Then, squaring his shoulders, he took a deep breath and drove back to the inn.

In the parking lot, he ran into Pete, who was bringing a large pot from the kitchen down to Ellen.

"I found out," Pete said. "They give me my job back

because some big guy's wife called up." Pete grinned at him knowingly.

They got into the funicular together and started down. Dade said, "You've been a great help and when my business here is done, I'll buy you a drink. I'll show you how to make an Old Fashioned."

"I don't drink alcoholic beverages."

"Not at all?"

"No, sir."

"Oh, that's very bad."

"It is?"

"It's the nondrinkers who become alcoholics. Proven fact."

"I never heard that."

"Time somebody told you."

"I don't understand it."

"I'll explain it to you. A gentleman, he knows his capacity. But nondrinkers never give themselves any chance to find out, and that's why they end up the way they do. Talk to any alcoholic and you'll find that, once upon a time, he started life as a bona fide nondrinker."

Ellen opened the door, Pete handed her the pot, waved good night and ran off.

Dade came in, grim-faced.

"Was it there?"

"No."

"Oh, Dade."

"I'll tell you something. I almost wish it had been. As is . . ." He trailed off.

"Valdez called. He's on his way over."

Dade mixed himself an Old Fashioned and sat down in front of the fire Ellen had built for him. The phone rang. A voice said, "This is Mary at the desk. The sheriff is in the lobby."

"Just go with him quietly." There was a loud click in his ear followed by a buzzing sound. Dade put down the phone, sipped his drink and then went to the door and let in Valdez. Dade gave him his imitation of an old lady's smile. "Well, what brings you to visit a lonely old shut-in at this hour?"

"Just cut the crap."

"Manners, manners," Ellen murmured from across the passthrough.

Valdez mumbled an apology, then turned on Dade: "Okay, we're ready to hear Welles' proposition."

"You speak as if I were in touch with him, Lieutenant."

"I'm just saying, should you happen to find yourself in communication with Mr. Welles—say, just after I leave here—give him a little message for me, will you do that?"

"What message?"

"Tell him we've identified the murder weapon."

"I think you'd better explain that."

"Gil Ransohoff was shot at close range with a thirty-eight. Bullet entered the right ear, traveling through the brain. Killed him instantly. Bullet itself was recovered from brain-case of deceased. Only one shot was fired. Bullet was given routine test by ballistics. Jensen Welles, Mr. Cooley, was a crack shot."

"You have not been describing a triumph of marksmanship."

"Just hear me out, please. It is well-known that Jensen Welles is an excellent marksman. What is perhaps not so well known is that he has a target-practice range in the basement of that big house. Quite an impressive collection of guns as well, all oiled, all in their cases mounted on the walls. Our men went through that place with a fine-toothed comb. They gathered together all the thirty-eight slugs from the targets and ran checks on every thirty-eight in the place. Among those slugs, ballistics found a number that matched up with the slug they dug out of Ransohoff. And they couldn't find a gun there which fired those matching slugs. You see my point?"

"That doesn't prove that the missing gun is the murder weapon. All you're telling me is that the gun which killed Ransohoff was once fired in the basement of the Welles house, on a target-practice range to which he might have invited anyone. If that were the case and his guest brought his own gun, that would explain why no gun matches those slugs." Dade's eyes flickered over the lieutenant's face.

Valdez nodded somberly. "Yeah. Excepting that there's

an empty gun case on the wall, just the size of a Webly thirty-eight."

"I see. That doesn't mean the missing gun is the presumed murder weapon."

"Nice try. I can't blame you for trying. But I'm afraid it's a pretty damaging case."

"All right, let's say the murder weapon was taken from the collection of Jensen Welles. You haven't yet been able to show who took it."

"In other words, you'd like us to catch Mr. Welles in the act of firing the same gun at someone else?"

"I'd like you to be sure of your ground. By the way, what was the motive?"

"It goes like this. Welles tumbled to his wife's game, caught her about to run off with the painting and killed her on the spot. He hid the painting, and when we called it an accident he figured nobody would ever know. Ransohoff figured it out and tried to brace Welles for a ton of money to keep his mouth shut—and Welles shut it for him for good. We know his game now. Welles', I mean. Welles figures he can plea bargain with that painting. Ten million dollars' worth of French national art treasure could buy him a lesser charge, that's his thinking, right? Wrong. I've been authorized by the D.A. to say, No deal."

There was a loud knocking at the door. Dade called out, "Come in."

The door banged open and Brandt burst into the room, breathless. He looked as if it were a stronghold he had just stormed. Then, to Valdez, he said, "It's that kid! The Greek!" Seeing their blank faces, he said, "The boyfriend! Levin, his name is."

"Russian," Dade said.

"That big guy works out all the time I'm talking about. Called up. Got me on the phone—now, just listen to this—and said the old man showed up at his apartment with a gun and tried to kill him, the kid lit out, promised to wait for us, we tore ass and got up there in five minutes—some bar where he called from—but he cut out of there—bartender remembers him—and I'll put my pee-pee on the line, that ties this thing up, Jesus Christ, lady, I just didn't see you." The sunburned face got redder. Turning to Valdez, Brandt said, "We went to the house figuring Welles had sneaked back. Maid let us in. We searched it again. Nothing. I thought maybe that lawyer had tried to reach him and maybe he did because she says some man called him twice tonight."

"That was a Mr. Dix," Dade said. "I was there both times. Mr. Dix does not talk like the Harvard Law School."

"Well, who is he?" Valdez asked.

Ellen said, "He's the Pinkerton man." They looked at her. "I saw his name on his badge that night we were there. I remembered because I thought of Richard Dix."

With a quick intake of breath, Dade seized the phone book, looked up Pinkerton's, dialed a number and asked for Mr. Dix.

"This is Dix," a voice said.

"My name is Cooley. I talked to you tonight when you called the Welles house."

"Mr. Welles, he ready for me now?"

"He said he wanted you?"

"Yes, sir, he did. He called last night."

"When?"

"Eight-thirty, sir. Asked me to be at the house last night at nine o'clock. When I got there, nobody was home. I waited in the car until ten P.M. but he didn't show up. That's why I called. I thought maybe he meant tonight."

"It's not tonight, either, Mr. Dix. But thank you very much." Dade put down the phone. The others were all staring at him.

Ellen said, "Why on earth call a Pinkerton man when he was by himself?"

"That's exactly the reason," Dade said. "There were no servants. Rosarita had the night off. He's got all his finest things in that lock room and he wasn't fool enough to have it open when he was alone in the house." Dade turned to Valdez. "But something else bothers me. Does it strike you as odd that Welles made an appointment at eight-thirty and then decided instead to shoot his wife's lover and went barreling out of there ten minutes later?" Valdez and Brandt exchanged looks. "When did you last search that lock room?" Dade asked.

"Well, the insurance people were in there Wednesday—" Brandt said.

Dade turned to Valdez. "Search it now," he said.

Valdez grabbed for the phone.

XXVIII

When Dade and Ellen arrived at the Welles house, the lights were on and the house was conspicuous by the flashing blue and red glow from a squad car's slowly revolving turret. Lieutenant Valdez met them at the door with a deputy, ushering them into the hall and then down the wide gallery to the library.

Valdez said, "Maid's in her room. Thought she might know something, but she doesn't. Spent Friday and Saturday nights in town with her family. Been here since this morning. We called the attorney for the combination. He's on his way."

Ten minutes later, Ballinger arrived. His thin iron-gray hair was carefully brushed, the thick lips were drawn into a reproving line, the protuberant eyes behind the thick glasses had a moist, injured look. He wore a pin-striped gray suit with a vest and a muted tie. His black shoes were not the fashionable slipons everyone wore but were laced and had closed vents. Everything about him was conservative except for his fingernails, which were not only highly polished but slightly rouged. On the little finger of his left hand, he wore a platinum ring set with a diamond. Dade felt an impulse to tap it with a forefinger and shake his head.

Ballinger said in a dry voice reminiscent of old papers rustling, which immediately told everyone he was not a trial lawyer, "I think we ought to have a court order."

"Why is that?" asked Dade.

"This is private property, sir. I don't have the authority—"

"The law gives you authority in cases where you must act to prevent a crime."

"Courts are divided on that interpretation. Myself, I see no probable cause of crime."

"You opened the lock room the day after the death of Mrs. Welles in compliance with a request from the insurance company as part of a general search of the premises, to see whether anything was missing."

"That search has already been conducted."

"But not concluded. Now, as the executor for Miriam Welles, I have decided that it is in the best interest of my late client's estate to open that lock room."

"You will assume all responsibility for this, sir." Ballinger glanced around at the others, to make sure they had heard this.

Dade crossed to the center of the wall at one end of the room, where he stood waiting. Surrendering, Ballinger followed him, touching the corner of a gilt-framed portrait of a young girl hung on the wall. It swung out, revealing the recessed dial and handle of the lock-room door. Ballinger took a slip of paper from a vest pocket and, studying the numbers, turned the big dial to the right, stopping at a number. The three deputies, the lieutenant and Ellen watched this performance. Behind them, Rosarita entered the room quietly, and stood at the door, waiting.

Ballinger now turned the dial carefully to the left, glancing at his paper again. He turned the dial one more time, then slowly put the slip of paper back into his vest pocket, grasped the handle and pressed it down. That part of the wallpapered wall with the girl's portrait on it now revealed itself as a door. Ballinger swung it open. Inside, a spotlight was on, shining toward them. A Chinese screen cut off their view. Over it, they could see a large room bathed in the glow from the spotlight.

There was a handle on the inside of the door. Valdez pointed at it and threw an inquiring look at Ballinger, who said, "He sometimes works in here. That was installed so he wouldn't be disturbed."

The lieutenant had taken out his gun. Motioning all of them back, he said in a loud voice, "This is the sheriff. Jensen Welles, if you're in there I want you to come out with your hands raised. Otherwise, we're coming in after you. I will count to ten." He began counting.

Ignoring him, Dade pushed by him and entered the room, making his way around the lacquered screen. Valdez, still counting, reached out to grab him but Dade was too quick for him.

In the hollow square of the center of the big lock room stood an easel with a canvas on it, its back to the door. Now, he caught sight of the painting for the first time. It was a portrait of a young woman, scarcely more than a girl. Dade thought of Danaë, whom Zeus had visited in a shower of gold. The shawl worn over her dark hair and her full shoulders, a shawl fine as Egyptian linen, was all dusted with dull gold. The necklace was gold. The huge silken sleeves were slashed with gold. The baroque pearl clasp which held the shawl to her hair was set in thick gold. And under the spreading dark wings of the thick soft hair, her complexion was suffused with the glow of gold, as if she had been painted sitting in a room sparkling with treasure. The expression itself was extraordinary. The young girl's lips seemed to tremble in apprehension, and the pupils of the large dark eyes were dilated with excitement. A long-fingered hand touched her breast as if she were about to protest her innocence. She was a woman taken by surprise. It was Raphael's "La Fornarina."

And there, apparently lost in contemplation before this vision, was Jensen Welles. He was sitting in a velvet wing chair. At his right elbow, a very small Duncan Phyfe candle table had been tipped over and a large brandy snifter now lay on the floor on the Shiraz rug, its contents spilled except for a small amber pool at the bottom of the bell. Jensen's head rested in the corner of the chair back. The eyes stared not at the painting but at Dade's shoes, as if Jensen had known that this was going to come, as if he now acknowledged defeat, as if he had known that this was how it must end. The adjustable spotlight on the stand behind him was aimed over his head, so that although it bathed the painting and the open doorway of the lock room behind it in a warm glow, it shadowed Jensen, even played tricks with his sardonic expression, deepening the ironic lines around the mouth, so that it was not until

Dade took another step that he could see the neat bullet hole in the temple, the thin line of blood. A gun lay on the floor just below his right hand.

Dade turned. The lieutenant was standing beside him, Brandt next to him. Seeing Ballinger about to enter, Valdez said, "Everybody out. Seal off this room. Get the camera crew up here and the fingerprint men before we do anything else." Dade walked out, Valdez beside him. Brandt was telling the others in a low voice what had happened. All of them went into the breakfast room and had coffee in silence.

Dade tried to reach Rachel at the number she had given him where she had been staying in San Marino and at her apartment. Neither number answered. Finally, they went back into the library.

Suddenly the room had come to life. The fingerprint men had arrived and were dusting the furniture. A photographer loaded down with equipment bustled in from the hall, the coroner was unpacking his bag and a young black deputy with the shoulders of a football player ran in and said, "Lieutenant, the media people are here."

"Keep them out. No questions, no answers." The deputy ran back out and they could hear him calling out the lieutenant's instructions. Valdez turned to Dade, and said, "I guess there's no point in your hanging around."

Ballinger swayed on his feet, looking pale. He sat down in a tufted armchair. Seeing this, Valdez gestured and said, "Hey! Somebody help him!" A deputy ran over and held his arm. The coroner pulled what looked like a small roll of gauze out of his bag and went over to Ballinger, breaking the thing in one hand and holding it under his nose. The smell of ammonia fumes filled the room. Valdez said to the deputies, "Okay, it's a wrap."

Dade said, "Is it?"

"Christ, we've just been handed a confession. At least that's how I read it. We'll review it, of course, before we go on record."

"I'll be grateful if you'll let me know your findings." Valdez gave Ellen and Dade a nod and was about to go back into the lock room when Dade touched his arm, saying, "Meanwhile, I remind you that that painting in there remains my responsibility."

"Don't you ever give up?"

Dade and Ellen walked to the door, Valdez accompanying them.

Rosarita was standing there, hands folded over her apron, face impassive. Valdez touched her arm. *"Hola!"* he said. She nodded mutely. *"Lo siento,"* he said. She nodded vigorously then turned away, but not before they had caught the glint of tears in her dark eyes.

Valdez said to Dade, "See, I knew you could find him if you wanted to."

The coroner came up to Valdez and said, "Any of your guys knock that glass over?" At a look from Valdez, the coroner said impatiently, "All right, I didn't think so. It looks to me as if the stuff might have spilled on his hand, which would tend to screw up a gun-residue test but I don't think we're going to need one. That's all until I get him downtown. Talk to me tomorrow. Late."

"Tonight," Valdez said.

"It's still Sunday, lieutenant."

"You put somebody on it. Priority. That's downtown talking."

"What are we supposed to be looking for?"

"You tell me."

"Guy's dead of a gunshot wound," said the coroner. "Self-inflicted. What is it, lieutenant? You think somebody poisoned him or drugged him? It's nothing like that. I'll do your P.M. I'll do it, I'll do it. But I'm telling you right now you'll come up with nothing."

"How about the time of death? Want to give me a guess?"

"Sometime last night. Room's air-conditioned. On the cold side, you know what I mean? Could be anywhere between eight and twelve."

"It wasn't eight," Valdez said.

"All right, so you already know, so don't ask me. Maybe I can come closer after I open him up, but right now I doubt it." He gestured. "Tell the photoplay boys to hurry it up. They've got more than they need and I don't want to be up all night long." The coroner gave them a brusque nod and strode out the door.

"Sons of bitches," Valdez said. "I mean it. All the M.E.s I've ever known. And the same goes for the lawyers." He caught himself. "No hard feelings, okay?"

"No hard feelings," Dade said. He caught sight of Jensen's belongings, which had been taken out of his pockets and laid on a table. Among them Dade saw what looked like a metallic credit card engraved with a sequence of numbers.

Valdez squinted at it. "What is that?"

"A code key."

"Come again?"

"From the way it looks, he never went back upstairs."

"Pardon me?"

"Nothing." Dade seemed lost in thought.

"What is it?" Ellen said.

He shook his head. Something bothered him. He couldn't say what it was. Turning, her arm still in his, he headed back down the hall toward the library, calling out to Valdez, "I want to see something in there."

"Go ahead," Valdez said.

Dade went back into the lock room, crowding past fingerprint men and the camera crew. Dade stopped in front of the Raphael. He frowned.

Valdez said, "What's the matter?"

Dade squinted at the scene, at the painting which stood on the lighted easel in the otherwise dim room, incongruously placed so that the spotlight over Jensen's head spilled over the gilded frame of the Raphael and onto the metal door of the lock room and wall of the adjacent metal storage cabinets visible above the Chinese screen.

Valdez said again, "What's the matter?"

Dade said, "I don't know what the hell I came back in here for." He started out, then hesitated, turning to Ellen. "You know something," he said, pointing. "There's the Botticelli. And with all this"—he searched for a descriptive word and couldn't find one—"with all *this* going on, I just realized something. We haven't even gotten a look at it. It'll probably outlast all our sorrows and we've never seen it."

Valdez turned to the photographers and fingerprint men and, gesturing at the Raphael said, "Can I move this?"

Two gloved technicians came forward and wordlessly lifted the painting from the easel, set it down carefully and then lifted the Botticelli from its hooks. They carried it over and placed it on the easel in front of Jensen's body. It was a much larger painting and they held on to it afterward to make quite sure it was balanced on the stand, then stepped back.

Dade looked at the Botticelli. This was not the Venus of the Primavera nor was it the Venus of the Birth. It did not really seem like a Venus at all. Instead, it was as if Botticelli had anticipated Lourdes, and what one now saw was the Virgin through the eyes of the astonished children.

Dade turned to Ellen.

"What do you think, honey? Just fills the room, doesn't it? When it's there, I can't seem to see anything else."

"Well, *I* can!" Ellen said with a shocked glance at the body sprawled in the chair. "What's the matter with you?" She took his arm and pulled him out of the room.

They left the house, as an ambulance and several squad cars were just arriving, turret lights rotating slowly. Outside the gates, reporters had begun to gather. Lights had been set up and were turned on as they came out the door. Minicams were lifted and aimed at them from a distance. A horn blew. A deputy made the crowd move to one side. The gates opened and they saw Rachel's car driving toward them. The car stopped and Rachel got out of it carrying her suitcase, looking around bewildered.

Seeing Dade and Ellen, she started toward them, then stopped abruptly when she saw the ambulance. She stood there frozen to the spot for a moment. Then, dropping the suitcase, she lowered her head and ran straight at Dade, arms outstretched. She seized the front of his jacket and began to scream hysterically, "Is it Nick? Is it Nick?"

"No, it's not Nick," he said softly. He took hold of her arms. She sagged in his grasp, letting out a little cry of relief.

"I warned him. He called me at the apartment and told me what had happened, I mean with Dad. I said, 'Go away. Go away until they find him.'" She caught sight of something over her shoulder and the hands on his coat tightened, a look of alarm on her face. He turned and saw the ambulance attendants carrying a stretcher toward the house. Her eyes searched his, fearful, questioning.

"It's your father," he said.

"Is it bad?"

"Yes."

Rachel pressed her hands to her mouth, stifling a whimpering sound.

Ellen said softly, "He's gone, Rachel."

"He's—gone?"

"He's dead," Ellen said. "Come on, sit down." Ellen led her over to a bench in the Japanese garden. Rachel looked back, uncomprehending, at Dade. He followed them.

"How did he die?" Her voice was wondering. She sat down, her eyes round.

Dade answered, "Now, just take it easy."

"Where did they find him?"

"Here," he answered.

"You mean he came back?"

"He was in the lock room," Dade said. "The painting was there."

"The painting," echoed Rachel, as if she did not remember the painting or could not for the moment see any connection. Then she seemed to realize what he was saying and said, "Oh, the painting!" Then the same bewildered look came into her eyes and she asked, "What was he doing in the lock room?"

"He shot himself," Ellen said gently.

"I see." Her face was blank for a moment, then she reacted with disbelief. "He *shot* himself? Then, that means . . ." She trailed off.

"There isn't any way to make it easy," Dade said.

"Why don't you come back to the inn with us?" Ellen said.

Rachel shook her head, asking, "Is he—in there now?"

"Yes." Ellen put an arm around her.

Rachel got up. "I'll go in to him."

"Why do that?" Ellen asked.

"I have to."

"There's no point in it," Dade said. "Don't."

"But it isn't right—just to leave him there!"

"Please don't go in there now," Dade said.

Ellen said, "He wouldn't want you to. Just go up to your room, Rachel. Do you want me to stay with you?"

"No, it's all right." Rachel turned away, a look of disbelief still haunting her eyes. She turned back toward them. "Did he suffer?"

"No," Dade answered.

"Are they sure?"

"He didn't suffer, honey."

"My God. My God." Her voice was expressionless. She started toward the house with them. Rosarita was waiting in the doorway. She came forward and took Rachel's arm. Rachel looked at her and patted her hand, as if Rosarita were the one who needed comforting. Rachel said, "I was sure that if he once got to know Nick—but he's not going to now, is he?" Then she began to cry quietly. "I want Nick!" she kept saying, "I want Nick!"

Ellen went to her and, with Rosarita's help, led her upstairs to her bedroom and put her to bed. Dade went into the bar and poured himself a stiff drink. It was half an hour before Ellen was able to leave Rachel. She came downstairs and took the drink from Dade's hand, helping herself to a large swallow from it. She clutched his arm.

"Let's go home, honey," he said.

"Yes. Oh, God, Dade."

Back at the inn, Dade was uncommunicative.

Ellen said, "It's over."

"Is it?"

"Dade, let go of it." It was almost eleven. She made him get in bed and offered to heat some broth for him. His answer was a low snore. She poured herself some milk, turned out the lights and got into bed. Dade was restless. He tossed and turned and mumbled, half-asleep. She stroked his broad smooth forehead, kissing it.

"Go to sleep," she murmured. "It's all right."

Dade dreamed. He heard a voice speaking. It was rapid, incoherent. He strained to make sense of the words but could not quite hear them. Then he was at a high school performance of *Our Town* with Abigail playing Emily. Miriam was in it with her, playing her mother. After that, he dreamed he was in the stacks at the library, searching for a book. He could not find it. Many books had been checked out and the shelves in that section were almost empty. After that came several brief dreams in rapid succession and he was aware in some part of himself that he was dreaming and that all these dreams were the same dream.

Then he was wide awake. He was thirsty. He got out of bed to get himself a glass of milk and fell over a chair, letting out a yell of pain, grabbing his shin and cursing. Ellen sat up, turning on the tubular reading light over her side of the bed. In the pool of light, he saw the chair lying on its side on the rug and straightened it up. He frowned in thought.

"What is it? Dade?"

"The light." There was a faraway look in his eyes.

"Dade?"

"I said something. About the Botticelli. What was it?"

"I don't know."

He sat down on the edge of the bed, running his fingers through his matted hair. "They put that picture up on the easel for us and I said—what?"

"I think you said something about how beautiful it was." He grunted. She said, getting up, "I'll pour you some milk. Come back to bed." She brought him a full glass and he drained it thirstily, then fell fast asleep and did not dream anymore.

In the morning, Dade had his dip in the ocean, then as Pete entered with breakfast, the phone rang. Dade answered it. "Hello?"

"This here's Motke."

"Hello, Arnie," Dade said, gesturing at Ellen.

"Just set it down here," Ellen said to Pete. He put down the tray and pulled a paperback out of his pocket.

"I can't read this, lady."

"One second, Arnie," Dade said.

"I tried."

"I'll tell him," Ellen said.

"I appreciated it, what he did, and I just want to tell him—" said Pete.

Dade looked at Pete. "Would you excuse me, please?"

"Go right ahead, sir."

Ellen took Pete's arm and led him to the door.

Dade spoke into the phone. "Okay, Arnie, what you got?"

"He's a cute guy. Real cute." Motke's voice had no carrying power at all. When he spoke, the sound seemed to come only from his mouth, with no resonance. Dade pictured him now, the ferret face expressionless, the thin lips scarcely moving. Dade listened, absorbed, as Motke said, "Levin started out with a hundred grand a few months ago. Been doing business all over town with lots of brokers. That's the key to all this. He makes money, all right. Lots of money. But he also loses money."

Instantly suspicious, Dade said, "How much, Arnie?"

"Exactly as much as he makes."

"Jackpot," Dade said, under his breath.

"That's it. Guy bets against himself. Buys puts as well as calls. Can't lose. 'Course, he can't win, neither. That tell you what you wanted to know?"

"That tells me what I didn't want to know." Dade sighed. "See you when we get back to the city, Arnie."

"So long."

Dade put down the phone and began wolfing down toast and bacon.

"What was that all about?" Ellen asked.

He told her, talking with his mouth full. "Surprised?"

"I've never met him, remember. But poor Rachel—you have to tell her, of course."

"Yes." The phone rang again. Valdez identified himself needlessly. Dade growled, "Morning."

"I've got the preliminaries from ballistics and the coroner. Welles killed himself with the same gun used to kill the lover, Gil Ransohoff. We figure it this way: Welles took his car to his office and left it behind that grill to get rid of the tail, picked up a company car there, drove it to Malibu Canyon to meet Ransohoff, then drove down through the canyon to the market. We found it in the parking lot there, which is just beside the creek. He walked on the footpath along the creek down to the ocean at the Colony, then north along the beach back up to his own house. That was so he could sneak back in without our tail spotting him. Must have decided to kill himself then. It tracks, all right. Shoes on the body muddy. Footprints found on the trail matching the shoes. But here's the clincher: Welles is a fastidious man. He must have wiped the frame clean. Only two sets of fingerprints on that painting—Ransohoff's and Welles'. That's it."

"You're going on record saying that?"

"You've got it. I wanted to break it to the daughter first. I mean, to let her know it's official. I just called there. I didn't get to talk to her. She's got two women friends there helping her. Maybe you'd like to tell her for me."

"What friends?"

"Mrs. Ransohoff and that French lady—uh, Mrs. Proulx."

The name Proulx conjured up an image of a gallery in his mind's eye, Nettie's, Jensen's, the lock room, and suddenly the image of the bare stage in *Our Town*. In that instant, he understood his dream.

"Valdez! I want you to meet me there with Tillie Monkhaus. And if her husband's out of the hospital, bring him along. Will you do that, please?"

"Just what the hell for?"

"I also want a wiretap on the house."

"We can't get one and you know it."

"The FBI can. And they're involved because of the art theft. Now, do what I tell you, otherwise those scrambled eggs on your cap are going to end up all over your face." Dade banged down the phone.

XXIX

Ten minutes later when Dade and Ellen got to the Welles house, Rosarita showed them into the breakfast room. Nettie, Chloe and Rachel were at the table together having coffee.

Rachel said, "Thank you for coming. Have you had breakfast?"

"We don't need anything," Ellen said.

"Have something, please," Rachel said. She glanced at Rosarita, who nodded and left the room.

Nettie said, "You're the one who ought to eat something."

"I can't."

"You heard from Nick?" Dade asked. Rachel shook her head. "You know where he is?"

"No."

"How do you plan to get in touch with him?"

"He said he'd call."

"When?"

"Today sometime. This is already on the news, isn't it?"

"No," Chloe said, "but it will be."

"He'll hear it. He'll call as soon as he does."

Ellen changed the subject and began talking about gardening. She continued talking about gardening while Rosarita brought in an omelet platter, sausages and toast, and went on talking about gardening all through breakfast, meanwhile managing to get Rachel to eat.

As they were finishing, Rachel heard the gate bell and rang for Rosarita, who went to the intercom. When she came back, Rachel asked, "Who is it?"

"Is the sheriff, *señorita.*"

"Then we'd better all go into the library," Rachel said, rising.

Chloe said uneasily, "Why is he here?"

"I suppose I have to sign things. You know, so they'll release the body. I don't know." They glanced out the window and saw a couple of squad cars driving toward the house.

Nettie said calmly, "We'll get it over with as soon as possible. Come on." She took Rachel's arm and all of them started to leave the room. Then Nettie hesitated, seeing something. In the driveway, Valdez was approaching, followed by two deputies and a man and a woman. Nettie said, "Isn't that Mrs. Monkhaus? I remember they showed her picture on the news after the shooting." Her husband was with her. He was white and drawn and he clutched her arm for support, walking stiffly. Nettie said, "Why are they here?"

Chloe said, suddenly shaken, "I don't know. I don't want to see them. Do you mind?"

"No, of course not," Rachel said. "Why *are* they here?"

All of them went down the hall and into the library, where another deputy was standing guard in front of the lock room. Nettie and Chloe sat down near Rachel. Ellen went over to a small chair and sat down by herself. Dade remained standing.

Tillie and Monkhaus entered the room. Tillie was dressed in a flowered print. She looked around at all of them with her wide, clear eyes. Addressing herself to Dade, she said in a husky voice, "The lieutenant told me—"

Dade gestured toward the sofa. Tillie and Monk sat down and looked up at him. Dade said, "Oh, forgive me. Miss Welles, Mrs. Proulx, Mrs. Ransohoff—Mr. and Mrs. Monkhaus." Somewhat taken aback, they all murmured greetings to one another. Dade said, "Ladies, I didn't mean to intrude on you at a time like this. I's just that, as Miriam's executor, I have to settle a matter that just won't wait, so I took the liberty of asking the sheriff to escort the Monkhauses here so we could resolve it."

They all looked at him blankly. He turned to Tillie and

Monk. "The late Miriam Welles bought a painting from you for thirty-five thousand dollars. The painting disappeared. You wanted it back. It has now been recovered. It's in there." Dade pointed at the lock room. "As her executor, it is now my duty to turn it over to you in exchange for the check, if you want me to." Startled, Valdez opened his mouth to object, but Dade held up a warning hand. "One moment, please, Lieutenant." Dade turned to the others.

Nettie said, "Really, I must protest. That was a bona fide purchase on the part of the gallery." She made a little French shrug of dismissal. Rachel and Chloe continued looking at him, their expressions unchanged.

Tillie and Monk had been caught off-guard. They looked at each other, then at Dade. He looked at each of them in turn, eyebrows raised inquiringly. Monk started to speak. Tillie put a hand on his arm, stopping him. Valdez and Dade exchanged a look. Dade turned back toward Tillie and Monk. They looked away.

Dade said, "I take it you would rather keep the money—which is indeed yours—than insist on having the painting back." There was no answer. Dade said, "You both know the painting is stolen. You didn't know that when you sold it. But you know it now. And you know if you take it back, the sheriff here will take it away from you and you'll end up with nothing. You also know it's a Raphael. You would have found that out when you looked up the works of Giulio Romano. They'd be in any book of the collected works of Raphael—because Romano collaborated with him on a few things. Anybody going through such a book would be bound to come across 'La Fornarina'—and you've lived with a copy of it hanging on your wall, since you were a kid. You would have recognized it instantly. My guess is you did."

Monk said nothing. Tillie said, "Yes, that's how he found out. How we both found out."

"Oh, yes, it's a Raphael, all right. And practically everybody connected with this case has known that from the word go." Now, he walked up and down, thumbs hooked into the armholes of his vest, not speaking for several moments, muttering under his breath, the bushy brows twitching, as if in the midst of some dialogue with himself. Then, he took a loud breath and faced them.

"You people have been through quite a lot lately. Very painful. No doubt about that. I got some information for you, sort of an explanation of how all this happened. Since all of you are greatly affected by it, it seemed to me only right that you should all have the chance to learn it firsthand, instead of having to read about it in the papers. The sheriff here has been kind enough to accommodate me. So I'll just plunge in.

"Oh, there is one thing I'd like to mention. Might make some people squirm, but it's necessary. From time to time, I'll be asking one or another of you for a bit of corroboration. I'd appreciate it if I could have it. See, you've told me some lies. You don't want to do that." At the end of his speech, his eyes came to rest on Nettie. He stared at her for a long time. Finally, she shifted her position, folding her plump arms.

"You're embarrassing me," she said.

"There have been three deaths in a short space of time. Your embarrassment has a low priority among my concerns." Turning suddenly to Monk, Dade said, "You went to Nettie's to search the gallery. That overturned furniture, that broken china—that wasn't vandalism, that was you running into things. I heard you doing it myself the day I was at your house.

"Nettie didn't have the painting. She let you in to show you that it wasn't there. When you couldn't find it, you weren't satisfied. You went upstairs to her apartment and searched that, too. My thought is, she followed you and tried to stop you from tearing the place apart. You were sure she knew where it was. You used force on her, trying to make her tell you. You must have knocked her down, she hit her head and you ran out of there. Yes or no?"

Monk's astonished face looked up. He said in his shrill voice, "I was trying to shake some sense into her. She fell and hit her head on the edge of a table. It was an accident!"

Dade turned to Nettie. "You pretended you never saw your assailant. You weren't protecting him. What you were protecting was your own interest. If the police dragged him in and questioned him, you were afraid they would find out what it was he was looking for. And you knew what it was. I know that because I've got me a witness who heard Miriam on the phone the day before she was killed saying to somebody, 'I *can't* move it,' and 'Those kids are still here.' Now, she was referring to the Raphael, obviously. Whoever was on the other end of that line knew she was talking about the painting and knew where it was. And whoever it was hung up without saying goodbye. That someone was you." He pointed at Nettie.

Nettie gave a shuddering little sigh. "Yes," she said, "it's the truth. I'd seen the painting once when she was cleaning it. She'd been working with trichloroethylene in that little room. I warned her about it but she got careless. She came out into the back courtyard and collapsed. I saw her and ran down the stairs. Fortunately, Nick was there looking for Rachel and he helped me. We brought her around. I wanted to call a doctor but she wouldn't let me. She was very pale, perspiring, really not well. But she insisted on going right back to work. It was all I could do to get some broth into her. We had brought her inside and put her on the sofa and Nick had gone out to make sure the fumes were gone. I went out to check."

"Did Nick see it?"

"I suppose so."

"Would he have known what it was?"

"Ask him."

"Did you know what it was?"

She gave him a little smile. "Anyway," she continued, "Miriam was herself in about five minutes and went back to work." Nettie gave a bitter laugh. "You know what I was going to do? I was going to wait until after Jensen had bought the painting and Gil and Miriam had gone off and then I was going to say, 'Jensen, I understand you have a Raphael now and I'd love to see it.' "

"You mean, you were going to blackmail him."

"That's such an ugly word. I was going to say exactly what I just told you. Sometimes, people can be unexpectedly generous."

Dade continued talking to Nettie. "After Miriam was killed, the painting disappeared. You knew Monk and Tillie didn't have it because Monk kept asking you for it. You knew you didn't have it. And it seemed unlikely that Chloe had ever heard of it—not in your mind. But she could very well have come to this house the night of the storm and killed Miriam to stop her from running off with Gil. Knowing nothing about the painting, she would have left it there, for others to find."

Chloe reacted with astonishment. "It never occurred to me that—!" Suddenly, she got up and stepped forward. The mask of the porcelain doll vanished in front of their eyes and her features twisted into an expression of outrage. She cried out in a furious voice, "How dare you presume to say such a thing to me?"

"I would like you to sit down," Dade replied softly.

"I will not sit down! I will not listen to any more of this!" Turning to the others, she clenched her fists and practically yelled at them, "I didn't kill her! I didn't kill Miriam! Whatever made you think such a thing?"

"I didn't think it. But someone else did."

Chloe rounded on Valdez. *"You?"*

"Not him," Dade said. "Her." He wheeled on Nettie and said loudly, "That's what *you* thought! You were the only one who knew Miriam was running off with Gil. You knew Chloe was desperate to keep her husband. You knew the whole story—because you were friends with both Gil and Miriam—you knew what had gone on a month before, when Jensen had gone to Chloe and between them they had broken up that affair, or thought they had. And you knew that if Chloe had found out the truth, she might have killed Miriam to stop her."

"No!" cried Chloe.

"You knew," Dade said to Nettie. "You knew the picture wouldn't have meant anything to Chloe and she probably would have left it behind. And that's why you came here the night of the funeral. Yes, you! The sheriff had sealed off the garage until the coroner had finished the autopsy and given his report and the insurance people had finished their inventory. You couldn't search the garage until Friday, and that was the day of the funeral, which you had to attend. The first chance you had was Friday night. And that's when you came here, knowing—or at least thinking—that the place was deserted.

"You were trained in the Resistance. You took no chances. You showed up here dressed in men's clothes, wearing a stocking mask and carrying a gun. And when you found the empty crate and knew the painting was gone, you were sure Miriam was murdered for it and in your mind there were only two people who could have done it: Gil or Jensen. And it wasn't until Gil showed up at your place last night and begged for your car, saying he'd figured out who the murderer was and was going to get the painting as the price of his silence, that you realized he meant Jensen. Yes, in your mind, Jensen had murdered his wife and stolen the painting—and now, he had killed Gil."

Nettie nodded, her head bowed. Rachel gasped.

Tillie said in an unsteady voice, "How can you do this to us after what we've been through?"

"Because it's time somebody told the truth," Dade said quietly. "And since I've taken you this far, I'm going to show you what I think happened." He walked toward the lock room. The deputy opened the door. Dade pointed at the easel behind the Chinese screen. "Can you fellas bring that out here? Oh, and that standing spotlight. And I'll bring the painting."

Valdez summoned another deputy and the easel and spotlight were carried out. Dade brought a shrouded canvas out himself, putting it up on the easel in front of all of them, and turned on the spotlight, adjusting it to light the canvas in a particular way. Then he dimmed the lights in the room. After that, he went back into the lock room and carried out a smaller painting and leaned it against a wall, its back to them. Dade walked up and down, glancing around briefly at all of them.

"It hit me last night," he began. "I saw it then but I didn't know what I was looking at. You know, Jensen was a connoisseur. Look at the way the paintings in this room are hung. Take a good look at the way they're lit. Well, the other night, he was going to show us the Botticelli. Easel set up in the library, lights in place. You understand what I'm saying, don't you? Well, Jensen's body was found in the lock room and the police came to the conclusion it was suicide. It looked like suicide. There was poor Jensen, sitting in his chair in front of his Raphael, just as if he'd put it up there so it'd be the last thing he'd see in this world.

"I didn't know what was wrong until they put up the Botticelli for us to look at. I said—now, I remember—when we looked at it, 'It just seems to fill the whole place.' I wasn't aware of anything else in the room. That's because Jensen had lit it. Like this." He flicked off the lights and then pulled the drape off the painting and turned on the spotlight. Botticelli's vision floated before them. Nothing else was visible.

Dade said, "All right," and Valdez flicked the lights in the room on again, covered the Botticelli, lifted it down from the easel, set it against a wall and then replaced it with the smaller canvas, still covered. He flicked off the lights in the room. They could hear a rustling as he unveiled the canvas. Dade's voice in the darkness said, "But when we found Jensen, we saw this."

The spotlight was turned back on. There was a murmur of awe and surprise in the room. Their eyes were now riveted on the Raphael. Dade walked toward it. The easel was so placed that the table with refreshments was behind it. To one side of the portrait, one could see rows of bottles of liquor and even read the labels. Boodles Gin, Ambassador Scotch, Martell Cognac. Dade walked over and switched the lights on..

He turned toward them and said, "The Botticelli's a much bigger canvas. But when the Raphael was put on the easel, the spotlight overhead was left the same way. The light spilled over the painting, do you get my meaning? It lit a lot of metal storage shelves and cabinets on the wall behind the easel and the Chinese screen, just the way this is lighting up that booze. Now, no man like Jensen Welles would do that to a painting, certainly not to a Raphael, certainly not if he meant it to be the last thing he saw on this earth. But Jensen had no such intention. He didn't put that Raphael up on that easel. And he didn't kill himself.

Jensen Welles was murdered—and by the same person who murdered Miriam and Gil."

They reacted to a sound. Monk had gotten to his feet and was walking unsteadily toward the Raphael. He made a groaning sound in his throat. Tillie was at his side instantly, taking his arm, cooing to him, gently leading him back again to his place.

Dade gestured at the canvas. Deputies moved the painting over to the wall and placed it there on the floor next to the Botticelli. Then Valdez collapsed the easel and gave it to one of the deputies in the gallery.

Monk sat apart, brooding, sunk in thought. Tillie stood by herself, looking out at nothing, her mouth open, arrested in motion. Chloe, Nettie and Rachel had gotten to their feet and were gathered together now, all talking at once.

Valdez said, "Okay, ladies, let's let him have his say, can we do that, please?"

The three women fell silent abruptly, all of them turning to look at Dade and communicating a sense that they had closed ranks, that the three of them, like the women in a Greek chorus, represented a common attitude. They looked at Dade with a mixture of astonishment and distaste, as if they were priestesses surprised at their secret rites by an intruder.

Dade said, "Until about an hour ago, the sheriff's theory was that Jensen Welles killed his wife in a fury when he found out what she was planning to do to him. Then, when Gil Ransohoff tried to blackmail him into giving him the Raphael as the price of his silence, he killed him, too, and then took his own life." Dade cleared his throat.

"But it couldn't have happened that way, because we now know that Jensen was murdered. Why? To silence him because he'd figured out who'd killed Miriam? Well, let's just examine the logic of that for a moment. He certainly hadn't figured it out at eight o'clock Saturday night, when I left him. He called Pinkerton's and sent for a guard to be here at nine o'clock, which meant that he had no plans to leave the house. Right after that, he sat down and wrote me a letter telling me he'd known Miriam was murdered as soon as he found out the Raphael was missing.

"Expecting the Pinkerton man, he opens the lock room. Enter the murderer. Oh, this was planned. This was carefully planned. My hunch is, he was killed then and there. It was the murderer who drove away in the Rolls, wearing Jensen's hat and coat and even his shoes, the murderer who changed cars in the private garage at the office, the murderer whom Gil had made plans to meet in Malibu Canyon.

"But why kill Jensen? To silence him? There's no evidence that Jensen knew anything that threatened anybody. Why was he murdered? To make it look as if he had first killed his wife, then Gil, then himself? Why? If it was just to make it seem that someone else was guilty, why not make Gil's murder appear to be suicide and leave it at that? Why was it necessary to kill Jensen? The answer to that one question is the key to the riddle.

"This whole mess is really very simple, once you see it straight. Here's where we went wrong. At first, everybody thought Miriam's death was an accident. It couldn't be murder. Nobody had any motive to kill Miriam. That's what everybody thought. So when Rachel came to me and said it was murder, I didn't have any reason to believe her. What was the motive?

"Then, we found out about the painting. There's your motive. A ten-million-dollar Raphael! There's your motive, right? Wrong!"

He sensed glances, like blinkers, signaling each other around the room. He turned away, reminded of something, trying to remember what it was. Then it came to him. In the Pacific, during the war, natives were airlifted out of Burma, fifty or a hundred half-naked men on the deck of an open cargo plane. There would be a quick glance of nomination, another seconding. Their glances flashed rapidly, opposing, assenting, yielding. Then in a gelid, unanimous argus-instant, one man was thrown a mile to his death. He turned back to them again, his eyes sweeping over them. He saw the truth. They were looking for a victim. He wanted then to step back, to withdraw.

Ellen sensed his dismay. He caught her eyes on him. He nodded, rubbing his big jaw.

"See, Miriam was murdered, all right," he continued softly. "But by mistake. Because she wasn't the intended victim. Jensen was."

XXX

There was dead silence. Valdez was staring at Dade open-mouthed, a look of astonishment on his face.

Dade continued. "The murderer couldn't very well stage a second accident. Forgive me, Refugio, but that might attract attention, even the sheriff's. The problem was how to get rid of Jensen. This required a certain degree of improvisation. After Miriam's death, the painting had been taken as insurance in case her death was thought to be murder. Any robber might have killed her for what she had with her. Remember, she was outside the fenced areas of the property in a narrow driveway all alone there on a stormy night. But now all of a sudden, there were a lot of suspects where the murderer had intended only one. That made for mischief.

"And here's the painting. With Gil Ransohoff's fingerprints on it. Sheriff here will confirm that." Valdez nodded. "Oh, he had the painting, Gil Ransohoff. My guess is he had it for about thirty seconds." There was a sudden surprised whispering. "That's right. Now, I'm going to tell you why I think that.

"See, Gil Ransohoff had the sheriff breathing down his neck. He'd been conspiring with Miriam to sell a ten-million-dollar stolen painting to Jensen Welles. He found Miriam dead. Told me so himself. Now all of a sudden, the sheriff, he's looking at Gil. Sheriff is thinking, She was killed for that painting and you've got it. That, my friends, is a rope around any man's neck. Now, here's what Gil must have thought: He knew damn well *he* didn't have it. Nettie had been assaulted by someone searching her place for it, so he would have ruled out Nettie. He knew Monk didn't have it because Monk had come to him demanding it back and gotten shot in the process. If Monk didn't have it, then neither did Monk's wife. He was damn sure Chloe never heard of it. Well, who did that leave? Jensen?

"Well, Jensen was the one with the strongest motive, the one they were afraid of. Everybody kept trying to think Jensen. But Gil didn't take the bait. This is only a guess. But what I think is, Gil found out from Monk that day he showed up that Monk and his wife had tried to get the painting from Jensen and had such damaging information about his movements that if Jensen had had it, he would have given it up to save his own skin." Dade looked at Monk for confirmation. "True or false?" Monk nodded dumbly.

"Gil guessed who the murderer was—and guessed right. And that cost him his life. He was so eager to make a deal with the murderer that he climbed out the bathroom window with the sheriff at the door. Left the house with nothing. Now, why was that? The answer, my friends, is indicated by Gil Ransohoff's fingerprints. He wanted that painting—and badly. That was ten million dollars' worth of bribe. Gil Ransohoff loved money. He couldn't live without it. His wife is the one who told me that. So to him, this must have looked like a chance well worth taking. And he was taking it. He knew he had to disappear. He was leaving the country, once he had that painting in his possession. The proof is, he had his passport with him. That's it. No suitcase, no possessions, nothing but that and a wallet full of credit cards that would have been good for, let's say, a few days. Oh, and an empty brief case. Just big enough to hold a folded canvas."

"He met the murderer in Malibu Canyon. Now, this wasn't like simple blackmail. This was going to be a one-shot deal. There was no chance that Gil could ever come back and ask for more. Once Gil took that painting, the murderer was off the hook and the risk was all Gil's. Here's the painting, the murderer says. Now, that must have been a very interesting moment, because if Gil had ever tried to get out of the country with it and gotten caught, there wouldn't have been a jury anywhere in the world that wouldn't convict him. Well, our murderer met Gil halfway. Accepted his silence, but gave him a bullet instead of a Raphael.

"Then if you were the murderer, all you had to do was put the painting where we found it to make Jensen's death look like the suicide of a guilty man. And suicide would work just as well for our murderer as accident. You catch my drift?"

Rachel got to her feet, an incredulous look on her face. She looked beseechingly at all of them, as if seeking support. Then she said to Dade, "What are you saying? What in the world are you saying?" She gave him a dreadful half-smile of disbelief, swaying on her feet. Chloe jumped up and took her by the arm, trying to make her sit down. But Rachel pushed her away, half whispering, "No, I have to hear it," as if she could only follow what he was saying by remaining where she was. A thin hand pushed her reddish hair back from the freckled forehead.

Dade said in a flat voice, "This was murder. This was murder three times. The district attorney will go into a court of law and show it was murder." They all looked up at him, motionless.

"There's a last piece of evidence that properly should come from Jensen himself, but since he's gone I'll have to submit it to you as amicus curiae. Rachel has a lot of money, that's true, but she can't touch it—I should say 'couldn't'—while Jensen was alive. She had the money but he had the income—the whole thing.

"Well, now, along came a young man named Nick Levin. Rachel fell in love with him. Jensen had the natural fears of a father with a rich heiress for a daughter. Every young man is looked on as a fortune hunter—unless, of course, he's got his own fortune. Fortunes are hard to fake. You can pretend to have a lot of money but men like Jensen can find out very quickly what you're worth.

"Nick never said he had a fortune, only that he was making one. And from all appearances, he was. He dealt in puts and calls. He'd buy a contract, say, for June wheat—that meant in March, he'd pay a broker ten thousand dollars against a hundred thousand, betting that the price of his wheat contract would be worth at least a hundred thousand in three months—and if it went up, well, every cent of it that went over that hundred thousand was pure profit. Of course, if it went down he could lose his investment.

"Well, Nick, he kept making money every month. Ten, twenty thousand dollars, month in and month out. He'd almost never guess wrong. He looked to everybody like a financial genius. Jensen was suspicious from the beginning. You know, it's a funny thing, but a man can be just too successful for his own good. Jensen's been around investments too long to buy a story like that. Still, he saw the receipts from the brokerage houses. No question about it, Nick was cleaning up.

"Jensen double-checked. Sure, Nick had made all those investments. Sure, he'd been paid. Nick was doing business all over town. Sure, they were delighted to have him as a customer. But Jensen was doing an awful lot of digging. It was only a question of time before he found out.

"I found out. Today. Two hours ago. Nick was betting against himself. Fact! He was buying puts as well as calls. He couldn't lose. 'Course, he couldn't win, neither. But he didn't care. All he needed to do was show Jensen those winning contracts to make himself look rich as Croesus. He spent six months looking like a real winner. Truth is, he was a real loser." Dade stopped.

Rachel was closer to him now, her wide eyes fixed on him in mounting disbelief. She said hoarsely, "It isn't true!" She turned away, leaning her arms on the back of a high chair for support, digging her fingers into her hair, slowly shaking her head. "Oh, no. There must have been a reason." She did not yet seem to absorb the implications of what Dade was saying.

Dade looked quickly at Valdez's face, caught a glance of amazement, then a look of appreciation from Ellen. Monk's perpetually surprised face sought his like a sunflower following the light, his head rotated slowly as Dade paced. Tillie seemed to withdraw into herself as she listened to him. Chloe, Nettie and Rachel drew close together, as if for support.

"I'm afraid it's true. Your father tried to steer you clear by just telling you Nick was a fortune hunter. You wouldn't listen. Said you were going to marry Nick and that it was your business and that was the end of the whole thing. When your father gave you a choice and said either you gave up seeing Nick or else you moved out and supported yourself, you packed up and left. After all, you didn't care about money. All you wanted was Nick. And all Nick wanted was your hundred million dollars, which he might not get his hands on for twenty years."

"No! No! No!" She clapped her hands over her ears to shut out the truth and shook her head as if to shake off suspicion.

Dade said, "It's true, all right."

"How can you attack him like this, behind his back?"

"I'll tell him to his face! Where is he, Rachel?"

She drew back and looked around as if the room itself held some secret hint of her lover's whereabouts. "Safe from you," she said with an uneven smile. Then anger reddened her cheeks and she yelled, "Safe from you!"

Dade continued. "After all, Jensen was hale and hearty and detested Nick." He turned to Rachel and said to her directly. "Well, what the hell were you going to live on? If you found out the truth, you might divorce him. You might exclude him from any settlement. You had a lot of weapons and he had already seen that you could be willful. He was trapped. And then you told him your father had threatened to kill him.

"Well, there wasn't much time. There it was, a hundred million on one side and an enraged father with a gun on the other. That's how things were on the night of the big storm, February fourteenth." Dade paused. They were all staring at him like a jury, weighing his arguments.

"That night, Jensen had to go out, in spite of the weather. He had urgent business affairs to attend to. The only person who knew what he was up to was Miriam. But that doesn't matter. Nick knew that Jensen had to go out. He knew from you, Rachel. You told me so.

"Now, the thing was, it had to look accidental. How does somebody improvise a murder by apparent accident at the last minute? That takes a kind of desperate imagination. We have already seen that kind of imagination in the story I've told you. Break the automatic door-closing device in the car by opening it up and bending it. When your victim drives out—remembering that he is a man who keeps attack dogs and lives in fear of being robbed—the murderer can be fairly sure his victim will get out of his car to close the door manually.

"Now, if you were the murderer, what would you do? You would lie in wait in the bushes, hidden by the trees in the turnabout, where your victim would have to stop the car to get to the garage without slogging through knee-high mud. You thank Providence for the blinding storm that keeps him from seeing you—but in this case, also keeps you from seeing your victim. Consider what Miriam was wearing: a long raincoat which hung in the garage, a Burberry with a hood. That's what you'd have seen—a Rolls Royce and a figure in a long raincoat." He paused and looked around at all of them. "I happened to have a look at it yesterday. You know what I saw? I saw a name tag in it, inside the pocket. Said the thing belonged to Jensen Welles. That's what Miriam was wearing: Jensen's raincoat. And that, my friends, is what the murderer saw.

"The moment has come. The clever murderer jumps in the Rolls and races forward, slamming the heavy car into the victim, and then discovering when it was too late that the victim was not Jensen but Miriam." Chloe gasped. Nettie sighed, covering her eyes. Rachel looked up, the horror dawning on her face. "Miriam had gotten out of the car not because the garage door opener wouldn't work, but to get the painting out of a cabinet, when suddenly she saw that huge car rushing down at her—"

"It isn't true," Rachel said, "it isn't true."

"Isn't it?"

"No, I don't believe it."

"And if I prove it to you?"

"Can you?"

"Where is Nick now?"

"Then you can't prove it!" Her face was flushed with triumph. "You can't prove it! I knew you couldn't!"

Dade whispered, "Where is he, Rachel?"

"I don't know."

"But he's going to call you."

"I don't have to help you!" Now her eyes blazed, she

was yelling at him. "I don't have to help you! We're married! He's my husband! You can't force me to testify against him!" The room was instantly filled with the sound of voices. Then, abruptly, silence.

Dade said to Rachel, "When he finds out we're looking for him, he'll know he's at your mercy. How long do you think he's going to put up with that? If he's killed not once, not twice, but three times—"

"You twist words!" She was desperate now, her arms locked, sitting on a barstool and writhing back and forth, as if to escape the torment of his conclusions. "Everybody here is guilty, according to you!"

"I did that to show you that everyone's innocent! To make you believe it! Rachel, Rachel, where is he?"

"I don't know! I told him not to tell me when he said Dad was out to kill him and I'm glad I don't know!"

"And when he hears on the news that Jensen was murdered? When Nick Levin finds out we're looking for him—to question *him?* Rachel, face it! He lied to you!"

"Take back what you said! It isn't true that he lied to me! It isn't!"

"Rachel, Miriam's dead. She was murdered. She died horribly. I didn't show you the coroner's report. She died in agony."

"No, no!"

"She was left to die!"

"I can't bear it!"

"Rachel, I will never rest until her murderer is brought to justice. I swear I won't. Rachel, you know where he is and you're going to meet him."

"No!"

"You are going to meet him, aren't you?"

"I won't do it!"

The phone began to ring. It went through all of them like an electric shock. Rosarita had entered to clear away the cups. She started toward the phone.

Rachel said, "Don't!" Rosarita backed off. Rachel whipped away from them. Dade went to her, took her by the elbow and steered her toward the phone. It continued ringing. He begged her with his eyes.

"No!" she said. "If you want it answered, you answer it!"

"If I answer it, he'll get suspicious. Rachel, please."

"No." She turned away, trying to avoid everyone's gaze and, by accident, looked straight at the smiling portrait of Miriam, hanging in the center of the room. The phone continued ringing. She kept looking at the painting until the ringing stopped. Then she said, almost to herself, "I can't! I won't!"

Dade nodded slowly, then straightened himself up and said to Rachel, "I'm afraid that conflict we spoke of has now arisen."

"But he's my husband, Dade."

"Exactly. And I represent all that a poor dead lady had to leave to this world. I must ask you to seek other representation." Dade offered Ellen his arm. They left the room together.

XXXI

Dade and Ellen got in their car and a moment later Valdez came up to them.

"Okay," he said. "Okay." He hesitated. "Want to meet over in my office? Talk a little?" Dade nodded. An earnest Brandt came up to Valdez and said something in his ear. Valdez shook his head. Brandt walked away a few steps.

Dade leaned forward and asked in an unemotional voice, "Get permission?"

"Yes," Valdez said. "We got a court order."

"They get anything?"

"They can't unless she answers the phone."

They drove to the station in separate cars. They sat down in Valdez's office. Valdez glanced at a wall clock. It was just twelve. Galvanized, he switched on a radio and after the familiar electronic sounds which announced the hourly news, an announcer read headlines and said that he would return ". . . with these stories and many more after this." A commercial followed.

The announcer came back and said, "And now for the news," and read the same bulletins over again. An electronic beeping in a higher key interrupted him. He said, "Now, here's news live and direct from Malibu. Jensen Welles, famed philanthropist and art collector, was found shot to death last night at his Malibu estate only five days after the freak accident which killed his wife. No details are available, but authorities are now searching for a man they want to question in connection with the death, Nick Levin, who disappeared sometime early this morning. And now, sports and the weather—"

Valdez switched off the radio, folded his arms on the desk and looked inquiringly at Dade. "Satisfied?"

"Yes."

"All right, it's a chance and we're going to take it." Valdez excused himself and returned a few moments later with three chilled cans of Coke and some large paper cups and paper napkins. He opened the cans and poured each of them one. The three of them sat in silence, sipping, waiting, watching a couple of young deputies on their lunch break playing Frisbee in their shirt-sleeves on the vacant landing pad of the helicopter.

After almost a quarter of an hour, Brandt banged into the office. He said, "There was a collect call a few minutes ago. Maid answered. Left the line for about a minute then came back and refused the call."

"Was it Levin?" Valdez asked.

"Yeah. Stayed on the line just long enough for us to trace the call. Came from a pay station up near Porterville."

"He'll call again," Dade said.

Valdez frowned. "She'll warn him. You know she'll warn him."

"Well, we can't help that."

"Up in the mountains," Valdez said. "Snow. Lots of it."

"You set up roadblocks?" Dade asked.

Brandt said, "We're doing it now." He nodded at Valdez and rushed out.

Valdez said, "They were all set to move, just waiting to hear. Weather's in our favor. Most of those roads are closed. He can't go higher. Car can't get through. If he tried it on foot, he'd freeze to death. He'll have to stick to one of the main roads and they all lead down to the highway. I guess there's nothing we can do but wait."

Dade said, "Well, as my granddaddy used to say, 'When God made time, he made plenty of it.'"

"She'll arrange to meet him," Ellen said abruptly. The two men looked at her. "She's a woman in love," she went on. "She's not going to wait here for him. After she warns him, she'll try to meet him."

"She's not stupid," Dade said. "It will occur to her that we've got the line tapped."

Ellen made a face. "For heaven's sake, of course she's not stupid! She'll just say something like, 'Where we went last Christmas.' I'm sure she's already got it worked out by now."

"And how are we supposed to know where that is?" the lieutenant grumbled.

Ellen made a birdlike little gesture. "She will also expect you to be following her."

"All right, my dear," Dade said, with a touch of annoyance. "What would you do?"

She said in a reasonable tone, "If I were going to meet him, I would drive to the airport, buy a ticket to San Francisco, mingle with the people and then join the crowd boarding the plane."

The lieutenant said gently, "I'm afraid we would have our people waiting to meet the plane in San Francisco."

"Oh, but I wouldn't be on the plane! You see, when you board a plane, you go through a door to one of those movable passageways leading to the boarding entrance of the plane. Well, right beside that entrance is a flight of stairs leading to the ground. On a crowded flight, I could slip away and you would never miss me. Once on the ground, I would get back into the terminal by a service entrance, keep out of sight and make my way to a cab stand. I would then take a cab into Westwood, rent a car and I'd be on the freeway while your agents were still waiting for me in San Francisco."

The two men stared at her. She shrugged and said, "Well, you asked."

"My dear," Dade said after a moment, "I never suspected you of such animal cunning—"

Ellen gave him a blue stare and said, "I'm not a mind reader but you mustn't underestimate the cleverness of a woman trying to save her husband's life. She may do the opposite and try to lead you away from where he's going. It all depends, really, on the telephone message—and, of course, on whether you can figure it out. Besides, I still think you're making a mistake."

"I've told you—" Dade began.

"I know what you've told me. I know what you think. What you both think. As for me—oh, I don't know what I believe anymore. We're all haunted by a sense of responsibility to find out the murderer's identity, just as we ourselves would want it found out if we were murdered. But it's dangerous, just as it was to Gil and poor Jensen and I'm afraid. I can't help it, I'm just afraid."

They were interrupted by the sound of a buzzer. Valdez picked up a phone and said, "Yes?" Then he flicked a switch on a speaker.

They heard the woman deputy's voice say "Deputy Brandt on six."

Valdez pressed a button on the phone and said, "Brandt?"

Brandt's voice said, "Phone rang again. It was not answered."

Valdez looked at Dade, then said, "Brandt, anybody else in there with her, besides the maid?"

"Negative, sir."

"You are monitoring all three phones?"

"All three, yes, sir."

"Report every message. Repeat: Every message."

"Yes, sir."

Valdez put down the phone, flicked off the speaker, and folded his arms. They waited an hour. Valdez sent out for lunch from the health-food store around the corner—thick slabs of homemade wheat bread buttered and filled with alfalfa sprouts, tomato, jack cheese and avocado and glasses of carrot juice. The hour stretched into two hours. There had now been perhaps a dozen calls, to be expected, of course, after the news of Jensen's death, but Rachel had answered none of them.

Valdez got an urgent long-distance call from Washington. He took it, his head in one hand, grunting and nodding, then, when someone else came on the line, got to his feet, as if unconsciously drawing himself to attention in the presence of a higher authority. "One moment, sir," he said. He covered the mouthpiece of the phone and said to Dade, "It's the French embassy in Washington. They want to take possession of the painting. Right away."

Dade shook his head, saying, "Sorry, they'll have to wait."

Valdez said into the phone, "I don't have authority to

release it yet, sir." He listened for a moment, then said, "The moment I do. Certainly. We have absolutely no wish to impound it. Yes, sir. Yes, sir." There was a click. Slowly, Valdez put down the phone. "I don't even know how they got this number—well—that's kind of a stupid thing to say, isn't it? But anyway, they want—" His face flushed. "I just take orders. You understand that, don't you?"

The phone rang again. Valdez snatched it up and said, "Valdez." Uneasy, clearing his throat and walking away from Dade, phone in hand as if wanting to insure the privacy of whoever had come on the line, he spoke in a low voice, apologetic, his forehead beginning to perspire. When he finally managed to extricate himself from the conversation, he put down the phone with a sigh, saying irritably to Dade, "That was the FBI. They want my cooperation." He looked at Dade helplessly. "They want the painting turned over to the French but have no authority to order me to deliver it. It's a big thing. They said there could be some big legal problem and had I heard about it? I haven't heard. What problem? What are they talking about? Please tell me. It would mean a lot if I could do them a favor."

"What they mean is, under the law, they don't know who owns the painting. The matter may have to go to court."

"What the hell are you saying?"

"When it comes to theft, there is such a thing as the statute of limitations."

"There's no statute of limitations in France! Not when it comes to art thefts! They said that up front!" Valdez was perspiring freely now.

"But there is in California," Dade pursued. "And it runs three years."

Valdez got out of his swivel chair, came around the desk and, sitting on his haunches, took Dade's big hand in both of his, squeezing it, and said, "I'm begging you—" Dade was taken aback. Valdez gestured at the phone as if at an idol. "These are really big people—breaking this case means, well, hell, you must know what it means to me! I can't go this far and lose that damn picture!"

"I understand you."

"Whose picture is it, if it doesn't belong to the French, will you tell me that?"

"Why, the picture was bought and paid for by Miriam Welles. It belongs to her heirs."

"Jensen Welles is dead! You mean to her stepdaughter?"

"No, she only left Rachel her personal things but she left her half of the gallery and any paintings she might own in whole or in part to Nettie Proulx."

"Well, hell, she's French. She wouldn't give her own people the shiv."

"Lieutenant, have you done much traveling?"

Valdez said, not following this, still squatting beside Dade, "If I've said anything to offend you in the course of this case, by God, I'm sorry. Look, I'm begging you, I'm on my knees—"

"I've already said—"

"You're one smart guy. Me, I've sweated—I mean, I've sweated—to get where I am. My pop, he picked grapes and hid from the *migra*. I want you to help me." The large dark eyes implored him. Dade felt like a plaster saint in a village.

Ellen said, "Of course he'll help you. Dade, help the man."

"Thank you, lady."

"Honey, he's got a problem. The FBI is right."

"I said, help him. Now, I mean it, Dade!"

Dade freed his hand, getting to his feet, and walked up and down, watching the crew work on the ever-present sheriff's helicopter. He was trying to dredge up a memory, thinking how strange it was that he remembered that he remembered, why, it was just like having a word on the tip of one's tongue. Then what he was hunting for came to him, he let out a hoot and his face relaxed into a down-home smile. "San Francisco!" he shouted. "Nineteen twenty-five! Anybody says no can kiss my ass downtown on Easter Sunday! You hear me, Refugio?"

"You got the answer?"

"Let me tell you just how the law reads, may I do that? It's covered under the Code of Civil Procedure—um, three thirty-eight subsection three, if memory serves. Yes, I'm right. The statute of limitations on theft runs three years in this state, no more, no less. But there's a couple of words gets us off the hook: You got to have 'notorious possession.' What that means is, if I steal a painting off of you and hide it under the bed, say, for three years and then pull it out and say, 'Now it's mine!' the law says, 'No, it ain't.' See, you can't conceal the thing. Under the doctrine of adverse possession, the statute is tolled until after the possession becomes open and notorious. Tolling the statute, of course, means just setting it aside till I pull that picture out from under the bed. Then, when I hang the thing up on my wall for all to see, the statute starts running again. Now, if it hangs there for three years and you never get around to saying, 'Hey, that's mine! I want it back!' why, once that three years is up, the painting's mine."

Valdez was uncertain. "But you said Monkhaus had the painting hanging on the wall of his house for years in plain view. Isn't that open and notorious?"

"It was overpainted," Ellen pointed out.

"But the overpainting was a copy of the Raphael underneath! Is that concealment?" Valdez still wasn't sure.

"It was intended to be," Dade said.

"Suppose Monkhaus argued the contrary?" Valdez pursued. "Suppose he said that was just a form of protection—oh, like hanging a fur coat in a mothproof bag. I'm just asking whether there's any way he could get around this—Monkhaus or his wife or that little French lady."

"Nope. Intent was clearly to conceal. Worked so well, it fooled Monk's mother, Monk, Tillie and presumably everybody who ever came by. Nope, no way you can argue that."

"So the painting is still legally stolen? Are you sure of that?" Valdez stroked his mustache.

"Let me show you how the statute works. Up in San Francisco, we once had us a famous case. That was back in nineteen twenty-five. Somebody stole a painting and fenced it. The fence hid it for . . . oh, seven or eight years, then sold it to an auctioneer who sold it publicly. Original owner saw it at the auction and sued the buyer. Buyer argued the statute of limitations. But the State Supreme Court held that the painting had been concealed all that time and every time there's a transfer of ownership, a new conversion, that starts the three-year statute running all over again. Result: Original owner got back his painting.

"See, the language is very specific. Possession must be 'open and notorious.' They got both words in there because they mean both words. Nope," Dade shook his big head, "in my judgment, that painting is still stolen. Statute of limitations doesn't apply. Refugio, you're a hero. You can rest easy."

Valdez grabbed Dade's hand and wrung it, then squeezed Ellen's. "I owe you," he kept saying, "I owe you."

Dade glanced at his watch. It was now after two. There was still no word. They continued waiting.

XXXII

That afternoon, Dade made occasional visits to the Welles estate, leaving his car at the gate and walking up and down outside the fence, looking at the grounds. The first time, he saw a gardener and his assistant arrive at the gate. They were let in by Rosarita, and began doing their chores, oblivious to what was going on. A truck drove up from a pool service and a pool boy, barefoot and wearing only shorts, began dragging equipment toward the pool, waving to the gardeners. He remained in plain sight all the time, his thin brown body visible at the edge of the pool as he backflushed it, working to get the prime up again, bleeding the filter and then vacuuming, rock music meanwhile blaring out of the speakers of the trucks' radio.

Later Dade caught sight of Rosarita coming out onto the service porch with bags of trash, filling a bucket, wringing out a mop.

The shoreline was being watched. Brandt told Dade that twice a deputy in a fishing boat reported that Rachel had come out onto the promontory behind the house, where the cliff plunged down a hundred feet to the breakers below, and had stood there, arms folded, shivering, staring out at nothing. There were steps cut into the rocky face of the cliff leading down to the water. The tide was going out. By nightfall it would be possible to walk along the beach to where it widened. The lieutenant expected her to try to get away then on foot, and deputies disguised as lifeguards were stationed at the nearby public beaches. The instructions to all of them were the same: If she tried to leave, they were to make no move to show themselves or intercept her, only to follow her and report her where-abouts.

But Rachel, Brandt said, had made no attempt to go anywhere. When the sun grew stronger in the late after-noon, she came out of the house wearing dark glasses and a bikini, carrying a big beach towel and a bottle of sun-tan lotion and, stretching out on an upholstered chaise placed on the edge of the pool deck overlooking the sea, she read her book, which a deputy with powerful binoculars duti-fully reported as, "some kind of religious book about an abbey by a guy named Austen."

Once Rosarita came out and spoke to her briefly, then returning with a tray and a pitcher and a tall glass of what looked like iced tea. Rachel sipped her drink and read her book, occasionally smearing herself with lotion from the dark bottle. She had the white skin of a redhead, rosy now from the sun and covered with scatterings of freckles. The sun would not be good for such skin and she clearly knew it, for after a while, she adjusted the umbrella so that she was protected by its shadow and covered herself from chin to toe with her big towel, afterward propping up her book on her middle and continuing to read it slowly.

There was a telephone at her elbow on the low table beside her. It was reported that she did not seem to react at all when it rang. It might have been no more than the sound of an insect. The deputies watching her became restless. The man in the fishing boat was hot under the canopy which protected him from the sun. Once or twice, he complained that he had almost fallen asleep. Finally Rachel lay the book across her middle, lay her head back and went to sleep.

The deputy in the boat stretched out on the padded bench along the gunwhale and began watching her through slitted eyes, after arranging with the lifeguard deputy to keep checking him to keep him awake. The whole thing reminded him of something, he told Brandt. After a while, he remembered what it was. Fifteen years before, when he was twelve, he had sneaked into what he thought was a dirty movie and it turned out to be a movie about a man asleep. Jeez, he just kept sleeping the whole fucking time, the deputy mumbled to himself, remembering. I thought I'd go outta my fucking gourd.

Brandt told Dade later that visitors had begun to appear at the gate, one after another, people paying condolence calls, members of the press after a story. To each of them, Rosarita repeated the same message over the intercom: Miss Welles was not at home, and the maid had no idea when she was expected. Inside the house, Rosarita wrote down all the names of those who had stopped by. The gate remained locked.

Some of the reporters waited around. A mobile unit from a television station parked in the drive and a cameraman with a minicam on his shoulder took up a station in a bend of the drive, where he could photograph visitors before they were aware of it. When the gardeners finished and loaded their equipment back on their truck and headed for the gate, several reporters tried to force their way in but found themselves suddenly intercepted by sheriff's deputies who told them to stand back. The gardeners departed, the gate locking behind them.

The shadows lengthened. It was after five. In an hour it would be dark. Dade still waited, now getting word from Brandt. The men on duty at the gates, the ones in the thick brush down the coast who had taps on all three phones, the men on the beach and the deputy rocking in his cradle of a fishing boat all waited as they had been waiting for six hours, looking impatiently at their watches, wondering when the relief men were going to show up, drinking coffee from thermos bottles, coffee that was always slightly rancid from the petroleum taste of the plastic of the cup, swearing under their breaths, sick of the whole business, none of them sure "why the hell we're birddogging this goddamn cunt and why the fuck don't she take a nude sunbath, she oughtta know nobody can see her out where she is anyway," this last from the deputy out in the fishing boat, after which an offshore wind made the water choppy. Within minutes, he was seasick, half falling out of his boat, vomiting, trying at the same time to keep his eyes on Rachel, who got up from her chair, throwing down her book and towel, and walked out to the very edge of the cliff, standing there with her hands digging into her thick hair, motionless, perfectly still, one foot in front of the other, poised and slender as a Giacometti statue, eyes on the sea, giving the seasick deputy, whose stomach was now knotted and cramped from the suddenness and violence of his nausea, the eerie impression that their roles had gotten reversed and she now watched *him*.

The setting sun flashed gold in the vaulted windows of the Welles house, touched Rachel's red hair, making it for a moment a radiant halo of molten metal. Then she relaxed, clasped her arms about herself, shivering, and collecting her book and towel, slowly went back across the flagstones of the pool deck and disappeared into the house.

Night fell. It was low tide now and the surf was scarcely more than a whisper. On the poolside table, the telephone began to ring again. A deputy stationed down on the beach in the shelter of the rocks could hear it distinctly. It rang repeatedly, for a long, long time, like the song of an unfamiliar bird piercing the night. No one answered it. Dade left.

Back at the inn, he sat in an armchair, eyes fixed on a small, leather-covered traveling chess game, the board now open, the magnetic chessmen in array, in his lap, an open copy of a paperback book in which great chess games were replayed, the final moves which spelled victory and defeat printed on separate pages at the back. Dade was replaying one of the games between Capablanca and Lasker, from the 1921 match in Havana, when Lasker had lost the title he had held for twenty-six years. He was playing Lasker's moves.

"I'm going to get your title back for you, Lasker, my boy." He pondered the little board, doubtful that he could do anything of the sort.

From time to time, Valdez called, giving Dade progress reports, or "no progress" reports, as the lieutenant had wryly taken to calling them, and asking, in a weary voice which indicated that he already knew the answer, whether Dade had yet heard anything.

At seven o'clock, when still nothing had happened, Ellen ordered dinner.

Dade said, "What happened to the lobsters?"

She gestured toward the ocean. "I set them free."

Dade made them both Old Fashioneds, then sat down to watch the news with the sound turned off. Ellen went into the bathroom to freshen up.

At 7:25, Pete arrived, putting down his tray and setting two places. He looked at the set, then at Dade, and said, "Sir?"

"Yes, my boy?"

"That the news you're watching?"

"Yes, it is."

"Don't you want the sound on?"

"No." Dade sat back, lacing his fingers across his middle.

Pete came over and watched with him. A ship blew up. The commentator's face once more filled the screen. "How come? I mean, that you don't want the sound on?"

"I happen to be thinking."

Dade signed the check and Pete left. Ellen came out of the bathroom and Dade seated her.

At a little after eight, the phone rang. There was something different in the tone, it seemed to Dade—the way a ringing phone sounds when one is afraid of receiving bad news.

"Hello?" he said into the phone.

"Dade?" said Rachel.

"Hello there."

"Dade, I have to talk to you."

"I must remind you that I don't represent you anymore, Rachel."

"I don't need an attorney, I need a friend. Dade, please—"

"All right."

"Not on the phone."

"All right." Dade put down the phone, picked it up again and punched out the lieutenant's number as he drank his coffee.

XXXIII

At the Welles house, he got out of his car and, seeing lights, walked over to the service entrance, which was screened by a trellis and bougainvillea. He tried the door and went inside, finding himself in a large empty kitchen, the walls done in Spanish tiles, with copper pans hanging from wrought-iron hooks.

A door was open to the breakfast room, where a light was on. In there, Rachel was sitting with her elbows on the table, her face in her hands. The table was French Provincial and made of fruitwood. In the center there was a big majolica epergne with half a dozen kinds of out-of-season fruit heaped on it. From a fixture of Tiffany glass, different-colored lights spilled down onto the fruit, onto the antique polished uneven tabletop and onto Rachel's auburn hair. It seemed for a moment as if she didn't know he had entered the room.

She got up wearily. She was wearing faded denims and an Aran Island pullover, and old tennis shoes with no socks. She had no jewelry on, not even a watch.

She turned toward him, the thick red fringe of her lashes blinked two or three times and then the blue eyes met his. "I don't know what to do," she said.

"What do you want to do, honey?"

"I don't want them to hurt him."

"Why would they want to hurt him?"

"If they come after him and he tries to get away."

"You think that's what he'd do?"

"I don't know. I can't take that chance."

"They're going to find him. Sooner or later."

"I know that."

"If they find him sooner, it might be the best way to protect him."

"I love him, Dade."

"It's hard, honey."

"Yes. But with the right defense—well, maybe he's sick or something."

"That's always possible."

"And there's plenty of money. It isn't as if he couldn't have the best defense in the world—"

"You should tell him that."

She drew away as if did not trust him. "You mean answer the phone? You know they've tapped the lines." She rubbed her eyes, trying to think. "They shouldn't have said on the news that they were after him. They're so stupid. If they'd said it was suicide, he would have thought it was safe to come back. They're trying to hunt him down like an animal! He'll run for his life. They'll corner him. And you know what they're like! When he won't surrender—" She took an uneven breath.

She went to the dark window and leaned her forehead against a pane of glass, as if cooling it, staring out blankly across the garden. Then her expression changed. Dade followed her glance. In the distance, he saw the knot of reporters gathered outside the gates, buying food from a sandwich truck near the mobile unit of a television station.

She turned, looking at Dade with the new expression in her eyes. Then, she opened the door and went out into the dark garden, crossing toward the high gates, Dade following her.

Reporters mobbed the gates when they saw her. The darkness was pierced with the brief flares of flash bulbs. The sound of shutters, like insects, clicked all around them. Rachel unlocked the wrought-iron gates and stepped through, followed by Dade. Reporters thronged around her, all of them speaking at once in a fugue of questions.

"I want to say—" she began. She took a step backward, a thin forearm raised to shield her eyes against the glare of the quartz lights which jumped into life, bathing the driveway in a whitish glow. A red light glowed like a baleful eye as a minicam on a shoulder was aimed at her and a reporter took up a position beside the lens, asking her questions.

Rachael said, "Please let me say something."

"Is it true that you are married to Nick Levin?" the reporter asked.

"Yes."

"Do you know where he is at this time?"

"No."

"Do you think he killed your father?"

"I think—" She turned to Dade, a bewildered expression on her child's face. "I want them to let me talk to him," she murmured.

"You just tell them that, honey."

"Can you give us any reason why he hasn't come forward?"

"He's afraid! I don't know what happened!" She twisted her hands together and leaned toward the camera, as if puzzled by her own flattened image reflected back at her from its convex lens. "Nick?" she said. "Nick, I beg you to give yourself up. I'm here. You'll be safe. Oh, Nick, please, I don't want you hurt. They just want to talk to you. I'm sure there's some explanation. Nick, please, please give yourself up, for both our sakes."

She turned away then, grabbing Dade's arm, and they walked quickly back together through the gates.

Back in the house she seemed dazed. He took her small hands to lead her to a chair and they were ice-cold.

He said, "I don't want you alone here."

"It's all right." Her voice was colorless.

"I'm going to go get Ellen and we're going to stay here the night."

"That's not necessary."

"I want to do it."

"All right." She rang for Rosarita and asked her to lay a fire in one of the guest rooms.

"You had any dinner, Rachel?"

"I don't want anything to eat."

Dade went to the cupboards in the kitchen, opening them until he found the canned goods. Rosarita watched him, trying to be of help. Forgetting that she spoke English, he said, "*Sopa?*" She found some canned soup. He chose beef bouillon and handed it to her, pointing at Rachel. Rosarita poured the bouillon into a saucepan and got out some crackers and cheese.

There was a small television set in the kitchen. At nine o'clock, Dade turned it on, flipping the dial until he found a channel with the news. He watched it with the sound off. Rachel sipped her bouillon, staring off into space. Suddenly the screen was filled with a picture of the gates to the Welles house as Rachel came through them, followed by Dade, the two of them dazzled by the lights, as if, like an echo, their own immediate past still reverberated. Dade turned up the sound. Like a revenant, Rachel watched herself, heard her own voice plead with Nick. Tears welled in her eyes.

"Will it do any good?"

"We'll see."

Dade left by the back door, getting into his car and driving back to the inn.

He said to Ellen, "You see the news?"

"No."

He told her what had happened, adding, "We're going over there and stay the night with her."

"Does she want us to?"

"I think we should."

"All right." She packed a small suitcase. Dade filled his pipe and walked out onto the deck, smoking it. The phone rang. Ellen answered it, then handed it to Dade, saying, "The lieutenant."

"Valdez?" he said.

Valdez's voice said, "They've spotted the car. That Pantera he drives."

"Where?"

"South of Porterville, headed west."

"Toward the highway."

"Right."

"They understand that they're to stay clear?"

"They understand."

"I thought we'd go stay the night with her."

"Yeah." Valdez rang off.

Ellen said, "What's going on?"

Dade answered, "Remember that story of the boy's

about the watchdog—the man who went back to that office to get some papers, and then when he was ready to go—"

"I remember."

"This is like that."

At nine-thirty, Dade and Ellen left the inn for the Welles house. When they got there, the reporters were gone. The place looked deserted after the crowds and sightseers of the afternoon. Rosarita let them in and took their suitcase, leading them upstairs to a large comfortable room next to Rachel's. A fire burned cheerily in a small marble-fronted fireplace. Rosarita had put the suitcase on a luggage stand and was now turning down the sheets on the fourposter bed.

Ellen said, *"Dónde está la señorita?"*

"Durmienda," Rosarita answered.

Rachel appeared in the doorway, dressed in jeans and a thin shirt. "No, I'm not. I was going to bed but I just couldn't." Excusing herself in whispered Spanish, Rosarita left the room. Rachel said to Ellen, "It's very kind of you to come be with me."

"You shouldn't be alone at a time like this." Ellen gave her a reassuring smile.

"Can I get you anything?"

"No, nothing, thanks."

"Have you had dinner?" Rachel asked.

"Yes. What about you?"

"I had a bowl of soup." She smiled wanly at them and stood there uncertainly. Then opening a pair of French doors, she led them out onto a balcony which ran along the back of the house and overlooked the sea. She pointed to a pergola on the bluff built like a Japanese teahouse and surrounded by boulders and Korean grass with a carp pond on one side. "I wanted flowers. The man Miriam got to do it was from Kyoto. He said, 'Flowers sad.' That was the end of my flowers. Nandina, *Juniperus prostrata* and five-needled pine. That was it. You're only supposed to have three elements. Oh, and all the rocks are placed where they are by tradition. They have names.

"See, by the chrysanthemum well there's a place to kneel, and then to the left, those rocks are called the candle stone, the shelter stone and the kettle stone. That's where we used to sit when we wanted to be alone and just talk, Miriam and I. Now, she's gone and all her special places are still here. That seems funny, doesn't it?"

The doorbell rang. Rachel went out and stood on the railed gallery. Below them, Rosarita looked out the peephole and opened the door. Valdez stepped into the entrance hall. He took off his cap and looked up at them. "Miss Welles?" he said.

Rachel glanced around apprehensively, saying to Ellen, "They've found him. That's it, isn't it? Oh, my God, do you think something's happened to him?"

Ellen said, "You'd better go down and talk with him." Rachel started to shiver. Ellen said, "Put something warm on."

Rachel called down to Valdez, "Just a minute." She disappeared into her room and returned a moment later, struggling into the baggy fisherman's sweater she always wore. Then, hesitating, she leaned a hand on the railing.

Ellen said, "Are you all right?"

"Yes."

"Come on." Holding her by the arm, Ellen walked her downstairs. Dade moved away.

Valdez came toward them. "I'm sorry to bother you at this late hour," he said, "but we want your permission to station a deputy here in the house, at least for tonight."

"Where's Nick? What's happened?"

"Miss Welles, do I have your permission?"

"Yes, yes, of course. Then you don't know anything?"

"There's nothing I can tell you at this time."

She sighed with relief. "All right. Thank you, Lieutenant. Rosarita will show the deputy where he can sleep."

"He's not going to be sleeping here, Miss Welles."

"No, of course not. How stupid of me. Well, good night, Lieutenant." She turned away and walked back upstairs with Ellen. Dade was waiting for them. She said good night. Ellen embraced her. Rachel walked slowly out of the room, bare feet soundless on the tiled floor.

Dade looked at his watch. It was ten o'clock. Ellen began to undress. "Coming to bed?" she asked.

"I think I'll read for a while." He made himself comfortable in a chintz-covered armchair by the fire, put his feet up on a stool and opened a travel book he had found on a shelf. Ellen gave him a kiss and then sat on the floor by the fire, leafing through magazines. When a porcelain bedside clock with an almost inaudible chime struck eleven, Ellen went to bed. Dade went on reading for a few minutes, then he put down the book, turned out the light and remained where he was, sitting in the dark, waiting.

Midnight struck, then one, then two. Dade got to his feet and stretched. Then he went through the open French doors onto the balcony and gazed out at the dark sea, watching the waves breaking white and phosphorescent at the bottom of the cliff on which the house was built.

From below came the labored sound of the surf, working its way up the steep coarse slope of the shallow beach. A scimitar moon rode in a halo of light. Below, the sea was almost black. Far out, he could see the running lights of a fishing boat riding at anchor. Somewhere, a dog barked.

A sound attracted his attention. He stepped back into the dark shadow cast by the overhang, trying to identify what he had heard. Then it came again—a creaking sound, almost like a hawser. He moved over toward the bay windows of Rachel's room and peered in. By the light of the moon, he could see Rachel asleep in bed.

Suddenly the light altered. Something dark blotted out the moonlight streaming through the French doors. Now Dade knew what sound he had heard. It was the doors being forced open. Whatever it was moved in the doorway slightly. Dade inched forward.

Rachel must have heard the same sound, for she awakened with a start, sat up and remained there motionless for a moment, then slipped out of bed. She glided away from the balcony toward the door, then seeing something, stopped, arrested in motion. The something moved, and now light from the moon played on it. It was something unreal, some gleaming black creature still dripping water from the sea.

Then the light caught the glint of a smile and a voice said, "Rachel!" It was Nick in a wet suit. He stepped into her room, pulling off his fins and then his black hood.

Dade watched. Nick shook his blond head and drops of
sparkling water showered down from him. He took a step
toward her, his bare feet white in the moonlight. "Rachel?
Is me!"

"Nick?" She was disoriented and glanced around involuntarily for the lighted face of the clock, as if a clock
were somehow also a compass.

He saw her eyes move toward it and followed her
glance. "Two o'clock in morning. Is late, huh?" She
seemed to feel an impulse to go to him. She took a step or
two, then drew back. "Rachel," he said, stretching out his
arms to her. "Do not be afraid." He moved toward her.
She shrank back. Now he stretched out his hand, as if to
take hold of her wrist. "You come with me. We go away.
I have boat."

"No!"

"Yes, Rachel. Is best. I am your husband. You will
come with me." He came closer.

"When they're looking for you?" She started to back
away slowly.

"Why do they look for me? I do not understand." He
took another step toward her, then another.

"I want you to talk to them."

"Why?"

"I'm trying to help you. Don't you want me to help
you?" She edged along the wall in the dark room, her
hands behind her.

"Is not good to talk to police, Rachel. What is it I tell
them?"

"Tell them how my father tried to kill you. How he
came to your apartment yesterday with a gun—"

"It is not the truth."

"But of course it is! You yourself said that to the sheriff!"

"You tell me to say that. You say, 'He is after you.
Don't say I tell you this. Is too dangerous. Say you saw it
yourself.' You tell me that, Rachel."

"But they're not going to believe that, Nick."

"I will not let you do this!" He took a step toward her.

From behind her back, she took Miriam's gun out of a

drawer and pointed it at him. He stared at her, incredulous. She said, "They'll say it was self-defense, Nick."

"You cannot do such a thing!"

She smiled at him then and pulled the trigger.

There was a clicking sound. She pulled it again and again. When the lights went on, she seemed oblivious of Dade coming into the room from the balcony, of Valdez in the doorway across the room. She kept trying to make the gun fire.

Valdez stepped to her side and began reading her her rights from a plastic-covered card he had taken out of his pocket. She seemed indifferent to everything he was saying.

Turning to Dade, she said, "It must have jammed. Don't you think that's what's the matter?"

"There are no bullets in it, Rachel." He took the gun from her.

"Oh. So that's what it is."

"We'll have to take you downtown with us now," Valdez said.

"I think I should get dressed," she said, looking down at her pajamas. "Don't you think I should?"

Dade said, "I'm sorry, Rachel, for putting you through all this. But, you see, we didn't have any proof"—he weighed the gun in his hand—"until now."

XXXIV

Dade and Ellen walked slowly across the driveway toward their car. Ellen turned for a last look at the Welles house. As Dade put their overnight case in the trunk, Ellen said levelly, "Why didn't you tell me?"

Dade faced her. He said, "The one thing I needed to disarm Rachel was your sympathy. And, honey, you were always a terrible liar."

"I see." Ellen nodded. Then something struck her and she asked, "But when could she have killed Miriam?"

"She only had one chance and that's the time when she said she went upstairs to look in on her. She never did. Because if she had, she would have found Miriam getting ready to leave. That's what hit me last night when I came back here alone. No, she couldn't have. Instead, she went out through the garage and waited on that slope to kill her father. When she found out it was Miriam she had killed—that must have been some moment—she kept her head. That was the test. If she could get through that, she could get through anything. My guess is, she didn't know her father was on the phone till she went back inside to head him off by saying she'd drive."

Ellen said, "She'd be soaking wet."

"No, she was wearing a waterproof poncho. She even showed it to me. All she had to do was pull it off and roll it up. She drove, all right. See, her car was in front and when she told Jensen the driveway was full of mud and the Rolls might get stuck, he agreed to take Rachel's car instead."

"She was taking a terrible chance."

"I'm not sure she was. If he'd insisted on taking the Rolls anyway, they'd just have found the body three hours sooner. It would still have looked like an accident, wouldn't it?"

She nodded somberly, then looked at him, puzzled. "But once the sheriff called it an accident, why on earth try to prove it was murder?"

"To frame her father. That was Rachel's game from then on. She must have seen him head back up north toward the house after she let him off at the Arco station that night to get Miriam's car. That would place him at the scene of the crime. That was all she needed. When Gil guessed the truth and tried blackmail, that—to her—was what the Japanese call a happy accident. She had to kill Gil, so why not make it seem as if her father had done it and then fake his suicide? Crazy as it seems, it worked perfectly. The sheriff bought it. If it hadn't been for that slip-up with the lighting—"

"That's the only mistake she made, isn't it?"

"Well, she has a gift."

"That's an odd thing to say."

"Oh, it's a gift, all right, and it's extraordinarily rare, something you almost never run into. It's what I'd call a gift for improvisation. You know, nothing in life ever works out quite as planned and that's the thing that trips most murderers up. They can't cope with the unexpected—especially under real stress. But that's Rachel's greatest talent."

"Was."

"Was. Hm. Well, we don't know, do we?"

As they were about to get into the car, Brandt led Rachel out of the house toward a squad car. Her arms were behind her back and she was handcuffed. Seeing Dade and Ellen, she hesitated. They went toward her. "I'm sorry," Dade said again.

Rachel frowned, looking away for a moment. Then she said to Dade, "You remember my mother, don't you?"

"Yes, Rachel."

"And you know how she died." Dade nodded. Rachel said in a flat unemotional tone, "What you may not know is why my father turned to other women. Mother had no feelings. No feelings at all. Not for him. Not for me. I saw the records at the Mayo Clinic. She was diagnosed as schizophrenic. Some authorities say it's hereditary. Do you believe that?"

"I'm not sure."

Taking her arm, Brandt said, "It's time to go now, miss."

Turning to Ellen, Rachel said, "Could you brush the hair out of my eyes?" Ellen reached over and smoothed back the reddish locks from the freckled face. Then Rachel turned away, not saying good-bye, and let herself be helped into the squad car.

As it drove away, Dade turned to Ellen and said, "See what I mean?"

XXXV

A week later, back in San Francisco, Ellen sat knitting quietly while Dade poked the fire. He sat down, stretched, yawned, picked up his book and resumed reading. After a while, he went to the windows and looked out. There was a dense fog. It seemed as if the house were swathed in it. All sound was muted, except for the intermittent moan of a foghorn, like the sound of a dinosaur trapped in a tarpit. He tried to see out. The mist was impenetrable. It seemed almost like a wall erected since morning to cut off their view of the Bay, except for the swirl of mist around the streetlights. He sighed. Ellen took another sip of tea.

He picked up an ad she had torn out of a department store catalogue for a Tibetan lamb jacket. "You thinking of buying this, honey?"

"Well—"

"Think we can afford it?"

"We've saved money lately. Remember when we didn't go to Mexico?"

"Why don't we not go around the world and then you can buy yourself sable."

She snatched the ad from his hands, stuffed it into her work basket and went on with her knitting, ignoring him. After a few minutes, she asked, "What news from town?"

"My driver on the number fifty-four bus, a nice man from Columbia—you know, that little town way up in the gold country—he just couldn't take city life anymore and he up and quit. Didn't even pack, just ran out of town, with a whole posse camping on his trail."

"He just went home? That isn't a crime," Ellen said.

"It is when you take the number fifty-four bus along with you, not to mention some seventy passengers. They caught up with the poor soul outside Knights Ferry. I doubt they'll give him more than six months, most likely suspended. Life here is difficult, my dear. Why, only today, one of our supervisors was caught *in flagrante delicto* with somebody's wife."

"That's not news anymore."

"It is if you ran on a gay ticket." He sat down again, picking up his book and leafing through it slowly. After a few minutes, he glanced up over his spectacles, reached out and lifted up a length of the dark-blue knitting and examined it. Ellen continued clicking away with her needles. "What are you knitting?"

"A man." He peered at her over the top of his book. She said, "Well, you're never home. Years ago, there was a cartoon in *The New Yorker* of an old maid doing just that and I decided if I were ever lonely, I'd knit one myself. I'm going to stuff it and, nights when you're not home, he'll sit in your chair, just like that inflated rubber man Tootie Featherstone drives around with when she has to go out after dark." He had gone back to his book. She said, "Darling, what are you reading?"

"I'm planning our trip."

"To Egypt?"

"This trip's in midsummer. Can't go to Egypt then. And with a whole atlas to choose from, why suffer the heat? Why should I do such a thing to my little flower? No, no, we can't go to Egypt in July. My dear, why are you looking at me in that way?"

"Where, then?"

"It's going to be a surprise. Where I'm taking you."

"Surprise me now."

"Someplace off the beaten track. Honey, this here's a gold mine of articles for you to write. Nobody's been there in forty or fifty years."

"Where?"

"Albania."

"*Albania?*" She put down her knitting and stared at him open-mouthed. "I never know when to believe you."

"I'm serious."

"I don't even think I know where Albania is."

"A little south of ancient Illyria. You remember your *Twelfth Night?*"

"Remind me."

"It's a little hard to explain. Maybe there's a map in this book. It's quite a place."

"How do you know?"

"I once had the pleasure of meeting the late King Zog at a reception. Full of enthusiasm for his native land."

"Oh, really? And what did he say about it?"

"I'm not sure. His language is almost unknown beyond his borders, so he learned several others but, alas, he was incoherent in all of them. Would you like to hear about Albania?"

"No."

"The coast is forbidding. And then there's this enormous marsh where malaria is still something of a problem. And that separates the coast from the rest of the country. There are almost no railroads and, as the *Britannica* says, 'No bridge crosses the Drin in its gorge section, and as it is too deep to be forded, the inhabitants usually cross it by swimming, supported by inflated skins.' "

"Oh, my God."

"The language, according to one of my sources, is 'seriously deficient,' or would be except for the borrowed Latin words, and so far as I can determine, it has no known literature. That's where you come in."

"Stop it, stop it!"

"And we'll just take us a little toot off to this sleeping beauty of a country, if I can just find a way into the place. I guess we'll charter us a plane into Tirana, but it seems like cheating."

"Dade—" She sharpened her glance.

The phone rang. It was Ballinger, calling from Los Angeles. The conversation was brief, Dade only listening and murmuring assent. Finally, he said, "All right, all right. Tomorrow." He put down the phone and said to Ellen with a slow smile, "We have to go back down south."

"What on earth for?"

"They want me to give them a deposition."

"But I thought you already—"

"This is a new problem."

"What?"

"About the will."

"Miriam's?"

"Old Arnold's."

"I don't understand."

"Rachel's going to have a baby."

"You're kidding."

"No, it happens."

"I would've thought she was impregnable." She sat looking at him steadily. Then after a long moment, he broke into a surprised smile, and carefully added the word to his list.

"Thank you," he said.

Ellen returned his smile, then she said, "Well, she can't profit from committing a crime. The money all goes to charity. You said so yourself."

"Not if there's a great-grandchild born within twenty-one years of the death of Old Arnold."

"You're not serious!"

"I am serious! Baby didn't commit the crime. Baby comes into the world innocent. This baby also comes into the world as sole heir to a very rapidly growing hundred million dollars. And guess who's going to sue for custody?"

"Who?"

"None other than the loving father, Nick."

Ballinger's office was in Westwood and, after the deposition, Dade and Ellen strolled with the crowds. In the last few years, a kind of *passeggiata* had sprung up there. Throngs of students filled the streets, swarming past long lines in front of the movie theaters, open-air cafés, boutiques selling handmade jewelry, incense, sandals, tarot cards, leather goods, clothes and book and record stores. Most of the shops, like the cafés and restaurants, were open late. Street musicians sang, accompanying themselves on guitars. The air had spring's softness. The young people were all athletic, suntanned and good-looking, as if Lysenko had been right, after all, and generations of nose-fixings and orthodonture had finally had genetic consequences. It seemed to Dade that the look he now saw in the streets was a race being born, a new breed sprung from the blood of the stars.

As they walked, Dade took Ellen's hand. "It's the damnedest thing. Nettie actually claimed the Raphael, saying she'd inherited it—which was perfectly true. Wouldn't give it up."

"But you said yourself you can't inherit stolen goods."

"Yes, but she said, 'All right, take me to court and prove that it was stolen.' For ten million dollars, that's a lot of proving. Nettie could have tied it up for years. The French authorities made a deal with her."

"Well, I'm just as glad. I hate to think of her broke. I couldn't bear pitying her. I would have to drop her."

"My dear, you are as sensitive as a mimosa. But you needn't fret. They gave her a staggering amount of money to drop the suit. Want to stop by and congratulate her?"

"Of course not!" She reflected. Then she gave him an impish smile. "But we could just pay a call . . ."

When they rang the bell at the gallery, Nettie opened the door. She wore a pink plaid couturier suit and her hair had been cut in a way that made her look surprisingly youthful. Her eyes sparkled. She greeted them both with kisses and a radiant smile. "Oh, my funny eyes! Are you looking at them?" She paused by a Venetian mirror, studying herself. "I look like a mongrel, don't I? I'm thinking of getting myself contact lenses and finally making them both the same color, but I can't decide whether to go blue or brown. Well, come on up!"

She led them through the gallery and up the covered stairway from the courtyard to her apartment. The living room was dim and at first they didn't see the figure sprawled on the floor, drink in hand, watching television. Then, the head turned toward them and they saw the handsome Baryshnikov face, the sudden smile. Nick scrambled to his feet, greeting them. Nettie sat down on a little sofa, motioning them to a velvet love seat. Nick squatted cross-legged on the floor.

"Well, how are you, Nick?" Dade asked.

"I am very sad. I am just now fighting to get the custody of my dear unborn baby. This so beautiful and matchless lady here, she is helping me."

"Is that so?" said Ellen.

"Is so." He pulled absent-mindedly at the threads in the rug.

Nettie stroked his head, running her fingers through his curly gold hair, saying, "I was going to get a cat."

When they left and the heavy door of the gallery closed behind them, Ellen said to Dade, "I want one, too."

"Now, that's enough." He shook a finger at her.

"Buy me one, Daddy."

"I said, that's enough."

"Please, Daddy?"

"One more time and you'll be sorry, Ellen."

"You won't take me to Albania?"

"No, I'll leave you there."

They walked out into the pale spring evening, crossed Melrose Place and headed toward Le Restaurant, arm in arm.

When they were seated, a balding waiter with a pencil mustache came up and bowed, saying, "My name is Victor."

"I'm Dade and this here's the little woman, Ellen—"

The waiter bowed again and hurried away.

Dade said, rubbing his eyes, "This whole thing is beginning to get on my nerves. Me, I've about had my fill of the Renaissance and that's where all these people ought to be living. I ever tell you that story about the good people of Siena? See, they had this fella who had freed them from foreign aggression and they were trying to figure out how to recompense him—tried every way under the sun—and when nothing seemed good enough, they decided to kill him and then worship him as their patron saint. That's the Renaissance for you." His features relaxed in a vapid smile.

She gave him a speculative glance. "What are you grinning about?"

"I think I'm going to take up modern art," he went on blandly. "I need a change. I didn't used to like it. Once I met Max Beerbohm. I ever tell you this? He didn't like it, either. He said to me—this here's a true story, honey—

said to me that someday, they were going to find out that not only was the emperor naked but that he had very bad skin."

"Dade—"

A wine steward filled their glasses.

"Well," Dade said, "I don't know about you but come summer, I'm leaving for Albania."

"I have a little going-away present for you."

"What?"

She made a familiar Italian gesture with her hand and said, *"Ciao!"* He looked at her, puzzled. Then his face lit up. He pulled out his little notebook and gold pencil and wrote down the word.

Then he said, "As a reward, I'm going to tell you the dirt about Chloe."

"What dirt?"

"I've been saving it. If I'd told you this afternoon, it would have been spoiled. But now—"

"What about Chloe?"

"Nick went to her first."

"He did what?"

"Fact. She was interested. But Nettie outbid her."

"Oh, my God—!"

"Honey, this here's a fancy place—"

"Oh, my God, oh, my *God*!"

A different waiter came up, a patronizing young man. He took out his pad and pencil and bowed.

"O tempora, O mores," Dade murmured.

The waiter consulted the menu to see where it was. He frowned and excused himself.

"I don't think I'm ready for Albania, Dade."

"Then where, honey?"

"Take me back to France."

"Honey," he said, "if that's what you want, I'll not only take you there but I'll even throw in a rendition of the 'Marseillaise.' Would you like that?"

"I'd love it."

"Well, here goes." He got to his feet, glass in hand, and turned toward the room, saying, "Ladies and gentlemen, I will now lead you in the French national anthem."

He began to sing. A number of customers struggled to

their feet. A black-suited headwaiter started toward them, his head lowered. Ellen ran around the table and tried to pull Dade back into his chair. He continued singing, his glass lifted. Everybody in the restaurant now joined in. The headwaiter, arrested in mid-career, began singing with them. Then they sat down again.

Ellen said under her breath, "I'm going to kill you."

"What's one murder more or less?"

"That's just how I feel."

They clinked glasses. A third waiter appeared and they ordered dinner.

ABOUT THE AUTHOR

GENE THOMPSON, a native of San Francisco, graduated from the University of California at Berkeley, after which he worked and studied in Europe for some time. Subsequently, he and his wife, also a writer, moved to Malibu with their four children and have lived there for the past sixteen years.

Ed McBain's Classic

87th PRECINCT

Mysteries...

"The best of today's police stories...lively, inventive, and wholly satisfactory." *The New York Times*

12   TA-14